PRAISE FOR RI

"A David-versus-Goliath, high-stakes legal thriller wrapped around a biomedical mystery. I was hooked from the start. Rick Acker delivers again with *The Enoch Effect*."

—James Scott Bell, bestselling author of *Romeo's Rules*

"This is a book that grabs you straight out of the gate. Centered around the suspicious death of a brilliant, eccentric scientist, the story drives you through a mercilessly paced, intricate plot with a rich cast of characters—it's a white-knuckled ride straight to the end. Make sure you're well rested before you start, because it will keep you up at night."

—P. J. Tracy, bestselling author of the Monkeewrench Mysteries series

"You love rocket-fast legal thrillers? Ones that also dig deep and make you wrestle with the bigger questions of life? Then Rick Acker is a must-read."

—James L. Rubart, bestselling author of *The Long Journey to Jake Palmer*

"Rick Acker has created a legal thriller that's fast-paced, suspense-filled, and better than John Grisham. I loved every minute I spent in the world of opposing lawyers Daniel Rubinelli and Leigh Collins and was sad to come to the end and say good-bye to these truly likable characters!"

—Lynette Eason, bestselling and award-winning author of the Elite Guardians series

"Reading a Rick Acker legal techno-thriller is like guzzling a Red Bull while riding a roller coaster. *The Enoch Effect* gave me all my adrenaline requirements for the rest of the year."

—Randy Ingermanson, physicist and Christy Award–winning novelist

THE
ENOCH
EFFECT

THE
ENOCH
EFFECT

RICK ACKER

Waterfall
PRESS

Published by Waterfall Press, Grand Haven, MI

www.brilliancepublishing.com

Amazon, the Amazon logo, and Waterfall Press are trademarks of Amazon.com, Inc., or its affiliates.

ISBN-13: 9781503942929
ISBN-10: 1503942929

Cover design by Cyanotype Book Architects

Printed in the United States of America

For my friend and agent, Lee Hough.
Three months after Lee was diagnosed with terminal
brain cancer, he and I brainstormed one last story. It
became the novel you are about to read.

PROLOGUE

February

Silence filled the lab, interrupted only by faint electronic murmurs from scientific equipment lining the walls. A Cray supercomputer whispered secrets to itself in a corner.

Moonlight spilled through cramped windows, carving squares and rectangles of silver white in the darkness.

The head and shoulders of an older man intruded into one patch of light. He lay slumped over an immaculate metal desk, his head pillowed on his right arm. His long, handsome face was perfectly still and white in the moonlight, a sculpture carved in alabaster.

A soft, powerful *whump*, like a giant pounding his fist into a huge feather pillow, shook the building and rattled the windows.

A yellow light flickered in one window. It flared and leaped. Then it shone through another window. Then two more.

Red-gold flames jumped into view. They brushed the windows. The glass quivered and warmed.

The man did not move.

The fire outside burned brighter and higher, clawing at the windows. They rattled and cracked.

The lab grew hot. Fans whirred to life as the temperature control system woke. The lab held tens of millions of dollars' worth of sensitive equipment that did not like heat or cold. And the data on that equipment was still more precious. More precious, perhaps, than anything else in the world.

The pallor melted from the man's face. A ruddy, wavering glow replaced it. But still he did not move.

The door of the lab burst open. A man ran in, but stopped at the sight of the fire roaring just outside. He took a tentative step into the room.

A wall of flame leaned against the windows. Streams of red, yellow, and orange writhed over them. The glass rattled violently, then broke.

The second man staggered back, throwing his arms in front of his face. Then he turned and fled.

A river of fire poured into the lab. It cascaded over the walls of equipment and priceless knowledge.

The temperature control system shrieked in protest, and then died. Gallons of specially designed fire-extinguishing foam gushed from spigots in the ceiling. It pushed back the flames and covered the lab and its unmoving occupant with a protective chemical shield.

But the fire still roared in through the shattered windows. It ate into the walls. It broke into rooms above and beside the lab. The ceiling began to sag as the supporting beams roasted and weakened.

The sound of distant sirens rose above the thunder of the flames. The sirens grew closer and louder. A fire truck screeched to a halt outside. A second pulled up beside it. Men leaped off and pulled out hoses and axes with practiced speed and precision.

But they were too late. The ceiling collapsed into the lab, crushing whatever equipment and data the fire had not already destroyed. And burying the man under a funeral cairn of flaming debris.

CHAPTER 1

May

Leigh Collins loved her job. She loved finding the case-winning e-mail that the other side had missed. She loved cross-examining witnesses—chatting with them and making them comfortable right up until the moment she sprang her trap. She loved weaving a web of complex facts together into a simple and powerful story that grabbed a jury.

And she loved winning, of course. Especially when she beat a man who hadn't taken her seriously. Winning was particularly sweet when her opponent said things like "Don't get emotional, sweetheart," when she argued with him during a deposition. Or tried to bully her by talking over her and standing close so he could use his nine-inch height advantage to intimidate her. Or who smiled and chuckled when she made objections. Or whose whole attitude said, "Aren't you a cute little thing, playing lawyer."

The man who had done all of those things during the previous six months happened to be standing next to her right now. His name was Bert Wells, and he wasn't smiling or chuckling now. In fact, he wasn't paying attention to Leigh at all. All his energy was focused on trying to persuade Judge Karen Bovarnick to grant a motion for a judgment notwithstanding the jury's verdict against his client. He'd been at it for about ten minutes, but it felt like at least half an hour.

He was rehashing the evidence he had presented during trial, trying to convince the judge that no reasonable jury could have reached the conclusions that this one had. He was exaggerating and misstating the facts—par for the course for him. Leigh jotted down notes like a shorthand taker on speed, cataloging all his lies so she could correct them when her turn came.

At last, Wells reached the end. "So it's clear—very clear—that the standard in *Palm Medical Group v. SCIF* is met. No reasonable jury could have come to this verdict, so clearly the verdict must be overturned. Does Your Honor have any questions?"

"No." Judge Bovarnick leaned forward and opened her mouth, but then shut it and leaned back.

"Yes, Your Honor?" Wells said.

"Nothing. I was just going to observe that the more a lawyer insists something is clear, the less likely it is."

Wells said nothing, but his face went red and a vein stood out on the side of his neck, just above his collar.

The judge turned to Leigh. "Any argument, Ms. Collins?"

Leigh weighed her options. She was tempted to forgo argument. That would be fun—like starting a chess game by taking a piece off the board and handing it to an opponent who thought he was better than she was. Or, rather, it would be fun if she won. She was pretty sure things were going her way, particularly after the judge's last comment, but still. Better to play it safe.

She stood and walked to the lectern as Wells sat down. "Thank you, Your Honor. I believe Mr. Wells may be, ah, misremembering some of the evidence. For example—"

"My memory is better than his," interjected the judge. "Anything else?"

There went 95 percent of what she had to say. "Just one point: based on the evidence, a reasonable jury *could* find for my client. In fact, that's the only decision a reasonable jury could reach." She scanned her notes. "That's all I have. Did you have any questions, Your Honor?"

Judge Bovarnick shook her head. "Nope. I sat through a two-week trial in this matter and listened closely to the evidence. It's very clear to me"—she arched an eyebrow at Wells—"that the jury's verdict was amply supported by the evidence. Accordingly, I'm going to adopt my tentative ruling and deny the motion for a judgment notwithstanding the verdict." She closed a folder on her desk and handed it to her clerk. "Okay, we're done here."

The judge stood and everyone in the courtroom got to their feet. "This court is now in recess," intoned the clerk.

Leigh savored the taste of victory, sweeter than a gallon of Cherry Garcia and totally calorie-free. She dropped her papers into her briefcase and looked over at her opponent. His face was still bright crimson and decorated with a lovely frown. He jammed a stack of briefs into the hands of a young woman in a new suit—a "spear carrier" in law firm vernacular. One of the briefs slipped through the spear carrier's hands, and Wells made a cutting remark. Leigh couldn't hear what he said, but it made the girl wince.

Leigh didn't like that. She had a soft spot for puppies and abused junior lawyers. As they walked down the aisle leading to the courtroom door, Wells was still chewing out his companion. Leigh stepped into the aisle with her back to them, causing Wells to pull up short.

"Watch it!" he snapped at her back.

"You need to be a little quicker on your feet, Bert," she said over her shoulder. "In more ways than one."

He let loose a stream of invective as she headed toward the door.

She stopped suddenly and turned, making him nearly run into her again. "Don't get emotional, sweetheart."

She gave him her sweetest smile and walked out of the courtroom before he could respond.

Life was good.

CHAPTER 2

Daniel Rubinelli hated his job. "Assistant general counsel" had sounded great three years ago when Biosolutions recruited him away from a promising career at Brown & Enersen. It had looked like a terrific opportunity, a chance for a young lawyer to step off the partner track and do something better than crank out billable hours.

But somehow the recruiters had failed to mention how much time he would spend dealing with HR's screwups and holding sexual harassment seminars for employees. On the few occasions when something interesting landed on his desk, he had to hand it off to outside counsel. His job? Review the outside lawyers' bills to make sure they weren't overcharging. What a great use of his Notre Dame law degree.

He gave up a $200,000 law firm salary to do this? Really?

If there was anything worse than unraveling HR messes, it was getting tied in knots by an insurance company. It was almost as much fun as whacking himself in the head with a two-by-four.

No, actually, the two-by-four would be more fun. The pain would be the same, but he wouldn't have to talk to the board.

He sighed and rubbed at the clump of pulsing ache forming an inch behind his forehead. The claims representative on the other end of the line was doing nothing to help his mood. "Sheila, Biosolutions bought these insurance policies—very expensive policies, I might add—because we wanted, you know, insurance," Daniel said. "Dr. Rhodes and his lab were very important to the company. If something happened to either of them, American Guaranty promised we would be paid. Promptly. Dr. Rhodes is dead and his lab is a pile of ashes. We need the money from those policies so we can start rebuilding. And we need it now."

"I understand your frustration, Dan," Sheila said, using a placating tone appropriate for an angry ten-year-old. "But these are large policies and we need to take the time to make sure that they're payable under these . . . unusual circumstances."

Daniel took a deep breath and silently counted to ten in Italian. "Four points. Number one, the lab had a state-of-the-art fire-prevention system, which your company knew when they wrote the policy. Any 'circumstance' that burns down a building like that is, by definition, unusual. Number two, the building policy expressly covers fire damage to the lab. That means the policy was intended to cover circumstances like this, even if they are unusual. Number three, Dr. Rhodes worked in the lab, which your company also knew. It can't be a shock that he was there when the fire started. Number four, both policies call for payment within sixty days of a claim. We submitted our claim seventy-five days ago. So, when can we expect the check?"

Silence.

"*Well?*"

Sheila cleared her throat. "We . . . um, we're investigating your claims as quickly as we can. It's . . . well, it's possible that the fire was set by a Biosolutions employee. It's also possible that Dr. Rhodes's death was—wasn't an accident or a crime."

So that's where they were going. If Dr. Rhodes had killed himself by burning down the lab with himself inside it, both policies would be voided. Not that they had any evidence that it happened that way, of course. Typical insurance company MO. Sleazy, outrageous, and borderline fraudulent. But typical. "I see what you're implying. What facts do you have to back it up?"

"We're still investigating. I'm just saying it's possible—"

8

"No. I didn't ask about investigations or possibilities. I asked about facts. You either have them or you don't."

"We're still—"

"Investigating. You mentioned that. No dice. You had sixty days to do that. It's day seventy-five. You either pay the claims in full or you deny them."

"I'm sorry, Daniel," Sheila said, sounding anything but sorry. "We are not in a position to pay Biosolutions' claims at this time. We'll let you know when we have made our decision." She hung up.

Daniel stared at the phone for several seconds, his jaw muscles clenching and unclenching.

"Want to go get a cup of coffee?" said a familiar feminine voice behind him.

Daniel turned and saw Sandy Hampton leaning against his door. Her office was right next to his, and the expression on her face said she had heard his phone call with Sheila the Insurance Troll.

He glanced out his window and saw that the morning fog had lifted, leaving a fresh blue sky. A flag rippled on a pole, and he could almost feel the crisp breeze blowing over the green hills. Then he looked at his in-box and realized just how much work he had to do. "I'd love to, but I just don't have time."

Sandy gave an easy grin that brought out smile lines around her eyes—one of the few clues that she was in her midfifties. "Sure you do. Those hiring guidelines can wait until tomorrow. Besides, the boss insists. She thinks you need a break."

Daniel felt the muscles in his neck and shoulders relax. He hadn't realized they had been tensed. She was right. He did need a break. "I know better than to argue with my boss."

She gave a motherly chuckle and shook her head. "If only that were true."

Ten minutes later, they were sitting at a little round table outside the Starbucks at the Hacienda Crossings mall. The breeze was colder than it had looked from his window, and the hot cup felt good in his hands. The chill didn't seem to bother a gaggle of skateboarders in baggy shorts and T-shirts, who provided free entertainment by attempting to commit suicide on an empty fountain at the far end of the plaza.

One kid with flaming-red hair rode in slow circles, watching the others and waiting his turn. It was a perfect metaphor for Daniel's legal career: he was in a holding pattern waiting to do something exciting.

"How are you doing?" Sandy asked.

He shrugged. "I'm good."

"Really?"

"Really."

She looked him in the eyes for several seconds. "I know you better than that."

Very true. She knew him better than anyone outside his family. To most of the company, she was the Iron Lady—a tough, intimidating lawyer and executive who was dangerous to cross. But she was something much different to him. Over the past three years, she had become a combination of surrogate mom, good friend, and boss. Painting on a fake smile and saying everything was fine wouldn't work with her.

He swirled his coffee and watched the brown whirlpool in his cup. "I didn't come to Biosolutions to argue with insurance companies and do sexual harassment trainings and review bills. I came to help beat cancer." Heat rose in him as he spoke. The words came faster, tumbling over each other. "No, I didn't—not, not just beat it—kill it dead. It killed my mom, my aunt, my uncle. I wanted to kill it. I came here to make a difference."

Sandy opened her mouth to say something, but Daniel's frustration was still boiling out. "Look, I know what you're going to say. What I do is important work. It needs to be done so the company can function— so our scientists can do the difference making and cancer fighting. Fine.

I accept that. But my job doesn't need to be done by *me*. All you need is a decent paralegal. Maybe even just a really good secretary. And anytime something interesting comes along, it's yanked out of my hands and given to some outside firm."

He looked up to see how she was reacting. There was sympathy in her face and a little frustration—at him or his situation?

Daniel pushed on. "You're great, of course, and I still believe in what the company is doing. But . . . I don't know. Maybe I'm not cut out to be in-house counsel."

He was a little surprised when those last words came out. But as soon as they did, he knew he meant them. He was through being a bureaucrat. It was time to be a lawyer again.

Sandy regarded him over the top of her cup for a moment, her face unreadable. She took a long sip and set her cup down deliberately. "I thought so. You're frustrated. I see it in your face and hear it in your voice—and not just when you're arguing with an insurance company. You think we've saddled you with a bunch of paper-pushing administrative jobs."

"It's not you. It's—" He started to protest, but she held up her hand to stop him.

"You're right about that. But you're wrong about everything else. To begin with, no secretary or paralegal could do the work you're doing. Not many lawyers could. You may not realize it, but I've given you a lot of the managerial work because you're better at it than I am."

He warmed at the compliment, but did his best to keep his poker face on until he knew where she was headed.

"But that's not what you came to Biosolutions to do, and it's a waste of your talents," she continued. "A lot of the most interesting work does go to outside counsel. We just don't have the resources to handle it ourselves. I think—" She stopped and paused for a moment. "Let's put a pin in this for now. No promises, but I may have a solution. Give me a few days to do some thinking and talk to some people."

Wood and metal scraped on stone, followed by a thud and a burst of loud cursing. Daniel looked up to see the redheaded skateboarder struggling to his feet. One shin bled profusely as he limped over to retrieve his board. Apparently, he had gotten his chance to skate and fallen flat on his face.

CHAPTER 3

Leigh deleted the last spam e-mail from her in-box, glanced at the clock, and sighed. It was quarter to eleven in the morning and she'd already done everything on her to-do list. And that really bothered her.

Winning a big case had been great, but it also made a hole in her schedule—which was a problem. Okay, maybe it hadn't been a problem for the first few days. She could come into the office a little late, do the odds and ends of work that had accumulated in her in-box overnight, take her time at lunch, and leave at five on the dot. She only billed a few hours on those days, of course, but she had been billing sixty or seventy hours a week for three months—and she had capped that with another win. So it was all good. For a while.

But then a new case had come in that was right up her alley—alleged financial fraud by a bank CEO. It didn't get assigned to her. Two days later, a couple more new cases came in. They also looked like good fits for her. And they both went to other lawyers. To make things worse, two of the three new cases went to Stephanie Fintzen, the new associate Jack Diamond hired last month.

Thinking of Stephanie ratcheted Leigh's worry level higher. Jack Diamond, the firm's founder, was famous for two things: the quality of his lawyering and the looks of his associates. Jack said he wanted lawyers who "look like they belong in a courtroom." Apparently, only tall and beautiful people belonged in a courtroom. Leigh was neither. She was five feet six inches tall, though her doctor's office wrongly insisted she was only five five. In terms of looks, she wasn't exactly a 10. Or a 9. On a good day, she was a 7, maybe an 8. And most days weren't good.

Stephanie was smart and ambitious and had been a varsity volleyball player at Georgetown while maintaining a 4.0. What if Leigh was only at the firm as a placeholder until someone came along who was equally talented and hardworking—*and* fit Jack's idea of what a litigator should look like?

"Early lunch?" asked a cheerful, familiar voice.

Leigh turned and saw her secretary, Andrea Jackson, in the doorway. It wasn't even eleven thirty and Leigh wasn't hungry, but she was glad to have an excuse to get out of the office. "Sure, how about that new Thai place in the Embarcadero Center?"

Andrea agreed, and five minutes later they were walking through San Francisco's Financial District, talking and laughing as they went.

Leigh liked Andrea. She was a large, comfortable woman of about forty. She had been at the firm since Jack Diamond and Louis Wang founded it and knew more about how the firm worked than anyone, including Jack and Louis. She was also fun, smart, loyal, and caring. And Leigh could relax around her. Conversations with other lawyers in the office were always just a little risky. Even an innocuous chat about what she had for breakfast could be tricky. If she mentioned that she had an egg-white omelet at the new restaurant on her block, would people start wondering if she was slacking off and coming in late? Would her meal sound pretentious or healthy? Andrea would only wonder how it tasted. In a word, she was safe.

Halfway to the restaurant, Andrea said, "You haven't been giving me much work recently. What's up?"

Leigh glanced around to make sure no one from the firm was nearby. "Nothing. Jack and Louis haven't been giving me anything, so there's nothing for me to give you."

"That's weird. What happened to those three fraud cases that came in last week?"

"Two of them went to Stephanie. I don't know about the third, but it didn't come to me."

"Interesting." Andrea looked at her for a moment. "Hmm."

"What?"

Andrea shook her head. "I shouldn't say anything."

"Oh, come on! After that, you have to say it."

"Well . . . those were run-of-the-mill cases, weren't they? A few million bucks each, right?"

Leigh nodded. "I've handled a dozen of those in the past year, and Jack and Louis were happy with the results. Or I thought they were anyway. So why did these go to Stephanie?"

"Maybe they're keeping your plate clear so they can give you the next really big case that comes in."

"Maybe," Leigh said dubiously. "Or maybe Stephanie is my replacement. She certainly fits the mold of a Diamond & Wang lawyer better than I do."

Andrea stopped and stared at her. "Are you serious? Is that what you've been thinking?"

"Well, it's possible, isn't it?" Leigh said a little defensively.

Andrea shook her head and laughed. "You poor, paranoid thing. I've been at the firm for twenty years. I know what it looks like when they're getting ready to fire someone, and this isn't it."

Leigh didn't like being laughed at, but relief overcame her irritation. "Okay, so what does it look like?"

Andrea chuckled again. "Oh, all right. First of all, they wouldn't fire someone in your shoes. They like you, so if they were trying to ease you out—which I don't think they are—they'd give you a hint and then try to land you a job with a client. Jack would do it. He'd be all suave and tactful, of course. He'd tell you what a great lawyer you are. Then he'd mention that there was a terrific opportunity someplace else—something tailor-made for you. He wouldn't just leave you sitting in your office with nothing to do."

Leigh nodded slowly, wanting to believe it. What Andrea said did make some sense, and she had been around long enough to know pretty much everything about how the firm worked.

"But I really don't think that's what's going on," Andrea assured her. "I'll bet they're holding you in reserve for something big."

CHAPTER 4

Sandy walked into Daniel's office. She held up a copy of his latest letter to Sheila. "Any word from American Guaranty?"

"Nope."

She frowned. "Yesterday was the deadline you gave them to approve our claims, right?"

"Yep."

"Sue them."

"Gladly." He pulled out his old-fashioned Rolodex and started flipping through it. "Who do you want me to use?"

"Yourself."

"Myself?"

"You wanted to handle some of the more interesting work, right?"

"Um, sure. Absolutely."

"Here's your chance. John and Ron were complaining about our outside counsel bills, so I talked them into letting us handle this in-house."

He stared at her, speechless. He felt like a boy who asks for a plane for his birthday—and suddenly finds himself at the controls of an F-22. The biggest case he had handled on his own at Brown & Enersen was a $10,000 pro bono matter. And of course he hadn't handled any litigation at all at Biosolutions. And now Sandy expected him to bring a $100 million lawsuit?

He finally found his voice. "So, uh, how are we going to staff this?"

She smiled. "Don't worry, I'm not going to make you do this on your own. I'll pitch in when I can, of course. I've handled big cases before, so I can help you with strategy and tactics—or just anytime you want a sounding board or a second set of eyes on something. I'll also take back some of the admin work so you'll have the bandwidth to do this right. We'll also hire a new paralegal to help you."

"Wow. That's great. Thanks. I just . . . thanks. I don't know what else to say."

She smiled and winked. "Say we'll win."

He took a deep breath. He had handled nine-figure litigation before—as the junior lawyer on a big team. It was great she had confidence that he could do this on his own, but that just wasn't realistic. And waiting to say so wouldn't make the situation any better. "I'm not sure we have the firepower to handle this on our own. I wonder if . . ." He swallowed hard. "Well, maybe we should consider hiring an outside law firm—just to help out."

Sandy's smile faded and she regarded him silently for a moment. Then she reached back and shut his door.

"I agree with you. You're great, but you're going to be outgunned. You are one lawyer working in the underfunded legal department of a biotech company. You're up against an opponent who can—and will—overwhelm you with their resources at every opportunity."

"So . . . we're going to hire outside counsel?"

"No."

"But . . ." He shook his head. "Okay, I'm clearly missing something. What is it?"

"If we hire outside counsel, they'll need access to Dr. Rhodes's files. American Guaranty claims that Rhodes committed suicide. Our legal team will have to go through his e-mail, read his diary, go through his notepads, and so on. We can't let outside lawyers do that."

"Why not?"

"Because of what he was working on. We can't risk anyone outside the company getting their hands on it."

A chill rippled up his spine. "What was he working on?"

She leaned forward on her elbows. "Do you know what gene therapy is?"

"Not really," he admitted. *Not at all* would have been more accurate.

"I'm not an expert either, but the basic idea is to treat diseases by changing genes in the sick cells. For example, the genes in cancer cells make them multiply out of control, creating tumors, right? If that multiplication gene could be switched off in all of the cancer cells, then the cancer would die."

"Can we do that?"

"Yes—in theory," Sandy said, smiling wryly at the last word. "We've had great successes in the petri dish. The trick is getting it to work in a living organism, especially a human."

Daniel's heart beat faster as he guessed where she was headed. "Did Rhodes figure out how to make it work in humans? Is that what he was doing?"

Sandy patted his arm. "Slow down, we'll get there. You need a little more background first. I said getting it to work in something living was a trick—but we know it can be done. There have been lots of experiments, mostly using genetically altered viruses to carry genes to sick cells. The viruses 'infect' the cells with a gene they need. Some of those experiments reached the point of human trials—and they *worked*. Or at least a few of them did. For example, BioVex is using modified herpes viruses to treat melanoma. Another of our competitors, Cellectis, is developing a leukemia treatment that uses a different method. And gene therapy doesn't just work on cancer. St. Jude's has successfully treated hemophilia using an adenovirus-based therapy. We're using a similar approach to develop a cure for certain types of sickle-cell anemia. There's even one company that's trying to cure male pattern baldness with gene therapy."

"I've got a cousin who'd be very interested in that."

She smiled. "All of these successes are limited and narrow. Gene therapy works on exactly one type of leukemia, but not others. It works in one patient, but not another. The virus carrying the therapy will put the corrective gene in the right spot on some cells and the wrong spot on others. It's very hit-and-miss. And it's expensive. *And* insurance companies don't cover it."

Daniel nodded. "So it's an exciting area for us but marginal right now. It has a lot of promise but not much profit."

Sandy nodded. "Well put."

"Is this where Dr. Rhodes's work comes in?"

"Yes." She looked him in the eyes. "What I'm about to tell you is very confidential. Not a word of this can be discussed with anyone, even inside the company."

"I understand."

"All right. Dr. Rhodes was working on two related problems. First, he wanted to create a reliable and effective delivery system—one that would work on every type of cancer cell and put its genetic payload in the right place every time. Second, he was trying to develop a genetic sequence that would halt replication of cancer cells—a kill switch. He thought he could make it work every time too—not just in some patients or on some types of cancer. He thought he could make a world without cancer."

Daniel felt light-headed. A world without cancer. He had come to Biosolutions to be part of something like this. "How . . . how far did he get?"

"He was making real progress. He could cure every type of cancer in rats, and the cure rate was one hundred percent. He was starting to work on more complex animals when he died." She paused, and for a moment she looked her age. "The fire also destroyed most of his research. We're not back to square one, but we've been knocked back a long way."

"Wasn't there an off-site backup?"

She sighed and rubbed her temples. "There was supposed to be, but Dr. Rhodes was the only one who knew where it was. We've looked everywhere and we can't find it."

"Wouldn't IT know where it was?"

She gave a sour smile. "You've unintentionally hit a sensitive spot. IT absolutely should have known. They should have set up the backup. But Dr. Rhodes was very protective of his work and insisted on taking care of the backup himself." She shook her head. "And as a result, it will take years to re-create what we lost in that fire."

"But we can do it, right?"

Sandy shrugged. "I hope so. We've got our best and brightest working on it, but it's slow and expensive. Getting that insurance money would sure help. And while we're doing that, we need to keep tight control over what's left of his research. We can't risk it leaking out to one of our competitors."

Now Daniel understood. "Outside counsel could be a security risk."

"Exactly," Sandy said. "I would rather lose the entire one hundred million dollars than have someone get hold of Dr. Rhodes's research. There's a good chance that an outside firm will work for one of our competitors sometime in the next few years. I can't let them have the future of our company in a file or database, where it could be 'accidentally' shared or even stolen. It's happened before, more times than I care to think about it." She shook her head and sighed. "I'm sorry, but we're on our own for this case."

CHAPTER 5

June

Someone rapped on Leigh's door, and she immediately recognized Jack's knock. "Come in."

He walked in and shut the door behind him.

He sat in one of her guest chairs and smoothed his immaculate gray wool slacks. "How are you doing?"

"Good. What's up?"

He gave a disarming and well-practiced grin and winked. "Have you been enjoying your little vacation in the office?"

She forced herself not to tense. "I didn't know that was intentional. Thanks."

"You earned it. That was a big win. Huge. And it was all you. I ran into Bert Wells at lunch today. He said you were fantastic."

Bert Wells said *what*? Not that, obviously. Maybe he said she was better than he expected or something similar, but there was no way he called her fantastic. That was spin from Jack. So why was Jack buttering her up? She realized he was still talking and focused back on him. ". . . one of my best attorneys. This is perfect for you. Perfect. I knew you'd be ready to go."

A pit opened in her stomach. "So, where am I going?"

"American Guaranty, of course. I'll send you the package. Give me a call after you've had a chance to read it."

His cell phone rang. He checked the number. "Gotta go. Talk to you later." He popped up from the chair and was gone.

Leigh stared at the chair he had just vacated. What exactly was she supposed to do at American Guaranty? It sounded like he wanted her to go work there, but his body language hadn't matched that message. He was too casual and peppy. Or had she read him wrong? She wished she hadn't blanked out after his Bert Wells comment. She hoped he would send "the package" soon. There was no way she'd be able to focus on anything else until it arrived.

Twenty-five minutes later, her e-mail chimed. It was from Jack, and the subject line was "American." Leigh took a deep breath and opened it. It was a summons and complaint. So Andrea had been right, Leigh realized with relief.

She turned to the complaint. A company called Biosolutions had sued American Guaranty for a hundred million on a couple of insurance policies. Stripped of histrionics and invective, it looked like the basic allegation was that American had issued a fifty million "key employee" life insurance on some scientist and another fifty million policy insuring his lab. Then a fire killed the scientist and burned his lab to the ground.

Leigh skimmed through the rest of the complaint, looking for a description or even a caricature of American's basis for the claim denial. Nothing. Just a lot of talk about how very clear it was that the policy covered the claims, how important Biosolutions' work was, how evil American Guaranty was, and so on. Blah, blah, blah.

She scrolled to the end of the complaint to see who was representing Biosolutions. To her surprise, it was in-house counsel. They couldn't find a law firm willing to take this case? Wow.

Did someone at Biosolutions have a personal vendetta against American Guaranty and the clout to force the general counsel to file a bad lawsuit? Maybe that was it.

Whatever happened, Leigh felt a little sorry for Daniel Rubinelli, the attorney who signed the complaint. The poor guy was clearly in over his head. She was almost going to regret beating him. Almost, but not quite.

CHAPTER 6

July

Driving up to the lab from the south, Daniel could almost imagine nothing was wrong. It was an elegant cube of tinted glass, gleaming in the morning sunlight. Biosolutions' stylized double helix logo stood out above a simple double door, seeming to hover over the building's smooth exterior. Achieving that effect had cost over twenty thousand dollars. The rock garden, hypoallergenic bamboo, and artificial stream outside had cost a lot more. Dr. Rhodes had allergies and therefore insisted that his workplace not be surrounded by anything that might trigger them.

The lab hadn't been designed just to please an eccentric scientist, however. It was Biosolutions' crown jewel—the first building visitors saw when they drove through the gate, the first stop on tours for big investors or important customers. Here they could see in tangible form Biosolutions' commitment to cutting-edge research. The ultraspeed centrifuges, supercomputers, scanning and fluorescence microscopes, incubators, and other equipment all testified to the company's prowess.

Or they had anyway.

The devastation became clear as Daniel and his companion, a private fire investigator named Tony Lopez, drove past the building on the right. The elegant gravel-and-flagstone patterns and pricey rock garden ended abruptly in an expanse of raw earth and vestigial ruins where the rest of the lab once stood. Most of the fire debris had been carted away, but reconstruction had not begun—and could not until American Guaranty paid on the insurance policies.

Lopez pointed to a spot near the center of the damage. "Park here."

Daniel complied and stepped out. The air outside the car was chilly and still smelled of burned plastic. He took out his cell phone and called Sandy to let her know he and Lopez had arrived at the lab. She had made it clear that this was his show, but she still wanted to hear firsthand what Lopez had to say.

A moment later, Sandy pulled up, driving one of the electric golf carts senior executives used to zip around the Biosolutions campus. She got out and nodded to Daniel to begin.

"So, is this where the fire started?" Daniel asked.

Lopez scratched his massive, white-bearded jaw. "It's where Jim thinks the fire started."

Jim Keller was the fire investigator assigned by the Alameda County Fire Department. The day after Biosolutions sued, he issued his official report on the fire. He claimed it was caused by arson, and the police promptly concluded that Dr. Rhodes was the most likely arsonist. That, of course, was a massive—possibly fatal—problem for Biosolutions' case.

As soon as they got the report, Daniel and Sandy scrambled to find a fire expert of their own. They found Tony Lopez, a retired deputy fire marshal who had worked at a nearby fire department.

Lopez had spent the past few days poring over Keller's report and examining the remains of the lab and other evidence. Now he was ready to give them his conclusions via a guided tour of the fire scene. Daniel hoped he had good news.

Carrying a heavily annotated copy of Keller's report, Lopez walked to a spot near a cement slab surrounded by the remnants of a bamboo grove. Gravel covered the ground around the bamboo stalks, and ornamental granite bordered the gravel. Lopez stopped and glanced at the report, then squatted and pointed to the gravel at the end of a long slab of red granite. "Here."

Daniel crouched beside him and Sandy leaned over to look, but Daniel saw nothing unusual. "Where?" Daniel asked.

"Right there." Lopez held up the report and showed Daniel a picture of this spot taken the day after the fire. "See how those pebbles are all pushed down, like someone made a little pool?"

Daniel saw it now and nodded.

"That's what Jim calls the 'accelerant reservoir' in his report. That's where he thinks the fire started." Lopez stood up. "Okay, now look at this long rock." He pointed to the granite slab that formed a low retaining wall for the gravel. "See how it still has burn marks along the bottom?"

Daniel nodded again.

Lopez stood and walked over to the concrete slab. He flipped to another page in the report. This one had a picture of the same slab, except with the exploded ruins of a diesel generator on top, surrounded by twisted shreds of blackened sheet metal. He jabbed a thick finger at a nozzle on the fuel tank. "Notice how those burn marks lead to where that generator used to be?"

"Yes."

"Keller thinks this was what we call a 'trailer.' His theory is that an arsonist opened the nozzle on the tank and let out a stream of diesel. It collected in that little pool—the accelerant reservoir—which the arsonist then lit. The fire traveled up the trailer to the generator tank, which blew." He gestured to the remains of a bamboo stand that had hidden the generator's steel enclosure. "This bamboo would have made a great torch. Notice how it was right up against the side of the building. I'll bet it reached up at least two floors. Rhodes was found on the third floor, right above the generator."

Daniel nodded, thinking ruefully that, while the little bamboo grove had been much more attractive than an exposed metal shed, maybe it hadn't been the best choice for concealing a tank holding hundreds of gallons of diesel fuel.

"After that," Lopez continued, "the fire knocked in the windows of the lab and got inside. It was all over then."

Daniel looked up at the remains of the building. He could see why someone would think the fire started here. And if he could see it, a jury could. "Is Keller's theory wrong?"

Lopez hesitated unnervingly. "There are some holes in it—and it sure doesn't support the PD's conclusions."

Daniel let out a sigh of relief. "I'm very glad to hear it."

Lopez gave a broad grin, which made him look like Santa Claus would if he had spent three decades fighting fires. "Let's start with what Jim says is an 'accelerant reservoir.' It could be a footprint or a natural depression in the gravel. There are at least fifty just like it."

Daniel nodded. "Okay. Anything else?"

Lopez swept a scar-covered hand over the scene. "Jim's arsonist didn't leave anything behind. No gasoline traces. No burned match. Nothing. That's unusual."

"Really?" Sandy asked. "Do most arsonists leave calling cards like that?"

Lopez nodded. "Over fifty percent of the time, they do. And the percentage is higher when you've got a suicide involved. People who are about to kill themselves don't usually bother to cover their tracks."

"All right," Daniel said a little dubiously. This was pretty thin evidence that the fire department and the police were wrong. Not much more than pure speculation, in fact.

"But here's the big problem with their theory," Lopez continued. "Let's say you're Dr. Rhodes. You just lit a puddle of diesel on fire. It's racing up toward the generator. You've got to get back into the building and over to your lab so you can be at your desk for the fire to kill you. How are you going to do it?"

Daniel looked back and forth, trying to reconstruct the devastated building in his mind. "Let's see. The nearest entrance was way around near the front." He started walking around the perimeter. "This would have looked different before the fire, but I'm pretty sure . . ."

"It still would have taken him close to half a minute to get to the door," Lopez said, finishing Daniel's thought. "Or at least that's my best guess after looking at the blueprints and coming out here. It's at least fifty yards, and there were obstacles—a concrete retaining wall and bamboo stands at the corners of the building, for example."

"And then he has to open the door and run at least another twenty yards down the hallway, go up two flights of stairs, open the door to his lab, and go over to his desk." Daniel paused a moment, making mental calculations. "How long do you think it would have taken the fire to reach the generator?"

"A few seconds. It might take a little longer for the tank to go. Then a little while longer for the fire to get into the building. Maybe a minute total."

"So he would have needed to light the fire and then sprint around the building, up the stairs, and back to his lab. Even if he could do that before the fire reached the lab, it makes no sense," Daniel mused. "If he wanted to burn himself to death, why not stay outside? And if he wanted to die at his desk, why come all the way out to the generator to light the fire—and then have to race back inside? Why not just pour gasoline around inside, sit down, and light a match?"

"All excellent questions," Lopez observed.

"So even if Jim Keller is right about how the fire started, the police are wrong about who started it."

Lopez nodded. "It doesn't make any more sense to me than it does to you."

"Do you think we could talk Jim or the police around?" Daniel asked.

Lopez shook his head. "Jim's report isn't really wrong. What you want him to do is add a paragraph saying that he doesn't think Dr. Rhodes could have been the arsonist. He won't do that."

"Why not?" Daniel demanded.

"Two reasons. First, it isn't his job. He's supposed to figure out how and where the fire started—cause and origin, as they say in the fire department. The police usually decide who did or didn't start the fire."

"But they're wrong," Daniel protested. "If Keller put more in his report, he could set them straight."

Lopez chuckled drily. "And that's the second reason. He's friends with a lot of guys in the PD. They work together on arson cases a lot. He's not going to set them straight about anything, particularly about something that's their job, not his. The police decided that Rhodes was the arsonist, which makes life easy for them because they can close the investigation the same day they open it. Jim's not going to contradict them unless it's impossible that Rhodes did it. It isn't impossible, so Jim's not going to do anything."

Daniel shook his head in frustration. "So we're stuck."

Lopez nodded and repeated, "So we're stuck."

CHAPTER 7

August

Leigh first started to hate Daniel Rubinelli on a Tuesday morning. At 8:37 a.m., to be exact.

The day had started out so promising. She woke up refreshed, was on time for her six o'clock yoga class. She walked into the office at seven fifty and was at her desk before any of the other lawyers. Not that she was racing them, but it was still nice to win.

By quarter past eight, she had finished her breakfast and was done clearing out the e-mail that had accumulated after she left last night. A clear ten hours stretched out in front of her, full of the promise of productivity. And Jack Diamond and Louis Wang were both gone for the day, so she was less likely to get interrupted by emergency projects. She started creating a to-do list on her new iPhone. She loved the new organizational app she had found—it was more fun than Candy Crush for an OCD lawyer.

At 8:16, her phone rang, just as she was on the verge of figuring out how to get her new app to sync with her work calendar. Some woman named Sheila Robinson was on the line. Leigh couldn't place her, but her name was vaguely familiar. A court reporter maybe? Or a client? Leigh decided to keep it vague and try to get the woman off the phone. "What can I do for you, Ms. Robinson?"

"Well, I got a call from Daniel Rubinelli. He wanted to ask me some questions and get some documents from me. Transcripts and stuff."

Transcripts. Must be a court reporter. Had she used Sheila's court reporting service in the past? Was that why she almost recognized her name? "Okay."

Several seconds of silence, as if Sheila expected Leigh to say something more. "So, uh, can I do that?"

"Is he asking about the Biosolutions case?"

"Yes."

"Then it shouldn't be a problem," Leigh said, her mind already half on the next task on her to-do list. "But if he asks for a transcript or exhibit we don't already have, please make a copy for us. Bill it to the firm account."

"Oh, we wouldn't bill you."

Diamond & Wang must be a good customer of Sheila's reporting service. "Great, thanks so much."

Click.

Leigh turned back to her to-do list, but she wasn't having fun anymore. Her mind kept drifting back to the call. It bugged her. Something about it was wrong. Court reporters sometimes called to say an opposing lawyer was ordering a transcript, but that was because they wanted to sell you a copy too—the message was basically, "If the other side is getting a copy, you'd better get one too." And when they did that, they *never* followed up by saying they would give you the transcript *for free*. They also never called to ask for permission to talk to other lawyers. And come to think of it, the Biosolutions case was too new for there to be any transcripts.

She put down her iPhone and searched "Sheila Robinson" in the Diamond & Wang contacts database. At 8:37, Sheila's entry popped up. She wasn't a court reporter after all.

Sheila Robinson was the American Guaranty claims adjuster who had processed Biosolutions' claims.

Leigh's stomach dropped straight down to her toes. She just told a key witness that it was okay to talk to opposing counsel with no one else around. Worse—infinitely worse—this witness was an employee of a client.

What was Rubinelli doing calling Sheila anyway? That was totally unethical. A lawyer couldn't directly contact someone who had a lawyer. Once Rubinelli knew that Diamond & Wang represented American Guaranty, he couldn't contact them. If he wanted to say something to the insurance company, he had to tell it to their lawyers. Period.

Leigh grabbed the phone and dialed Sheila's number. Voice mail after the first ring. Fear gripped Leigh's heart. "Sheila, this is Leigh Collins," she said, keeping her voice as calm as she could. "Please give me a call as soon as possible. We need to talk before you speak to Daniel Rubinelli."

She hung up and immediately dialed Rubinelli's number. Voice mail again. Cold horror strangled her as she realized he was probably on the phone with Sheila *right now.* "Mr. Rubinelli, this is Leigh Collins." It was a struggle to keep her voice level and professional. "I represent American Guaranty and its employees. Please do not contact any of them without speaking to me first." She left her number and hung up.

Leigh then banged out e-mails to Sheila and Rubinelli mirroring the voice mails she had just left each of them. Maybe they would check e-mail while they were still on the phone. She put red flags on the e-mails and hit "Send."

Now all she could do was wait—and stew in her own juices. She had screwed up. Badly. Worse than she had ever feared possible. She probably would be looking for another job soon—if she could find one after a debacle like this. How could she have made a mistake this massive?

Simple. She had assumed that her opponent would play by the rules, more or less. What he did was unthinkable to an honest lawyer—which was why Leigh didn't think of it. Maybe she should have recognized Sheila Robinson's name, but no one could blame her for not anticipating that her opponent would do something so brazenly unethical. But they would blame her. She had no doubt about that.

The more she thought about it, the angrier she got. Rubinelli's conduct really was appalling. Going behind a lawyer's back to talk to her client was as bad as destroying evidence or trying to bribe a judge. And to make matters worse, his slime was going to rub off on her because she didn't spot it fast enough.

She pulled up the state bar's website and found the ethics complaint page. She started scrolling through the standards for the different types of punishments. Maybe she could get Rubinelli sanctioned or even disbarred. That would be fun.

Leigh had just started filling out the online ethics complaint form when her phone rang. She looked at the caller ID. Him.

She picked up the phone. "Daniel Rubinelli?"

"Uh, yeah."

"What do you think you're doing?"

"Excuse me?"

"You know that I represent American Guaranty, right?"

"Yes. So?" He didn't sound the least bit apologetic, or even defensive.

"So why were you calling my client to talk about the Biosolutions case?"

"I didn't call your client—or at least I don't think I did."

That threw her off track. "You . . . Didn't you just call Sheila Robinson?"

"I did. Do you represent her personally?"

Leigh exploded. "I represent American Guaranty! She is an American Guaranty employee. You knew that. And yet you deliberately contacted her to talk about the exact subject of my representation. Do you deny any of that?"

"No."

His insouciance flabbergasted her. "I . . . I have never in my career come across such blatantly unethical conduct."

He was momentarily silent. "Uh, what are you talking about?"

Was he fresh out of law school? An idiot? Both? "I represent American Guaranty, and Sheila Robinson is an American Guaranty employee," she said slowly. "And you just admitted that you knew both those facts before you called her. So you just violated the rule against contacting represented parties."

"Um, did you bother to read the rules before calling me?" he asked, irritation in his tone.

"Which rules?" she asked, then immediately gritted her teeth at how stupid she sounded.

"The California ethics rules." She heard the sound of book pages flipping. "Rule 2-100 in particular. I'm pretty sure you think I broke that one. I didn't. It says I can communicate directly with an employee of a company you represent unless 'the subject of the communication is any act or omission of such person in connection with the matter which may be binding upon or imputed to the organization for purposes of civil or criminal liability or whose statement may constitute an admission on the part of the organization.'"

She frantically searched for the rule he was quoting. She found it and parsed through the unwieldy wording as he spoke. The blood drained from her face as she read. Oh, no. No, no, no.

"So I can contact any American Guaranty employee I want," Rubinelli continued, "as long as I don't ask them to say anything that could bind American Guaranty or be imputed to it. I did nothing of the sort—and frankly I don't appreciate you accusing me of being unethical."

She instinctively stayed on offense. "Who else have you interviewed?"

"My interview list is attorney work product and therefore protected from disclosure," he said, the annoyance in his voice growing. "Would you like me to read that rule to you too?"

She hung up. Then she realized she'd let him get the best of her a second time. He was probably laughing at her right now. She clenched her fists and gritted her teeth. She desperately wanted to scream and throw something. Preferably at Rubinelli.

She dashed off a quick e-mail to American Guaranty's legal department alerting them to Rubinelli's calls and asking them to warn their employees not to talk to him. After agonizing for a minute, she added Jack Diamond as a cc. To her relief, she got an immediate autoreply saying he was out of the office and couldn't check e-mail today.

She calmed herself enough to log on to Westlaw and pull up cases dealing with Rule 2-100. Rubinelli must be wrong. Lawyers on opposite sides of a case didn't go behind each other's backs like that. She'd been practicing long enough to know that wasn't how the world worked.

As her research progressed, her fury and righteous indignation leached away. A black fog of despair crept into her soul. Rubinelli was basically right—or at least he wasn't as clearly wrong as she had hoped. He had been more aggressive than most judges would probably like, but had he actually broken any rules? Maybe, maybe not. It was a gray area, so a judge would likely give him a pass.

She slumped back in her chair and closed her eyes. Of course Rubinelli was laughing at her. She deserved to be laughed at. She deserved to be fired. She had never had an opponent use this tactic before, so she had assumed that it couldn't happen, assumed that it must be against the rules. And when you assume . . .

She winced and sighed. Okay, so Rubinelli had caught her unprepared and embarrassed her. Now what? She wasn't going to just wallow in defeat until Jack and Louis got around to firing her. As long as she was a Diamond & Wang lawyer, she would act like one. By the time she talked to Jack, she would have a strategy thought out and ready for his approval. And it would be good.

But before she started planning her counterattack, there was something she needed to do. She went online and found a picture of Daniel Rubinelli on Biosolutions' website. He was wearing a suit and a confident grin. The same grin she knew he had all over that ridiculously square jaw while they were talking. She copied the picture to her desktop. Then she pulled up Zombie Hunter 3 and opened a hack a friend had installed that let her put whatever face she wanted on the zombies. Five minutes later, she was hunting undead Rubinellis through a Louisiana swamp.

CHAPTER 8

Daniel smiled as he hung up the phone. He knew he had won that little exchange, and it felt good. The thought of going up against Leigh Collins and Diamond & Wang no longer seemed quite so overwhelming. Maybe he *could* take them on with help from Sandy.

He pulled up Collins's Diamond & Wang bio, which had intimidated him when he first saw it: Stanford BA—with honors—and JD, four jury verdicts in her favor, and she was just named a Rising Star by *Super Lawyers* magazine. Her picture showed a slender young woman in a navy suit with shoulder-length sandy blonde hair. She was leaning against a bookcase filled with gilt-lettered volumes with her arms crossed and a small, coolly professional smile on her face.

He enjoyed savoring his little victory, but he needed to get back to work. He sighed and turned to his in-box. Sitting in it were two weathered accordion folders stuffed with copies of documents from Dr. Rhodes's personnel file. Plus, he had finally been given access to Rhodes's online HR file. That was a lot, even for someone who worked for the company for twenty years. What had he done to attract so much attention from HR? Hopefully nothing that would help American Guaranty argue that he was a suicidal arsonist.

Two photographs were stapled inside a manila folder in the first accordion file. One picture showed Rhodes when he joined Biosolutions two decades ago. The other must have come from his most recent ID.

He had been a handsome man, but not particularly pleasant looking. He looked more like an artist than a scientist—intense blue eyes, strong cheekbones and chin, longish brown hair, Vandyke beard. His beard and hair had gone mostly gray by the second picture, but otherwise he had aged well. He wore the same irritated, let's-get-this-over-with expression in both pictures. He didn't look happy, but he didn't look crazy or depressed either.

Daniel flipped through the contents of the accordion files, looking for anything relating to Rhodes's mental health. There was a lot, unfortunately. Nothing indicating that Rhodes was suicidal—but plenty indicating he was strange.

For starters, he fought an epic—and paranoia-fueled—war with Biosolutions' IT staff. The fight over the backup of his research was only a skirmish in context. Rhodes claimed that IT was spying on him, so he locked them out of his work computer and e-mail. They tried to break into his account. So Rhodes retaliated by locking them out of the Biosolutions network entirely. He refused to let them back in until he was directly ordered to do so by the CEO.

When IT finally got access to Rhodes's computer and e-mail again, they discovered that he had apparently cleared them out. His personnel file contained a memo and three e-mails pointedly reminding him that company policy required him to keep all records relating to his work on company servers. Daniel couldn't tell whether Rhodes ever complied.

Rhodes apparently didn't trust his superiors any more than he trusted IT. More than once, he had ignored requests from the CEO and CSO for updates on his work. He either blew them off completely or replied with vague brush-offs like "Continuing to work on development of gene therapy protocols. Nothing new to report." That didn't sit well with them, especially since they had just given Rhodes a very expensive lab and he continually demanded a larger budget to fund his research.

Rhodes also seemed to have been a joy to work for. Several of his lab assistants complained about him insulting them and making unreasonable demands. For example, he insisted on having their home and cell numbers—which he called regularly. He called one woman at two in the morning because he couldn't find a draft report she had given him three weeks earlier. That got him reprimanded. So did his habit of throwing things when he was annoyed.

Rhodes even got himself arrested once. He drove off after a collision— while a police officer was preparing an accident report. The cop pulled Rhodes over and threatened to ticket him for leaving the scene of an accident. Rhodes said he had important work to do and shouldn't have to stay since the crash wasn't his fault and his car was drivable. He drove off again, and was arrested five minutes later.

How did Rhodes get away with so much? Daniel knew Biosolutions' HR policies well and had even written some of them. Any employee who behaved like Rhodes should have been canned years ago. The man had committed half a dozen obvious firing offenses, been warned repeatedly, and then committed more. Yes, Rhodes was valuable to the company, but no one was valuable enough to hijack the IT system and blow off the CEO and CSO.

And why hadn't Daniel ever dealt with Rhodes? It looked like all the complaints about him went straight to Sandy, even though HR problems were below her pay grade. Weird. And even weirder, it looked like she basically gave him a pass each time—even though she was usually a stickler when it came to personnel rules.

Then Daniel found a copy of Rhodes's résumé. Twenty-six patents, more published papers than Daniel cared to count, and even a National Medal of Science. And, doubtless of particular interest to the executive committee, a chemotherapy drug Rhodes invented in 2004 made more than $3 billion in profits for the company. Two other drugs made more than half a billion each. So maybe Rhodes *was* that valuable. For four-plus billion, the CEO probably would have let Rhodes blow up the executive helicopter.

Daniel turned to the family and friends section of Rhodes's file. This part of the file was mostly a security analysis: Biosolutions profiled everyone close to employees who had access to highly sensitive company information. Daniel wasn't at all surprised to learn that Rhodes never married and didn't have any close friends, just professional colleagues. There was a lot on his family, but none of it was troubling—no suicides or evidence of serious mental illness. They were an interesting bunch, though. Rhodes's father had been an intelligence agent in World War II, working behind Nazi lines to help resistance groups in German-occupied territories. After the war, he had been an accomplished chemist, though nothing compared to his son. Rhodes's mother had been a guerrilla fighter in wartime Ukraine, where she killed more than a dozen Gestapo agents. When Stalin's forces rolled back in, she disappeared. Then she popped up later in America with Rhodes's father, who was her fiancé by that point.

Daniel finished the file and stretched his neck, which had developed a crick. He glanced at his watch and realized that he had just spent over three hours reading about Rhodes. The man certainly had been unique.

Daniel stared at Rhodes's file. There were important clues in there, he was certain of it. But what were they? Rhodes had certainly made enemies. Did a disgruntled former lab worker kill him and set the fire to cover up the murder? Or was the killer a humiliated IT worker? Or maybe Rhodes had been embezzling all that money he demanded for his lab, which would explain why he had been so vague about what he was working on.

Daniel frowned. There were a lot of possibilities to follow up on, but there was only one of him.

CHAPTER 9

Leigh had never been to an estate sale before. She didn't particularly like it. It felt creepy to go tramping around a dead person's house and checking out their stuff. It seemed like a combination of a garage sale and grave robbing.

But when one of her Google Alerts picked up an announcement for the estate sale of Dr. Elijah Rhodes, she knew she had to be there. So she signed up as a bidder and blocked out the afternoon.

Rhodes had lived in an old, modest bungalow on a large lot—probably at least a quarter acre. A neighborhood of McMansions had grown up around it, and the land under the house was probably worth several times the value of the structure and everything in it.

About a dozen other people milled around the little house, most of whom appeared to be professional buyers. They checked the backs of paintings and the undersides of furniture, counted plates and silverware, checked the models and years on electronics, and so on. They pulled an antique baptismal gown and wedding dress out of their boxes to examine the stitching and look for signs of yellowing. Then they dropped them back carelessly like discarded tissues.

Leigh winced inside and scoured the house for anything that might be useful to her case. A diary, cell phone, computer, or anything that might shed some light on Rhodes's mental state at the time of his death. Was he suicidal? Angry at Biosolutions? Mentally unstable in some other way that would make him kill himself and burn down his lab?

After half an hour, she had checked every room in the house and found nothing. She was a little surprised that a scientist wouldn't have a personal computer, but she was sure there wasn't one in the house unless it was hidden under his mattress or something. There was no reason to stick around for the auction, which was something of a relief.

She was on her way out the door when a black Mercedes pulled up outside the house. A tow truck followed, pulling a battered, ugly pea-green Volvo, which the tow truck deposited at the curb behind the Mercedes.

A white-haired man got out of the Mercedes. He greeted several of the bidders, laughing and clapping them on the shoulder like old friends. He opened the rear door to the Volvo and pulled out a cardboard banker's box, which he brought to the house. Leigh looked into the box as he passed and caught a glimpse of a laptop and a stack of papers.

She followed the auctioneer back into the house. He went into the dining room, where other bidders gathered around him. "We have a few late additions," the auctioneer announced. "The deceased's car was found in a parking lot, and it's outside now. It's a Volvo S40 with just over sixty thousand miles on it. We'll save that for last so that you all have a chance to bring over a mechanic if you want. And we'll start with what we found in the car."

The auctioneer reached into the box and pulled out a stack of CDs. "Wow. K-tel Top Hits of 1978, and here we have 1979 and 1980 too. I didn't even know these were on CD. Prime ironic retro-chic. I'll bet they're hard to get. Do I have a bid?"

Several of his listeners chuckled, but no one bid.

"No?" He shook his head sadly. "I see we don't have any music lovers here today. All right, the next lot is a collection of notebooks and papers, most of them handwritten." He held up an untidy stack. A couple of bidders drifted away. "Come on. This guy was a scientist—what secrets of the universe are locked in here?"

Finally, something worth buying. Leigh held up the numbered card she'd been given when she arrived. "Fifty dollars."

"A hundred," said a woman's voice behind Leigh. She turned and saw a tall young woman with dark hair pulled back at the neck. Leigh hadn't seen the woman among the other bidders, and she was sure she would have noticed. The woman had high cheekbones and striking green eyes. Her skin was perfect except for a mole on her right cheek. She wore an elegant cream suit that made everyone else in the room look underdressed.

"That's more like it!" the auctioneer said with a grin. He looked past Leigh to the woman behind her. "I'm sorry, I didn't see your card. Could you hold it up again?"

The woman hesitated for an instant. "I don't have a card. I thought the auction was open to the public." Her voice was deep, and she had an accent Leigh couldn't place.

"It is," the auctioneer assured her. "You just need to register with my assistant. She'll need to see your driver's license and a major credit card. Then you're welcome to participate."

"I don't have those with me," the woman replied, "but I do have cash."

"I'm sorry," the auctioneer said, "but we need to register all bidders. If you'd like, I can hold this lot until the end so that you can go home and get your license and a credit card."

She thought for a moment and glanced at Leigh. Then she shook her head. "Thank you for your offer, but that won't be necessary." With that, she turned and walked out of the house.

"All right," the auctioneer said. "Are there any other bids for the scientific secrets of Dr. Elijah Rhodes?" He paused, eyes sweeping over the bidders. No one moved. "Sold!"

He reached into the box again. "And here we have the grand finale." He paused for effect and with a flourish pulled out a battered silver laptop. "A MacBook Pro!"

CHAPTER 10

By the time Daniel pedaled to the top of the hill, he was puffing hard. Which was embarrassing because Sandy wasn't. He consoled himself with the thought that her bike was newer and lighter than his. Also, he was carrying a pack and she wasn't. Nonetheless, he resolved to make it to the gym more often. There was no way a woman twenty years his senior should be in better shape than him.

Sandy pulled to a stop in a little clearing at the hilltop. She pointed her chin toward the right side of the road. "So, did I lie?"

Daniel stopped next to her and inhaled a deep breath so he wouldn't be panting when he spoke. "Nope. It's amazing."

The rolling hills of Napa County spread out below them. Well-groomed vineyards covered the landscape like an emerald carpet. Groves of trees lined little streams and slopes too steep for grape growing. Here and there, Victorian mansions or wine tasting rooms nestled into nooks in the land. It had rained that morning, leaving the air bright and clear. The whole scene looking freshly washed.

It was as pretty as a picture—which was why they were there.

Daniel leaned his bike against the end of a bench made of wrought iron and redwood slats. He slipped off his backpack and took out a collapsible easel, watercolor paints, brushes, and a portfolio holding art paper. As he got set up, Sandy parked her bike and sat down next to him. She pulled out her iPhone and started going through e-mail as he painted.

They sat like that for the better part of an hour. Sometimes they talked, and sometimes they didn't. They had done this a dozen times before. They would hike or bike to different scenic spots in the Bay Area, and Daniel would paint while Sandy relaxed. Sandy enjoyed watching him work, and he enjoyed the company.

"This is odd," Sandy said, breaking the comfortable silence.

Daniel didn't look up. He was struggling to capture the color and feel of sunlight on a cream-colored adobe winery building. "What's odd?"

"I just got an e-mail from Ron asking if we should put in a bid at the Rhodes estate sale."

"Ron . . . our CEO Ron?"

"Yes, Ron Thompson."

Daniel put down his brush. "It might be useful to go through his stuff to see if there's anything we can use to show he wasn't suicidal. Maybe we could bid on any letters or diaries he had."

"And any personal computers," Sandy immediately added.

"Right. Of course. So, when is the sale?"

"Good question." She dialed and held her phone to her ear. "Hi, Ron. It's Sandy. Thanks for the e-mail about the estate sale. We might want to buy his computer and a few other things. Do you know when the sale is?"

She stiffened as she listened to his reply.

"What's the number?" She snapped her fingers at Daniel and pointed to a blank sheet of paper. He took the hint and yanked out a new sheet. She called out numbers and Daniel jotted them down with his brush. "Thanks. I'll let you know what happens."

"The sale is going on right now," she reported as she dialed again. "They found Ron's name and number in a stack of papers that someone bid on, so they called him."

"Who would want to buy a stack of papers?"

But Sandy was on the phone again and ignored him. "Mr. Hansen? This is Sandra Hampton, the general counsel for Biosolutions, Inc. I believe you spoke with our CEO, Ron Thompson. It's possible that Biosolutions property may have made its way to Dr. Rhodes's home. Do not sell anything with a Biosolutions logo or letterhead."

Sandy's eyes widened as she listened to his response.

"Who bought it?"

Her mouth hardened into an angry line. "I see. What's left? Any computers?"

Pause. "Yes, but his personal computer might have Biosolutions data on it."

Pause. "I understand, but we need to examine the hard drive before it's reformatted. Dr. Rhodes might have saved Biosolutions files there."

She stared into the middle distance as she listened, her face stony. "You have no legal right to do that. Biosolutions does not have to bid for what might be its own property."

Pause, followed by a sigh. "One thousand."

She had her Iron Lady face on now. Her voice went neutral and flat. "Three thousand . . . Five."

Who was she bidding against? One of Biosolutions' competitors?

"Seven . . . Eleven."

Another possibility flashed into Daniel's mind. Not even a real possibility—more of a paranoid fear, but . . . a bead of cold sweat rolled down his spine.

"At this price, it's almost worth going to court," Sandy said, still using that monotone voice.

Daniel discovered that he was fidgeting with his brush and forced himself to stop.

"All right, sixteen. But if you don't stop this auction right now, we'll see both you and her in court tomorrow morning. Oh, and we'll sue you personally and seek attorney fees." Still icy and calm. Daniel wondered if Hansen was intimidated yet.

"My colleague will come by before five to pick it up."

She hung up and turned to Daniel. "Art hour is over," she snapped, heat coming into her voice and face. "You need to get to Rhodes's house by five o'clock to pick up his computer. Ask for the bloodsucking auctioneer. His name is Jim Hansen."

Daniel was already packing as she spoke. "I'll be there. Do I need to bring a check?"

She shook her head. "He insisted on a wire transfer. I'll talk to the accounting office and make sure it's ready to go."

"Got it."

"By the way, the other bidder was Leigh Collins. She had already bought a stack of Rhodes's papers before I called."

Daniel's stomach dropped. He nodded. "I was afraid it might be her. I wonder how she knew about the estate sale."

"Me too. I also wonder why we *didn't* know. You and I need to talk about that. But first, we need to get those papers back."

Daniel felt himself flush with embarrassment and anger. "I'll put together an *ex parte* motion tonight and get it to you by first thing tomorrow morning." An *ex parte* motion was one where the other side didn't get the required advance notice (usually at least two weeks)—typically because the motion was an emergency.

"I want you in *court* first thing tomorrow morning," Sandy snapped. "Get the draft to me by midnight. And make sure you've got plenty of coffee. We're going to have a long night."

CHAPTER 11

Leigh sat in her car, flipping through the stack of paper she just bought. It looked like she had just wasted fifty bucks of the firm's money.

Based on a quick skim, she had purchased three Biosolutions memos about protocols for conducting animal experiments and about three hundred pages of mostly illegible notes. Maybe the auctioneer was right and the secrets of the universe were in there, but Leigh could only read about one word in five. And there weren't even many words. Diagrams of molecules, long strings of math, and columns of random numbers filled most of the pages. There were no suicide notes or rants against Biosolutions.

In short, there was nothing that would be useful in beating Biosolutions' case. She tossed the documents in the backseat and pulled away from the curb.

It hadn't been a total waste, she reflected as she drove back to the office. At least she had been able to pay Rubinelli back for his stunt with Sheila Robinson. Leigh had only heard the auctioneer's end of the conversation with the Biosolutions lawyer—she assumed it was Rubinelli—but it was clear her opponent had been caught by surprise.

Leigh savored that thought until she pulled into her usual parking garage twenty minutes later. Then she checked her e-mail. She had a red-flagged message from Rubinelli titled "Ex parte motion." She clicked on it and read, her blood pressure rising. The gist of the message was that he was going to be filing and arguing an *ex parte* motion tomorrow morning complaining about her conduct at the auction today. He'd send her the papers when they were done, but didn't think they'd be ready until shortly before the hearing.

She couldn't believe it. He went behind her back to talk to her client's employees, and then he had the nerve to complain about *her*? What a hypocrite!

Brimming with righteous indignation, she checked the time. Four minutes until the deadline to give notice of an *ex parte* motion. Good. She called Rubinelli.

"Hello?" he said.

"This is Leigh Collins. I got your e-mail. In light of your past behavior, I'm surprised that you're accusing me of underhanded conduct. Very surprised."

He chuckled. "I take it you'll be opposing our motion."

"Oh, we'll be doing more than that. We're going to bring our own motion."

"Really. And what is this motion going to request?"

She hadn't thought that far ahead; she only knew she needed a motion—any motion—on the calendar at the same time his motion was set to be heard. "We're going to bring your misconduct to the court's attention," she improvised. "We'll . . . well, we'll ask for sanctions, of course. And an injunction preventing you from doing it again."

"Okay," he replied calmly. "See you in court."

She ended the call and got out of her car. She walked to the office, fuming and planning her motion. When she reached her building, she realized that she had left the box of documents in her car. She hesitated for a moment, then decided that she couldn't waste the ten minutes it would take to go back and get them.

She had cleared her calendar for the auction, so she had been hoping to leave early tonight. But that wasn't going to happen. She was going to be spending a very long night in the office thanks to Daniel Rubinelli. And also thanks to him she was going to miss yoga class for the third time in a row. She added that to his list of sins and went inside.

◆ ◆ ◆

At three thirty the next morning, Leigh and Andrea stumbled out of Diamond & Wang, bleary-eyed with fatigue and jittery with caffeine. The motion, supporting declarations, proposed order, and all the other papers were finished, edited, and proofread. And that was just the start. If Biosolutions wanted to go to war, American Guaranty would be ready.

Fortunately, they had both parked on the same floor of the garage, so neither of them would have to be alone before they were in their cars. The neighborhood was relatively safe, but it was the middle of the night.

They reached Leigh's car first. Leigh took one look at it and froze. Andrea stopped beside her and gasped.

The rear driver's side window had been smashed in. The stack of papers she bought at the auction was gone.

CHAPTER 12

Daniel took a swig of room-temperature coffee and rubbed his eyes. He sighed and pulled up the Word "Help" menu for the dozenth time, searching for an explanation of how to get the lines of text in his brief to line up with the numbers going down the left margin. He knew there was an easy way to do it because the secretaries at his old law firm had been able to make it happen by pressing a button. But he didn't have a secretary with him tonight. All he had was Rich Johnson.

When Daniel had gotten back to the office that afternoon, Sandy informed him that she had hired the help she promised. She said that Rich was a paralegal, so Daniel had assumed that Rich had actual paralegal skills. Daniel had been too busy working on the brief and other *ex parte* papers to read the résumé Sandy had e-mailed to him. Once he did, he realized that Rich had essentially no legal experience. He was basically a lab tech who was a couple of years out of college and wanted to go to law school.

Daniel could see why Sandy had hired Rich. He seemed bright, hardworking, and interested in the case. Plus, he was already at Biosolutions and had worked with Dr. Rhodes, so he was pre-vetted and could start work immediately. And on top of that, he knew the company and Rhodes's work. But it turned out that he *didn't* know how to handle even the most basic legal tasks. He was an expert with an electron microscope but couldn't format a Word document to save his life. Daniel eventually had to banish Rich to the copy room and take over.

A shiver ran through him. He was still wearing his biking clothes, and fatigue and air-conditioning left his skin chilled and clammy. He rubbed his arms and decided to pay a visit to the chai machine in the break room. He passed the empty office he was using as a war room for the case and glanced in.

He stopped. Rhodes's laptop was gone.

Daniel remembered leaving it on the desk when he came back from the auction, but it wasn't there. He went into the office and looked around to make sure he hadn't left it somewhere else. Nope.

That was strange. Access to this floor was keycard controlled, so no one could have wandered in off the street and stolen the laptop. Besides, the gray metal exterior was festooned with dings, scratches, and dirt. Its black-market resale value couldn't be very high. Unless the thief knew who had owned it. But the only people who both knew that and had Biosolutions keycards were him, Sandy, and Rich. And Sandy had left hours ago and was working from home.

Daniel went looking for Rich. He wasn't in the copy room, the break room, or the bathroom. Daniel finally found him in his cubicle. His tall, slender form was hunched over a laptop.

Rich turned as Daniel approached. "Oh, hi," he said, a disarming smile on his handsome, youthful face. His blue eyes were still alert and he looked fresh despite the hour. "I finished the copies, so I thought I'd take a look at Dr. Rhodes's laptop."

"Why?"

"I thought there might be something useful on it. The insurance company's lawyers may argue that the documents they bought were purely personal and that they therefore don't belong to Biosolutions. If we can show that Dr. Rhodes's personal computer—which was found in the same place—contains Biosolutions research, that strengthens your argument that the documents probably do as well, doesn't it?"

Daniel tried to force his fatigued brain to think through what Rich had just said. It seemed to make sense—but he still didn't want Rich messing around with the laptop. "Thanks for your initiative, Rich, but please check with me before doing anything like this in the future."

Rich nodded. "Will do, Mr. Rubinelli. I apologize for not talking to you first. You looked busy and I didn't want to disturb you."

"Don't worry about it," Daniel said with a sigh. "And don't call me Mr. Rubinelli. Daniel is just fine. So, did you find anything?"

Rich shook his head. "The computer requires a password. I made a few guesses based on my acquaintance with Dr. Rhodes, but none of them worked."

"Okay. We'll have an expert give it a try." Daniel yawned. "For now, I want you to go home and get a couple of hours of sleep. There's nothing more you can do to help me, and we've got a busy day ahead of us."

Rich left and Daniel took the laptop back to his office. He put it in the bottom drawer of his file cabinet, piled some old personnel files on it, and locked the cabinet.

CHAPTER 13

Leigh sat on a bench in Judge Bovarnick's courtroom, drumming her fingers on her notepad. She and a scattering of other lawyers waited for the judge.

Daniel Rubinelli was on the other side of the aisle, several rows up from her. He looked like a typical jock in a suit—a little over six feet tall and muscular. And from the way he carried himself, she guessed he was a former athlete. He had thick, slightly unruly brown hair, and his jaw didn't look quite so ridiculous now that she saw him in person. He would have fit in perfectly at Diamond & Wang—at least based on appearance. But she hoped Jack and Louis would never hire someone with Rubinelli's questionable ethical standards.

The Honorable Karen Bovarnick was still in her chambers, doubtless going through the stack of *ex parte* motions waiting for her when she came in.

For regular motions, the judge issued tentative rulings the day before and heard argument on them promptly at the scheduled time. *Ex parte* motions, however, were for emergencies that couldn't wait the weeks it took to get a regular motion heard. So the judge read the papers while the lawyers waited. And waited.

Leigh wasn't the only one from her team waiting. Behind her sat Sheila Robinson of American Guaranty, a Diamond & Wang paralegal with a box of exhibits, an IT guy with a PowerPoint projector and related equipment, and Andrea—who somehow managed to be just as bright and cheerful as usual despite the fact that she couldn't have gotten more than three hours of sleep.

All Rubinelli had was a slightly bewildered-looking guy who kept glancing around the courtroom like he'd never seen one before. Probably a student intern or something. She smiled—if this was decided by a full-scale evidentiary hearing, Rubinelli clearly wasn't prepared. And she was.

She hoped it wasn't decided just on the briefs. She had read Rubinelli's *ex parte* papers twice since he had handed them to her an hour ago. Not bad. The formatting was sloppy, but the content was strong. Much as she hated to admit it, he had done a good job on short notice. Simple, to the point, well researched. All the qualities she liked to think her briefs had. He also had gone for an understated tone—no outrage, no claims that she acted unethically. Just clean, straightforward argument.

Her own brief hadn't been nearly so restrained. It had been a little embarrassing to hand her fire-and-brimstone papers to him after she read his cool-and-professional filing.

"All rise," announced the bailiff.

Everyone in the courtroom got to their feet when Judge Bovarnick walked in. She motioned for them to sit down as she made her way to her raised seat behind the bench.

Leigh started to sit, but the first case the clerk called was *Biosolutions v. American Guaranty.*

The judge shook her head. "Hold that one for last. It's going to take a while."

Leigh sat down, wondering what that meant. Was the judge going to chew her out? Rubinelli? Was she going to force them to negotiate their differences in open court?

Judge Bovarnick was in rare form today. She always ran a no-nonsense courtroom and refused to let lawyers push her around. But this morning she didn't even let most of them speak, ruling on their motions with crisp dispatch. She denied all of them, which Leigh hoped was a good omen. She could live with losing her motion if Rubinelli lost his too.

The judge finished the last motion, which really hadn't been an emergency. That earned the lawyer who brought it a lecture. As the attorneys from that case left the courtroom, the clerk called the Biosolutions case again.

Judge Bovarnick watched them over the top of her glasses as they took their positions at the counsel tables on either side of the lectern. She did not look happy.

"All right." The judge flipped through the papers on her desk. "We're here on two motions. Biosolutions has moved for an order requiring the return of certain papers. They also want sanctions in the amount of sixteen thousand dollars plus attorney fees. American Guaranty wants an injunction barring Biosolutions lawyers from having any contact with current or former American Guaranty employees, and they also want sanctions." The judge's eyebrows shot up. "Including an award of attorney fees against Mr. Rubinelli personally. Wow."

Leigh winced internally. That request had sounded a lot more reasonable at one o'clock in the morning.

The judge put down the briefs and looked at the two lawyers. "I'm going to rule on both your motions—if you really want me to. But first we're going to have a little chat." She turned to Rubinelli. "If the situation were reversed, how would you feel about opposing counsel calling your client's employees and interviewing them behind your back?"

Rubinelli went red and stammered. "Your honor, the . . . California law is clear that, uh, it is permissible to—"

Judge Bovarnick waved her hand as if shooing away an annoying insect. "I didn't ask you what California law says. I asked you how you'd feel about it if she did that to you. Wouldn't you say that she was violating the spirit of the rules even if she was complying with their letter?"

Rubinelli cleared his throat. "That would depend on . . . on . . ." He stopped and took a deep breath. "Yes, I guess I would."

Leigh would have been enjoying this if she hadn't known her turn was coming. The judge had been merciful in calling all the other cases first so that there were no witnesses. Other than the ones she had brought, she remembered with an internal cringe.

"I thought so," the judge said, her expression lightening slightly. "I appreciate your candor, counsel." She turned to Leigh. "Ms. Collins, could you tell me exactly what you were shopping for at that estate sale? You weren't there for Dr. Rhodes's baseball card collection, were you?"

Leigh chuckled and gave what she hoped was a relaxed smile (ignoring the judge's joke wasn't an option, of course). "No, Your Honor. My client believes that Dr. Rhodes may have set fire to the lab and then committed suicide. We were looking for a diary or other evidence indicating that he was depressed or mentally unstable."

"And you thought that you might find that in a stack of documents with the Biosolutions logo? How many people keep diaries on their employer's letterhead?"

"A lot of people are unhappy at work. We thought there might be evidence of that in those documents. Also, most of the documents were handwritten notes and weren't on Biosolutions letterhead."

"And I suppose you'll make the same argument about his computer—that you thought it might contain evidence of his state of mind?"

"Yes, Your Honor."

"But when you learned that Biosolutions was concerned that there might be confidential company documents on that computer, you didn't suggest any steps to allay those concerns, did you?"

"Biosolutions wasn't present, Your Honor, so that wasn't possible."

The judge's eyebrows arched in disbelief. "The auctioneer had no trouble contacting them. Are you telling me you couldn't do the same thing?"

"No, Your Honor, but—"

"Did you have reason to believe their confidentiality concerns were unfounded?"

"We don't know what Biosolutions considers confidential, Your Honor."

"So the answer to my question is 'no,' correct?"

Leigh would have a lot more sympathy for witnesses going through cross-examination in the future. "That is correct, Your Honor."

"And instead of trying to find a solution, you started a bidding war. Is that also correct?"

"We wanted to be able to examine the documents we purchased and the data on the computer, Your Honor. We were concerned that we might not be able to."

"But you didn't call Mr. Rubinelli to ask for assurances that the computer's memory wouldn't be erased before you had a chance to run searches."

"No, Your Honor. Events moved very quickly once Biosolutions' lawyers called the auctioneer."

The judge frowned. "So they were already on the line at that point. It didn't occur to you to ask the auctioneer to let you talk to them?"

"No, Your Honor."

"Instead, you bid on the computer, eventually costing Biosolutions sixteen thousand dollars, correct?"

Leigh didn't like where this was going, but arguing with a judge was difficult and dangerous. "In the heat of the moment, bidding for the computer was the only path we could see to obtain the potentially critical data it held."

The judge glared down at her. "I asked you a yes-no question, counsel."

Leigh flushed, but she managed to keep her voice even. "The answer is yes."

"I thought so." The judge leaned back. "All right, let's turn to the motions themselves. I can rule on these motions. Or you can both withdraw your motions. Your choice."

Leigh turned to Rubinelli, who looked back at her uncertainly. Getting both motions withdrawn would be a win for her. Getting his motion denied would be better, of course, but withdrawal wasn't bad. She turned back to the judge. "Your Honor, we have a witness here to testify to the facts set forth in our motion. We also are prepared to put on additional documentary evidence demonstrating the inappropriateness of Mr. Rubinelli's conduct." She gestured to the back of the courtroom and saw Rubinelli's gaze flick to the group on the rear bench. "However, in the spirit of compromise, we're willing to withdraw our motion if the plaintiff does the same."

Judge Bovarnick turned to Rubinelli. "Counsel?"

He shifted his weight from foot to foot and glanced at the back of the courtroom again. "Um, we would be withdrawing without prejudice, Your Honor?"

The judge shrugged. "Sure. If you want to refile your motion at a later date, be my guest."

"And can we get a protective order that bars disclosure of the documents Ms. Collins purchased to anyone outside Diamond & Wang until Biosolutions has a chance to review them?"

The judge turned to Leigh. "Counsel, will you stipulate to a temporary attorneys'-eyes-only order?"

"I wish I could, Your Honor," Leigh said. "The documents were stolen from my car last night." She watched Rubinelli as she spoke. He looked genuinely surprised.

"We, uh, we will of course work with the police and opposing counsel to recover the missing documents," he said.

The judge glanced at her watch. "Will you also withdraw your motion?"

"Um, yes."

"Okay." The judge lifted the stack of papers off her desk and handed them to her clerk. "Mr. Rubinelli, draft an order stating that both motions are withdrawn without prejudice."

The judge nodded to the bailiff, who intoned, "This court is now adjourned and will be in recess until one o'clock p.m."

Leigh turned and headed down the aisle, eager to get out of the courtroom. She was happy with the result, which was basically what she had hoped for—though she could have done without the judicial tongue-lashing. But she wasn't sure what she should do next, and she didn't want to talk to Rubinelli until she figured it out.

"Counsel," the judge called from the bench.

Leigh stopped and turned to face the judge. So did Rubinelli. "Yes, Your Honor?" she said.

The judge held them each with her gaze for a second. "One more thing: play nice."

CHAPTER 14

Daniel sat in his office, trying to figure out what had happened to him back in Judge Bovarnick's courtroom. Everything seemed to be going his way. He had worked hard on his motion and knew he had done a good job. Then Collins handed him hers, and it was an emotional, over-the-top screed. Exactly the type of thing judges hate. He had seemed to be well on the way to a nice win.

But then he got in front of the judge and . . . He shook his head at the memory. Somehow things fell apart. He suddenly found himself admitting he'd done something wrong when he'd done exactly what the rules allowed. And then he withdrew his motion without even arguing it. He had let the judge push him around because he was too surprised and inexperienced in court to know how to push back. His only consolation was that Collins hadn't done any better, though she was clearly more experienced at fencing with judges than he was. Or *had* she done better?

He replayed the hearing in his head, particularly Collins's exchanges with the judge. She had certainly seemed polished and collected the whole time, like everything had been going according to her plan. Had it? Had she filed her motion simply so Judge Bovarnick could deny both motions and appear to be treating them equally? And who stole those documents from Collins's car? Was it a random theft or was it somehow related to the case? Should he have tried to call her out in front of the judge for not keeping the documents in a safer place?

The questions bounced around in his skull without finding answers. His brain was a fatigued jumble. He had worked sixteen of the last twenty hours, fueled by caffeine and adrenaline. Those were wearing off now, and he still faced an afternoon in the office.

His cell phone buzzed to let him know he had e-mail. He pulled it out. Dad wanted to know when Daniel would be landing at O'Hare Airport on Friday. Good question—he still needed to make flight reservations. He had been too focused on today's motion to think about his upcoming trip to Chicago.

He stopped by the break room for a double espresso from the Keurig machine and headed back to his office. He had to start someplace, and Dr. Rhodes's laptop was as good a spot as any.

He needed expert help, of course. Fortunately, he knew exactly who to call—but first he needed to get Sandy's permission.

He walked next door to her office and stuck his head in the door. "Hi, Sandy. We need to get into Dr. Rhodes's computer, but it's password protected."

She looked over at him and smiled. "Of course it is. Do you want to have IT take a look at it? They have password-cracking software."

"Didn't Rhodes have a major run-in with them? What if he booby-trapped his computer somehow?"

"Good point," she said, drumming her nails on her desk. "What do you recommend?"

"Well, I was thinking of calling my cousin. He's the best guy I know for computer stuff."

She nodded thoughtfully. "Is he the same one who fixed my laptop in ten seconds when the IT guys couldn't figure out what was wrong with it?"

"Yes, that's him. And he's not a security risk. He'll never work for one of our competitors, he has federal security clearances, and he's impossible to bribe. Trust me."

She thought for a moment, her face blank. "I do trust you, and I have no reason to distrust your cousin. But that computer could contain very, very valuable information. So we need to have our people involved. Let's hire your cousin, but have him work with our IT department. He'll do the work and they'll monitor what he finds."

Daniel nodded. "Okay, I'll get him started."

He went back to his desk and dialed his cousin Bruno—who had the misfortune of being the eldest male Rubinelli of his generation and therefore was named after the founding patriarch of the American Rubinellis, Bruno Antonio Augustus Rubinelli.

Bruno picked up on the second ring. "Danny Boy. What up, cuz?"

"Hey, B. Listen, I've got a computer that I need to get into, but it's password protected. Think you can help?"

"Did you look under the keyboard? Lots of idiots keep their passwords there. Or on a sticky note in their desk drawer or something."

"I checked. Nothing there. This belonged to a scientist who worked here, and I'm guessing he put some pretty heavy-duty security on it."

"Hmmm. A challenge. I'm listening."

"So, think you can help? We'll pay you for your time, of course."

"No worries. I'll be right over."

Daniel felt the muscles in his stomach relaxing. He hadn't realized he'd been clenching them. "Excellent. I'll meet you out front and walk you through security."

"One more thing: don't touch the computer again. You're lucky it's password protected. You would've messed up the metadata just by getting into it."

"Uh, sure thing."

"Good. On my way."

Daniel went outside and enjoyed the sunshine as he waited for his cousin. It was in the upper eighties, but the heat was dry and there was a nice breeze. The golden-brown grass waved on the hills and the cloudless sky was a pristine and smogless blue. A typical pleasant summer day in the East Bay.

During spring, when the hills were still brilliant green from the winter rains, he could almost imagine that Dublin, California, actually did sit in the Irish countryside. It never lasted, though. When summer came and the hills turned brown and the thermometer hit one hundred, the painted shamrocks on every street corner looked as out of place as a leprechaun in a spaghetti Western.

Ten minutes later, Bruno rolled up in a black BMW M6. He looked about twenty years younger than his real age of thirty-five—shaved head, hoodie, ragged jeans, lumpy backpack, multiple tattoos. He was the same skinny misfit Daniel remembered from family gatherings in his youth, except that Bruno had less body art back then. Also, in those days family members referred to him as "weird" or (after he dropped out of college) "underachieving" and even "delinquent." Then he sold his first company to Microsoft for nearly ten million dollars. After that, he was "colorful" and "free-spirited."

Fortunately, Daniel had always gotten along with him, though he was just a little jealous of his rebellious cousin.

Daniel gave Bruno a quick man-hug and escorted him past two surprised and suspicious security guards. Then they went upstairs to a conference room. Bruno pulled a laptop, a couple of external hard drives, cables, and other equipment out of his backpack. He gave Daniel an odd drink order (who puts Red Bull in a Jamba Juice smoothie?) and shooed him out. An IT guy in a Biosolutions polo shirt stood awkwardly in the corner, being ignored by Bruno.

Daniel answered his secretary's questions about their unusual visitor, relayed Bruno's drink request, and answered questions about that. Then he went into his office, shut the door, and pulled up a turgid set of new OSHA regulations that he'd been meaning to look over.

Five minutes later, he was taking a well-deserved nap.

"Ha! I always figured this was what my lawyers were doing when they billed for twelve hours of 'document review' in one day. Now I know."

Daniel opened his eyes to see Bruno standing in his doorway, a triumphant smile on his face. Daniel sat up and stretched. "I don't bill anymore, B. Besides, I was doing research, not document review. So, were you able to get into Dr. Rhodes's computer?"

Bruno's cue ball head gleamed as he nodded. "Dude was a freak, man."

Daniel nodded wearily. "What did you find?"

"Come on down and I'll show you."

They walked down the hall to the conference room where Bruno had set up shop. Dr. Rhodes's battered Mac had sprouted wires, which led to other computers and odd-looking electronic boxes. The IT drone hovered in front of it, but wasn't touching anything. He stepped out of the way when Bruno walked in.

Bruno pointed to one of three monitors he had set up. It displayed what looked like a list of file names—but they had titles like "I Will Survive," "Le Freak," and "Disco Inferno." "Check it out. Every seventies disco song. Four gigs of Abba and crap like that. He even had bootleg Bee Gees concert tapes. I mean, who makes bootlegs of the Bee Gees?"

"Anything else? Any hint that he might be depressed or, you know, suicidal? Anything about where he might have backed up his research?"

Bruno shrugged. "Don't know yet. I'll need to image the hard drive before I start poking around. All I did so far was beat the first layer of encryption—which was pretty intense—and skim the file catalog."

"First layer," Daniel repeated. "You mean there are more layers of encryption?"

"Oh, yeah. Definitely. Lots of other security too. Rhodes put some serious black ice on these. Not off-the-shelf stuff either. Custom. And nasty. I think it's set up to wipe the hard drive clean if you step on a trip wire."

"Think you can pick its locks without stepping on any of those trip wires?"

Bruno took a deep breath and blew it out. "Maybe. I never met a computer I couldn't hack, but I also never met this particular setup." He scratched his neck and looked doubtfully at the machines. "So maybe. No promises."

Daniel nodded. Bruno did freelance work for the NSA and FBI as a hobby, so if he couldn't get into Dr. Rhodes's machines, no one could. "I'll tell my boss. I'm pretty sure she'll give us a green light, but wait until you hear from me, okay?"

Bruno nodded. "Cool. Hope she does. I'm curious now. There's a good ten gigs of stuff locked down on there. All I can see is the folder name."

Maybe Sandy or Rich would recognize it. "What is it?"

"Enoch."

CHAPTER 15

After leaving Judge Bovarnick's courtroom, Leigh sent Jack Diamond a quick text with the results. Then she and Andrea strolled down to the farmers' market two blocks from the courthouse. Andrea loved to cook and stopped at every farmers' market or fresh produce stand she could. Leigh viewed food—particularly the rich dishes her secretary created—the same way postmen view dogs: a fact of life, but one that could do real damage to her rear end if she wasn't careful.

"That lawyer this morning—Daniel—he's cute, isn't he?" Andrea commented as she examined organic bok choy arranged in a bushel basket.

"I suppose," Leigh said with a shrug. "I didn't really notice."

Andrea looked up from the vegetables. "How could you not notice? You were in court with him for almost an hour."

"I guess he's not really my type. Hey, look at those." She pointed to some random piles of fruit. "They look terrific, don't they?"

Andrea didn't bother looking at the produce. "So what is your type?"

Leigh sighed. "I'm not sure what my type is. All I know is that I can't seem to find it."

"Well, I'm glad the last one wasn't your type," Andrea replied. "You had me worried, girl."

Leigh winced at the memory. "That was only two dates."

"It should have been zero dates. Any guy who forgets your first date shouldn't get one."

"I know, I know. That should have been a warning."

"Now that Daniel Rubinelli," Andrea said with a sly smile. "I'll bet he wouldn't forget. He seems like a nice young man. And he was so respectful to that judge. She liked him."

Leigh rolled her eyes. Andrea was right about the judge, which further annoyed Leigh. "Trust me. He's not a nice man."

"I can tell about people," Andrea went on. "And I think he's nice. He's the kind of man who visits his mother."

CHAPTER 16

Gray rain fell on the living and the dead at Chicago's Holy Sepulchre Cemetery. It blew on a fitful wind, gusting under the black umbrellas and wetting mourners and gravediggers. Graveside ceremonies were moved inside.

Daniel was soaked five minutes after he got out of his car, but that was okay. The weather reminded him, and that was good.

It had rained two years ago on this day. The weather had slowed traffic to a ridiculous crawl, and the cab ride from the airport to the hospice had taken an eternity. He had left as soon as he got the call, of course, but Maria and Dad had gotten there ahead of him. Maybe they had spent the night—he never thought to ask. Maria had met him in the hallway outside Mama's room, her face wet and blotchy, and he knew before she said a word. He went into the room and saw Dad hunched over the bed, embracing the withered, shrunken thing that used to be Mama before the cancer started eating her.

Suddenly, Daniel had needed to leave. He couldn't be in the same room with his mother's death and his father's grief. He ran outside and stood gasping for breath. Rain drenched him, streaming down his face like a flood of cold tears.

Like it did today. Standing at his mother's grave in the rain brought back all the agony of her slow death. And the other deaths. Uncle Antonio. Aunt Sophia. Each of them roasted over a slow fire of illness and pain. They looked like concentration camp survivors by the time they died. He looked around the field of crosses and stones surrounding him. How many of them went like that?

"It still surprises me." The voice was gravelly and soft.

Dad's voice reminded Daniel that he wasn't alone. Maria hadn't come back to Chicago this year, so it was just the two of them. Daniel turned to his father. His granite face was gray and tired. "What surprises you?"

"That she's dead. I'll make coffee in the morning and start to get out two cups before I remember. Or I'll be at the store and catch a whiff of her perfume. For just a second, I'll think she walked up behind me— and I turn, but it's not her. Each time, it's like . . . like ripping open a cut that had been sewn shut."

Daniel nodded, dislodging raindrops from his eyelashes. "I know. Whenever something good happens at work, my first instinct is to call and tell her. But I can't, and suddenly whatever happened doesn't seem important anymore. All I can think about is Mom."

"But it is," Dad rumbled.

Daniel had long ago stopped trying to decipher his father's cryptic remarks. "What is what?"

"Your work, Danny. It's important."

Daniel started to mumble something self-deprecating, but Dad interrupted. "You know one of the things I say to myself when I remember she's dead? I say, 'Danny's out there fighting what killed her. And he's going to beat it.' That always makes me feel better."

No pressure there. "I'm doing what I can."

"See, cancer isn't just a disease. It's an enemy. But it's one I can't fight." Dad held out his hands. They were a boxer's hands: big, powerful, scarred from decades as a beat cop in a rough neighborhood. "There's nothing I can hit or grab hold of. But your company—I read about what they're doing. And you—" A coughing fit seized him.

Daniel reached an arm around his father's massive shoulders. It was easy to forget that this tank of a man was pushing seventy and not in the best health. He had quit smoking twenty years ago, but his habit had left him with chronic obstructive pulmonary disease, or COPD. And it had been getting worse as Dad aged.

"Come on," Daniel said. "Let's get out of the rain."

Dad shook his head. "Go on back to the car. I'm going to stay a little longer."

"Then so am I."

They stood there side by side, not speaking and not needing to.

◆　◆　◆

Back at his father's house, Daniel lounged on the sofa, watching a Cubs game on the same TV he had watched growing up. Dad was a thrifty man.

Daniel's cell phone rang. It was Bruno.

Daniel hesitated. Dad had never liked Bruno, whom he considered "an overgrown delinquent with too much money." On the other hand, Bruno knew where Daniel was and wouldn't call without a good reason.

Daniel picked up the call on the third ring. "Hey, what's up?"

"Bad news. You know that MacBook you asked me to look at? Stolen."

Daniel froze. "What? When?"

"Last night. Your boss told me to leave it in the secure room at Biosolutions. I said it would be safer at my place, but no."

Daniel sucked in a breath and blew it out through his teeth. He didn't relish the thought of an I-told-you-so conversation between his cousin and Sandy. Bruno must have read his mind: "Don't worry, man. I was cool about it and so was she."

"Do you know who took it?"

"Whoever did it wore a hoodie and a ski mask, so the security camera pictures aren't much good—but I'm looking at the keycard log right now. According to this, Doctor Elijah Rhodes entered the building at one thirteen this morning and left at quarter to two. Looks like we've got a dead man walking."

CHAPTER 17

Leigh tried not to get too excited. The coroner's report contained a lot of medical jargon, and she might have misunderstood it. She reread it slowly, looking up three words on merriam-webster.com just to be sure she hadn't gotten anything important wrong the first time through.

Nope, she had read it right. This was big news. So big that it needed to be shared right away. She went looking for Andrea—then recalled that her secretary was at some cooking convention today. She considered telling Jack, but he was out of the office too. Well, that was frustrating. She had to tell someone, but whom?

A wicked thought occurred to her. She picked up the phone and dialed.

"Hello, Daniel Rubinelli."

"Daniel, Leigh Collins here. I was wondering whether we could work out a deal on that computer your side bought at the Rhodes estate sale. We'll need access to the hard drive." She could get that simply by sending a demand for inspection under the Code of Civil Procedure, but this gave her an excuse to call. Then at the end of the conversation, she could mention the report in an oh-by-the-way tone.

Rubinelli didn't answer for several seconds. "It was stolen two days ago."

"It was?" she asked stupidly. "What happened?"

"We're still trying to piece that together. Have the police made any progress on catching whoever broke into your car?"

"I don't think so. It's probably a pretty low priority for them. Do you think the same person might have stolen the computer?"

"Good question. It does seem like a major coincidence that someone would steal Rhodes's notes and his computer in the same week. Can you think of anyone who might be interested enough in his research to risk two burglaries?"

Was he implying that her client or her firm were guilty? "No."

He was silent for a moment. "Me neither. Well, I hope the cops solve both crimes fast. I'll let you know if I hear anything."

"Likewise."

"Was there anything else you wanted to talk about?"

She looked down at the report in her hands. She found that she couldn't quite bring herself to mention it. He was being nice enough today, and it would be mean to ambush him. She almost wished he had been a jerk on the call so that she could feel good about sucker punching him with this. "No, nothing else."

He would find out soon enough that the coroner had determined that Dr. Rhodes committed suicide by overdosing on barbiturates.

CHAPTER 18

Daniel stared at the phone after he hung up. He hadn't been entirely honest during the call. He actually did have an idea of who might have stolen the computer—and possibly the stack of documents Leigh bought at the auction.

The thief had hidden as much as possible from the Biosolutions security cameras by wearing an oversize hoodie, ski mask, gloves, and baggy pants. Even with repeated viewings and digital enhancement, it was impossible to tell the intruder's race, age, hair color and length, or gender. The only thing the outfit didn't conceal was height and general build: the thief was on the tall side and slender. Daniel could think of someone who fit that description and had already tried to get into Rhodes's laptop.

But why would Rich do it? He had worked closely with Rhodes as a lab tech for nearly two years. If he had wanted to steal Rhodes's secrets, couldn't he have done it then? Why wait until Rhodes was dead?

His train of thought was interrupted by the arrival of the morning mail. He flipped through the stack quickly, sorting it into smaller piles—legal newspapers and magazines for reading and forwarding when he had a few free minutes, sections from a draft employee handbook with comments from Sandy, letters from outside counsel that he had already received by e-mail, junk mail, and a manila envelope from an address he didn't recognize. He tore it open and pulled out a stack of documents. It was the coroner's report, autopsy protocol, and toxicology results for Elijah Rhodes.

Daniel read intently for half an hour. Then he sat back and stared into space.

So the coroner thought Dr. Rhodes died of a barbiturate overdose. Not good news. If Rhodes killed himself, that would void the "key person" insurance policy and cut the size of the case in half.

Daniel needed to get a medical expert for a second opinion—and hoped it wouldn't confirm that Rhodes committed suicide. So that was now the number-one item on his to-do list. Was there anything else he needed to do because of this report?

He flipped through the report again, pondering its implications. How else could it hurt him? And was there any way he could use legal jujitsu to turn the report to his advantage?

An intriguing thought popped into his head. He turned to the toxicology results and reread them carefully. Then he went to the autopsy protocol and read the internal examination section again. A smile slowly spread across his face. His to-do list had a new number-one item: take Jim Keller's deposition. Immediately.

CHAPTER 19

Leigh's mind kept coming back to her conversation with Daniel Rubinelli. It bothered her, and for once that wasn't because he did or said something obnoxious.

He had asked whether she knew anyone who might be interested enough in Rhodes's research to commit two burglaries. She said no, but that wasn't entirely true now that she thought about it.

Her mind went back to the auction at Dr. Rhodes's house and the woman who tried to bid on his papers. Maybe she had followed Leigh back to the office and then broken into her car. And maybe she had also stolen Rhodes's laptop from Biosolutions.

Leigh turned the idea over in her head. The woman *had* acted strangely. She showed up late to the auction, and she hadn't been prepared to bid. It was almost as if she had wandered in off the street after seeing a sign for the estate sale. But if that's what happened, why would she bid a hundred dollars for a random stack of papers? Wouldn't she be a lot more likely to try to buy a chair or a TV or something else with obvious value?

The woman's actions only made sense if she knew what was in those papers or at least knew about Rhodes. But if that was the case, why wasn't the woman a registered bidder like Leigh? And why did she show up late?

Maybe the woman hadn't known the papers would be for sale. The auctioneer said the papers came from Dr. Rhodes's car, which had just been found. Maybe the woman had searched the house after Dr. Rhodes died, but hadn't known about the car. She didn't realize that the papers or the laptop existed until the auctioneer pulled them out of that box.

That might make sense if the woman had been monitoring the auction somehow. Maybe she had been hiding in the house or had bugged it. Or maybe she was watching from a car parked on the street outside. She would have had to be nearby because she showed up at the auction a minute or two after the auctioneer first held up the stack of notes.

The woman might be working for one of Biosolutions' competitors. They could have heard about Dr. Rhodes's death and hired her to search his house and get anything she could about his research.

So if all that was true—and Leigh wasn't convinced that it was—why did the woman simply leave when the auctioneer asked her to register? If she were a professional thief, she presumably would have had a fake driver's license. And if there were any chance that she might have to make a bid at the auction, she probably would have looked into the rules. As it was, all the woman did was show up, act suspicious, and leave. That made no sense at all.

The theory collapsed and Leigh was back to square one, except now she had even more questions.

CHAPTER 20

Daniel sat staring at the bar exam booklet, panic rising in his chest. He hadn't studied. He also hadn't brought any pencils. And he wasn't wearing any pants—which he desperately hoped no one would notice. All of that would have been okay if he could only concentrate. But how could he concentrate while sitting under an alarm bell that kept going off continuously? And why was the alarm playing the marimba?

He opened bleary eyes and realized his phone was ringing. He looked at the clock on his bedside table. The glowing numbers read 6:45 a.m. He didn't recognize the number on the caller ID but picked up anyway. Anyone calling at this hour had better have a good reason for it.

"Hello?" he croaked.

"Danny, it's Bruno."

He groaned and rolled onto his back. "Dude, I didn't get to bed until after one o'clock."

"I broke the second encryption layer last night."

"What?"

"The second layer of encryption on Rhodes's computer. I'm through it. There's still more—he encrypted each folder separately. Still, this is major progress."

It took a moment for Daniel's sleep-fogged brain to process that. "Wait, what? His computer was stolen—wasn't it?"

"Yeah, but I copied the hard drive before I gave it to your boss. Made it easier for me to work on it, and I trust my security more than hers."

Daniel sat up, stretched, and looked for something to write with and on. "Can't say I blame you, though it would've been nice to know about the copy."

"Sorry, force of habit. I'm used to working strictly on a need-to-know basis. Speaking of which, keep this as quiet as you can. Remember that the original drive got stolen from your company. Could have been an inside job."

So Bruno had the same basic suspicion Daniel did. "You think so?"

"Not sure what to think. Which is why the fewer people who know about this, the better."

Daniel decided to tell Sandy but definitely not Rich. "Okay."

"There's more: it looks like Rhodes had another lab."

Daniel wasn't sleepy anymore. "Seriously? Where was it? What was he doing?"

"Don't know. So far, all I've got is a folder labeled 'Animal Trackers—Lab Two.'"

"What's in it?" Daniel asked.

"Like I said, it's encrypted," Bruno said, a trace of annoyance in his voice. "I won't know what's in it until I break the encryption."

"Any idea how long that will take?"

"Not really. Could be tomorrow, could be a year from tomorrow. I'm starting to get a feel for how Rhodes thought, so I should get in eventually. Just don't know when."

"We need to find that lab, B. Can you tell where it is?"

"Nope. All I've got are three folder names. The other two are 'Compound E Formulations and Protocols' and 'Lab Two Documents.'"

Daniel thought for a moment. "If we're looking for the address, the documents folder sounds the most promising, don't you think?"

"Yep. I'm on it."

"Is it possible he kept an off-site backup there for the research he did in the lab that burned?"

"Sure," Bruno said. "The backup could be anywhere. Might even be nowhere—he could have kept the backup in the cloud. But probably not. He was too security conscious. I'm guessing he had a server somewhere. This second lab of his would be a good place to look."

"Is there, uh, any risk that whoever stole the laptop will be able to get past the encryption faster than you can?"

"Not without the encryption keys. If they don't have those, they're not getting in at all."

That was a comforting thought—for about three seconds. "What would the keys look like?"

Bruno was silent for a few seconds. "Depends on the form. You can store an encryption key on a disk or a USB drive or really anything. Even paper. Written down, a key would look like a string of gibberish. The longer the string, the stronger the key. Rhodes was using pretty heavy-duty encryption, so we're talking a few pages for each key."

So the keys could have been in that stack of documents stolen from Leigh Collins's car. "If someone had the keys, how long would it take them to get into the folders on Dr. Rhodes's computer?"

"If they have the keys, they got in five minutes after they turned on the computer."

CHAPTER 21

Biosolutions wanted to take the deposition of Jim Keller next week? That was weird—not that they would depose Keller, but that they would do it now. Keller was the fire investigator who wrote the official report on the Biosolutions lab fire, so he was an important witness. That meant his depo would normally be one of the last ones taken.

Plus, depositions usually didn't come until after document discovery was done. Witnesses normally could only be deposed once, so lawyers generally waited until they were sure they had all the documents potentially relevant to a witness before taking their shot. You didn't want to have the smoking gun memo show up *after* you had deposed the guy who wrote it.

But Daniel Rubinelli had subpoenaed Keller's deposition now—even though Biosolutions and American Guaranty had only just started their document productions. Why? Leigh debated whether there was a reason not to ask what he was doing, decided there wasn't, picked up the phone, and called him.

"Daniel Rubinelli."

"Daniel, Leigh Collins here. I got your subpoena for Jim Keller's deposition. Why are you taking his depo now?"

"Because I want his testimony."

Leigh tried to ignore his snippy answer. "Is there a reason you can't wait until we're done with document discovery?"

"Is there a reason that I have to?" he countered. "I'm ready to take his deposition now. I've got everything I need for him, and I see no reason to delay."

"I'd like to wait until we have all the documents. I'm still waiting for Biosolutions to finish producing documents about their fire protection systems, for example."

"Those are all irrelevant. Keller is a third-party witness who never saw those documents. I don't plan to ask him about them."

"Yeah, but what if I do?"

"Then you can depose him again later."

Was he being stupid or intentionally obnoxious? Leigh took a deep breath. "Are you familiar with the one-deposition rule, counsel? What happens when Keller's lawyer asks for a protective order when I send out my subpoena in two months?"

"You can explain to the judge why you weren't ready to ask all your questions now," he replied. "If you've got a good reason, it shouldn't be a problem."

"Or we can go to the judge now and you can explain why this depo can't wait until we're both ready," Leigh snapped.

"You really want to bother Judge Bovarnick again?"

"No, but you're not giving me much choice." *Firm but calm,* she told herself. *Firm but calm.* "Give it some thought and let me know by the end of the day whether you've changed your mind. If I don't hear from you, I'll have to go to court on an *ex parte* motion."

She hung up without saying good-bye. By this point she knew Rubinelli well enough to know that she didn't need to wait for the end of the day to start on the motion. "Hey, Andrea," she called through her office door. "We're going to be doing another *ex parte* in the Biosolutions case. Could you set up a motion template?"

"I already did," she replied as she walked in and sat in one of Leigh's guest chairs. "Check your in-box."

Leigh swiveled back to her computer. There it was. "Have you been reading my mind again, Andrea?"

"Just listening to you yell at Mr. Rubinelli."

"You wouldn't believe what he did this time. He—" She paused. "Was I really yelling?"

Andrea gave a motherly smile and patted her arm. "I'm sure he deserved it. I also called the court to check on the *ex parte* calendar. It's pretty full tomorrow morning. Can this wait until Thursday, or do you need to be in court tomorrow?"

Leigh thought for a moment. The deposition date set by Rubinelli wasn't until next week. That wasn't enough time for a normally scheduled motion, so she would need to go in on an *ex parte* basis—but she didn't necessarily need to go in tomorrow. "Thursday will work." She sniffed. "What's that smell?"

Andrea gave a broad grin. "You mean the chocolate macaroons I brought in? Would you like some?"

Leigh recoiled. "The same ones you brought in last month? Those things have like three hundred calories each."

"You don't want any?"

"I didn't say that. Bring them in here. But don't make them again for a few months, okay? It's still summer."

One hour and four macaroons later, Leigh was in a much better mood. She would pay for the cookies later, but right now her soul basked in a warm, chocolaty glow. It also helped to talk and laugh with Andrea for a while. It brought her blood pressure down and made it a lot easier to deal with petty nuisances—like Daniel Rubinelli.

But she would have to deal with him eventually, and "eventually" might as well come now. She said good-bye to Andrea, brushed the crumbs off her desk, and started working on the *ex parte* motion.

CHAPTER 22

Daniel scribbled notes furiously as Leigh Collins argued.

"And so, Your Honor," she said, her voice enviably calm and reasonable, "Mr. Rubinelli refused to explain why he insisted on taking Mr. Keller's deposition now, before document discovery is complete. He also refused to postpone Mr. Keller's deposition to a mutually agreeable date. We therefore had no choice but to bring this motion. We ask the court to enter a protective order barring the deposition of Jim Keller until document discovery is complete. Thank you." She gathered her papers from the lectern and sat down.

Judge Bovarnick nodded wearily at Daniel. "Mr. Rubinelli?"

He bounced up. "Yes, Your Honor. I'm sure Ms. Collins would like to know why I want to depose Mr. Keller now. For that matter, I'm sure she would like to know why I do everything in this case."

He allowed himself an ironic smile. The judge didn't smile back. "She'd be delighted to hear my entire strategy. But I don't have to tell it to her. The Code of Civil Procedure doesn't make me do that. It also doesn't let her schedule my discovery. If I want to take Mr. Keller's deposition now, I can do it. If Ms. Collins has a scheduling conflict on the day I picked for Mr. Keller's deposition, I will gladly work with her to find a mutually convenient date. But I won't put off the deposition for months simply because she isn't ready to take his testimony now. If she later wants to depose him a second time, she can move for leave to do so. Thank you."

He sat down. Collins rose and stepped to the lectern. "Your Honor, I would like to correct several misstatements in Mr.—"

The judge held up her hand. "Let me ask you this: Did you ever contact Mr. Keller to ask whether he would agree to a second deposition if it proved necessary?"

Collins paused for a heartbeat, as if weighing whether to argue with the judge. "No, Your Honor."

"Well, I did. Jim Keller has testified in my courtroom several times, and we happen to be friends. So after I got your motion, I called him. He said that he would be willing to do it if you're willing to buy him dinner. The conversation took no more than five minutes. So, are you willing to buy him dinner in the event that you do need to depose him again after you finish document discovery?"

Collins looked flustered. "We . . . uh, I'll need to check with my client, but I think so. Would we be splitting the bill with the plaintiff?"

Judge Bovarnick looked at Daniel with arched eyebrows. "Mr. Rubinelli?"

Daniel nodded. "Of course, Your Honor. I can recommend several excellent Italian places in the Dublin area."

"Good, he likes Italian," replied the judge. "Here's my order on the motion: it is denied. In the event that the defendant determines that a second deposition of Mr. Keller is necessary, the parties are to treat him to dinner at a good Italian restaurant and split the bill, including a twenty percent tip, evenly. If the parties cannot agree on a restaurant, they shall submit to binding baseball-style arbitration with professional arbitrators chosen from the roster at JAMS. The costs of arbitration will be split evenly. Ms. Collins, please draft the order."

Daniel chuckled at the mental image of using an arbitration panel to pick a restaurant. He started putting papers in his briefcase.

Judge Bovarnick cleared her throat. "Just a minute. We're not done yet."

Not done? Daniel looked up in surprise. The judge's face wore an expression that reminded him of the look he used to get from nuns at his elementary school when he had been misbehaving—the look that came just before he was ordered to hold out his hand to be whacked with a ruler.

The judge looked back and forth from him to Collins for a few seconds, then leaned forward. "This dispute could have been avoided by a few minutes on the phone and a minimal amount of professionalism. All you needed to do was agree to a second deposition if it was necessary. Then the two of you could have called Jim to see if he would agree. That would have taken, what, ten minutes total?

"But instead you decided to waste hours writing briefs on this completely unnecessary motion. Worse, you wasted over an hour of *my* time reading your briefs, calling Jim, and holding this hearing. I don't appreciate that." She paused for breath and her look softened some. "It's not entirely your fault, I suppose. Young lawyers are so combative these days. Maybe it's because you all seem to communicate by e-mail and phone, never face-to-face. But whatever the cause, it's got to stop."

Judge Bovarnick leaned back and crossed her arms. "The last time you two were here, I suggested that you play nice. Now I'm going to order it. First, I hereby order both parties to engage in an information exchange like that contemplated by Federal Rule of Civil Procedure 26. If you have anything that is relevant to the case and not privileged, you need to produce it without being asked. You also have to exchange lists of witnesses who are likely to have relevant information. And if something *is* privileged or otherwise protected from disclosure, you have to create a log describing it and provide that to the other side. Second, when you contact third-party witnesses, you must do it together so that we can avoid the sort of thing that led to this hearing. Third, neither party can bring any further motions until the lawyers have met face-to-face for at least half an hour to negotiate a resolution. That's my order. If either of you violates it, I will come down on you like a ton of bricks. Do I make myself clear?"

Daniel and his opponent exchanged nervous glances. "Yes, Your Honor," they said simultaneously.

"Good," said the judge as she got up. "*Now* we're done."

CHAPTER 23

September

Leigh sat at a conference room table at Biosolutions, waiting for Jim Keller's deposition to begin. Since Rubinelli had issued the deposition subpoena, he got to pick the location. Not surprisingly, he had picked a location about twenty feet from his office.

Leigh wasn't complaining. She would do the same thing when she started taking depositions. Besides, Rubinelli (or more likely his secretary) had ordered a carafe of Philz coffee and a plate of Specialty's cookies. She poured herself a cup and picked a chunky oatmeal-and-chocolate-chip cookie, which she left sitting on a napkin in front of her. For now.

Jim Keller sat immediately to Leigh's right. He looked nothing like Leigh's mental image of a fire investigator. He was a slight, bookish man of about thirty-five with long, thinning black hair. He wore a double-breasted black suit with a little too much padding in the shoulders, a bright yellow shirt, and a black tie. Leigh wished she had been more specific when he asked her what he should wear. She had said "a suit," thinking that since he had done this before he would know what kind of suit to wear. Especially since this would be videotaped. He really should be dressed to look as dull and respectable as possible. Like she was.

Leigh didn't represent Keller, but he had opted to come without a lawyer. He was an important witness to her side, so Leigh would need to be on her toes to assert objections and make sure Rubinelli didn't cross any lines with his questioning.

Rubinelli walked in thirty seconds before the deposition was scheduled to begin. He sat down opposite Keller and had the court reporter swear him in. Then Rubinelli started with the routine background that most lawyers used to start a deposition.

Rubinelli then had Keller walk him through the fire investigation from start to finish. After that, Rubinelli turned to the report Keller had written on the fire, which he went through in detail. Then he turned to the police report, which he also went over with a fine-tooth comb. By the time Rubinelli neared the end of the police report, Keller was getting noticeably snippy in his answers. And Leigh had started working on the cookie and her second cup of coffee to help keep herself awake.

"So, to summarize, you conclude in your report that the fire was caused by arson, correct?" Rubinelli asked.

"You read very well, Mr. Rubinelli."

"So that's a yes?"

Keller rolled his eyes. "Yes."

Rubinelli nodded. "Okay. And you're aware that, based in part on your report, the Dublin police believe the person most likely to be the arsonist is Dr. Elijah Rhodes?"

"Objection, asked and answered," Leigh put in. Repetitive questioning was typical of an inexperienced attorney, and she wanted to encourage him to move along.

"She's right," said Keller. "You asked almost the exact same question fifteen minutes ago."

"I'm just summarizing to make sure I understand your testimony before we move on. I only have a few more of these questions, and Ms. Collins did not instruct you not to answer." He paused. "So is your answer yes?"

"Yes," Keller snapped.

"Thank you. The police concluded that Dr. Rhodes opened the fuel tank on the backup generator, lit the fuel, ran inside the lab, and sat down at his desk, correct?"

Keller held up the police report. "That's what this says."

"And you have no reason to disagree with it, correct?"

Keller pointedly looked at his watch. "Correct."

Leigh glanced at Rubinelli as she popped another piece of cookie in her mouth. He was leaning forward and studying his notes. His fingers were a blur as he fidgeted with a pen cap. She realized that he was as tense as a cat about to pounce. Weird. What was he up to?

"But if Dr. Rhodes were dead—or at least unconscious—before the fire started, then he couldn't be the arsonist, right?"

She drew in a breath to object—and a cookie crumb went down her windpipe. She instantly went into an uncontrollable coughing fit.

Hack! Hack! Hack! She bent over the table, totally helpless. Keller patted her on the back.

The deposition video would later show that her coughing fit lasted less than a minute, but it seemed to go on for an hour. When she finally caught her breath, she croaked, "Objection, assumes facts not in evidence."

"You can answer," Rubinelli said to Keller. Then he turned to Leigh. "After he does, would you like to take a break?"

Leigh's face burned. "No, I'm f-fine," she forced out, stifling another cough.

"I suppose the answer to your question is yes," Keller said, shifting uneasily in his seat. "But I'm not aware of any evidence that Dr. Rhodes was either dead or unconscious before the fire started."

Rubinelli nodded as if he had expected exactly that answer. He handed a document to the court reporter, then distributed copies to Keller and Leigh. "Let the record reflect that I have given the witness plaintiff's exhibit number three, which is the autopsy protocol prepared for the Coroner's Bureau concerning the death of Dr. Elijah Rhodes. Mr. Keller, please read the first full sentence on page eight."

Keller flipped to the page. So did Leigh. What had she missed when she read it before?

"'Examination of the esophagus and lungs revealed no visible injuries or disease process,'" Keller recited.

"Is it typical for fire victims to have smoke damage in their lungs?" Rubinelli asked.

Keller stared at the report. "I . . . I'm not a doctor, but that is my understanding."

"Okay, next I'm going to mark plaintiff's exhibit number four, which I'm handing to the witness. This is the coroner investigator's report regarding the death of Elijah Rhodes. Mr. Keller, please look at the section titled 'Death.' Could you read the first cause listed in that section?"

"Sure. 'Cause A: barbiturate overdose.'"

"Thank you. So, since Dr. Rhodes was either dead or dying from a barbiturate overdose when the fire started, do you still think it's possible that he set the fire?"

So *that's* where Rubinelli had been heading this whole time. And Leigh hadn't seen it until now. She had been so focused on how she could use the coroner's report and related documents to beat Biosolutions' case on the life insurance policy that she had missed how Rubinelli could use it against her client on the building insurance policy. She felt like an idiot.

Keller sat silently for over a minute, poring over the autopsy protocol and coroner's report, then glancing at his fire report and the police report. At last, he put them down and looked up. "I'm sorry, could you repeat the question?"

"Sure," Rubinelli replied. "Since Dr. Rhodes was either dead or dying from a barbiturate overdose when the fire started, do you still think it's possible that he set the fire?"

Keller slowly shook his head. "No."

CHAPTER 24

October

Daniel's morning mail included a CD of documents from Leigh Collins. According to her cover letter, it contained all of the documents required by Judge Bovarnick's "play nice" order. Daniel had been expecting this—the deadline for them to exchange documents by mail had been yesterday. He had mailed a disk to Collins with a similar cover letter, which was probably arriving in her office right about now.

He had expected to receive a bunch of insurance company forms and other mostly useless stuff. Collins's CD did hold lots of bureaucratic crud, but there was more. A lot more. After an hour of reading, Daniel knew he needed to talk to Sandy.

He walked over to her office and looked in. She was on the phone, but she caught his eye and motioned for him to come in. She finished her call as he sat in one of her guest chairs.

"What's up?" she asked as she typed up a note from the call.

"I've got an update for you."

She stopped typing. "Has your cousin decrypted more of the hard drive?"

"Not yet, but I just got the insurance company's initial document disclosure, and I think I figured out a couple of things."

"Like what?"

"Well, to begin with, about a month before he died, Dr. Rhodes set up an anonymous bank account in the Cayman Islands and put six million into it. I'll bet whoever owns that account now—or owns the money anyway—could tell us something about his death, and they might be able to tell us about a lot more. Like how the fire started, for example."

"Or where that second lab might be," Sandy mused. A frown creased her forehead. "Why were you able to figure this out from the other side's documents?"

"Because they figured it out first," he admitted. "They got Dr. Rhodes's probate file and they did some other digging, which they then turned over to us under Judge Bovarnick's order."

Sandy shook her head slowly. "I don't get it. Why isn't that work product?"

Daniel had asked himself that same question half an hour ago. Attorneys could ordinarily protect the results of their investigation and analysis—known as "work product"—from the other side, particularly if turning it over would disclose the attorney's thoughts and impressions. But there were exceptions.

"It probably *is* work product," he said. "But they have to turn it over anyway if they want to use it at trial, right?"

"Right. Do you think they plan to put this stuff into evidence?"

Daniel nodded. "They've got pretty good evidence that Rhodes committed suicide, which means they've got a good chance of beating us on the life insurance policy. Now they're focused on the building policy. We've basically proved that Rhodes didn't start the fire—"

"Thanks to your good work," Sandy put in.

Daniel smiled at the compliment. "But the arsonist is still out there. If it's someone from Biosolutions, then the insurance policy is void."

Sandy gave him a sharp look. "You think someone here burned down the lab?"

He shrugged. "I think American Guaranty could make that sound like a plausible theory to a jury. Someone broke in using Dr. Rhodes's keycard and stole his laptop. That person knew our building, knew we had the laptop, and may have gotten the keycard from Rhodes. Based on that, American's lawyers could argue that the thief is a Biosolutions employee." He chose his words carefully. He didn't have the evidence to explicitly accuse Rich. Yet. But at the same time, he wanted Sandy—and the rest of Biosolutions—to be on guard. "Also, the laptop contained some of Rhodes's research. So did the lab. So they'll be able to claim that the person who took the laptop might also have burned the lab."

Sandy frowned. "What does all that have to do with his estate?"

"I'm not sure yet," he admitted. "A month before he died, he decided to give everything he owned to someone, and he seems to have given the bank instructions to keep the identity of that someone secret. It feels like there's a connection to his death there, though I'm not sure what it is. There's also a connection between his death and the fire, but I'm not sure what that is either."

"But the other side may know something we don't," Sandy observed.

Daniel nodded. "I'll bet they do. They wouldn't be planning to put on evidence about Rhodes's money if they didn't."

Sandy drummed her nails on her desk, making tiny clicking sounds. "So how do we find out what they know?"

"We 'play nice' like we were ordered to," Daniel responded. "We say that we've noticed that they're looking into something that's on our radar too and we see that they've already started contacting witnesses— they've been in touch with the bank that has Rhodes's money—and we say that we're happy to work together wherever possible. In fact, we have to under Judge Bovarnick's order. There's a decent chance that they'll drop some clues while we're cooperating."

Sandy nodded and smiled. "Good thinking. I knew we hired you for more than your art skills. Okay, go play nice."

CHAPTER 25

Leigh listened to Rubinelli's proposal with growing discomfort. He was effectively giving her two options: either give him an up-close view while she built her case on the arson issue or risk the near-certain wrath of Judge Bovarnick—and then have the judge order her to do what Rubinelli was suggesting or something very similar. Not much of a choice.

"Okay," she said when he finished. "The judge ordered us to share information and set up joint interviews, and I'll do it—but I expect this to be a two-way street."

"Of course."

Oh well, best to just get it over with. "I'm sure it won't shock you to know that we've been looking into Dr. Rhodes's personal life, including his finances. As you've already figured out, he funneled his entire estate into an offshore bank account that's being held in trust."

"Is there anything more you can tell me about that trust account?" he asked. "We may be able to help each other out a little on this one. Do you know how much is in the account? Or whether any money has been taken out?"

"We've been trying to figure that out," she said. "But it's tough. There are lots of restrictions on obtaining personal financial information, particularly in California and the Cayman Islands."

"Send what you've got to me. I'd like to see what we can do. And I promise to share our results."

She hesitated. "I don't know. Why do you think you'll have better luck than we did?"

"Let's just say I've got a guy who's good at this sort of thing."

"Who?"

"Why does it matter? We'll pay his bills, and we're not asking you to vouch for him in court or anything."

She gritted her teeth. This went entirely against her grain, but she was stuck. "Okay, fine. Just don't do anything that embarrasses me or my client."

He laughed. "Trust me."

◆ ◆ ◆

A week later, Leigh was embarrassed. She sat in a conference room with Daniel Rubinelli's "guy who's good at this sort of thing," deeply wishing she had insisted on getting his name before she agreed to this.

Bruno *Rubinelli*? Seriously?

A quick Google search revealed that Bruno was very active in the "free skateboard community." Also, he was somehow involved with "Whacktastic, Inc.," an unlisted company with no website. An Accurint check turned up nothing on him—no assets, education, or qualifications. Not even a current address.

She looked at him across the conference table. He sat slouched down in one of Diamond & Wang's handmade leather chairs, nearly disappearing into an oversize black hoodie that sported a grinning Guy Fawkes mask. His ratty sneakers rested on another chair, and an expensive-looking skateboard leaned against the wall. His eyes were closed and he seemed to have fallen asleep while waiting for Daniel, who had called to say he was stuck in traffic on the Bay Bridge. Ordinarily, Leigh would have left Bruno in the conference room and stayed in her office until Daniel arrived, but she was half afraid her guest would steal office supplies from the conference room credenza.

The door opened and Daniel walked in. "Hi, sorry I'm late. There was a jackknifed semi on the Bay Bridge, and it took them forever to clear it."

Bruno stirred and yawned hugely. "No problem." He glanced at his watch. "But let's get started if you don't mind. I'm meeting the boys for some tubing in an hour and a half." He glanced at Leigh.

Unfortunately, it was too late to call this off. She nodded. "Your show. Go ahead when you're ready."

Bruno produced a much-used backpack from under the table and pulled out a stained portfolio. He opened it and produced several sheets of expensive-looking bond paper, which he flipped across the table to Leigh. "By the way, here's my résumé. You've been running searches on me, and you won't have found anything useful on Google or Accurint."

Okay, maybe Bruno Rubinelli did know what he was doing after all.

She glanced at Daniel and saw him watching her with an amused smile on his face. He caught her eye—and had the gall to wink. She felt herself go red and looked down at Bruno's résumé.

Reading it made her feel even more foolish. Bruno had started a network security company when he was twenty and sold it to Microsoft two years later. He started a second company the next year, which he later sold to Apple. His current job description was "Philanthropist and amateur skateboarder." His list of hobbies included "cybersecurity consulting and Internet privacy." She suspected he threw in that last item just to tweak her.

Fortunately, Bruno went on without waiting for her reaction. "So, Daniel has asked me to brief you on what happened to Dr. Rhodes's money. You already know that it went into a bank account in the Caymans, but that account is now empty and dormant. It was just a pass-through to hide the final destination of the money. That was another account, a trust account. The trustee is Aegis Bank on Grand Cayman. The trust money is mostly in treasuries and other supersafe fixed-income investments. It throws off about ten K a month, which goes into an account at Wells Fargo here in San Francisco."

"He could easily have set up a trust account at Wells," Leigh said. "But he went to a lot of trouble to put the money in the Caymans. I'm no expert in banking law, but I know there are lots of hoops you need to jump through to do something like that. He probably had to pay extra fees and taxes in the bargain."

Bruno bobbed his head. "Yep. But as I'm sure you know, Cayman banks are a lot tighter on customer privacy than US banks."

"But not tight enough to keep you out, apparently," Leigh observed.

He shrugged and gave a half smile, but said nothing.

"Has anyone made withdrawals?" she asked.

He flipped a page in his portfolio. "Money goes out of the Wells account pretty regularly. Most of the withdrawals are for rent and utilities for an apartment in Twin Peaks. Rhodes put those on autopay before he died. Someone has also been making withdrawals using an ATM card. Before he died, it was mostly Rhodes. Since then, it's been her."

He took a sheet of paper out of his portfolio and handed it to Leigh. It was a grainy black-and-white picture that looked like it had been taken by a security camera. It showed a woman wearing a broad-brimmed sun hat and dark glasses. Her face was mostly obscured, but Leigh could see a long, elegant neck, a strong chin with full lips, and a lock of dark hair that had escaped from her hat.

It was the woman from the estate sale auction.

"She's careful about not letting the ATM cameras get a good shot of her," Bruno continued. "That's the best one I found."

Leigh fought to keep her voice casual. "Do you know her name?"

Bruno shook his head. "The bank account is in the name of the trust, not her. She's not on the lease or the utility bills for the apartment. There's not even a library card for that address."

"So, the question is what we do next," Daniel said. "We're not likely to be able to learn much about our mystery lady online—are we, B?"

Bruno shrugged. "Can't even find her online, man."

"So, what do we do? I'd like to know more before we try to talk to her."

Leigh tore her eyes away from the ATM picture. "I . . . I know someone who may be able to help."

CHAPTER 26

As they walked out of the building, Daniel glanced around to make sure they were alone, then turned to Bruno. "Nice job, B."

Bruno swiveled his head around on his long, skinny neck, looking like a bird hunting for bugs. "Thanks, Danny. So, can I still do corporate suit-speak?"

Daniel chuckled. "Oh, yeah. It was funny listening to you turn it on and off depending on which of us you were talking to. It was pretty clear who you wanted to impress."

Bruno snorted. "Sorry to break it to you, man, but she's way better looking than you. Not my type, though. At all. Looks like she's not sure if she wants to be a nun or an accountant. Right up your alley, though."

"She's on the other side of this lawsuit, remember?"

"No fraternizing with the enemy, huh?"

"Nope."

Bruno nodded. "Probably best. She's outta your league anyway."

"Dude. You have no idea what league I play in."

"Neither do you, obviously."

Daniel punched his cousin in the shoulder. "Careful, or I'll bring up those girls you found at the *Star Trek* convention and Comic-Con."

Bruno shrugged sheepishly. "So I'm a sucker for Klingons and stormtroopers. Sue me."

"Love to, but I've already got my hands full suing American Guaranty. Speaking of which, do you have a few minutes? I'd like to talk about a couple of things."

"A few," Bruno responded, glancing at his cell phone as he spoke. "Like five. I'm guessing you want to ask about that paralegal, Rich Johnson?"

Daniel nodded. "If you've got anything on him. I know you've had other things on your plate."

"Yeah, but Johnson turned out to be pretty easy. I didn't need to do a deep dive on him—just a quick check of bank records and a little graphics work. It only took a couple of hours to have an answer."

"Which is?"

"He didn't steal Rhodes's laptop."

Good. "How do you know?"

"Two reasons. First, you said he's at least six feet tall. I did a little more image analysis of the security camera video, and the thief is no more than five ten. Second, Johnson used his ATM card to take out money from a machine near the War Memorial building at one o'clock in the morning on the night the laptop was stolen. That's only thirteen minutes before your thief walked into the building. No way he could've made it across the bay to Dublin that fast."

Daniel was simultaneously relieved and disturbed. "Thanks. Uh, you've never gone poking around in my records online, have you? Hacked my e-mail or my phone or my bank account or anything like that?"

Bruno laughed. "Danny, remember what I said about operating on a need-to-know basis?"

"Yeah, well, I need to know."

Bruno laughed again, hopped on his skateboard, and was gone.

CHAPTER 27

November

Leigh studied the stack of pictures in her hand and compared them to the ATM security camera shot that Bruno Rubinelli had found. They were the same woman, and unquestionably the woman from the auction.

She dropped the pictures and looked up at her detective. "Nice work, Aunt Phyllis. As always."

The detective gave a sunny smile at the compliment. "Why thank you."

Phyllis Higgins was actually Andrea's aunt, not Leigh's, but her friends and better clients all called her Aunt Phyllis. She looked the part. She was a sweet-faced lady of about sixty-five with long gray hair and a penchant for comfortable clothes. Today she wore a slightly faded floral-print sweatshirt, baggy mom jeans, and pink tennis shoes. You would never know from looking at her that she had spent nearly thirty years in the Oakland Police Department, where she had been one of the most effective undercover cops on the force. But then, that's why she was so effective—she looked nothing like a detective was supposed to. The bouncer at the door of the illegal casino would see a little old lady who wanted to play the slots with her friends, not a detective. The drug dealer in the park wouldn't pay any attention to the woman out walking her yappy lap dog and carrying her big, overstuffed purse. And never in a million years would it occur to him that the purse contained a gun bigger than her dog.

"Now we know what she looks like," Leigh said. "What else do we know about her? Name? Connection to Rhodes? Background? Where she works? What she drinks? Her favorite color? What can you tell me?"

Aunt Phyllis chuckled. "She dresses well—reminds me of Audrey Hepburn—and she likes Earl Gray tea with sugar and a little milk. Other than that . . ." She shrugged. "Nothing. No name, no job, no background."

"Really? How is that possible?"

"It's hard to do, but it is possible. She pays cash for everything, so there's no credit or debit card trail to follow. Nothing is in her name. The bills for the apartment are all paid by that trust. There's no phone listing for the apartment. I got her prints and a DNA sample from a plastic cup she threw away, and I had a friend run them through the FBI's databases. No hits on the prints. I'm still waiting on a DNA analysis—but I'll bet you ten bucks that there's no match on that either." She held up her hands helplessly. "I've got nothing to work with."

"What does she do with her days?" Leigh persisted.

"Nothing that I could see," Phyllis said with a shrug. "I staked out her apartment for a week. One day, she walked two miles to a cafe, ordered tea, and sat with her computer for an hour and five minutes. Then she left, took a different route home, and went back into her apartment. Another day, she went grocery shopping and saw a movie at the Roxie. An old foreign movie—it was called *Persona*, I think. The rest of the days, she stayed inside."

"Hmm." Leigh drummed her fingers and looked at the pictures. She noticed that the mystery woman wasn't smiling in any of them. "Did she meet anyone?"

"No. She was always alone."

"Seriously? She didn't talk to anyone?"

"Not other than ordering her tea. A couple of guys tried to chat her up, but she shut them down in under a minute each time."

"So she's alone by choice then. I wonder why."

Aunt Phyllis leaned forward and looked like she was about to say something. But she didn't.

"What?" Leigh asked.

Phyllis pressed her lips together for a moment. "I'm not sure how to put it, but she gave off a weird vibe."

"What do you mean? Like she was crazy or something?"

"No, not crazy." Phyllis gave a short laugh. "Believe me, I know the crazy vibe, and this wasn't it. No, it was more . . ." She looked into the middle distance for a few seconds. "Depressed, I guess. Like she was just going through the motions, sleepwalking through life."

CHAPTER 28

Daniel's phone rang, and he recognized Leigh Collins's number on the caller ID.

He pushed the speakerphone button. "Hello, Leigh."

"Hi, Daniel. I've heard from my investigator. She wasn't able to find out much more about our mystery woman than Bruno was. She appears to be kind of a hermit—she doesn't seem to have a job or friends, and she doesn't leave the apartment much. The investigator got her fingerprints and ran them in the FBI's database, but there were no matches."

"Okay, thanks. I guess the next step is to talk to her. Hopefully, she'll let us record the interview, but I can bring my paralegal to take notes in case she says no."

"Before we do that, there's something else you should know: she was at the estate sale auction. She tried to bid on those papers I bought, but she hadn't registered and couldn't—or wouldn't—show ID."

"Huh." Daniel digested that bit of news for a moment. "Think she stole the documents from your car?"

"It's certainly possible."

A thought popped into his head and he leaned forward in his chair. "Is she tall?"

"Yes."

"How tall?"

"I don't know—five nine or ten, I'd guess. Why?"

He sat back, mind whirling. "That's about how tall our thief was—the one who stole Dr. Rhodes's laptop."

"Hmm. What an interesting coincidence."

"No kidding. Did your investigator take any pictures? Someone around here might recognize her. Also, I'll bet Bruno can run a search for her face on the Internet."

"Sure. E-mailing them to you now."

"Thanks. I'll start asking around."

Leigh's e-mail appeared in his in-box as the call ended. He opened it and clicked on each of the half-dozen JPEGs it contained. There were three close-ups of her face and three distance shots. The pictures were good—focused, clear, high resolution. They could almost have been a modeling photo shoot. And their subject could certainly have been a model. She had glossy black hair, brilliant green eyes, and perfect skin. She was dressed in a conservative green dress, but it didn't hide the fact that she had the body of a *Sports Illustrated* swimsuit model. If she had visited Rhodes at Biosolutions, Daniel was sure someone would remember.

He hit Rich's speed dial, and the paralegal answered on the first ring. "Hey, Rich," Daniel said. "Could you come in here for a minute?"

"On my way."

Rich appeared in his doorway thirty seconds later.

"Have a seat," Daniel said, gesturing to his guest chairs. As Rich sat down, Daniel pulled up one of the head shots Leigh had sent. "Know her?"

Rich stared for a moment, then grinned. "No, but I'd sure like to."

"Ever see her before?"

Rich looked intently at the screen. "I may have, but it's been a while. I think she visited Dr. Rhodes once a few years ago, right after I started. Do you have any other pictures, by chance?"

Daniel clicked through the rest of the slide show.

Rich gave a low whistle. "That's her all right. But would you mind going through the pictures again a little more slowly—just to be sure?"

Daniel laughed and went back to the first slide.

"Okay, what's going on in here?" a familiar feminine voice asked. "Are you two putting together a skit for our next sexual harassment training?"

Daniel looked up to see Sandy watching them with arched eyebrows. He smiled sheepishly and wondered how to respond. He wasn't quite sure whether she was just joking around or whether he might be in a little trouble.

But before Daniel said anything, Sandy caught sight of the picture on Daniel's computer screen. "Who's that?" she asked.

"The woman who's living off of Dr. Rhodes's estate," Daniel said. "The one from the ATM picture. And there's more. She was at the Rhodes estate sale, according to Leigh Collins. She tried to bid on that stack of papers, but she couldn't because she hadn't registered and couldn't or wouldn't show ID. Those papers were later stolen from Leigh Collins's car." He pointed toward the screen with his chin. "She also happens to be the same height as the person who broke into our building and stole Rhodes's laptop."

Sandy nodded. She fixed Daniel with her gaze. "Thoughts?"

An idea that had been floating half-formed in his mind gelled. "She got to be very close to him and she's very interested in his research, but Rich only saw her at the lab once. Also, she's obviously trying to keep her identity secret. Leigh's story from the auction is just one example of that, there are several others."

He paused for a moment, thinking. Sandy and Rich watched and waited for him to go on.

"Putting all of that together," Daniel continued, "maybe someone—probably one of our competitors—caught wind of what Rhodes was working on. They knew they'd have trouble planting a spy with the company, so they planted one with Dr. Rhodes. Based on his personnel file, he was probably a pretty lonely guy. He might have been vulnerable to the charms of a beautiful young woman who overlooked his, um, quirks and was interested in him and his work. So she went to work on him, gaining his trust, learning his secrets. It took a long time—years— but in the end she had everything he could give her, even his money. So then she killed him and burned down his lab to set us back and leave the field wide open for her employer. Since then, she's been hunting down anything that could help us reconstruct Dr. Rhodes's research."

Daniel's office was silent for several seconds as Rich and Sandy pondered what he just said.

"Should we contact the police?" Daniel asked.

Sandy shook her head. "We have enough for them to question her, but not enough for them to arrest her. She would vanish the moment they left. No, we need to talk to her first, and search her apartment if we can find a way to do it safely." She paused and looked each of them in the eye for a heartbeat. "And we need to be very, very careful about how we handle this."

CHAPTER 29

Leigh sat at a table in a Starbucks a block from the mystery woman's apartment, pecking at a muffin. Her stomach was in knots, and she regretted agreeing to try a surprise interview before calling the police.

Aunt Phyllis sat beside her, sipping a pumpkin spice latte and surfing Facebook on her phone. "Relax. We're going to go to her apartment and ask her a few questions. What's the worst that could happen?"

"I don't know. That's why I'm worried. I mean, we know virtually nothing about her. She could be a psychopath."

"You're afraid she'll kill you and turn you into mince pies?"

"Something like that," Leigh admitted.

Phyllis shook her head. "That's not going to happen. Do you know how many mince pies you and Rubinelli would make? Where would she put them all?"

Leigh forced a smile. "I'm so relieved."

The detective laid a hand on her arm and gave her a sympathetic smile. "I'll be just down the street listening. If anything goes wrong, just say my name and I'll be there in less than half a minute. Besides, I really don't think anything will. This woman is hiding, remember? Killing you would attract attention. She would much rather get you out of her apartment quickly and smoothly, without raising any red flags. The real risk is that she'll try to disappear after you leave—but we've planned for that too."

"I know." They had been over the plan several times, and her brain knew perfectly well that she would almost certainly be safe. The problem was that her stomach disagreed. But talking it through again did help.

Daniel walked in, spotted them, and came over, accompanied by the spear carrier who accompanied him to court. The spear carrier was about twenty-five and carried a leather briefcase while Daniel only had a portfolio. They both wore gray suits.

"Hi, Leigh." Daniel turned to Phyllis. "Daniel Rubinelli." He gestured to the spear carrier. "And this is my paralegal, Rich Johnson."

After a minute of shaking hands and pleasantries, they all sat down around the table. Daniel turned to Phyllis with an appraising look. "So you're the security Leigh mentioned?"

She gave a single nod and smiled. "Yes, I am. Thirty years with the Oakland PD. And no, I didn't sit behind a desk. I did undercover, mostly organized crime."

He laughed. "Thanks for saving me the trouble of asking." He turned to Leigh. "Let's talk a little bit about how to handle this. I was thinking that I could start off and go through my outline. Then you can ask any follow-up—"

He broke off and his gaze shifted to a point somewhere behind her left shoulder.

Leigh turned. There she was. The mystery woman was fifteen feet away, standing in front of the cashier. And she had just noticed Leigh staring at her.

CHAPTER 30

Daniel's brain locked up when he saw her. What should he do? Go over and talk to her now? In public? Wait and follow her back to her apartment? But what if she had already noticed him? She had looked their way for a couple of seconds.

The woman stepped out of line and started walking toward the door. Daniel was rooted to the floor, still uncertain what to do. He turned to Leigh, but she was gone.

He turned back and saw Leigh talking to the mystery woman. He couldn't hear what they were saying, but Leigh was smiling. The woman hesitated and replied to whatever Leigh had said. Leigh continued talking and gestured toward the group. The woman glanced around the cafe, seeming uncertain what to do. Leigh touched her arm and spoke in a reassuring tone. The woman smiled and walked over to the table. As she walked, she slipped her right hand into the pocket of her black trench coat.

Out of the corner of his eye, Daniel noticed Phyllis unobtrusively drop her right hand into her purse. Did she have a gun in there? Her bag was big enough to hold a grenade launcher.

Rich immediately got out a notepad and pen. He was there to take notes of the interview so that Daniel wouldn't have to. Also, if anyone ever needed to testify in court about what happened during the interview, Daniel could put Rich on the witness stand and have him read from his notes. Otherwise, Daniel would be forced to testify himself, which would be awkward.

Daniel put on what he hoped was a friendly, nonthreatening smile as Leigh and the woman walked up. He stood and put out his hand. "I'm Daniel Rubinelli. Pleased to meet you."

"My name is Anne Smith," she replied, shaking his hand with a firm grip, then slipping her hand back into her pocket. She had a throaty alto voice with a faint, hard-to-place accent.

"I'm Phyllis Higgins," Leigh's detective said with a nod. She smiled, but she didn't get up or take her hand out of her purse.

When Anne's eyes reached Rich, she seemed to pause for an instant and mentally recalibrate—like she recognized him, but didn't expect to see him. "Do I know you?" she asked.

"Not yet," Rich replied as he stood and extended his hand. "I'm Rich Johnson. There, now you know me."

She laughed and shook his hand. "Pleased to meet you, Rich."

"Likewise, Anne," Rich said. "Actually, I wasn't quite fair to you just now. I worked in Elijah Rhodes's lab at Biosolutions, and you may have seen me there. I remember you visiting at least once."

"And I remember you from Dr. Rhodes's estate sale," Leigh said.

"Yes, I thought you looked familiar as well," Anne said. "So, what can I do for you all?"

"Could we have five or ten minutes of your time?" Daniel said, gesturing to an empty chair. "Ms. Collins and I have a few questions we'd like to ask you. We're lawyers, and we think you might have information about one of our cases."

She hesitated for a moment, then sat down. The rest of them did the same. "I will have to leave for an appointment soon," she said. "But I can talk to you for a few minutes."

Leigh leaned forward to speak. Daniel didn't like her seizing the initiative with a key witness, but it was more important to get Anne talking than to bicker about who would lead.

"Thanks so much, Anne," Leigh said. "I know you don't have a lot of time, so I'll get right to the point. Mr. Rubinelli represents Biosolutions and I represent American Guaranty, an insurance company that issued some policies to Biosolutions. Those policies covered a lab building at Biosolutions and the life of Elijah Rhodes. The lab was destroyed in a fire a few months ago. At about the same time, Dr. Rhodes died. We're trying to figure out whether my client's policies cover either the damage to the lab or Dr. Rhodes's death."

Anne's face was impassive. "I'm not sure I understand. Why do you want to talk to me?"

"To begin with, we know Dr. Rhodes paid for the apartment you live in," Leigh said.

A slight crease marred the smooth skin between Anne's perfectly formed eyebrows. "I don't see the connection between where I live and these insurance policies. Are you asking whether I know anything about Dr. Rhodes's death or this fire?"

Leigh smiled disarmingly. "You put it better than I did. Yes, that's exactly what we're asking. Would you mind answering your own question?"

Anne smiled back, revealing perfect white teeth. "Certainly. I know only what was in the newspapers and on the television."

"Do you have any idea whether he might have been depressed or angry about something at work?"

Daniel was about to object, but Anne shook her head. "I don't. Dr. Rhodes did not discuss his work with me."

"Did he seem at all depressed or moody?"

Anne paused as if searching her memory. "Yes, now that you mention it, he was in a black mood the last time I saw him."

"And when was that?" Leigh asked.

"Three days before he died."

"Did he say anything that indicated he might be considering injuring himself or others?" Leigh asked.

"Not precisely, but he was certainly in a dark humor."

"Do you remember anything specific?" Leigh asked.

"I'm sorry, no."

"Let's switch gears," Leigh said. "Why were you at the estate sale?"

"I hoped to buy some mementos of him."

"But the only item you bid on was a stack of papers from his job," Leigh noted. "Why?"

"Well, that was the first item that came up for sale after I arrived. I hoped to find some of his thoughts in those pages, a window into a part of his life that I never saw."

Leigh nodded sympathetically. "Of course. I can understand why that would be important to you, particularly after his death. So why didn't you take the auctioneer up on his offer to halt the bidding on those papers until you could come back with your driver's license?"

Anne was silent for a moment. Daniel could hear the faint sound of Rich writing beside him. "I . . . I don't have a driver's license," Anne said at last.

Leigh shrugged. "I'm sure the auctioneer would have taken some other form of ID."

Anne's nervousness increased and her gaze flicked around the table. "Do any of you work for the government?"

"None of us do," Leigh replied. "Why do you ask?"

Anne relaxed slightly. "I was not born here and . . . I don't have all of my papers. So I would rather not show identification if I don't have to."

Leigh nodded. "We won't call the immigration authorities. If that's why you didn't show ID, why didn't you just wait to see who bought the documents and then contact them afterwards and make an offer?"

"I was nervous when he asked to see my license, so I left—but that is a good idea. Do you know who bought the papers?"

"I did."

"What a lucky coincidence!" Anne said with a bright smile. "Will you sell them to me?"

"Unfortunately, they were stolen from my car," Leigh replied.

"Oh," Anne said. "I'm sorry to hear that. Are the police investigating?"

"Yes," Leigh said. "Do you know anyone who might be a witness or a suspect?"

Anne shook her head. "No one comes to mind, but there were other bidders at the auction. Perhaps one of them?"

"Perhaps," Leigh said. "By the way, what exactly was your relationship with Dr. Rhodes?"

"I apologize, but that is personal information and I really must go," Anne said, looking at her watch. "Good luck with your case."

Anne stood gracefully, and the rest of them followed suit. Daniel pulled out a card and handed it to Anne at the same time Leigh did. Not that she would ever actually call either of them. Unless he could think of a way to pique her interest . . .

"Thanks for your time, Anne," he said. "One last quick question: Does the name Enoch mean anything to you?"

For just the tiniest fraction of a second, her eyes widened and a shadow of fear crossed her face. Then the mask was back in place. "No, not the name by itself. Could . . . could you give me some context?"

He shrugged. "It's just something we found on Dr. Rhodes's computer. We think it might be related to his work, but we're still sorting that out. Ring any bells?"

"There is . . ." She paused and bit her lip. "It is very vague in my memory. Perhaps if I could see the computer?"

"I'm sure we could arrange something. A company called Whacktastic is decrypting it now, but they should be done any day. Give me a call or send me an e-mail, and we'll arrange a time and date. By the way, what's your e-mail and phone number?"

But she was walking toward the door now. "Sorry, I am almost late." She flashed him another brilliant smile. "I will call you."

Then she was gone.

Chapter 31

Leigh watched Anne walk out the door. She moved quickly and confidently, like a woman who really was on the way to a routine appointment. She didn't look back at them as she walked out the door and past the plate-glass window of the coffee shop.

"I'd better get some surveillance on her in case she tries to disappear," Phyllis announced. "I don't think she will, though. Not until she gets a look at that computer of yours. Nice work." She nodded toward Daniel and slipped out the door.

Leigh turned to him. "I have to admit, that was pretty smooth. Let me know if she calls you, okay?"

"Of course, and vice versa."

"Sure. So, what's this Enoch thing you mentioned?"

He shrugged. "I have no idea. It's the name of something on Rhodes's computer. All the files are encrypted, so I don't know what it is. I was afraid we'd never see her again if we didn't catch her interest, so I just threw the Enoch thing out there and hoped she would bite. I hope it worked."

"I'm pretty sure it did." She paused. "I thought Rhodes's computer was stolen."

"It was, but we had already imaged the hard drive."

"I see. When were you planning to tell me about that?"

He shifted his weight from one foot to the other and glanced out the window. "I wasn't really. The hard drive itself doesn't have anything to do with the case. If we find something relevant while we're decrypting it, we will log or produce it, of course."

He really should have told her about it already, but she decided not to make a big deal out of it. "Well, okay." Another, larger problem occurred to her. "Wait—aren't you worried that she'll try to steal the drive now that she knows where it is?"

His face split into a broad smile. "I really hope she does. That's why I told her. Whacktastic is Bruno's company, and I'm pretty sure their security is light-years ahead of anything she has seen. I'm going to give him a call after we're done here and ask him to cook up something special for her."

CHAPTER 32

Daniel sat quietly while Rich recounted the afternoon's events for Sandy. His notes and memory of the interview were very good—it was almost as if he were reading a transcript. She jotted down a few notes as he spoke, but said little until he was done.

"You said she had an accent. Could you identify it?" Sandy asked.

"Sorry," Rich replied, shaking his head. "It wasn't very strong."

"It was sort of a singsong in the vowels," Daniel added, "and she sometimes put the emphasis on the wrong part of a word."

Sandy looked out of her office window for a few seconds, then turned her gaze back to them. "Could her accent have been East European or Russian?"

Daniel thought for a moment, trying to remember the speech patterns of the handful of East Europeans he had known. "Yes, it could have."

Sandy nodded. "I'm not surprised. We have competitors in that part of the world, and they don't always play by the rules. Did you ask her who she was working for?"

"No," Daniel admitted. "We didn't get a chance."

"And you didn't look around her apartment, correct?"

"Uh, no. We wound up talking to her in the Starbucks. That wasn't the plan, of course, but she surprised us."

"Why did you decide to meet so close to her apartment building?"

Daniel felt himself flush. "It was a convenient spot. It didn't occur to any of us that she might walk in."

Sandy looked down at her notes for a moment. "Okay, those are all the questions I have for now. Thanks."

They got up to leave, but as they reached the door, Sandy said, "Daniel, could you stay for a moment?"

"Sure. What's up?"

"Please shut the door."

He did as she asked, feeling a little nervous. He turned back to Sandy—and saw the Iron Lady. She watched him silently as he walked back across her office and sat down again.

"How did this happen, Daniel?"

"I'm sorry."

"Think about it. You picked a meeting place that was much too close to her building and far too high traffic. Then you let Collins take the lead during the interview and hardly asked any questions. The two of you basically told her that you were after Rhodes's notes and computer, so she knows to hide those if she has them. And you ended the interview by letting her walk away—but only after you mentioned Enoch. Oh, and when she was gone, you told Collins about our copy of Rhodes's hard drive, which she is no doubt going to say should be turned over to a neutral third party for searching." She paused and pinned him with her stare, her blue eyes glacially cold. "What were you thinking?"

He looked at the floor. "I . . . I . . ." He sighed. "I guess I wasn't thinking. I'm really sorry."

"I'm sure you'll do better next time," she said, her voice softening slightly.

"I will," he assured her. He looked up and saw that the sternness had largely left her face. "Should we call the police now that we've talked to her?"

She gave a half shrug and rubbed her eyes. For a moment, she looked old. "It won't do any good. Even if Rhodes's papers or laptop were in her apartment when you talked to her, they're gone now. No, the best thing we can do at this point is wait to see whether she walks into the trap you and Bruno set."

"Okay. Was there, uh, anything else you wanted to talk about?"

She smiled. "Don't take this too hard, Daniel. You're a good lawyer, and you'll get better with experience. You're in over your head right now, so you're going to make mistakes. It's unavoidable. Just learn from them and don't repeat them and you'll be fine. Really."

She gave him a reassuring look, but he didn't feel very reassured. "Thanks," he said and went back to his office.

Back behind his desk, he stared at his monitor without really seeing it. Sandy was right: he was in over his head—and had been since the case started. Judge Bovarnick had rapped his knuckles hard each time he was in front of her, and he was pretty sure Leigh Collins had gotten the best of him whenever they were in court. And now he had fumbled the ball yet again—and let Collins get the upper hand. Par for the course.

He leaned back and swiveled to look out the window at the autumn landscape—hills covered in dead brown grass under a leaden sky that refused to rain. He wasn't surprised that Sandy let him have it just now, only that she had waited so long. He was letting her down, slowly losing a case that Biosolutions needed to win. And he was accidentally leaking company secrets along the way.

Maybe he should go back to proofreading HR policies and answering questions on overtime regulations. At least he could do that without messing up.

CHAPTER 33

Leigh walked out of Jack Diamond's office and headed straight for Andrea's desk. "Lunch?" she asked as Andrea looked up.

"Of course. Just give me a few minutes to get these bills in final so Carmelita can send them out."

"Okay, let me know when you're ready."

Leigh went in and sat down at her desk. She couldn't focus, so she did mindless busywork while she waited for Andrea. But as she skimmed advance sheets and cleared out her e-mail, her thoughts kept going back to her meeting with Jack about the Biosolutions case.

Ten minutes later, Andrea appeared in her door. "Lunchtime!" she announced cheerily. Leigh allowed herself to be talked into getting their meal from a food truck dubiously named Señor Fishface.

Fifteen minutes after that, they were strolling along the Embarcadero, dodging lunchtime joggers and enjoying the view of San Francisco Bay as they munched fish tacos. The name of the truck notwithstanding, the tacos were really good.

"So, what happened in your meeting with Jack?" Andrea asked between bites.

"I gave him a report on the Biosolutions case, and he said he wants me to try to settle it."

"So what do you think about it?"

"I don't want to settle. Not yet, anyway."

"Why not? You settle cases all the time."

"I don't like to settle cases until I understand them—and I don't understand this one. I can't start negotiating unless I know the important facts and can see the strengths and weaknesses of the case. I have no idea what it's worth until then. But in this case I feel like the more I find out, the less I know."

Andrea arched an exquisitely tweezed eyebrow at her. "Seriously? I read your update memo to Jack. You said you were quote-unquote making good progress. Aren't you?"

"I've gotten most of the documents I'd want if this were an ordinary insurance case, and I've started talking to the key witnesses. So I am making progress—but I've got more questions than I did when I took the case."

"Such as?"

"Such as when I first got the case, we had a fire inspector's report and a police report that said Dr. Rhodes set the fire and then killed himself. Now we know he couldn't have been the arsonist, so who was? And who broke into my car and stole that laptop from Biosolutions? Was it 'Anne Smith'—or whatever her real name is—or someone else?" Leigh stepped to the side to avoid a pack of spandexed runners with grimly determined expressions on their faces. "I've never had a case like this before."

"And you're not willing to let it go," Andrea observed.

"Maybe not," Leigh admitted. "I can't put my finger on it, but there's something big here that I can't quite see. I mean, this is a hundred-million-dollar case, but I sometimes feel like the money is almost an afterthought. I want to know what's really going on."

"Plus, you're having fun."

"Well, that too."

"And I haven't heard you yell at Mr. Rubinelli in a long time," Andrea said with a mischievous wink. "Is he growing on you?"

Leigh laughed. "Like a tumor. Seriously, he has been behaving better. Judge Bovarnick must've scared him into acting nice. Or nicer, anyway."

Andrea smiled smugly. "So I was right about him."

"For the moment," Leigh conceded. "Things could get ugly if we have to take this case to trial. We'll see what happens."

"Oh, I know what'll happen if this case goes to trial," Andrea said with utter confidence. "You'll have another notch in your belt and he'll have a learning experience. But I'd like to think that he'll be a better loser than that awful Mr. Wells."

"I hope you're right," Leigh said. "That's what makes it all worthwhile."

Andrea finished her taco and rubbed her arms against the chilly breeze that always seemed to blow on San Francisco's waterfront. "Is it?" she asked.

Leigh looked at her secretary quizzically. "What do you mean?"

"Is winning cases what makes it all worthwhile?"

Leigh shrugged. "I guess. Is that a bad thing?"

"No," Andrea said. "I was just wondering, you know, what it's all about for you."

"My life goals and that sort of thing?"

"Yeah, pretty much."

Leigh weighed Andrea's question for a moment, then decided to give an honest answer. "Cone of silence?"

"Of course."

"Okay. First, I want to be the youngest partner in the history of the firm."

"So . . . by the time you're thirty-one," Andrea said. "That gives you less than two years." She appeared to do some sort of mental calculation, then nodded. "I think you can do it. Any other goals?"

"I want to join the billion-dollar club by the time I'm thirty-five."

"Wow. A billion dollars' worth of wins in the next six years? Well, if anyone can do it, you can. Anything else?"

"My name on the door by my fortieth birthday."

Andrea whistled. "You're an ambitious girl. But if you're a partner by thirty-one and have a billion in wins by thirty-five, Jack and Louis will probably make you a name partner by forty. Otherwise, they'll risk losing you, and they won't want to do that. Anything else?"

"Isn't that enough?" Leigh asked in surprise.

"Well, it's all work related," Andrea said.

"So is my life," Leigh said with a smile.

Andrea laughed, but Leigh thought she saw a hint of sadness in her friend's eyes.

CHAPTER 34

January

Daniel jerked awake.

His cell phone was ringing. He made a clumsy grab for it and knocked it to the floor. It kept ringing, muffled by the carpet.

Daniel leaned out of bed and picked up the phone. He looked at the screen with sleep-bleared eyes. Bruno. Of course.

He sighed and answered the phone. "I assume you know what time it is, B."

"She broke into Whacktastic half an hour ago."

Daniel was suddenly wide awake. "Anne Smith? Did you call the police? Have they arrested her?"

"I thought you might want to talk to her first."

"What . . . Where is she?"

"Locked in a storage room at Whacktastic," Bruno said matter-of-factly. "I figured you wanted more than a picture of her stealing Rhodes's hard drive. Again."

"Uh, yeah. Thanks. On my way. Oh, and I need to let Leigh know, so she may be showing up too."

"Seriously? Why do you have to tell her?"

"Because the judge ordered me to." Daniel rubbed his eyes. He wasn't entirely sure that Judge Bovarnick had this particular situation in mind when she ordered him and Leigh to conduct all witness interviews together. But he wasn't going to take any chances.

He tumbled out of bed and pulled on jeans and a faded green Notre Dame Law School sweatshirt. Then he called Collins, who had her usual polish despite having just been woken up. He downed a five-hour energy drink on his way out the door and grabbed a couple of granola bars to eat as he drove.

It wasn't until he was on the road that his brain really began to function. That's when it sank in: it had worked. The trap he had set for Anne Smith on the spur of the moment in that Starbucks had actually worked! He punched the steering wheel in excitement.

"Yes!"

Then he realized that he had left his interview outline back in his apartment. He'd just have to wing it—and hope he didn't forget something important. They weren't likely to get another shot.

◆ ◆ ◆

Half an hour later, Daniel walked into Bruno's "office" in downtown San Francisco. The door had a faded sign reading "Whacktastic!" over a cartoon image of a crazed-looking boy holding an enormous sledgehammer. Inside, it looked vaguely like the party room of an upscale frat house. There was a large open room with a pool table, a foosball table, several leather chairs and sofas arranged around scarred coffee tables, and a huge television surrounded by several gaming consoles. Several doors opened off of the main room. Incongruously, a wheeled garbage can stood near the middle of the room, a bucket of cleaning supplies hanging off its side.

Bruno lounged in one of the chairs facing the TV. Leigh and Phyllis sat next to each other on a sofa, tense as caffeinated cats. He almost didn't recognize Leigh—her hair was pulled back in a ponytail, she had no makeup on, and she wore yoga pants and a sweatshirt instead of a power suit. She had clearly just rolled out of bed and she didn't have her usual professional polish. Daniel actually liked her better like this. She was more human.

They all looked over when Daniel walked in.

Bruno yawned. "Nice of you to join us."

"Sorry, I had to drive in from Dublin," Daniel said. "Where is she?"

Bruno glanced in the general direction of a closed steel door. "In there. We had a live video feed until she spotted the camera and took it out. Here's some footage from about an hour ago."

He picked up a remote control from his lap and clicked it. It showed the room they now sat in. A woman in a baggy janitorial uniform entered the picture, pushing the wheeled garbage can. She looked around, then walked toward the camera. Just before she disappeared out of the bottom of the frame, Bruno froze the image and blew it up. A slightly grainy picture of Anne Smith's face filled the TV screen. Her hair was now short and blonde and her eyes were brown, but it was her.

"She got a job with the night cleaning service for the building," Bruno explained. "That got her past the building security and gave her an excuse to be in here. But then she went into that room"—he pointed at the closed door—"where she *didn't* have an excuse to be. And once she got in there, she picked up a hard drive labeled 'Rhodes.' That triggered a silent alarm, which called every phone I own. It also instantly shut and locked that door, which is tougher to get through than most bank safes." He paused. "So, shall we let her out and have a little chat?"

Daniel swallowed hard. "Well, that's what we're all here for."

Leigh jerked a nod.

They all stood and Bruno started toward the door, but Phyllis held up a hand. "Just a sec." She walked over to a blocky chair against the wall a few feet to the side of the door. Then she crouched behind the chair, pulled a Sig Sauer P226 pistol out of her purse, and braced her arms against the arm of the chair. She nodded to Bruno.

He opened the door. Then he jumped back, arms in the air. Anne Smith stepped out, holding a gun pointed at his head.

"Drop it!" Phyllis barked from behind the chair, sounding every bit like a police detective.

Anne glanced at Phyllis. A spasm of fury and panic twisted her face, and for an instant Daniel thought she was going to try to shoot her way out of Whacktastic. But it passed after a second and was replaced by a cold mask.

Anne dropped the gun to the floor.

Phyllis didn't relax. "Kick it away."

Anne did as ordered. Leigh picked up the weapon and held it tentatively, like she was afraid it would go off spontaneously.

"Do you know how to use one of those?" Phyllis asked.

"You just point and pull the trigger, right?" Leigh said with a nervous smile.

"I think that's a Glock 19," Daniel said. "I've fired at least a hundred rounds with one of those." His father's idea of father-son bonding had involved a lot of Saturday afternoons at the shooting range. Daniel used to resent the fact that he routinely spent so much of his weekend stuck in noisy, windowless rooms. Not anymore.

Phyllis and Anne both gave Daniel appraising looks.

"Give him the gun," Phyllis told Leigh. She did, looking grateful to be rid of it.

"Sit down," Phyllis said to Anne, nodding in the direction of a chair in the middle of the room.

"What do you want?" Anne asked.

"I want you to sit down," Phyllis responded, raising her voice slightly.

Small lines of frustration formed around Anne's mouth and eyes for a moment, but she shrugged and walked over to the chair. She sat with fluid grace and crossed her legs. Phyllis stood slowly and walked over to stand facing her from about ten feet away, her gun never wavering from Anne's head. Daniel, Leigh, and Bruno all moved into a rough crescent beside Phyllis.

Anne regarded them with an icy stare. "Well, aren't you going to call the police?"

Daniel cleared his throat. "We have some questions for you first."

A small smile momentarily quirked Anne's lips. "I thought you might. I have some questions of my own."

"Who do you work for?" Daniel asked.

She shrugged. "Why does it matter?"

"Answer my question," Daniel said.

"Answer one of mine first," she shot back.

Daniel was momentarily at a loss. He'd never faced a witness who simply refused to answer his questions—and he never would have guessed that he'd face one for the first time while he was holding a gun. But she very likely realized that he wouldn't shoot her, and he couldn't credibly threaten to call the police if she didn't talk. She had preemptively called his bluff on that front. He would have to persuade her to talk to him—and she knew it.

He thought for a moment. He might learn more from her questions than from her responses to his. "So go ahead. Fire away."

She looked surprised. "Thank you. My first question is whether the hard drive in that room is real."

Bruno glanced into the storage room. Then he stared. Wrinkles climbed up his forehead. "It *was* a real hard drive," he said. "Now it's garbage."

Daniel risked a quick look into the room. The smashed case of the hard drive lay on the floor, surrounding a heavily dented silver disc.

He turned back to Anne, staring at her in confusion. Why had she destroyed it? How could she be sure that she already had whatever was on the drive? He thought back to their conversation at Starbucks. He hadn't said anything about the hard drive being a copy of the one from Rhodes's laptop. All he said was that they had a hard drive, that it held information about Enoch (whatever that was), and that the drive was at Whacktastic. So for all she knew, the drive she just wrecked held key research records that were now lost forever.

But maybe that was the point.

"This isn't about stealing Enoch, is it?" Daniel said. "This is about destroying it."

She replied with stony silence.

"You killed Rhodes and burned his lab," Daniel continued. "Then you somehow realized that you missed his laptop and notes, so you stole those. I'm guessing those are gone too, right?"

More silence. He hadn't really expected an answer, though he had hoped that her body language would tell him something. But she didn't even flinch.

A loose end occurred to him: the second lab. He had set up automated searches of news and police websites for reports of mysterious abandoned laboratories. A fire or explosion at one almost certainly would been have mentioned on the sites he was monitoring. "But you didn't destroy Rhodes's second lab, did you? Why not?"

She still didn't say anything, but he thought that last question surprised her. Maybe she hadn't destroyed the lab because she didn't know about it.

Daniel sighed. "Okay, any other questions you wanted to ask us?"

"You still haven't really answered my first question. You knew perfectly well that I was asking whether that was Dr. Rhodes's hard drive."

"You seriously expect us to tell you that?" Daniel asked.

She gave a small smile. "Not verbally, but your reaction told me what I needed to know. That was a fake, meant to lure me into your trap." She nodded toward him. "Well played, Mr. Rubinelli."

"Thank you. Any other questions?"

"I only have one more: Do you want to know where that second lab is?"

"Do you know where it is?" Daniel countered.

"I know where it *may* be."

"Where?"

She shook her head. "I'll take you there."

Daniel scoffed. "And try to escape on the way. No dice."

She shrugged. "Then this conversation is over. Go ahead and call the police."

Chapter 35

An hour later, Leigh sat in the backseat of Daniel's car. He was in front, driving down unfamiliar roads somewhere north and east of Oakland. Anne sat beside him, giving directions. Her hands were folded in her lap, bound together by a plastic zip tie. Her face wore a small, victorious smile.

Phyllis sat in the rear passenger-side seat, her gun aimed at a point in the seat directly behind Anne's heart. Leigh was behind Daniel. Bruno had also decided to come, but he was in his own car, following them.

After Anne refused to budge from her ultimatum, they had put her back in the storage room while they debated what to do. They ultimately decided to agree to her demand that she go with them, though only after Phyllis collected some equipment, including the zip tie on Anne's wrists.

Anne took them away from the glittering tech campuses, new subdivisions, and bustling retail centers. They entered an older, grimier part of the East Bay. They drove along streets lined by decaying warehouses, vacant lots, and boarded-up storefronts. Intermittent streetlights cast pools of light on dark, largely car-free roads. Most traffic lights either blinked yellow or were dark, victims of wire thieves.

"Turn left in two blocks," Anne said. "I do not recall the street name, but there is a bakery on the corner. Or at least there used to be."

Daniel slowed down as he approached the unlit intersection. One corner held an abandoned gas station, two were vacant lots, and the fourth had a graffiti-covered lump of a building that could have been anything. "Is this it?"

"Yes," Anne replied, a tinge of sadness in her voice.

They turned onto a narrow, completely dark road. It led to a large rusty arch. A faded sign over the arch read "NorCal Chemicals." Beyond the sign, a wilderness of decrepit pipes, storage tanks, and buildings stretched as far as the headlights reached. A perfect place for an ambush, Leigh realized uncomfortably. A sea breeze carried clumps of fog through the industrial ghost town, increasing the ominous feel of the place.

"There's a parking lot—on the right," Anne said, pointing to a cracked and weedy expanse of asphalt. "From there, we must get out and search."

"This place is huge," Leigh objected. "How are we supposed to find a hidden lab here?"

"We must look," Anne replied. "I don't know where—if it is even here. I told you, I am only guessing."

Leigh scoffed. "Well, why do you guess that he would have hidden a lab here?"

"Because Dr. Rhodes knew this place and it would be easy to conceal a lab here," Anne replied.

"I may be able to help," Phyllis said from the backseat. She reached into a voluminous canvas bag and pulled out bulky, complicated-looking binoculars with odd-looking lenses. "Thermal imaging," she explained. "Buildings that are being used usually give off more heat than abandoned buildings, particularly on a cold night like this." She handed the binoculars to Leigh. "Careful with these—they're expensive. Daniel, go ahead and drive around. Leigh, just look through these and let me know if you see any bright spots."

They drove slowly through what looked like an abandoned alien city, made all the stranger by darkness and neglect—and stranger still by the spectral palette of the thermal imaging binoculars. Weird spherical structures lined the road at one point. Then they passed a complex tangle of rust-stained pipes and smokestacks that stretched over a hundred yards. After that came huge buildings that resembled blocks from a giant's toy set. And then a remarkably normal office campus.

Then came a tiny concrete building—hardly larger than an outhouse—about fifty yards to their left. And it glowed like it was radioactive. "Hold on," Leigh said. "I think I see something."

Daniel pulled over to the side of the road and stopped the car. He squinted into the murk. "Okay, what are we looking at?"

Leigh lowered the binoculars and pointed to the little building.

Daniel cocked a skeptical eyebrow at Anne. "*That* is a secret lab?"

She shrugged. "Your words, not mine," she said, her voice tense.

"Only one way to find out what it is," Phyllis said from the backseat. "Leigh, look around and tell me if you see anything else. A person or a warm car engine should glow like neon."

Leigh held the binoculars to her eyes and slowly swept them to the right and left. "I don't see anything nearby."

"Okay, let's go," Phyllis said, opening her door as she spoke.

Leigh followed her lead reluctantly, half expecting an ambush as soon as she stepped out of the car. The whole place felt threatening.

A moment later all four of them stood by the car. Bruno joined them and they filled him in. He frowned into the darkness as if he too mistrusted it. "I didn't bring a flashlight."

"I've got an extra," Phyllis said, pulling a heavy black flashlight out of her canvas bag. "Here you go." Leigh noticed that Phyllis had on something stiff and black—body armor?—under her baggy pink sweater. She suddenly felt underdressed.

Daniel heaved a deep breath. "All right, let's go."

They walked along an uneven, cracked cement path, keeping their flashlights on the ground ahead of them to avoid tripping. The fog had thickened, turning beams into blurry cones of gray light.

Anne took the lead, and Phyllis consistently stayed several feet behind her, gun pointed at Anne's back. Daniel and Bruno followed, and Leigh brought up the rear. She took a quick peek through the binoculars every few seconds.

Leigh stopped. There was a noise just on the edge of her hearing. "What's that?"

They all froze and listened. Leigh could identify it now: a low hum coming from ahead of them, to the left of the shed. Bruno pointed his flashlight in the direction of the sound, illuminating a thick, new-looking black cable snaking from a manhole to the back of the shed.

"Looks like someone put that in fairly recently," Daniel observed. "Maybe that little building is a lab after all."

Bruno played his flashlight beam over the shed. A large, shiny lock secured a rusty steel door.

They started forward again, and in a few seconds they were at the door. Phyllis reached into her bag and produced short-handled bolt cutters, which she wordlessly handed to Daniel.

"I'm surprised you don't have a blowtorch and welder's mask in there," Daniel said, nodding toward her voluminous purse.

"Fire hazard," she replied. "Get cutting."

The lock was too strong for the cutters, but the door wasn't. After ten minutes of work that left his face sweaty despite the chilly night air, Daniel managed to cut through the door flange that held the lock.

Breathing heavily, he handed the bolt cutters back to Phyllis and tried the door handle. It opened easily.

Inside, a steep metal and cement staircase descended into darkness. A puff of warm, stale air wafted out. It smelled faintly of ammonia and decay.

CHAPTER 36

The five of them stood around the top of the stairs, looking down uncertainly. Daniel and Bruno swept their flashlight beams over the interior. They saw nothing but the stairs and bare cement walls. There appeared to be a barred gray metal door at the bottom, about thirty or forty feet down.

After a few seconds, Daniel steeled himself and said, "Well, this is what we came here to see." He walked in and, after a moment's hesitation, the rest of them followed. Leigh handed the binoculars to Phyllis as they went down the stairs and clutched the railing that ran along the left wall.

They reached the gray door, which appeared to be made of heavy steel. It was held shut by thick horizontal bars operated by a large rusty lever. Faded red lettering said "KEEP DOOR SHUT AT ALL TIMES."

"Maybe that's good advice," Leigh commented, pointing toward the sign.

"Could be this place was used to manufacture or store explosive chemicals," Bruno said. "That'd explain why it's underground."

Daniel's stomach was clenched tight, but he nodded. "Makes sense." He got a good grip on the lever. Then he turned to the rest of them. "I'd like to have someone shine a flashlight in there so I can see where I'm going, but the rest of you really don't have to come."

Anne smiled. "That is chivalrous, but unnecessary. I will come."

The rest of them muttered their agreement with varying degrees of enthusiasm.

"Okay, here goes." Daniel yanked on the lever, putting his back into it. To his surprise, the bars slid back easily, causing a loud clang. Several of the party jumped. "Sorry, I expected it to be stuck. Someone must have oiled it."

He pulled Anne's gun out of his waistband and pushed the door open. Then he stepped into a long, low-ceilinged hallway. Several doors opened off of the hall, each made of windowless gray metal. The smell was stronger down here, and the air was close and thick. The place felt like he imagined a tomb would.

Daniel started down the hall, his and the others' steps echoing on the bare concrete floor. He was about to try the first door when a click sounded behind them and the dark hall was suddenly bathed in flickering fluorescent light.

"What the—" He jerked back from the door and looked around wildly. He found Leigh watching with a grin on her face.

"Sorry," she said, not looking the least bit sorry. "After you banged the door open like that, there can't be much harm in turning on the lights, right?"

Daniel recovered and grinned ruefully. "I guess not."

He opened the door and found himself looking into a climate-controlled room that was empty except for several floor-to-ceiling towers of complicated-looking electronics that emitted a dim blue glow.

"Servers," Bruno said, walking past Daniel to give the electronics a critical look. "Looks like we found Rhodes's system backup."

"Excellent!" Daniel said. So Rhodes's research hadn't been lost after all. They would still have to rebuild the lab, but at least they wouldn't have to re-create years of research by a now-dead genius. That was huge.

"There are lots more doors," Phyllis observed from the hallway.

"There are indeed," Daniel said, turning back into the hall. He felt a little like an explorer who just discovered a long-lost treasure cave.

He walked up to the second door and opened it.

Stale air puffed out, carrying an unclean smell. Daniel coughed and stepped back. Bruno pointed his flashlight into the dark room. Cages full of dead rabbits lined the counters. There must have been over a hundred animal corpses. Many of their cages showed gnaw marks on the gates and bars. A table in the center of the room held syringes, bottles, testing equipment—and dishes of rabbit food. Enormous unopened bins of food stood stacked along one wall.

"Oh, the poor things!" Leigh exclaimed when they had recovered from the smell. "They must have all starved to death when no one came to feed them. Maybe there are some still alive in the other rooms."

Without waiting for a response, she walked down the hall to the next door and opened it. Then she screamed.

CHAPTER 37

For a few seconds, Leigh's mind couldn't quite grasp what her eyes saw. It was another darkened lab like the room full of dead rabbits—except that the food bins were full of holes and empty. Water sprayed from a hole chewed into a plastic pipe that ran along one wall, puddling around a drain in the middle of the floor.

Before she could wonder what had happened, she noticed there was something wrong with the counters and floor. They were covered with something gray, splotchy, and lumpy—like piles of lint. Except that it moved and writhed like turbulent smoke or . . .

Rats. Hundreds of rats crowded every surface. Many were clearly dead, their bodies partially eaten by the survivors. But many were still alive. Their eyes gleamed in the dark as they looked at Leigh.

She screamed and tried to slam the door, but the rats were already racing through it. The door wouldn't shut. It hit something with a crunching thud and bounced back open.

Dozens of them were already out, and more poured through in a rising stream. Tiny feet and hairy bodies ran over her feet and brushed her ankles. A chorus of high-pitched squeaking filled her ears.

Several people shouted at the same time. Leigh looked up to see her companions running for the door to the stairs. She turned to follow them, but stepped on a rat. It shrieked in pain and she stumbled. She took an awkward step and came down heavily on the side of her left foot. Agony shot through her leg and she fell in a heap.

Instantly starving rats were all over her. Pain pierced her left hand as one bit her. Then others bit her ankle and neck.

She screamed again and tried to knock them off, but there were too many. She somehow pushed herself to her feet and limped toward the door. She couldn't put any weight on her left leg, so she braced herself against the wall and hobbled with desperate speed. But her hand was bloody and it slipped. She fell again, and again the rats were on her, biting and squeaking and scratching.

She heard shots and someone yelling her name. She felt hands bat the rats away from her and hoist her into the air. She caught a brief glimpse of Daniel's face as he threw her over his shoulder.

A jolt ran through his body as he hit his head against something. He staggered and cursed. She clutched the back of his shirt instinctively and braced for another fall. But he managed to catch his balance and jogged down the hall.

Then they were pounding up the stairs. Each step was a painful punch to her stomach from his shoulder. She flopped like a rag doll, watching helplessly as he ran. Rats followed them up the steps, but he ignored them. Her pulse hammered in her ears, almost drowning out his ragged breathing and the incessant squeaking.

They burst out into the night. The door to the little concrete hut slammed shut behind them.

He slipped her off his shoulder and gently lowered her to her feet. Pain lanced through her left ankle again. She closed her eyes and leaned against the wall for support, sucking in huge breaths of cool air.

Daniel's hand steadied her. "Are you okay?"

"I—I think so. My ankle hurts and the rats bit me, and—" Her voice was suddenly uneven as the memory rushed up. She fought to stay in control. "But I'm fine. I—"

She opened her eyes and found herself looking at his hand on her shoulder. Blood welled out of several bites. She looked up at his face. The entire right side was covered in black-red streaks from a cut over his eye.

Her eyes widened. "Look at you! I'm so sorry."

He shrugged. "Slammed my head on the edge of the door. Not your fault that I'm clumsy."

"Hey, where's Anne?" Bruno asked.

"She ran off that way," Phyllis said, pointing into the darkness to their left. "I think she was chasing the rats that came out with us."

"She was chasing *them*?" Leigh asked.

Bruno peered into the dark, then flicked on his flashlight and swung the beam in a wide arc. "I don't see her . . . Anne!"

No response.

"Anne, are you all right?" he called.

Still nothing.

He turned to Phyllis. "Do you still have those night vision binoculars?"

She rummaged in her purse for a moment and pulled out the binoculars. She brought them to her eyes and scanned their surroundings. "There she . . . No, wait—that's not her." She paused and reached for her gun. "Kill the flashlights. There are at least two guys out there, and they're armed."

CHAPTER 38

Phyllis's words didn't immediately penetrate Daniel's throbbing head, so Bruno took the flashlight from his hand and switched it off. The night was moonless and starless, and the darkness folded around them like black velvet. Everyone stood silently, listening. Nothing but a whispering breeze and the hum of the power cables.

"They know we've spotted them." Phyllis's voice was a soft hiss to his right. "They've got their guns out and they're heading this way. They didn't bring night vision gear." She plucked gently at his sleeve. "We can dodge them. Follow me."

She moved off silently, barely visible even though she was less than a yard in front of him. He followed, trying not to stumble on the cracked cement and uneven ground. He could hear Leigh and Bruno behind him. Leigh's breath was ragged and she seemed to be limping.

Daniel turned and looked back. His eyes had adjusted to the dark and he could dimly see Leigh struggling along the path. He offered her his arm, but she either ignored or didn't see it.

They walked for what seemed like a mile, Phyllis leading them like blind children. She stopped them suddenly once and pushed them down below a low wall. Footsteps passed a few seconds later. And a minute after that, Phyllis motioned for them to start moving again. Daniel wished he still had the Glock, but he had lost it back in the lab.

At last, they approached the spot where they had left their cars. But Phyllis stopped them again and pulled them to the ground. "Cars are staked out," she whispered softly. She looked around. "Wait here. Don't move." Then she was gone.

Phyllis reappeared a few minutes later. "Here." She pressed a small cylinder into Daniel's hand. "Laser pointer," she said, inches from his ear. "Point it here." She positioned his hand on a small rise. "Okay, this is pointed at his head. He's about ten yards in front of you. Count to thirty and turn it on. Then say, 'Drop the gun and kick it away.' But don't say it too loud—we don't want the others to hear."

She disappeared again. Daniel counted. He reached thirty and clicked the on button. "Drop the gun and kick it away." His voice didn't shake, but the red dot from the pointer danced in time to his pounding heart.

Silence. The guy wasn't buying it! Daniel braced himself, waiting to be shot.

"Don't," said Phyllis's voice from the darkness somewhere to his left.

A few seconds later, Daniel heard the most beautiful sounds he could imagine: a soft thump followed by the clatter of something metal tumbling across the ground.

"Tom, you okay?" a man's voice called from behind them.

There was a second of silence, then running footsteps and confused shouting. Daniel glimpsed shadows darting through the darkness, but couldn't make out anything.

"Go!" he hissed. He ran toward the cars, his footsteps sounding like drumbeats in his ears. He pulled out the keys and unlocked his car as he ran. An amber blink from his running lights told him he had succeeded. His back tingled as he yanked the door open, expecting a bullet any second.

A gunshot went off beside the car as he started the engine. Leigh tumbled in beside him, and he heard Bruno's car roar to life. The rear left door opened and Phyllis plopped into the car. "Okay, they're running back to their car. Let's go."

Daniel already had the accelerator floored.

"Whoa, slow down, big fella," Phyllis said. "They're not following us."

"How do you know?" he asked, scanning the rearview mirror. No headlights.

"I slashed their tires. Oh, and could you give me back that laser pointer when you have a minute? My puppy will miss it."

Daniel handed the laser pointer back to her and eased off the gas. "Any idea who they were?"

"No," Phyllis said, "but I did get the license plate. That might tell us."

He slammed on the brakes. "Anne! We have to go back for her."

"No, we don't," Phyllis said firmly. "She disappeared before those guys showed up, remember? In fact, I wouldn't be surprised if they're friends of hers."

Daniel wasn't convinced. "I still think—"

"Besides, we need to get you two to a hospital."

"I'm fine," he insisted. "And Leigh . . ." He glanced to his right, then stared. Leigh was using a flashlight to examine her ankle. Her lower leg looked like an enormous sausage, and it was streaked with blood from a dozen rat bites. "Wow. You look awful."

"Why, thanks." She smiled, but he could see the pain in her face and hear it in her voice. "You look like an extra from a slasher movie. A dead extra."

He looked in the rearview mirror. Whoa. The cut on his head had bled more than he realized.

"All right, we'll go to the hospital," he conceded.

CHAPTER 39

Leigh's left ankle throbbed, sending a jolt of pain through her leg with each heartbeat. She gritted her teeth and looked out the window so she could grimace without anyone seeing her. The drive to the hospital seemed to take forever, but whenever she glanced at the dashboard clock, it had barely changed.

Twenty minutes later, they finally pulled into the hospital parking lot. Leigh opened her door and stepped out with her right foot. She felt a touch of pride when she managed to get out of the car on her own, but she nearly fell when she tried to take a step. Her left leg was a useless lump of agony.

The sidewalk leading to the ER entrance had rails on both sides and it was only a few feet away. She started to hop over on her one good leg. Even that hurt, but she could do it.

But before she reached the rail, Daniel was there beside her.

"I've got it," she said through gritted teeth.

"It's okay." He put an arm around her waist. "Here, you can lean on me."

The pain was so bad that she didn't argue. She grabbed his shoulder with her left hand and let him half carry her into the ER. He set her down in a chair and went to check them in.

Phyllis sat down beside her. "How are you?"

Leigh really didn't feel like talking. "I'll be fine."

"Are you sure?"

"Absolutely," Leigh said, making an effort not to grimace. "Go on home and I'll call you in the morning."

Phyllis glanced toward the other side of the ER. Leigh followed her gaze and saw two policemen lounging against the wall. "Well, all right. I'm pretty sure we lost those guys. Even if we didn't, you should be safe enough here. But be careful when you leave."

A wave of fear rippled through Leigh's stomach. She hadn't focused on the fact that she was still in danger. "Shouldn't we tell the police what happened?"

Phyllis gave a grim little smile. "You mean tell them that we were wandering around in an old factory—probably trespassing? That we saw someone following us, shot in their general direction, and slashed their tires?"

Leigh opened her mouth and then shut it. That wasn't how she had thought of the evening's events. But now that Phyllis mentioned it, the police might see things that way.

Bruno walked in and came over to them. "I just took a lap around the block," he said. "No one followed me, and there were no new cars in the parking lot when I came back around."

"Good thinking," Phyllis said. "You can head home now if you want. Oh, and you should call SFPD about the Whacktastic break-in. That's all we want to do, though."

"What about those guys who were following us?" Bruno asked.

"I got their license plate, and I'll check it"—Phyllis stifled a yawn—"tomorrow. They're probably just PIs who had been assigned to tail us. I hope I didn't shoot at anyone I know. No need to mention any of that to the police."

Bruno nodded. "Okay, I see your point."

Phyllis patted Leigh's good knee. "Get well soon. I'll talk to you tomorrow."

Bruno and Phyllis left. Leigh slumped back in her seat and realized just how exhausted she was. Today had been stressful even before they went hunting for Dr. Rhodes's secret lab and she hurt her leg. Vivid images of swarming, biting rats filled her mind. She shuddered and did her best to push those memories away.

She suddenly realized that she hadn't thanked Daniel for getting her out of there. If he hadn't come back . . . She tried not to think about what could have happened, but couldn't stop herself. Hundreds of ravenous little animals scrambling over her, tearing at every inch of exposed skin with needle teeth. She couldn't beat them all off, couldn't move fast enough to get away from them. Eventually, one would bite an artery and she would bleed to death while they ate her. She looked at a bite mark on her wrist and multiplied it by a thousand, gnawing all the way down to the bone.

She squeezed her eyes shut. Panic and nausea rose in her throat. Her breath came shallow and fast. *It's over*, she told herself. *That didn't happen. You're safe now.*

Daniel's voice broke into her thoughts. "They'll call us. The nurse said the exam rooms are all full, so—hey, are you okay?"

She opened her eyes as he sat down next to her, concern in his eyes. "I'm fine," she said, hearing the brittleness in her own voice. She swallowed hard and tried to steady herself. "I just . . . Thank you for coming back for me. If you hadn't, I . . . I . . ."

Her vision blurred and she couldn't speak. Sobs convulsed her, and she couldn't stop them. She buried her face in her hands and wept.

One part of her watched in horror. There she was, bawling like a little girl. Right in front of an opposing lawyer. How unspeakably humiliating.

But most of her didn't care. She was exhausted and in pain, and she had just gone through an experience that would give her nightmares for years. She had a right to cry—and she really couldn't care less who was watching.

"I, uh, I'll be right back," he said.

A few seconds later, she heard him having a heated conversation with someone. She looked up and saw him at the front of the ER lobby, arguing with the nurse behind the ER desk. Leigh couldn't make out everything they were saying, but she caught snippets:

". . . in severe pain . . . just look at her . . ."

". . . sorry, sir, but . . ."

". . . sorrier soon if no one helps her fast . . . we're both lawyers, by the way . . ."

Leigh's face, already hot from crying, went hotter with embarrassment. He was being nice, but she really didn't want him doing this for her. Except that she kind of did.

That thought annoyed the part of her that didn't like her crying in front of him. So now she wasn't just fragile and emotional, she was helpless too? She needed a big strong man to go talk to the scary nurse? Pathetic.

Whatever—it worked. Two minutes later, the nurse came hurrying over with a paper cup of water and a box of Kleenex.

Ten minutes after that, they put her in a wheelchair and rolled her back into one of the examining rooms. It had walls full of complicated and vaguely ominous equipment and a linoleum floor that looked like it had been sterilized rather than cleaned.

She waited there for another ten minutes, but it felt like she was making progress, which helped. By the time the doctor arrived, Leigh was checking e-mail on her cell phone and starting to wonder when she would be able to leave.

The doctor was a harried-looking man of about thirty with a short dirty-blond ponytail. He asked how she got her injuries, and she made up a lame story about helping clean out her aunt's garage and stumbling into a nest of rats. The doctor looked a little skeptical, but he just took notes and didn't question her story.

The doctor gave her a rabies shot and firm instructions to get several more, ordered an X-ray for her ankle, and hurried out of her room. A nurse appeared and cleaned the rat bites with sadistic thoroughness. There were a lot of bites, so this went on for an excruciatingly long time. Finally, the nurse left.

More waiting, followed by an X-ray. Then some more waiting.

The doctor reappeared for about five minutes to tell Leigh that her ankle wasn't broken, but that she had a severe sprain and would need a boot and crutches for a few weeks. He also gave her a prescription for antibiotics.

More waiting. Her leg had subsided to a dull ache by now. Maybe it was the painkillers or maybe it was the psychological effect of knowing that it wasn't broken. Either way, she really wanted to go home now. She finished her e-mail and nearly fell asleep on the examining table before a nurse appeared to fit her with a boot.

Finally, at five thirty in the morning, she hobbled back toward the lobby on her new crutches. She wondered whether there would be cabs outside at this hour. Probably not. And it was awkward to use her cell phone to call a taxi while she was on crutches.

She pushed her way through the lobby doors and found a seat. She was about to call a taxi company when she noticed Daniel. He was slouched down in a chair on the other side of the room, his eyes closed and his chin on his chest. He had a big white bandage tied to his forehead with a ribbon of gauze. His head had been shaved around the bandage, revealing an enormous, lumpy bruise.

Leigh realized that he was probably waiting for her. Well, that was nice, but he shouldn't have. She decided to call a cab, then go over and say good-bye to him five minutes before the cab was scheduled to arrive. But as she pulled out her phone, he opened his eyes, saw her, and walked over.

"How's the leg?" he asked.

"Sprained." She lifted up her booted foot. "I have to wear this thing for a few weeks. How's the head?"

"It looks worse than it is. I've got some stitches, but that's all. If there's a scar, it won't be visible unless I shave my head."

So her stupidity and clumsiness back in the factory had given him stitches and maybe a scar. Great. She hated owing people, particularly opposing lawyers. "Well, thanks for everything—for getting me out of there and bringing me here. Go on home and get well." She smiled. "I don't want you to have any excuses the next time I beat you in court."

He gave a tired chuckle. "Likewise. Come on, I'll give you a ride back to your car. I'm headed that way."

"No, that's okay."

"I'd appreciate the company. I could use someone to help keep me awake."

She reluctantly agreed. She hobbled out to his car—without help this time. As he drove out of the parking lot, he started telling a story about how he had sprained his ankle once while playing football, but she had trouble focusing on what he was saying.

The next thing she knew, the car had stopped and he was shaking her gently. She jolted awake and opened her eyes. "Hey, we're here," Daniel said.

"Thanks." She stifled a yawn. "Sorry. I guess I wasn't very good company."

He smiled. The first rays of the dawn were on his face and gave his brown eyes a warm glow. "I had a great time," he said. "I never get to tell my old jock stories without someone interrupting and changing the subject. So thanks."

She returned his smile. "Well, goodnight—or good morning, I guess. See you in court."

Chapter 40

Daniel just wanted to go to bed, but he knew he needed to talk to Sandy. He called her cell. It rang through to voice mail. She was probably at the "holistic health" place she went to for her morning workout. "Hi, Sandy. It's Daniel. Sorry to bother you so early, but something urgent came up. Please give me a call."

Sandy had told him that they confiscated cell phones before workouts started, so he didn't expect to hear from her for a while. He thought about taking a nap, but opted for a long shower instead. The hot water felt good on his bruises, though it stung a little on his bites and he had to lean his head to the side to keep from getting water in the gash on his head.

He toweled off, pulled on some sweats, and collapsed on the sofa in his living room while he waited for Sandy to call back. The sun slanted in through the window, and he thought of how Leigh looked with the sunrise on her sleeping face. She had been curled up in his passenger seat, her head pillowed against her right arm. Her face was peaceful and naturally pretty—though slightly smushed by her arm. She had none of the poise and polish he was used to from her. She was just a regular girl who had been through a very rough night and fallen into an exhausted sleep when it was over. Actually, the best word to describe her at that moment had been "cute." Not a term he had ever thought to apply to her before. He hadn't wanted to wake her.

His phone rang at seven thirty. Sandy.

He picked up the phone. "Thanks for calling," he said.

"I got your message," she said, slightly out of breath. "What's up?"

The words tumbled out of him in a rush of scattered sentences. "A lot. Anne Smith tried to steal Dr. Rhodes's hard drive last night, but Bruno caught her. We questioned her. She wouldn't tell us anything, but she did lead us to Rhodes's second lab. It's in an old chemical plant near the refineries up north. We think we found his backup server. And he was doing some kind of animal testing there. The rabbits were all dead, but the rats got out of their cages and attacked us. They—"

"Whoa, whoa, whoa," Sandy broke in. "Who is 'we'? What lab? Which rats? Take a deep breath, slow down, and try it from the top."

Daniel took a deep breath, slowed down, and described yesterday's events in a more coherent, linear narrative.

Sandy listened without interrupting. When he finished speaking, she said, "Okay, first things first: you and Bruno are not the Hardy Boys. Never do something like this again. Never. If you get into a situation that needs detective work, tell me. I'll hire a detective. Do you understand?"

That hadn't occurred to him, but maybe it should have. "I . . . yes, I understand."

"Good. Second, we have to secure that lab. We need to know what Rhodes was working on—and why he was hiding it from the company. I'll talk to whoever needs to be talked to—the police, the owner of the factory, anyone else like that. I'll also line up some animal control experts to deal with the rats. Once they're done, we'll have our IT guys or a consultant take a look at those servers you found."

"Okay."

"You get some sleep, then be ready to head back to that lab by ten. I may need your help there."

"No problem."

She hung up. Daniel sat back and closed his eyes for a minute before heading to bed. Two minutes later, he was snoring on the sofa.

CHAPTER 41

Leigh left messages for Andrea and Jack, then tried to get some sleep. She failed. The pain in her ankle flared every time she moved at all. And the few times she actually dozed off for a moment, she had vivid nightmares of demonic rats chewing on her. Those jolted her awake in a cold sweat, usually accompanied by a friendly reminder from her ankle that she shouldn't move it. Then she would lie awake, staring at the ceiling and replaying the all-too-real events of last night in her head. If Daniel hadn't come back for her . . .

She did her best not to let her thoughts travel too far down that path. He had come back. That's what mattered. And then he had waited for her in the ER lobby. The memory of him slouched asleep in that vinyl-covered chair with that slightly ridiculous bandage on his head brought a smile to her face. Then she remembered the sound of his voice as she relaxed into the passenger seat of his car, feeling safe for the first time that night. That set her drifting off to sleep as she lay in bed. Until the rats and her ankle woke her up again.

She gave up around ten o'clock and got out of bed. She took an awkward and painful shower and headed into the office.

Shortly after Leigh arrived, Andrea floated into her office, wearing a bright smile and carrying a plate of enormous cookies. She deposited the plate on Leigh's desk. "I made you a little 'get well' present."

Leigh eyed the cookies apprehensively. Dark chocolate and macadamia nuts. Her favorites. And they must have three hundred calories each. Apparently, Andrea viewed "get well" and "get fat" as synonyms.

Andrea watched her expectantly, so Leigh had no choice but to pick one up and take a bite. "Mmm! These are good." Lethally good. "Thanks!" She held the plate out to her assistant. "Here, you have one too. You baked them."

Andrea waved them away. "No, no. Those are all for you." She patted her ample stomach. "I had some already and I'm stuffed. Besides, I need to watch my figure, but you're a skinny little thing."

Leigh rolled her eyes. "A skinny thing who can't get her skinny jeans over her hips."

"Well, you won't be wearing jeans for a while, so don't worry about it." Andrea eyed Leigh's boot critically. "How long did the doctor say you had to use that thing?"

"He wasn't sure," Leigh responded. "Maybe three weeks."

Being reminded of the boot made Leigh notice that the rat bites inside it itched. She took a pencil from her desk and pushed the eraser end into the boot to get at a particularly annoying one. "Sorry for being gross."

"Go ahead and take that thing off. I'll bet that would be more comfortable."

"It would, thanks," Leigh conceded. She unbuckled the boot and slipped it off. Her lower leg was pale, bruised, and puffy. It looked like an enormous, overripe, bloated albino banana. With scabs.

"Oh, wow," Andrea said. "That looks horrible."

"Gee, thanks."

"No, I mean what happened to your poor leg was horrible." She shivered. "Are those the rat bites you told me about?"

"Yeah, and I don't want to talk about them, okay?"

"Sure, I—"

Leigh's phone rang. It was the receptionist. She picked it up. "Hi, Lilly."

"Phyllis Higgins is here for you."

"Thanks. Andrea will be right out for her."

Andrea bustled out. A moment later, Leigh could hear Phyllis's voice coming down the hall. ". . . over his shoulder."

"Really? She didn't mention that to me," replied Andrea.

They appeared in her door. "How come you didn't tell me Mr. Rubinelli carried you away from those awful rats?" Andrea demanded.

Leigh felt her face burning. "It must have slipped my mind. Have a seat, Phyllis. Good-bye, Andrea."

Phyllis smiled, but switched to business. "I'm still working on that license plate, but I thought you might be interested in these." She handed Leigh two bound documents of about twenty pages each. "Here are the DNA and fingerprint reports on Anne Smith."

"Thanks." Leigh gestured toward the plate. "Have a cookie or ten. If you don't eat them, they'll force themselves on me."

"Don't mind if I do." Phyllis took one of Andrea's saucer-size creations and broke little pieces off it while Leigh skimmed the reports.

The labs had been able to get a good DNA sample, three full fingerprints, and two partials from the plastic cup Phyllis had fished out of the trash can when she was first tailing Anne. But contrary to Phyllis's comment, the results didn't look particularly interesting—no criminal record, no prior security clearances, nothing really.

Leigh finished the report and looked up. "What's so interesting in here?

Phyllis swallowed and brushed crumbs off her copy of the report. "The third tab—the one labeled 'Ancestry and Ethnicity.'"

Leigh flipped to the third tab and started reading. Anne Smith was probably East European, possibly Russian. That explained her accent. Near the back of the tab was a section about probable relatives with profiles in the FBI's database. Anne had one: Elijah Rhodes, whose

DNA sample had been taken when he was booked for resisting arrest after a traffic incident.

Leigh looked up. "She's . . . she's related to Rhodes?"

Aunt Phyllis nodded. "Closely related."

"How close?"

"Very close, according to the DNA tech I talked to." Phyllis paused, shaking her head slightly in disbelief. "She's probably his daughter."

CHAPTER 42

The road to the old chemical factory complex looked much different during the day. Last night, it had seemed alien and ominous to Daniel. Now it just seemed run-down and a little sad. The factory complex itself was an industrial ghost town—an enormous jumble of rust-streaked pipes and tanks, cracked streets and loading docks sprouting weeds, and derelict buildings with peeling paint and broken windows.

He was supposed to meet Sandy's animal control contractors in a parking lot a block from the complex gate. They were specialists at working with biomedical companies. Specifically, Sandy said, they were experts at handling situations where lab animals with infectious diseases got out of their cages "and that sort of thing." Daniel's job was to observe and make sure that Animal Experts—the company Sandy had hired—caught the rats without damaging them.

He turned onto the street leading to the complex's main entrance. He spotted two white vans in a parking lot with "Animal Experts" painted on their sides. He pulled in and parked next to one of the vans. Four men got out, each wearing a matching shirt with his name sewn over the left pocket: Tom, Zhang, Danny, and Jeong.

"Mr. Rubinelli?" asked Jeong, who appeared to be in charge.

Daniel nodded. "What's the plan?"

Jeong looked confused. "Well, ah, we were hoping you could tell us. All we know is that we're supposed to meet you here and that you have an animal problem that needs to be solved nonlethally."

Daniel was itching to go. "That's right. Some lab rats have escaped, and we need you to catch them. There may also be other animals in there, but we're not sure. Come on, I'll show you where they are."

Daniel started to get back in his car, but Jeong hesitated. "Is there anything else you can tell us about these animals? You know, do they have any infectious diseases?"

"Nope, no diseases that I'm aware of."

"Have they been given any chemicals or treatments that might affect their behavior?"

"I don't think so. But they are very, very hungry."

Jeong relaxed and smiled. "Good. That will make them easy to catch. How many of them are there?"

Daniel shrugged. "I'm not sure. Hundreds, maybe thousands, of rats. There may also be some caged rabbits in there. I don't know about any other animals—but I didn't see any loose when I was there yesterday."

Jeong's smile faded. "Thousands of rats? It's, ah, possible we may need backup. But why don't you show us the problem first."

"Sure, just—" Daniel became aware of a rapidly approaching siren. He stopped in midsentence and turned just as a fire truck roared around the corner. It drove past at high speed, heading into the factory complex.

Daniel looked in the direction that the truck was heading and noticed a column of black smoke rising from somewhere in the middle of the factory complex. His muscles tightened and apprehension coiled around his spine.

"Just follow me," he said. He got in his car and drove in after the fire truck. His stomach sank. The truck was leading him to Dr. Rhodes's hidden lab.

He turned the last corner and got his first clear view of the little building that formed the gateway to the underground laboratory. Oily black smoke poured through the doorframe of the lab entrance and out of ventilation slits that Daniel hadn't noticed before. The fire truck was parked by the side of the street. Firefighters were already pulling equipment off the truck with practiced speed.

Daniel stopped the car in the middle of the street. He opened his door and started to get out, but the car started rolling again. He realized that he hadn't put it in park or turned off the engine. He slammed the car into park, drawing a nasty crunch from the gearbox. He yanked out the keys and jumped out, leaving the car in the center of the deserted road.

The two white vans pulled up behind him as he ran over to the fireman who appeared to be in charge. The man paused from giving orders and looked up as Daniel approached. He pointed to the building. "Do you know whether anyone is in there?" he asked Daniel.

"Not that I know of," Daniel admitted. "But there are animals inside."

"Animals?" The fireman glanced toward the vans, where Jeong and company stood in an uncertain clump as they watched the smoking building. "What kind of animals?"

"Lab rats." As the words came out of Daniel's mouth, he realized how trivial that sounded. "Uh, valuable lab rats. Maybe other animals too. They're part of important research that was going on in there. And there's very valuable equipment in there."

The firefighter gave the building an appraising look. "Well, we'll do what we can. What can we expect inside? Fuel tanks? Chemicals?"

"I'm not sure. I didn't see anything like that, but I've only been in part of the building."

"Hmm." The fireman looked at the building. The door was open now and thick smoke billowed out, forcing back the firefighters. "Mind telling me why exactly that research is so important?"

179

Before Daniel could answer, one of the men who had opened the door came up to them. "There's nothing in there except stairs going down," he reported.

The first fireman nodded and turned to Daniel. "Most of that building is underground, right?"

"Yes."

"Thought so. I've seen this sort of thing before. Sometimes they build labs underground like that. It prevents fires or explosions from starting a chain reaction and spreading to the whole complex. Makes my job a real pain, though. Getting at the fire can be almost impossible." He pointed to the little building with his chin. "Is that the only entrance?"

"There might be others, but that's the only one I've seen."

The fireman looked at the building for several seconds, then shook his head. "I can't send my men into that. We can try to seal the ventilation ducts to starve the fire of oxygen, but other than that we'll need to let it burn out." He gave Daniel a sympathetic pat on the back. "I wish there was something I could do. Sorry about your lab."

Chapter 43

Leigh wasn't happy to see Daniel Rubinelli, at least not under these circumstances. But there he was. He and his paralegal, Rich, stood at the window of a conference room at Diamond & Wang with their backs to the door, sipping coffee and admiring the panoramic view of the San Francisco Bay.

Daniel and Rich were here because Jack had essentially ordered Leigh to hold an in-person settlement meeting. Once he got her report on recent events, particularly her visit to Ratopia (as she had started thinking of Dr. Rhodes's secret lab), he had decided that it was time to end the case. She wasn't sure whether he was more disturbed by her harrowing ordeal or by the fact that he'd have trouble billing American Guaranty for her time.

Leigh had protested that the case wasn't ready to settle, that she needed to know more before she could justify recommending that their client shell out tens of millions of dollars to resolve the case. Jack hadn't cared. "Get a demand from them," he had ordered. "If it's reasonable, great. If it's too high to counter, that's also fine. We'll tell the client. It'll be tougher for them to moan about our bills if they know we're fighting against extortionists."

So now she had to make a serious effort to end a case that she didn't want to end. And leave Anne Smith and a hundred unanswered questions still out there.

For once, she really hoped that Daniel Rubinelli would be unreasonable.

She cleared her throat from the doorway. Daniel and Rich turned. The bandage on Daniel's head was smaller than the one he had worn home from the ER a week ago, and the bruise on his scalp was starting to fade.

"Good to see you," Daniel said as he stepped around the conference room table to shake her hand. His grip was warm and gentle, and he was careful not to touch her half-healed rat bites.

"You too," Leigh said as she slipped into one of the leather chairs around the conference table and leaned her crutch against another.

Daniel and Rich took seats across the table from her. "How are you doing?" Daniel asked.

"I'll be stuck in this boot for a couple more weeks and I'll never look at Mickey Mouse the same way again, but I can't complain. It could have been much worse. I'm glad you were there."

"Thanks, though I'm not exactly glad either of us was there," he said with a smile. "Any word on the police investigation?"

The police had interviewed all of them and claimed to be searching for Anne, but nothing much seemed to be happening. Leigh wasn't even sure they had searched Anne's apartment yet. She shook her head. "Phyllis put out some feelers, but nothing yet. If I hear anything, I'll pass it along." She took a deep breath. "Okay, let's get started. I've been instructed to explore whether settlement is possible. So let's explore. What do you think, Daniel?"

"We're willing to be reasonable," he said without hesitation.

Nuts. "Let's talk about what that means. For example, when we were at Whacktastic, you accused Anne of murdering Dr. Rhodes. Being reasonable, wouldn't you say that accusation no longer holds water?"

He leaned forward and rested his elbows on the table while Rich took notes. "You mean because your DNA test shows that she and Rhodes are closely related?"

Leigh nodded. "Very closely. Probably father-daughter. You're welcome to do your own test if you doubt the results."

He shook his head. "We know the lab you used, and they do good work. No, I was just thinking that close relatives do sometimes kill each other."

"Cold, but true," Leigh acknowledged. "Though it's also pure speculation. You're going to need a lot more than that to win at trial. You're going to need to be able to show that the most likely cause of Dr. Rhodes's death was something other than suicide. All you have now is your unsupported theory that maybe his daughter killed him. You'll need evidence to back up that theory, and you don't have it."

"Yet."

Leigh resisted the urge to smile. "Well, until you get it, your claim on the life insurance policy isn't worth very much."

"But—being reasonable yourself—you have to admit that the building insurance policy is worth a lot, right?"

"Really? Why is that?"

"Four reasons," Daniel responded. He held up one finger. "First, your theory that Dr. Rhodes was the arsonist fell apart." Two fingers. "Second, I accused Anne of setting the fire, and she didn't deny it." Three fingers. "Third, we have at least one known example of her destroying Rhodes's research—the dummy hard drive at Whacktastic." And finger number four. "Fourth, someone burned Rhodes's second lab within hours of Anne's escape. So it's pretty clear that she burned the first lab. She's not a Biosolutions employee, so the insurance policy applies and your client is on the hook."

"But was she being paid by a Biosolutions employee—say, Dr. Rhodes?" Leigh countered. "Unless you can prove she wasn't, I don't see my client paying out on the policy—at least not the full amount." Not exactly a ringing defense, but the best she could do. Time to cut to the chase. "On a related note, are you prepared to make a settlement demand?"

He looked at her in surprise. "Uh, sure. If that's going to be your client's defense on the building insurance policy, we feel pretty good about our chances at trial—so we're going to demand the full value on that one. For the life insurance policy, we'll give you a twenty-five percent discount to reflect the, um, uncertainties you noted. We'll also waive most of the prejudgment interest and attorney fees we're entitled to. So all told, our demand is ninety million. Are you prepared to make an offer?"

Leigh shook her head. "Not now. I'll take your offer back to my client, but I doubt they'll be willing to offer more than a few million dollars."

Daniel looked slightly annoyed. "If they're that low, I doubt we'll make a counteroffer. It sounds like the parties are just too far apart."

She nodded and smiled. "It looks like we're stuck with each other for a while longer."

CHAPTER 44

February

Daniel woke to the sound of his cell phone ringing. He pushed himself up onto one elbow and looked at the clock on his bedside table. 4:23 a.m. Then he looked at his phone and rolled his eyes.

He groaned, flopped onto his back, and answered the phone. "This better be good, Bruno."

"I broke the encryption on the Animal Trackers folder last night."

"It's *still* night, dude. Can't you work during the day like normal people?"

"Can't concentrate. So do you want to hear about it or do you want me to call back after naptime is over?"

Daniel sighed. He'd never get back to sleep now. "Fine, tell me about it."

"The tracker is an Excel spreadsheet with pages for different kinds of animals. It looks like he wasn't just working on rats and rabbits at that lab. He had fruit flies, nematodes, and dogs too."

"There were dogs down there?" Daniel squirmed a little. He had always liked dogs.

"Looks that way, but that's not the real news: the tracker has info for animals in both a control group and in groups that had been given something called Protocol E."

"What kind of info?"

"All sorts of stuff—there are about fifty columns. Most of 'em are for diseases and health problems—cancer, arthritis, cataracts, dementia, and so on."

"So mostly age-related stuff?"

"Bingo," Bruno said. "And here's the kicker: a lot of them stayed healthy for a really, really long time. Know what the average life span for a fruit fly is?"

Daniel yawned. "I'll bet I'm about to find out."

"About six weeks. They never live more than three months. Rhodes had six flies that lasted more than five years. Two of them were still alive the last time he updated the tracker."

"Wow." Daniel was wide awake now. "How about the other animals?"

"He got the same kind of results for nematodes, most of the rats, and some of the rabbits. He had trouble with dogs, though."

"What kind of trouble?"

"They all got cancer. Most of 'em died within six months of getting Protocol E. Same thing happened with some of the rats and most of the rabbits."

"You mean the ones that didn't stay young forever?"

"Exactly. They wind up like Tom Cruise or they die of cancer. Doesn't look like there was much middle ground."

Daniel sat silent. He caught a glimpse of himself in the mirror on his closet door. His mouth hung open and his eyes stared vacantly. He looked like he had been drugged. He felt like it too. The magnitude of what Rhodes had done threw his mind off kilter. He couldn't get a sense of perspective. The sensation reminded him of the vertigo he felt when he visited the Sears Tower as a child and stood right against the base of the skyscraper, staring up.

"You there?" Bruno asked.

"Yeah. I just . . . I don't know what to think."

"Well, I've had a little time to think about it," Bruno said, "and I know what I think."

"What's that?" Daniel asked.

"That someone needs to talk with Rich about exactly what Dr. Rhodes was doing."

CHAPTER 45

Phyllis called just as Leigh was hobbling into her office. She pushed the speakerphone button as she sat behind her desk. "Good morning, Phyllis. What's up?"

"I finally got a report back on that license plate," Phyllis said. "There was a delay because the records seem to have gotten misfiled at the DMV. Maybe it was a random bureaucratic mistake or maybe someone got paid to make that mistake, but it meant that I had to put a lot of effort into finding out who owned that car—more effort than a traffic cop would probably bother expending, coincidentally."

"So what did you find?"

"As I guessed, it's owned by a detective agency. They're called Stillwater Security."

"Do you know anything about them?"

"I do." Phyllis clicked her tongue. "Good investigators; bad people. They've got a reputation for hiring former cops and FBI agents who have top-notch skills, but have been terminated for cause or forced to retire early. They've also got a military contracting wing full of special forces guys who got dishonorable discharges. There are also rumors that they do work for organized crime, but I don't know whether that's true. What I do know is that they're very expensive and that they'll do things other companies won't."

A chill went up Leigh's spine. "What kind of things?"

"Oh, illegal surveillance—wiretaps, hacking, and that sort of thing. The security side of the company has been accused of doing mercenary work. And worse stuff. The only stories I know anything about for certain had to do with a case where two people accused a Stillwater agent of false imprisonment. They claimed both incidents were misunderstandings and that their guy was just trying to interview reluctant witnesses. They make a point of staying very connected with law enforcement, so they called in some favors and managed to avoid getting charged. It was a total whitewash, though."

"Great, they sound like a fun bunch. Any idea who hired them?"

"Nope, and I don't think we'll find out. They also have a reputation for being very discreet."

Leigh sighed. What a wonderful way to start her morning. "I hope they don't take the slashed tires and gunshots personally."

"Professional hazard," Phyllis said. "If you pull a gun and stand in front of someone's car in the middle of the night, you run the risk that something bad might happen—particularly if you start cracking shots off. They're lucky I only slashed their tires and fired a couple of warning shots into the dirt. If the roles had been reversed, I bet they would've shot me and claimed self-defense."

"Think we should try to make peace somehow?" Leigh asked. "Maybe explain what happened to someone in management and offer to pay for the tires?"

"No. At best, that won't make any difference. At worst, they'll view it as a sign of weakness."

Leigh groaned. "This just keeps getting better. I need to give Daniel a call and tell him about this. We were in his car, so they must know he was involved."

"When you call him, there's some other news you should pass along."

"What's that?"

"The SFPD executed a search warrant on Anne Smith's apartment. They're going to be calling both of you and asking you to come in and look over some stuff they seized. They'll want to know whether any of it was stolen from your car or Biosolutions."

"Did they catch her?" Leigh asked.

Phyllis laughed. "What do you think?"

It wasn't hard to guess. "Nope."

"Nope," Phyllis confirmed.

CHAPTER 46

Daniel took a deep breath and walked over to Rich's cubicle.

Rich saw him coming and stood to greet him. "Hey, Daniel. What can I do for you?"

"We've been asked to go up to a meeting on the fifteenth floor."

Rich tensed slightly. The fifteenth floor was where the C-level executives had their offices. "When?"

"Now. Come on."

Daniel started to walk toward the elevator, and Rich fell in step beside him. "What's the meeting about?"

"Confidential. I can't talk about it until we're in the meeting. Sandy's instructions. Don't worry—you're not in trouble."

Rich relaxed slightly. "I've never been up there."

"We'll be meeting with the chief science officer, Prakash Gupta," Daniel said as they stepped into the elevator. "Sandy will be there too."

Rich's eyes widened. "Dr. Gupta? The guy is a genius."

Daniel had only met Dr. Gupta once. He remembered the CSO mostly as a small man with an exceptionally large nose and intense eyes. Other than that, Daniel knew of him mostly from Dr. Rhodes's personnel file, where he featured as one of Dr. Rhodes's many corporate antagonists—primarily because Dr. Gupta wanted to know what Dr. Rhodes was working on and Dr. Rhodes refused to tell him.

The elevator doors opened, and they walked out onto the fifteenth floor. It was an intimidating place. Instead of the utilitarian tile and carpet of the lower floors, the halls up here were floored with polished maple, and matching paneling covered the walls. Ansel Adams photographs hung on those walls, each an original—Daniel knew because he had handled the insurance policies on them.

The fifteenth floor had its own receptionist. She gave them a brightly inquisitive look. "Can I help you?"

"Yes, we're here to see Dr. Gupta," Daniel said.

She called someone, and thirty seconds later a secretary materialized and whisked them into Dr. Gupta's office. Actually, "office" didn't really do the room justice. It was more of an open executive suite, with its own conference table and waiting area.

Sandy and Dr. Gupta were sitting at the conference table when Daniel and Rich arrived. Dr. Gupta was at the head of the table and Sandy was to his right. "Please have a seat," Dr. Gupta said, gesturing to the chairs at his left.

"Thank you for coming so quickly," he said, as if they'd had a choice. "Mr. Johnson, we'd like to talk to you about some of Dr. Rhodes's research."

"Of course," Rich said as they sat. "What can I tell you?"

"To begin with, what role did you play in his research?" Dr. Gupta asked.

"I was a lab tech. I checked the equipment to make sure it was calibrated and functioning correctly. I helped prepare and monitor experiments. That sort of thing."

Dr. Gupta nodded. "Did you ever create spreadsheets to track lab animals during experiments?"

"Yes, I did that several times."

"Did you create this one?" Sandy asked as she slid a document over to Rich, her voice and face neutral.

She had just handed Rich a copy of the animal tracker Bruno had decrypted last night, except that the life-span column had been deleted.

Rich examined the spreadsheet carefully. His face was focused and calm, but Daniel noticed tiny drops of perspiration along Rich's hairline. He could sympathize. Being cross-examined by the GC and CSO would make anyone nervous, particularly a twentysomething lab tech turned paralegal.

"I don't think so," Rich said at last. "I don't remember working on this experiment. It looks like this was for a gerontology study, but I only worked on cancer research."

Sandy and Dr. Gupta exchanged a quick look. "Why do you say that?" Dr. Gupta asked.

Rich pointed to the top of the spreadsheet. "The headings for these columns. They're tracking dementia, arthritis, cataracts, and so on. That's not the sort of thing we would track for cancer research."

Dr. Gupta leaned forward and folded his hands on the table. "Was there any possible gerontology crossover with the experiments you were working on?"

"I . . ." Rich stopped and looked into the middle distance for a moment. "Well, hypothetically."

"What do you mean?" Dr. Gupta asked. He leaned farther forward, his sharp nose and sharper eyes making him look like a bird of prey.

"The link between cancer and aging has been known for a long time, of course," Rich began. "As people get older, their risk of developing various types of cancer goes up dramatically. A number of factors may be to blame. For example—"

"Yes, yes," Dr. Gupta interrupted. "But what was it about Dr. Rhodes's research in particular?"

"He was working on telomere stabilization," Rich replied. His gaze flicked to Daniel and Sandy for an instant. "Should I provide a little background on what that means?"

"Explain for the benefit of Ms. Hampton and Mr. Rubinelli," Dr. Gupta said. "But be concise."

Rich nodded and turned to Sandy and Daniel. "Whenever a cell divides, the DNA gets copied—but a cell can't make a complete copy of its DNA. The molecular structure doesn't work. The end of the DNA string gets left off. Telomeres fix that problem. They're strings of nucleotides on the ends of your DNA. They don't have any genes in them, so it doesn't matter if part of the string gets lost during copying."

"Except that the telomere is shorter the next time the cell divides," Sandy observed.

"Exactly," Rich replied. "Eventually, the telomere gets too short and the cell can't divide anymore. It becomes senescent and dies. As organisms get older, more and more of their cells become senescent. That's a major cause of aging."

"But what does it have to do with cancer?" Daniel asked.

"Cells with short telomeres are more likely to become cancerous," Rich answered. "I know what you're thinking—the short telomeres should mean the cancer cells can only divide a few times, right?" He paused and looked expectantly at Sandy and Daniel.

Actually, Daniel was thinking that he wished he had taken more biology classes in college. But he simply nodded for Rich to go on.

"For a lot of tumors, the cancer cells' trick is that they lengthen their telomeres by making an enzyme called telomerase. That's why they can reproduce out of control. They basically make themselves immortal by creating unlimited amounts of telomerase."

"I think I understand," Sandy said. "So Dr. Rhodes was trying to stabilize the telomeres in lab animals. If he could do that, he could both stop cancer cells from making too much telomerase and keep regular cells from senescing."

Rich nodded approvingly, like he was a professor and Sandy was a clever student. "You've got it! That's a very high-level summary of what we were doing."

The implications of what Rhodes had been doing percolated through to Daniel's brain. "So you were making cells that could live forever?"

"Theoretically," Rich cautioned. "Just stabilizing the telomeres would only make cells immortal if their DNA was never damaged. DNA damage happens all the time for various reasons—radiation, contact with harmful chemicals, and so on."

"But wasn't Dr. Rhodes also working on strengthening cell self-repair mechanisms?" asked Sandy.

Rich nodded. "Yes, I was about to get to that. We'd had success with that too. Cells have lots of different DNA repair tools, so we just needed to make them a little more active. Fortunately, stabilizing the telomeres seemed to help with that as well."

"But you were only working on single cells or small cultures," said Dr. Gupta, who had been listening with a sort of intensely thoughtful expression. He gestured to the spreadsheet in front of Rich. "This indicates that Dr. Rhodes was working on actual animals."

"Maybe." Rich picked up the spreadsheet. "I wasn't part of this experiment, so I don't know exactly what he was doing. But if he *was* doing telomere stabilization and so forth on animals, he would have had to develop a completely new delivery vector. That would have been hard. Really hard."

"What about that Harvard study?" Dr. Gupta asked. "I thought they managed to reverse aging in mice by altering the lengths of their telomeres."

Rich nodded. "That's true, but they didn't do it through gene therapy. They used mice that had been specially engineered to have short telomeres, and the structures that produce telomerase had been engineered so they could be activated by an estrogenlike drug, not by introducing curative genes into the mice's cells."

Rich turned to Daniel and Sandy again. "Gene therapy only works if you can get the therapeutic genes into each cell that needs them and put the genes where they belong in the DNA. That's a lot easier to do with single cells under a microscope than with trillions of cells in, say, a rat or a monkey. The most common technique is to use a virus. The researcher puts the therapeutic DNA into the virus and then infects the test animal with the virus. But I don't think that would have worked for something as complicated as telomere stabilization. Also, you would need something that could deliver the genes to every cell in the body, and I'm not aware of a virus that will do that." He paused for a moment, then shook his head thoughtfully. "I wonder how he did it."

"Well, couldn't he have done the same thing the Harvard team did?" Dr. Gupta persisted.

"I doubt it," Rich said. "Our approach was different. They weren't trying to put new genes into the mice's cells. All the Harvard guys did was inject the mice with a drug. We were actually changing the genes in our test cells—but only individual cells, nothing more. But based on this"—he pointed to the spreadsheet—"Dr. Rhodes managed to apply those changes to actual living animals. That can be done, but not using the Harvard team's methods." He paused, staring at the spreadsheet. "Stanford managed to extend the telomeres on human muscle cells," he said, as if musing to himself. "But they did that *ex vivo*. Maybe a combination of *ex vivo* and *in vivo* . . ." His voice trailed off.

The group was silent for several seconds. Then Dr. Gupta cleared his throat. "Thank you, Mr. Johnson. You may go now. You will keep everything we have just discussed strictly confidential. Do not discuss it, even within the company. Mr. Rubinelli, please remain."

"Of course," Rich said. He got up and walked slowly toward the door, his face still pensive. He stopped and turned. "It would be an honor and a privilege to work on reconstructing Dr. Rhodes's research."

Dr. Gupta smiled and nodded. "Thank you for your enthusiasm, Mr. Johnson. I will keep it in mind."

"Thank you, sir," Rich said. He turned again and left.

"A very impressive young man," Dr. Gupta commented. He picked up the spreadsheet. "Unfortunately, if this is all we have, we will have great difficulty re-creating Elijah's research." He turned to Daniel. "When can we expect the remainder of the hard drive to be decrypted?"

Daniel shrugged. "I wish I knew. I can ask if you like, but I'm pretty sure my cousin will say the same thing he told me before—that he doesn't know when he'll break the encryption. It could be tomorrow or a year from tomorrow."

"Your cousin," Dr. Gupta echoed. He frowned. "I would feel more comfortable if the company had full control over that hard drive."

"I'm not, uh, sure our IT department has the technical ability to decrypt it," Daniel said. "That's Bruno's—my cousin's—area of expertise."

"Maybe Bruno can keep working on it," Dr. Gupta said, "but the hard drive really should be kept here. The information on it may be vital to the company's future." He glanced at Sandy. "And I understand that there was a recent attempt to steal the hard drive, and the thief is still at large."

Daniel began to feel a little indignant on Bruno's behalf. "That attempt failed—unlike the attempt here. I understand your concern, but I think the hard drive is probably safer with Bruno."

Dr. Gupta shook his head. "We've tightened security since then, and this time the hard drive won't be sitting in something as easy to break into as a locked storage room." He gave a thin smile. "Trust me, it will be safe here. Please get it to me as soon as possible."

Daniel knew better than to press the point. "Will do."

Back in his office, Daniel stared at his phone for a full minute, wondering what he would say to Bruno. Then he chickened out and wrote an e-mail instead:

> B—
> Sorry, but we need Rhodes's hard drive back
> ASAP. When can I come over and pick it up?
> —D

He looked at the draft e-mail, replaying the conversation from Dr. Gupta's office in his head. Something about it bothered him, though he couldn't quite put his finger on it. Something about Rich. The paralegal and former lab tech had acted . . . not quite how Daniel expected a paralegal and former lab tech to act. Nothing specific, but Rich seemed a little too nervous before the meeting started, and then a little too eager later on. Bruno said he hadn't done a "deep dive" on Rich last time. Maybe he should.

Daniel revised the e-mail to read:

> B—
> Sorry, but we need Rhodes's hard drive back
> ASAP. Can I come over to pick it up?
> Unrelated: Could you run a full background check
> on my paralegal, Richard C. Johnson? He's a UC
> Berkeley grad, if that helps.
> Thanks!
> —D

Then he hit "Send."

CHAPTER 47

As Phyllis had prophesied, a police officer called Leigh to say that they had searched Anne Smith's apartment and might have found documents stolen from Leigh's car. He asked her to come down to the station to take a look.

At least some of the stuff taken from her car came from Biosolutions, so she called Daniel to see whether he wanted to come. He did, and he offered to give her a ride since her office was on his way to the police station.

Forty-five minutes later, he pulled up outside her building. She stowed her crutch—she was down to one now—in the backseat and got in.

"Want some coffee?" he asked as they pulled away from the curb. He nodded toward two cups in holders between them. "I stopped by Philz on the way, and I hate to drink alone. One is Wonderbar and the other is Mint Mojito. I love them both, so your choice."

"Mmm, thanks!" She picked up the Mint Mojito and took a sip, savoring its fresh sweetness. "This is a lot more fun than the last time we carpooled."

He nodded and smiled. "I figured you might want something to help you stay awake this time."

She laughed. "I plead extenuating circumstances." She took a look at his head. The bandage was gone, his hair was growing back, and the cut was little more than an angry red line. "You're looking a lot better than you did last time."

"Yeah, I looked like—what was it—a dead extra from a slasher movie?" He shot her a grin. "Now I just look like a guy with a blind barber."

"Hopefully, we're in for a lot less excitement today."

He nodded. "Hence the coffee."

Leigh had the foresight to bring her disability placard, so they were able to find a decent spot to park.

Ten minutes later, they were in a slightly dirty, very utilitarian room in the station. They sat in front of a scarred Formica-topped table, which held three boxes of paper. A bored-looking cop sat on the other side of the table, ostensibly there to answer questions, but probably also to make sure they didn't damage or take anything.

The first box contained user manuals for random appliances. The second box was mostly news magazines in what appeared to be Russian. The third was slightly more interesting—it held the lease for the apartment (signed by Elijah Rhodes) and financial documents, largely bank statements from the Wells Fargo account Rhodes had set up for Anne. Daniel and Leigh pored over these for about half an hour, but ultimately concluded that there was no meaningful new information in them. And none of the boxes held any of the papers stolen from Leigh's car.

When they were finished, Daniel turned to their uniformed chaperone. "I was wondering—did you find any electronics when you searched the apartment?"

"We looked for a MacBook laptop and didn't find one," the officer said.

"Did you look for other electronics?" Daniel asked. "This wasn't a normal computer theft—I'm pretty sure she only wanted the drive, not the machine as a whole. She might have removed the hard drive and thrown away the computer. In fact, that probably would have been the smart thing to do—the hard drive would be smaller and harder to identify."

The policeman frowned. "I'll check." He put the boxes on a hand truck and wheeled them out of the room. A few minutes later, he reappeared without the boxes. "We weren't searching for computer components, only the stolen MacBook."

"You didn't search for the hard drive?" Daniel's eyes widened. "Then we need to see the apartment. The data on that hard drive is vitally important. Biosolutions needs to get it back right away."

The policeman shook his head before Daniel finished speaking. "I don't think that will be possible."

Leigh was pretty sure Daniel was using the missing computer as an excuse to get a look at Anne's apartment. Clever. She decided to help him out. "Let me give Detective Higgins a call and see if she can work something out."

Phyllis was something of a legend in the Oakland Police Department, and invoking her name could have near-magical results with the OPD. Leigh hoped her reputation had crossed the bay to San Francisco.

The officer's face darkened. "Wait here," he said and walked out again.

Daniel turned to Leigh and whispered, "Thank you."

Ten minutes later, a man in his fifties wearing a suit walked in. "My name is Detective Frank Jameson. I've talked to Phyllis and she vouches for you two. Since we've already processed the apartment, we'll take you there and you can look around."

◆ ◆ ◆

Anne Smith lived on the fifth floor of an impeccably maintained 1940s brick building in the Twin Peaks neighborhood of San Francisco. Her apartment was decorated to match the era—dark wood paneling with simple carved accents, furniture upholstered with black leather and brass nails, polished wood floors almost entirely covered by Persian rugs. Leigh could almost imagine Bogart and Bacall living there—except for the microwave oven and other modern touches.

The apartment wasn't big, but it was cozy rather than cramped. It had a fireplace, a large bay window, and a tiny balcony on which Anne had managed to fit a single chair and a very small table that would have looked at home outside a Paris cafe.

It only took Leigh and Daniel about ten minutes to search the entire place, all under the watchful eye of Detective Jameson. The apartment was neat and had only about a dozen drawers and a mostly empty walnut file cabinet that had probably been the source of the documents they reviewed at the police station.

When they finished, Leigh still hadn't found either the papers stolen from her car or anything resembling a Mac hard drive. But she had learned more about Anne—though she wasn't sure how useful it would be. Anne liked cognac, for example, and had two expensive bottles and four crystal snifters in her kitchen. She spoke at least French, English, and Russian, based on the contents of the bookshelf in her living room, which was stuffed with classics in all three languages. She actually seemed to read them, judging by what appeared (based on Leigh's limited ability to sound out Cyrillic letters) to be a Russian copy of Dostoevsky's *The Idiot* on Anne's bedside table. She also had a well-thumbed Russian Bible by her bed, so she was probably religious as well. And she had a flair for retro decorating, of course.

To Leigh's surprise, Anne seemed to be married. Or at least she had posed for a couple of wedding pictures that sat on her bedside table—black-and-white and 1940s-themed, naturally. But there was no hint that a man had ever set foot in the apartment—no men's clothing in the closet, no male toiletries in the bathroom, no James Bond or *Avengers* DVDs by the TV.

She went back out to the living room, where Daniel was already. "Find anything interesting?" he asked.

Leigh shrugged. "Sort of. No hard drive or stolen documents, but . . . Well, this place is interesting. I don't know what the apartment of a pistol-packing burglar usually looks like, but I'm guessing this isn't it."

He nodded. "Yeah, I was thinking basically the same thing. I mean, look at this stuff," he said, making a sweeping gesture that encompassed the living room. "Why all the old books and antique furniture? And where are the high-tech burglar tools, disguises, and so on? Maybe I watch too much TV, but it seems like there should be at least some of that stuff. It all feels weird somehow."

Leigh nodded and looked around the room. She noticed something she had missed before: two photo albums in a corner of the bookshelf. She walked over, pulled one out, and started flipping through it. The pages were yellowed and crackled faintly as she turned them. The pictures were . . . odd. They looked at least sixty years old—old cars, old fashions, old hairstyles. Even the paper they were printed on seemed old. But a lot of them showed Anne and the man from the wedding pictures. Had they spent their honeymoon at a "travel back in time" resort?

Daniel noticed her looking at the album and walked over.

"This is now a little weirder," she said, holding it up for him to see. "I thought she had a retro style, but I'm starting to think she had a retro obsession."

He stared at the pictures wordlessly for half a minute. Then he grabbed the second album from the shelf. He turned the pages rapidly for several seconds, stopping at a series of color pictures that appeared to have been taken at a graduation. He froze and went pale.

"That's Elijah Rhodes in the middle," he said softly.

Leigh leaned over for a closer look. The pictures all showed three people outside on a sunny day. In the middle was a handsome young man in his early twenties wearing a graduation robe and mortarboard. He held a diploma, and a happy smile split his long face. To his right stood an older version of the man from the wedding pictures, wearing a suit-and-turtleneck combo that would have been popular around 1970. On his left was an attractive woman of about fifty with strong cheekbones, glossy black hair, brilliant green eyes, and a mole on her right cheek. Anne.

CHAPTER 48

Anya Shevchuk Rhodes woke in an antiseptically bright room. She squinted and blinked, then tried to sit up.

She couldn't.

She looked down and saw a padded belt across her waist over a thin white sheet. Two similar bands held her wrists. She appeared to be in a hospital bed of some sort. A tube ran down to a needle in the inside of her right elbow. It connected to a bag of clear liquid hanging from a stand.

She looked around. She was alone. Institutional wood cabinets lined the wall to her left above a utilitarian steel sink and a white counter. A pulse oximeter stood by the bed, beeping softly. A wire ran from it to a clip on the index finger of her right hand.

She could see no doors or windows in the featureless gray-white walls. There must be a door behind her somewhere.

The last thing she remembered was going back to Elijah's secret lab to burn it. She had managed to set the fire, but two men caught her as she tried to leave. She had struggled, of course, but one of them had hit her hard in the left temple with a blackjack or club.

Her head didn't hurt anymore.

She couldn't touch her scalp to check for a lump, of course. So she turned her head to the left and pressed down as hard as she could. No hint of pain.

So she had been unconscious long enough for her head to heal. How long did that take? A day or two? She healed faster than she used to, so it was hard to estimate. But at least a day, and maybe a lot longer. The tube in her right arm was probably at least partially for feeding and she could feel a catheter between her legs.

A cold fog of fear crept through her as she realized that whoever had captured her planned to keep her here for a long time. Maybe forever.

The inside of her left elbow was bruised and stung slightly when she moved her arm.

Someone had been drawing her blood.

She yanked at her restraints, straining to pull her arms free. Sharp pains sliced through her abdomen, but she ignored them. She had to get out! Now! This could not happen!

"Please don't do that."

She looked around, searching for the voice.

"Even if you managed to get out of your restraints, you would never be able to leave that room," the voice explained patiently. It was mechanical, slightly disjointed, and feminine—like the voice in an elevator. She realized it was coming from a small speaker on the counter. A tiny camera perched on top of it. "You might also tear open your incisions."

She looked down at her abdomen and saw that there were bandages underneath the sheet. Her horror grew.

"Stop this," she begged. "Please stop now."

"You are awake because we have questions for you. If you help us, you will stay awake. If you don't, you won't. In fact, you may never wake up again."

"I have no fear of death," she said—and meant it more than her captors likely suspected.

"Oh, we won't kill you," the flat android voice said. "You're far too valuable for that. We simply won't let you wake again. Ever."

Panic rose in her. She gripped it with the iron hands of her will and throttled it. She needed to be able to think clearly and fast, and she couldn't do that if her mind was clouded with fear. "What do you want?"

"Tell me everything you know about Dr. Elijah Rhodes's Enoch project."

"I don't know what you're talking about."

"Of course you do," the voice said. "You are Dr. Rhodes's mother. You are also ninety-seven years old. Not only do you know about Enoch, you participated in it."

So they knew. She had assumed they knew as soon as she woke in this place and found evidence of what had been done to her. But now she was certain.

She needed to play for time. The longer she could keep them talking, the more likely it was that they would make a mistake or she would come up with a workable plan. Several Nazi soldiers had died because she managed to keep them talking past the point when they should have killed her.

She sighed. "Very well. He named it Enoch after a man in the Bible who went straight to heaven without dying. Elijah thought his invention would create heaven on Earth. Not only had he cured cancer, but no one would ever get old again. Everyone in the world would be perpetually young and healthy."

"So why did you burn his lab?"

"Because he was wrong."

"He was right about you."

She shook her head, looking around the room as she did so. She didn't see a door, but there must be one. Where? How strong was it?

She coughed. "My throat is dry," she said, making her voice rough. "Can I have some water?"

There was no reply, but about a minute later, she heard a door open behind her head. She listened carefully, concentrating on the direction of the sound. It seemed to come from the left.

Masculine footsteps walked up and stopped directly behind her head. Then a hand wearing a blue latex glove appeared to her left. It held a small plastic cup, which it pushed against her lower lip. She raised her head and drank.

Her gaze rested on her bed and body as she drank. The sheet and her gown had become disheveled during her thrashings, so she looked like she had just woken from a night of tossing and turning. Also, her IV tube had gotten caught on her arm restraint. The tension on the tube wasn't high because she was lying still, but . . .

She drained the cup and the steps retreated to the door, which opened and closed again. Definitely on the left, and it sounded heavy and solid.

"Proceed," said the artificial voice. "Why was he wrong about you?"

"Does this look like heaven on Earth?" she said, allowing heat to creep into her voice. She didn't really expect them to listen. Elijah had never listened. He had blinded himself to all truth that could not be measured with a machine or tested in a laboratory. Worse, for him and people like him, the question was always whether they *could* do a thing, never whether they *should*.

But it was still worth talking to these people, even if their hearts and minds were closed. She had discovered long ago that when she spoke passionately, people focused on her face, not the rest of her body. That had proven useful more than once.

She held her head up and stared into the camera. "Death at the end of a full life is not a tragedy. Trust me on that—I know it well." She gestured as much as the restraints allowed, her arm tugging against the tubing. The surgical tape holding the needle in place tugged against her skin, but it didn't come loose. She would need to put more pressure on it. Somehow.

"And eternal youth is no blessing," she went on. "Imagine being trapped forever in an amusement park. What is entertaining and exciting for a short time becomes a horror when—"

"So he wasn't wrong about the science," the mechanical voice broke in.

"Science is more than genetics," she countered. "Have you thought about what will happen to Earth's population if no one ever gets old? Imagine the millions—billions—who will die from starvation or war in the next fifty years."

"But you have no reason to believe he was wrong about you personally, correct? You were old and sick, and Dr. Rhodes used Enoch on you. Afterward, you were young and healthy."

"I suppose so," she said. "Physically healthy, at any rate."

"Describe the protocol he used on you."

"You mean what he did?"

"Yes. Tell me precisely what he did at every step."

Another idea occurred to her. She squirmed. "I'm sorry. I've developed a terrible itch on my right leg. It's very distracting. Could someone come scratch it for me?"

"No," came the immediate response. "Proceed now with your answer."

"My memory is not very clear. I was old and on many medications." She stretched her right arm down as she spoke, reaching for the nonexistent itch. The IV tube tightened. She could feel it straining against the single piece of surgical tape that held the IV in place. "I recall him giving me several injections and pills to take." She contorted her body, pulling hard against the restraints and reaching as far down her right leg as she could. The IV came out of her arm and fell between it and her body. She scratched her thigh vigorously, then flopped back and sighed. "Got it. Then he gave me more injections. After that, he treated me with some sort of machine. Radiation, I think."

In fact, the treatment had involved him giving her injections and taking blood and bone marrow samples, treating them somehow, and then reinjecting them. No pills or radiation. It would be interesting to see whether her inquisitors knew the truth.

They apparently did. "I'm going to give you one more chance," the calm robotic voice said. "Tell me the truth or this conversation will end and you will go back to sleep."

That threat didn't bother her now, of course. In fact, now that the IV was out of her arm, she wanted the conversation to end as quickly as possible.

"I told you, my memory isn't very clear. But I do remember that Elijah took detailed notes. I know where they are, and I can take you to them." Not a particularly good lie, but that was fine.

"If you knew where they were, you would have destroyed them," the voice said. She almost thought she caught a hint of anger and frustration in its mechanical monotone. "You ignored my warning. Sleep well."

"Please!" she cried, putting fear into her voice. "I've told you everything I know. Please let me go."

The door opened behind her. The same steps, except this time they went straight to the IV bag beside the bed. She turned to her right, straining for a glimpse of the intruder—and covering the loose IV tube with her sheet and pressing her right arm against her body.

A tall, slender man in a blue hospital uniform and mask appeared.

"Please don't do this," she pleaded. She kept her eyes on his face, trying to make eye contact and keep his gaze away from her right arm.

He took a syringe out of his shirt pocket, uncapped it, and poked it into the IV tube where it joined the bag.

"Please," she said again.

His eyes flicked down to her face for an instant. They were blue and she had the impression he was young.

He pushed down the plunger on the syringe. She felt a dribble of cool liquid on her right side, then a spreading wet patch under her back.

She closed her eyes and sobbed quietly.

The footsteps retreated and the door opened and closed again.

She stopped crying gradually over the next two minutes and slowed her breathing to a steady, even rhythm.

The speaker uttered a sharp click and went dead. Then the lights went out.

She waited about five more minutes. Nothing changed.

She began to work free of her restraints.

CHAPTER 49

"We have to find her," Daniel insisted. He had been in Sandy's office for the past half hour, planning next steps. Dr. Rhodes's personnel file lay on one of Sandy's guest chairs, the section on his family history out. The shock of discovering the truth about Anya Rhodes had worn off a little, and Daniel had realized just how much needed to be done—and needed to be done right now. But he was getting the sense that Sandy didn't really think he should be doing it, which bothered him.

Sandy nodded. "I absolutely agree. Anya Rhodes is incredibly important. That's why we need professionals looking for her."

"That's great," Daniel said. "But while we're figuring out who to hire and then waiting for them to get up to speed, Bruno and I can get the ball rolling. For instance, we can—"

But she was already shaking her head. "We've been over this. Remember how I said you two aren't the Hardy Boys? You still aren't."

"I understand. But I'm not talking about going out and trying to hunt her down. All I'm suggesting is that we do a little discreet poking around. Some cybersleuthing and—"

"I said no and I meant no," she said, a warning look in her eyes. "To be blunt, the first time you tried this sort of thing, she walked into the Starbucks where you were plotting and you all stared like preschoolers in a zoo, right?"

His face burned and he looked down at her perfectly organized desk. "Okay, that's on me. Bruno wasn't involved."

"That's right. Once Bruno got involved, we went from an awkward scene at a coffee shop to a burning lab full of priceless servers and animals. How is that an improvement?"

He couldn't look at her, so he stared at a beautifully carved amber paperweight on her desk. "That wasn't Bruno's fault," he said. He heaved a sigh. "I guess that one was on me too."

"Hey, I don't blame Bruno and I don't blame you," she said, her voice softer. "You're a lawyer and Bruno is a hacker, or whatever you call someone who does what he does. You guys did the best you could, but neither of you are detectives—and some things went wrong as a result. So now we're bringing in professional detectives, and you can go back to being a professional lawyer. There's still a hundred-million-dollar lawsuit that needs your attention, remember?"

He looked up and saw that she was smiling at him. Her eyes were now warm and had little crinkles at the corners. He discovered that he was smiling back. "Yeah, I guess it does. I never would have guessed that a nine-figure case would be an afterthought in one of our conversations."

"Speaking of which, did American Guaranty ever get back to you with a response to our settlement demand?"

"No, though Leigh Collins said they'd probably only offer a few million, so I wasn't exactly holding my breath."

She nodded. "That's fine, but let's follow up with them. If you can persuade them to make a decent settlement offer, that would be great. Dr. Gupta is talking about pulling Rich back into research, and there are some urgent projects I may need your help with."

"I'll do some tactical thinking and give her a call this afternoon."

"Good—but first go to Whacktastic and pick up that hard drive from Bruno."

"She seriously compared us to the Hardy Boys?" Bruno shook his head in disgust. "Whatever."

"I didn't like it either," Daniel said. "Still, we don't have much choice."

"*You* don't have much choice. You work for her; I don't. She doesn't even understand what I'm doing. If Anya Rhodes shows her face on any security camera I've, um, accessed, I'll know. Then I'll just tell Phyllis and she can take it from there."

"You've been talking to Phyllis?"

"Don't want to tell you anything you can't hear, but . . ." Bruno shrugged his skinny shoulders. "It would make sense, no? I do the new-school techno stuff and she does the old-school street stuff."

Daniel hesitated. Did he want to know more or didn't he? Curiosity won out. "How does that 'techno stuff' work, hypothetically? I mean, security cameras in airports and places like that aren't connected to the Internet, are they?"

"No, but a lot of them are connected to systems that are connected to the Internet. All you need to do is ask the system to have the cameras look for a particular face, and then send an e-mail or text when it finds that face."

That sounded a little too simple to Daniel. "Is that kind of like saying that all you need to do to fly to the moon is build a rocket and space suit?"

"No, moon shots are easy. They're just expensive, which is why we stopped doing them. But you're missing the point: I've got this thing up and running already. Why shut it down?"

"Because she told us to. The message was crystal clear."

Bruno leaned back in his chair and put his feet up, resting his dirty Vans on an expensive-looking but abused desk. "Yeah, well you can tell Nancy Drew 'message delivered.' Next?"

Daniel decided he had done all he could on that front. "Sandy also wants the hard drive. Or, more accurately, our chief science officer wants it, so Sandy has to get it."

"So you have to get it. I saw your e-mail." Bruno rolled his eyes. "Man, am I glad I don't work for a company."

Daniel braced himself for another argument, but Bruno reached into a desk drawer and pulled out a hard drive, which he tossed to Daniel. "Here you go. I hope they've found a safe place for it this time."

"Thanks, B," Daniel said as he slipped the hard drive into his briefcase. "They're going to keep it in the CSO's personal safe, or at least that was the plan the last I heard."

Bruno laughed. "And nothing *ever* goes missing from executive safes."

"Or tech companies," Daniel said.

Bruno took his feet down and leaned forward. "Hey, nothing ever went missing from here." He shrugged and leaned back. "But no big deal." He pointed toward Daniel's briefcase. "That thing isn't my problem anymore."

"Thanks, man."

"By the way, before you give that hard drive to your boss, you may want to let her know that you guys have another security breach."

Daniel's stomach sank. "We do? What happened?"

"You hired Richard C. Johnson—or some guy claiming to be Richard C. Johnson anyway. I ran that background check you asked for, and the dude doesn't exist."

CHAPTER 50

The door opened and the lights came on, turning the insides of Anya's eyelids orange-red. She lay still, keeping her muscles as relaxed as possible. The sheet covered her body, so it should be virtually impossible to tell that her restraints were no longer fastened and her catheter and IV were out.

She knew her odds were best if she lay there until the most opportune moment—but it was hard. She felt an unreasonable urge to roll off the table immediately and bolt for the door.

Steps approached from behind. They were quicker and lighter than those of the man who came in earlier. Hopefully, it was a woman this time.

The steps went to the foot of the bed, where the catheter bag hung. Anya heard a faint sound of fabric shifting, and she guessed that her visitor was checking the bag. She opened her eyes and saw a strongly built woman in blue scrubs bending over at the end of the bed. She appeared to be about Anya's height, but probably outweighed her by at least thirty pounds, little of it fat. Still, Anya wasn't likely to get a better chance.

She tensed, waiting for the best moment. The woman started to stand. Now!

Anya grabbed the wrist restraints for leverage and kicked hard. Her heel hit the woman in the side of the head. She grunted in surprise and staggered, but didn't go down.

Anya was on the woman's back before she could recover, an arm around her neck. A gurgling cry struggled from her lips and she flailed ineffectually at Anya with meaty arms. But she still didn't go down.

Anya kicked at the woman's knees. The blows didn't have much force, but they were enough to throw off her balance. She fell heavily, with Anya still on her back, forcing her head down.

The woman's head hit the floor hard. She went limp and Anya rolled off of her. She came to her feet in a fighter's crouch, ready to strike again. But the woman didn't move.

An alarm squealed from the pulse oximeter, which was no longer attached to Anya's finger, of course. She yanked the plug out of the wall, silencing the machine. But she had to assume that it had also triggered an alarm somewhere outside the room. That meant more enemies on the way, ones who wouldn't be taken by surprise. She had to be gone by the time they got here.

Anya quickly examined the woman on the floor. She still hadn't moved, though she was breathing. She didn't have a gun or other weapon, but she did have a keycard on her waistband, which Anya grabbed. She was only wearing a hospital gown, so she yanked off the woman's scrubs and pulled them on. They were too big, as were the woman's scuffed white sneakers, but they'd have to do.

Time to go.

She pulled the door open and cautiously looked outside. An empty hallway. Linoleum tiled floor and concrete walls. Pipes on the ceiling, mingled with buzzing fluorescent lights. It looked like the basement of a large building, so the first thing she needed to do was find a stairwell that would take her to ground level.

She stepped out and turned left, walking quickly but not running. Her right side stung and she felt something trickling down her ribs. She reached under her shirt and touched her side. Her fingers came away smeared with blood.

One of the incisions her inquisitor mentioned must have torn open during the fight. How many were there? How deep? She tried to do a mental examination of her body as she walked. Little jolts of pain went through her torso with every step, but she couldn't be sure precisely where they came from. There seemed to be at least two in her abdomen, maybe more.

A shout behind her, then running footsteps. She glanced over her shoulder and saw two men racing toward her.

She ran.

Agony arced through her body. She ignored it, sprinting around a corner. Another empty subterranean hall stretched in front of her.

There! A glowing orange exit sign above a door at the end of the corridor. She ran toward it, heart pounding and breath gasping. Her pursuers' footsteps were closer. Much closer.

She put on a final burst of speed and pushed through the door. Dimly lit cement steps ascended in front of her. She went up two steps, then wheeled as the door opened again behind her. A man's head appeared in the opening door just as she threw all her weight against it. The door slammed into his head, then shut. A cry of pain came from outside the door, followed by cursing.

She turned and ran up the stairs. The door opened again as she reached a landing. She turned and looked up the next flight of stairs. A door was at the top, "FLOOR 1" stenciled on it in black. She willed herself up, forcing her body forward despite the pain and exhaustion.

Her shirt was wet from wounds in both her back and her side. It stuck to her, and she could smell the blood. Static fuzzed the edges of her vision and she knew she risked losing consciousness. But she kept moving. She had to make it through that door.

She reached the door and fumbled with the handle as her pursuers closed in. She could hear them behind her, almost feel them.

Hands grabbed her from behind. She tried to pull away, but she couldn't. They pinned her and a needle jabbed into her arm.

Dear God, please— she began, but darkness took her before she could finish the prayer.

CHAPTER 51

As soon as he got in his car, Daniel clipped his Bluetooth headset over his right ear and called Sandy.

She answered on the first ring. "Do you have the hard drive?"

"I do, but that's not the big news," he said.

"What is?"

"It looks like Rich is a corporate spy."

The line was silent for several seconds as she absorbed the news. "Why do you say that?"

"During our meeting with Dr. Gupta yesterday, Rich seemed a little . . . well, not like a paralegal or a junior lab tech, so I asked Bruno to check out his background. It turns out that there is no Richard C. Johnson living at the address he gave us. Also, the birth certificate he gave us for his I-9 was forged."

"Do you know who he really is or who he works for?" Sandy asked.

"Not yet, but Bruno is working on it." Daniel paused, half expecting her to tell him she'd have professionals take it from here. But she said nothing. "We think there's some connection at UC Berkeley. The transcript he gave us actually came from the Office of the Registrar at Berkeley—they really do have grades and other info for a Richard C. Johnson. But it's fake. Someone got into their system and created student records for him. Bruno is trying to figure out who did it and when."

"Okay, we need to have a chat with Rich ASAP. Where are you right now?"

"I'm on the Bay Bridge," he said, watching the Oakland shore inch closer as he drove. "Traffic is pretty heavy, but I should be back at the office in about an hour."

"I'll tell security not to let him leave. A guard will meet you at the door. I want you to go to Rich's desk as soon as you get in and escort him to my office."

"Will do."

Fifty-five minutes later, Daniel took a deep breath and walked through the sliding glass doors of the Biosolutions headquarters building. A burly armed man in a blue uniform walked up to him. Daniel recognized him as one of the regular security staff, but didn't know his name. Fortunately, the man had a nameplate.

"Okay, Cyril," Daniel said as the guard fell in stride with him. "We're going up to legal on the fourth floor. Then we'll escort an employee to the general counsel's office."

Cyril nodded. "Yes, sir, Mr. Rubinelli."

They got into the elevator and rode up in silence. Questions whirled through Daniel's mind. Who was Rich really working for? How many secrets had he already stolen? Or was it possible that this was all somehow a false alarm—that Rich had some innocent explanation that would make Daniel feel like an idiot once he and Sandy started grilling their paralegal?

The elevator doors opened. Daniel walked to the small warren of cubicles that contained Rich's desk. Cyril trailed after him.

Rich wasn't there. His computer was turned off.

Daniel turned to the occupant of the cubicle next to Rich's. "Janet, have you seen Rich today?"

She shook her head. "No. I haven't seen him since yesterday afternoon."

Daniel looked over Rich's desktop. It held nothing but office supplies and schedules for the Warriors and A's. No pictures or other personal effects. He pulled open the drawers. All empty.

"Cyril, could you check the keycard logs to see whether Richard C. Johnson ever carded in today?" Daniel asked.

"Yes, sir." Cyril pulled his walkie-talkie from his belt and had a brief conversation that Daniel couldn't make out. Then he turned back to Daniel. "Mr. Johnson carded out at three thirty-five yesterday afternoon and hasn't carded in since."

Chapter 52

Leigh took a bite of surprisingly good vegan pad thai. She, Phyllis, and Andrea sat in a semiprivate booth at Golden Era, an Asian-themed vegan restaurant in a dubious neighborhood on the edge of the Tenderloin. Andrea had chosen the restaurant because she was on a diet and had decided that eating vegan counted as dieting—even though she was eating a dish called "Spicy Mongolian Delight" and drinking her second mango smoothie.

Phyllis's office was nearby, so she took the opportunity to give Leigh an informal report on the search for Anya Rhodes.

The conversation started off casual, but hit a lull as they neared the end of their meals. Phyllis glanced around the restaurant, apparently making sure that no one was in easy earshot. "Okay. Ready to talk some business?"

"Sure," Leigh said.

"It's been a busy couple of days, so I'll just give you the highlights and save the details for my written report. Sound good?"

Leigh nodded.

"Where to start—" Phyllis frowned in thought for a moment. "World War II is as good a place as any. Anya Rhodes got a medal in 1995 for stuff she did during the war."

Andrea's pencil-perfect eyebrows went up. "Seriously? What did she do?"

"What didn't she do might be a better question," Phyllis replied. "She killed a dozen Nazis, mostly Gestapo agents. She watched Nazi bases and sent secret radio messages to the Red Army. She even blew up a railroad bridge."

"Sounds like quite a lady," Leigh said. "Why did they wait until 1995 to give her a medal?"

"Because she worked closely with an American agent," Phyllis said with a smile. "*Very* closely."

Andrea put a hand on her aunt's arm. "Let me guess—his last name was Rhodes."

"Very good," Phyllis said. "Yes, his name was Theodore Rhodes, and he was a lieutenant in the US Army. The Cold War started as soon as World War II ended, so the Russians suddenly got suspicious of anyone who was friendly with Americans. Plus, Anya is Ukrainian, not Russian, and the Russians were worried about Ukrainian independence guerrillas. They decided they didn't want a killer Ukrainian with an American boyfriend on the loose, so they sent her to a prison camp."

Andrea shook her head. "Nice."

"How did she wind up in California?" Leigh asked.

"Lieutenant Rhodes called in some favors from his Russian war buddies to help her escape," Phyllis said. "She made it to Finland, and he met her there and got her to Britain. They got married in London and then came back to the US. Sometime between 1947 and 1963, they moved to Oakland, and that's where they settled."

"Got it," Leigh said. "And Theodore Rhodes got a job in that old factory where we found Ratopia, right?"

Phyllis nodded. "He worked there for about thirty years, and he was chief chemist when he retired. I'll bet Rhodes knew that place pretty well growing up."

"His mom too, probably," Leigh said. "That's one reason it was so easy for her to ditch us that night."

"Well, that and we were all a little distracted," Phyllis responded, perhaps a touch defensively.

"True," Leigh said with a smile. "Sorry about that. I've learned my lesson about opening random doors in creepy abandoned factories."

The server came to clear empty plates. "I wonder what it's like to be Anya Rhodes," Leigh said. "To be twenty-five basically forever."

"I'd love to be twenty-five again," Andrea said with a chuckle. "I could be skinny without dieting. No more gray hair. No more falling asleep in front of the TV at nine o'clock on a Friday night. And Ken would have all his hair again and lose his gut. He'd look just like he did on our wedding day."

"But what if Ken was still forty-five and only you were twenty-five?" Leigh asked. "And what if he kept getting older and you didn't?"

Andrea's face grew serious. "That might not be so much fun."

Leigh nodded. "I think I'd feel like everyone else was leaving me behind. They'd all get old and die, and I'd still be exactly the same." She shook her head. "Anya must be very lonely."

Phyllis leaned forward and put her forearms on the table. "When I first started doing surveillance on her, I thought she might be depressed. But I'm not sure that's quite right. Now that I know what's really going on, I think it's more . . ." She paused for a moment, then went on. "I've gotten the same sense from people at a funeral. They're going through the motions, doing what they need to do. They're not smiling or talking, and you know they'd rather be someplace else. They've got something they need to do and that's why they're there. They aren't crying or acting out—or at least not the ones I'm thinking of. But there's just a . . . Well, you feel the sadness and loneliness and tiredness in everything they do. That's the vibe I got from Anya. It's like the whole world is a funeral for her, a funeral that never ends."

They were all silent for a moment. Then Andrea said, "Okay, but what if everyone was twenty-five forever? The whole world wouldn't be a funeral then."

"The population would explode, though," Leigh said. "Or we'd need to make having babies basically illegal."

Phyllis shook her head. "I'd hate to have to enforce that law. Can you imagine? Arresting women and hauling them in for forced abortions like they used to do in China."

"That's a good point," Andrea said.

Phyllis leaned back and crossed her arms. "Plus, being twenty-five again would feel . . . I don't know, like going backwards. I'm done with that part of my life and I like where I am now." She shrugged. "Maybe I'd feel different if I looked like Anya."

The server arrived with the bill. Leigh took a quick look at it and handed the server her credit card.

Once the server was gone, Leigh turned to Phyllis. "So where is Anya now? And what's she doing?"

Phyllis took a deep breath and blew it out. "Those are really good questions. Bruno and I see basically two possibilities: either she's hiding somewhere around here and managing to stay away from security cameras or she left town."

"Which possibility is most likely?" Leigh asked.

"That she's still around," Phyllis said without hesitating. "She wanted that hard drive at Whacktastic and she didn't get it. I don't think she'll leave until she does. But we're covering our bases—I'm pulling some strings to see if we can get archive video from security cameras in the airports, train stations, and so on. We'll start with the last day we saw her and move forward, running Bruno's facial-recognition computer program on the video from each day. One way or another, we'll find her eventually."

CHAPTER 53

Daniel's cell phone buzzed. He pulled it out and saw Bruno's number. "Hey, B. What's up?"

"I'm passing through Dublin and I've got a couple of things to talk to you about."

"No problem. Come on over. I'll reserve a conference room."

"Actually, I'm hungry. I'll pick you up out front in fifteen minutes."

Daniel glanced at his watch. It was only quarter after ten. "I've got a meeting at ten thirty. How about we meet for lunch instead?"

Bruno heaved a sigh. "Dude, I'm almost there and we need to talk. It's more important than your meeting. Trust me."

What was going on? "Uh, okay. See you in a few."

Bruno pulled up ten minutes later, driving his black BMW M6. "Give me your cell phone," he said as soon as Daniel opened the door.

Daniel handed it over without bothering to ask why. Bruno dropped it into a thick-walled metal box, which he deposited in the backseat.

"Bugged?"

"Better safe than sorry," Bruno said as he sped out of the Biosolutions parking lot.

"Safe from what?" Daniel asked. "I canceled an important meeting with a board member on ten minutes' notice because of a 'family emergency.' This better be good."

"'Good' isn't the right word, Danny," Bruno said, shooting him a glare. Bruno took a deep breath and drove in frosty silence for half a minute. "I'm mostly mad at myself for not catching it sooner."

"Catching what?"

"Why do you think I called you on your cell phone instead of your office line?" Bruno asked in exasperation. "Why didn't I want to meet in your conference room? Why is your phone now in that box?"

A chill ran through Daniel. "It's bugged? My office and the conference room too?"

Bruno nodded. "Wouldn't surprise me one bit. Your e-mail sure is. Someone set up a bot to run searches over the company's system and send copies of e-mails to a hidden mailbox. It was a thing of beauty, but when you guys upgraded your system last month, no one updated the bot. That's how I found it. It became obvious—if anyone was looking. Which no one was. Morons. I can't believe I didn't check earlier."

"How did you get into our—"

"Not important," Bruno said flatly. "The point is that someone has thoroughly hacked your e-mail system. Oh, and guess what search terms the bot was looking for?"

Daniel thought for a moment. "Rhodes? Enoch?"

"Very good. Also Rich within five words of Johnson and Fred within five words of Stein. Every e-mail that had one of those got copied to that hidden mailbox."

"And Rich had access to it, right?"

Bruno nodded as he drove. They were on the highway now, and Bruno seemed to be relaxing a little as the traffic thinned and the landscape turned from strip malls to green hills dotted with wind turbines. "So your e-mail asking me to run a backgrounder on him got bcc'd to him."

"Which explains why he cleared out his desk and left the office about half an hour after that," Daniel said. He thought for a moment. "I'll bet someone else set up the bot, someone outside the company. Rich would have known we were getting system upgrades—there were a

232

couple of blast e-mails about it—but if his hacker wasn't at Biosolutions, then that person wouldn't necessarily know about the upgrades." He glanced over at Bruno, who was nodding as his cousin spoke. "Might that person happen to be named Fred Stein?"

"He might indeed," Bruno said. "The person who created Rich Johnson's records at Berkeley used a dummy account, but that dummy account was set up by a Professor Frederick F. Stein. The hacking at Berkeley isn't as good as the job at Biosolutions, but it wasn't bad. I'm still not done tracing everything he did."

"A professor, huh?" Daniel chewed on that for a moment. "What does he teach? Computer science?"

"Did," corrected Bruno. "Stein taught genetics, biochemistry, and microbiology for over thirty years. He probably taught Rhodes when he was at Berkeley."

The puzzle pieces started to come together. "So he might have known about Dr. Rhodes's work after he graduated. And there's a good chance he knew Rhodes personally."

"Oh, they knew each other," Bruno said. "Even wrote some papers together. And it gets better—the papers were on possible techniques for telomere stabilization."

A possibility occurred to Daniel. "Where is Stein now?"

"No one knows," Bruno said. "He retired suddenly right after he hacked the Berkeley registrar—and I'm guessing your e-mail system. Sounds like he'd been acting erratic before he vanished—missing lectures, acting weird in public, disappearing for days at a time without telling anyone where he was going. Then he disappeared and never came back. Most people thought he died. Wandered out into the desert or jumped off a bridge or something."

"But he's not dead, is he?"

Bruno shook his head. "Nope. Or if he is, someone managed to get into his bank account. And he's been making regular transfers to Rich Johnson's account."

Which was consistent with the picture that had been forming in Daniel's brain. "Did any of the money go to a company called Stillwater?"

"The hired guns from the rat factory? Could be. Lots of cash withdrawals, which would make payments hard to trace."

Daniel nodded. "That would be consistent with Stillwater's business model."

"They're still watching me, by the way," Bruno said casually. "Or trying to anyway. Bet they're doing the same with you and Leigh."

Daniel's stomach muscles tightened. "Not a surprise." He took a deep breath and blew it out. "Okay, so what's their plan? I'm guessing Stein got wind of Rhodes's work on Enoch and wants to steal it. So he set Rich up as a mole at Biosolutions. When Rhodes died and the lab burned to the ground, Rich managed to work his way onto our team. And the minute our CSO began talking about restarting Rhodes's research, Rich tried to worm his way into that too." He paused and shook his head in reluctant admiration. "Impressive. Evil, but impressive."

"Sounds right to me," Bruno said. "One question—where does Anya fit into all this? She working with Stein and Rich, or is she doing her own thing?"

Daniel pondered that for a full minute. "Don't know," he said at last. "It doesn't make a ton of sense either way. If she's working with Rich, why didn't she know you'd set a trap for her at Whacktastic? But if she's not working with Rich, what's she doing? Why destroy everything her son did? He should get a Nobel Prize for this, so why is she running around burning his labs and smashing his hard drives?"

Bruno nodded in agreement. "Makes no sense. Guess we'll need to find one of them and ask. Or, excuse me, have your boss's 'professionals' ask." He glanced at Daniel with a sardonic grin.

Daniel grinned back. "You're never going to let that go, are you?"

"Nope."

CHAPTER 54

Dr. Frederick Stein peered through the eyepiece of the microscope. He saw human skin cells. They looked perfectly normal—well formed, well organized, regular nuclei. But they had abnormally high levels of telomerase, which typically indicated cancer. And although he couldn't see their telomeres, he knew they weren't shrinking with each cell division. How were they doing it?

A complete and reliable answer to that question would require a full, high-quality sequencing of the entire genome of those cells. Sequencing technology had come a long way since Dr. Stein first used it in the 1980s. Back then, it was all done manually, but now he could send a DNA sample off to a commercial lab that could do an automated sequencing in short order. However, an automated commercial sequencing would take a lot of shortcuts—and might miss crucial details as a result. So Dr. Stein had ordered the raw sequencing data and would do the actual sequencing himself. If he had time.

He sat back and rubbed his eyes. Time to stretch his legs a little. It would help him think. He got up and wandered out of the informal lab he had created.

His footsteps echoed from the cracked tile floor. Fluorescent lights buzzed overhead. Boxes of supplies—some new, some decades old—cluttered his path. He picked his way to the door, which squealed on unoiled hinges as he opened it.

He walked along the long, dimly lit corridor. The atmosphere was stale and sour—and it wasn't just the musty air. The building felt dead and sad. He remembered it as a place buzzing with activity and conversation. Now it was this semi-abandoned warehouse.

Rooms aboveground had better light and ventilation, but he couldn't risk going up there, where he could be seen. Going outside just to take a walk was out of the question, of course.

Had Elijah felt the same way in his secret lab? It had been underground too, in the middle of an abandoned place he knew from happier days. Of course, he hadn't been stuck there day in and day out. He had his state-of-the-art lab at Biosolutions, stuffed with all a geneticist could want—a Cray supercomputer, nanopore sequencing technology, and so on. Dr. Stein felt a twinge of jealousy, imagining what he could accomplish with those tools.

So why hadn't Elijah done all of his work there? He could be difficult and paranoid—Dr. Stein knew that all too well from working with him. Elijah always wanted to be in control of his research and was intensely sensitive about getting all the credit he felt he was entitled to. That was why his name went first on every paper the two of them published together, he was the listed inventor on every patent that came out of his lab, and he had absolute hiring control over everyone who worked in that lab. So why had he felt the need for a second lab?

Enough leg stretching. This wasn't accomplishing anything. He knew more or less what he needed to do. It was time to get started.

He turned around and walked back to the room where he had started. He made the final preparations on the adenovirus solution and filled a dozen syringes. Then he took those into an adjoining room filled with squeaking cages and he began injecting rats.

CHAPTER 55

Daniel ended a call with his sister, Maria, and started to pace around his apartment. Living room, kitchen, bedroom, second bedroom, living room again. If it hadn't been raining, he would have gone for a run to clear his mind.

But wandering around his apartment wasn't going to accomplish anything. He knew what he needed to do, and he was just delaying now. He braced himself, walked back into the kitchen, picked up his phone, and called his father.

"Danny, it's good to hear from you," Dad said a moment later. Daniel thought his father's voice sounded rougher and weaker than usual, but maybe that was his imagination.

"Hey, Dad. Sorry I haven't called in a while. Things have been crazy busy at work. How are you doing?"

"Oh, I can't complain. Tell me about work. Are you doing anything interesting?"

"Actually, yes," Daniel said, relieved to have the conversation on a painless topic for the moment. Plus, he could do a little overdue intra-family diplomacy. "I'm still working on that big insurance case. And you won't believe who's helping me—Bruno! We hired him to help us get access to a hard drive, but he has been pitching in on all sorts of stuff."

"That's great," Dad said without enthusiasm.

"We're lucky to have him on our side. He's one of the best hackers in the world, and he's semiretired. He usually only works on national security stuff, but he made an exception for us because I'm a Rubinelli." That wasn't precisely what happened, but Dad appreciated family solidarity.

The line was silent for a moment. "Are you sure you want him hacking for you, Danny? Isn't that illegal?"

"I haven't asked him to do anything illegal, Dad. Besides, he's a white hat hacker and he does most of his hacking for the FBI and the NSA. He can't talk about it much, of course, but I'm pretty sure he does stuff like break into terrorists' computers and stuff like that." Technically, that probably made Bruno a "gray hat" hacker to the Silicon Valley cognoscenti, but Daniel didn't want to muddy the moral issue.

"Yeah, which is why the feds don't bust him when he does other stuff," Dad rejoined. "White hat, black hat—it doesn't matter. He's breaking the law. We used to have guys like that—informants who we wouldn't bust because they were helping us take down guys who were even worse than them. They're necessary. I understand that. I just don't like having one in the family."

Daniel had heard this argument from Dad before, and he was ready for it. "The guys you're talking about did bad stuff, Dad. Bruno doesn't. He's not selling crack to kids or fixing horse races or any of the other stuff your informants used to do. He just breaks into computer systems that are supposed to be secure. He doesn't steal anything or do any damage—that's what black hats do. In fact, Bruno often tells the people who run the system what he did so they can fix the holes in their security."

"So he's like a burglar who doesn't steal anything, right? He just breaks into your house and wakes you up at three in the morning to tell you that you need to lock your downstairs windows." Dad sighed. "Maybe you're okay with that, but I'm not."

"But if the streets are crawling with people who will come in through your downstairs windows and rob you blind, the burglar is doing you a favor, don't you think?"

"Huh." Dad mulled that over for a few seconds. "Maybe you've got a point."

Daniel felt the warm glow of victory. That was the closest Dad would ever come to admitting that he'd been wrong. With luck—and a few more well-placed Brunomercials—the two of them might actually be on speaking terms the next time they saw each other.

Time to move on to the real reason for the call. "So, what's up with you, Dad? Any news on your end?"

"Nothing in particular," Dad said. "I've got a cold, but I'm on the mend."

"Um, Maria described it as more than a cold."

Silence. "You know how your sister blows little stuff out of proportion."

"Dad, pneumonia and congestive heart failure are not little stuff."

"Walking pneumonia, and the doctor didn't say I had congestive heart failure. He said I had *signs* of congestive heart failure. Not the same thing at all. Besides, he gave me prescriptions for three drugs, and I'm taking them all. And I really am on the mend. I'm a little tired, but other than that I feel fine."

"But you're not fine, Dad. You should come out here for a while. I've got an extra bedroom and I'd love to have you. Besides, it'll be a lot easier on your lungs."

"That's nice of you, Danny. It's great to come visit you and all, but I'm a Chicagoan. I was born here, and I'm gonna die here."

Which was precisely what Daniel was afraid of.

CHAPTER 56

The phone on Leigh's desk rang, and Daniel's number appeared on the caller ID screen. Good. She hadn't spoken to him in the three days since they had found Anya Rhodes's photo album. She was curious to hear his thoughts, particularly since he must know a lot more about what happened to Anya than Leigh did. Plus, she was kind of looking forward to talking to him again.

As she reached for the phone, she realized that she was smiling. She paused, hand in midair. He was opposing counsel, she reminded herself. She needed to be professional and—if necessary—adversarial. She'd never had a soft spot for the main lawyer on the other side of a case and it unnerved her a little. Soft spots were vulnerabilities, and she couldn't afford those.

She put on her game face and picked up the handset. "Hi, Daniel. What's up?"

"Hey, Leigh. I was just calling to follow up on a loose end from that settlement meeting we had at your office. Weren't you supposed to give us a counteroffer?"

He was calling to talk settlement? Seriously? "Um, yeah. I guess we were. I'll have one for you by next week. Does that work for you?"

"Sure, that's fine," he said. "I'll look forward to hearing from you by next Friday."

"Okay. Is there anything else on your mind?"

He chuckled. "Well, now that you mention it, yes. I was in the middle of planning a trip back to Chicago. I always take my dad to opening day at Wrigley Field, but I waited too long to buy tickets this year. Decent seats at the ballpark are going to cost more than my seat on the plane."

She was pretty sure he knew what she really wanted to talk about and was being genially evasive, but she decided to let it go for the moment. "I thought I recognized a Chicago accent."

"Likewise. There's lots of us out here, in case you hadn't noticed."

"I notice every time the Cubs play the Giants," she replied. "I actually grew up in Wrigleyville."

"No kidding. I love that neighborhood."

"I know some people who may be able to help with opening-day seats. Let me make a couple of calls."

"That'd be great! I'll owe you one. Want me to bring you back a box of Fannie May Mint Meltaways or something?"

Her mouth watered. "I love those, but let's not turn this call into a Windy City nostalgiafest."

"Why not? How many people in this state can really appreciate Mint Meltaways or a Vienna Red Hot with all the fixings?"

She discovered that she was smiling again. "True, but let's talk about something else right now. Anya Rhodes, for example."

The line was silent for a few seconds. "Um, I'm not sure what happened to her after she disappeared that night. Which reminds me: Has Phyllis found out any more about those Stillwater guys whose tires she slashed?"

More evasion. Did he not want to talk about Anya for some reason? Or was something else going on? "No, but I haven't asked her to try. They're a combo PI and security company, so I'm guessing she won't be able to find out much, and they might figure out that we're investigating them, which probably wouldn't be healthy. I don't think we want to poke that particular hornet's nest."

"Good point," Daniel said. "I just don't like the idea of those guys being out there—probably still watching us and ticked off about that night—and we have no idea who they're working for."

"Maybe Bruno could take a look at them," Leigh suggested. "He probably knows some angles Phyllis doesn't, and they might be less likely to catch him."

"Uh, maybe. Let me think about it."

Did his evasiveness have something to do with Bruno? Tough to tell over the phone when she couldn't watch his body language. Maybe if she could talk to him in person . . .

"Thanks," she said. "About that settlement offer, it might be best to have another face-to-face meeting. Negotiations always seem to go better if you're in the same room with the other side—at least if you get along with each other. So how about we grab lunch and talk?"

"Sure, that sounds great. My schedule is pretty full, but I'm open next Thursday. I'll be in the Financial District in the morning, and we can get together after that. How about the Waterbar at, say, eleven thirty?"

"Deal. See you then."

CHAPTER 57

Daniel was in the middle of his morning workout when his cell phone rang. He put his PowerBlocks down gently—his downstairs neighbor liked to sleep in—and picked up the phone. Yep, it was Bruno. At least this time his cousin waited until after dawn to call.

"Good morning, B," Daniel said. "What's up?"

"I found Rich."

"Congrats! Where is he?"

"Lots of places, but mostly around the Bay Area. Looks like he's staying at different hotels every night, and paying cash each time. He wears a hoodie all the time, but he couldn't avoid showing his face to a camera a couple of times."

Daniel wiped his face with a towel. "Huh. Any idea what he's up to?"

"Not really. He disappears into an older part of Berkeley most days. Even stays overnight sometimes. No security cameras in that area—or at least none I can hack—so I don't know where he's going. He bought a disposable cell phone, and I think I've tracked down the number for it. I also spotted him coming out of a medical supply store. Maybe he's setting up another lab or something."

"Wouldn't surprise me." Daniel thought for a moment. "How about Professor Stein—any sign of him?"

"Nope. He must be lying low, like Anya."

"So what's in that part of Berkeley?"

"Kind of a mishmash of stuff: old houses, a couple of small office buildings, some apartments. A lot of it seems to be connected to the university somehow, though I haven't looked into it."

"Stein worked at UC Berkeley," Daniel mused. "I wonder whether there's a connection. I remember there being some news stories a few years back about all of the university's real estate. They've been there for a long time, and they own all sorts of buildings in town. I wouldn't be surprised if they've sort of lost track of some of it."

"What do you mean?" Bruno asked.

"Say they bought a building in 1950, but they stopped using it in 2000. Now they're not doing anything with it, but they're holding onto it as an investment because prices keep going up."

"Stein might know about it because he worked at the university," Bruno said. "He could set up shop there, at least for a while."

Daniel nodded. "Exactly."

"And he's tech-savvy enough to stay away from networked security cameras wherever possible, so an older building in an older neighborhood would be ideal."

"So what about Rich? Why is he letting himself be spotted?"

"Good question—maybe he doesn't have a choice."

"Hmmm." Daniel kicked absently at the base of his weight bench. "Maybe it's just him and Stein. If so, one of them probably has to go out sometimes. Might as well be Rich."

"That's what I was thinking," Bruno replied. "Probably more of a risk that someone would recognize Stein around Berkeley, so Rich is the natural choice."

"Sounds like we need someone to check it out in person," Daniel said. "I'll tell Sandy and she can have one of her 'professionals' go take a look."

"I'd, ah, rather you didn't, Danny."

"Why not?"

"I've already got someone working on it."

"Who? He'd recognize Phyllis, so you can't use her, of course."

"Of course," Bruno echoed. "I hired someone she recommended."

An uncomfortable thought occurred to Daniel. "Um, I'm not sure that's covered by our contract with you. You, uh, may not get reimbursed."

Bruno laughed. "Don't worry about it, dude. This is fun. I'd rather lose a few thousand than turn this over to someone else."

Daniel relaxed. "Thanks, B."

"No problem. It'll be worth it to be there when we finally get to the bottom of this thing."

CHAPTER 58

Leigh's e-mail chimed. She pulled up her in-box and opened the new message, which was from Aunt Phyllis and was titled "Anya Rhodes."

The body of the e-mail said, "From a gas station near I-80:" followed by a black-and-white picture of a gas pump. Part of a dark SUV showed at the edge of the image. A man in a hoodie appeared to be changing a tire. Anya's face was visible in the rear passenger-side window. She appeared to be asleep, slumped against the door with her head resting against the glass. A time stamp in the lower right corner showed that the picture was taken a little over three weeks ago at 6:43 a.m. That was about three hours after she vanished into the night at Ratopia. But where she was now?

Her phone rang. Phyllis. She picked it up. "I just got your e-mail. Nice work."

"Thanks," Phyllis said. "It's been a slog. We checked with all the airports, Amtrak stations, and bus terminals, but didn't find anything. I happened to know a guy who owned half a dozen gas stations, and we got lucky." She paused. "Did you notice anything unusual about her?"

Leigh took a closer look at the picture. There *was* something slightly off about Anya. The way she was leaning against the window looked awkward and uncomfortable. There was something around her eye too—a bruise?

An icy ripple ran down Leigh's spine. "Is she asleep or unconscious?"

"I was wondering the same thing," Phyllis said. "I was a cop long enough that it's easy for me to see crime scenes everywhere, so I wanted a second opinion. Which you just gave."

"What should we do? Call the police?"

"I thought about that," Phyllis said. "All we have is a picture of a woman in a car. I'm guessing that most cops would be a little disturbed by it, but there's no hard evidence that she's been kidnapped—no missing person report, no video of her being abducted, nothing. So nothing will happen—except that we might get asked some questions about why we've been collecting pictures from security cameras."

"Yeah, I see what you mean."

"But this does give us a couple of new leads. The first is that guy in the picture. There's another picture from the gas station that gives a decent look at his face. Bruno is working on enhancing that."

"Great—what's the second lead?"

"Kidnap victims don't tend to survive for very long, so I have a new place to look for Anya: morgues."

CHAPTER 59

Daniel turned off his cell phone and swiveled to stare out his window. He had just finished talking to Bruno, who insisted on calling his cell phone even though the Biosolutions phones were checked yesterday and declared clean.

For the first time, Bruno had laid out what he and Phyllis were doing—or, more accurately, had done. It was a lot more than Daniel had realized. He had known in a general sense that his cousin was trying to find Anya at the same time he was looking for Rich, but that was all. So when Bruno called to say that he had found them both and was handing them to Biosolutions as a "gift-wrapped present with a bow on top," Daniel was more than a little surprised.

And now he needed to go tell Sandy.

He wished he could take some time to think through exactly what he would say, but this news wouldn't wait. He printed the pictures Bruno had sent him, took a deep breath, and walked over to her office.

She noticed him in the doorway before he could knock, and she smiled. "Come in."

He shut the door behind him. "What's on your mind?" she asked.

"Let me just start by saying that I know you have professionals looking for Anya Rhodes," he said as he lowered himself into one of her guest chairs. "And I passed that message along to Bruno. I also told him that we should stay out of the way and let your professionals handle it.

We're not the Hardy Boys, as you rightly pointed out. But Bruno is—" He lifted his palms up in helplessness. "Well, he can be stubborn."

"What did he do?" she asked, her voice and face neutral. At least she seemed to be reserving judgment. For the moment.

"I just got a call from him. This is literally the first time I—"

"What did he do?" she repeated, a little heat in her voice this time.

"He found her—or at least it looks that way," Daniel said. "Here's a picture of her taken a few hours after the fire at Dr. Rhodes's secret lab." He handed her the picture of Anya in the SUV at the gas station. "She hasn't been seen since, as far as they can tell—but that SUV has."

He handed her a second picture, which showed the SUV driving out of the gas station. "This is the same car, but you can see the license plate," he explained.

He gave her another picture, this one showing an SUV driving down a narrow, tree-lined street. "This was taken two days ago in Berkeley. The license plates match. They checked the plates and found out that the SUV belongs to a company called Stillwater Security."

"You keep saying *they*," Sandy noted. "I thought Bruno was the only one doing this."

"Sorry—he's been working with Phyllis Higgins. She's a retired police detective who we met through the American Guaranty case."

Sandy's mouth tightened in a slight frown. "I see. Go on."

"Okay," he said, giving her a fourth picture, this one showing a nondescript cinder-block building. "This is two blocks down the street from where the picture of the SUV was taken. It used to be an off-site lab for the plant biology program at UC Berkeley. They haven't used it in years, but they still own the building. It should be abandoned, but it's not."

Another picture, this one showing Rich wearing a black hoodie and emerging from a side door of the old lab. "Our old friend Rich Johnson is doing something there. Bruno and Phyllis don't know what it is, but Rich has been buying medical supplies at different stores around the Bay Area, and he brings them back to that building. They think Dr. Frederick Stein—the guy who created Rich's fake identity and hacked into our e-mail system—is inside. And Anya Rhodes might be too. The Stillwater guys caught her after she set that second fire, and they might have brought her there. She would . . . Well, it's terrible to think about, but if Dr. Stein is trying to re-create Dr. Rhodes's research, he'd probably want to run tests on Anya. What her son did to her must have left clues in her DNA."

Sandy nodded slowly, looking down at the pictures. "This is all the evidence you have?"

Daniel shrugged. "It's circumstantial, but it makes sense. The first picture proves that Stillwater had Anya in an SUV. It might be a coincidence that the same SUV is in the neighborhood where that lab is. And it might also be a coincidence that Rich is bringing medical supplies to the lab. But I doubt it. More likely, Rich and Stein have Anya in there and Stillwater is patrolling the neighborhood."

"Mm-hmm," Sandy murmured, still examining the pictures. "Could be."

"Bruno is still working up the Stillwater angle. He's hacking into their system as we speak. But it might take some time and he thought that Anya was probably in danger, so he wanted to bring in the people you're working with—and maybe the police—now."

She looked up. "Good. I'm glad to hear it. What do you say we give him a call? I've got some questions for him."

The prospect of Sandy talking directly with Bruno unnerved Daniel, but he couldn't immediately think of an excuse to keep it from happening. "Uh, sure," he said.

She moved her phone to the middle of the desk. Daniel pushed the speaker button and dialed, hoping his cousin wouldn't pick up. To his relief, the call went to Bruno's voice mail. Sandy leaned forward. "Bruno, it's Sandy Hampton. Please call me when you get this message."

She ended the call and Daniel stood, eager to get back to his office and call his cousin's cell before Sandy talked to him. But before he could move, Sandy's cell phone rang.

She looked at it and her eyebrows went up. "It's Bruno." She pushed the speaker icon, answered the call, and placed the phone on the desk between her and Daniel. "Bruno, thanks for calling me back so quickly. I have Daniel here with me."

"Saw that you called," he said. "Thought I might be hearing from you. What's up?"

"Daniel just briefed me on your hunt for Anya Rhodes. I'm not going to ask you to stop because that obviously doesn't work."

Bruno chuckled dryly. "But you are going to ask me something. What is it?"

Little lines of irritation formed around her mouth. Daniel's stomach churned. "I'm actually going to ask you two things. First, please keep me in the loop. I'd like to avoid your efforts getting in the way of ours. For example, if we both have people doing street surveillance at the same time, that increases the risk that we'll be spotted."

"Makes sense," Bruno said. "What do you have planned?"

"I'm sorry, but I'm not in a position to reveal that."

The line was silent for a moment. "Okay. I guess it doesn't matter. All I'm doing now is working on some electronic stuff."

"Daniel mentioned that—you're working on Stillwater's computer system. How long do you think it will take before you're done?"

"Not sure. Maybe a day, maybe a month."

She picked up the pictures Daniel had given her and shuffled through them again. "You have an interesting theory, but the evidence isn't that strong. I'd like to have more before we bring this to the authorities."

"Are you serious? She could be dead by the time I'm done."

Daniel winced, but Sandy stayed calm. "I understand your concern, Bruno," she said in a placating voice. "Trust me, I want to find her at least as much as you do—probably more. But I'd like to know more before we go to the police. Which brings me to my second request: Is there a time when one of our investigators could meet with you? If you're coming over to our office to work on Dr. Rhodes's hard drive soon, that would be perfect."

"Ah, no. I'd like to finish the Stillwater thing before I go back to work on the hard drive. But I should be around here more or less all week."

"Terrific. Someone will give you a call as soon as we can coordinate schedules on our end."

She ended the call and looked at Daniel. Her face was unreadable for a moment, but then she smiled. "I know you're doing the best you can, stuck between Bruno and me."

He relaxed and smiled back. "I'll be happy when it's all over."

"It mostly is, at least as far as you and I are concerned. Bruno will sit down with our team, and they'll take it from there. Then it should be just a matter of tying off some loose ends and giving this to the Berkeley police. That shouldn't take long once they talk to Bruno. But in any event, it's off your plate now, so don't worry about it."

He chuckled. "Easier said than done."

CHAPTER 60

Dr. Stein was running out of time, and he knew it. He was fairly certain someone was watching the lab.

He did everything he could to accelerate his research. He ran multiple staggered trials using different viral vectors and different formulations of the compounds he knew Elijah had been using. And he didn't just run animal tests. Though it made him intensely uncomfortable, he needed a daily supply of human tissue samples.

He worked through the night. He slept on the lab floor, lying on flattened cardboard boxes and using a seat cushion ripped from an old chair for a pillow. His muscles were perpetually sore and his eyes were rimmed with red.

And still it wasn't enough. He looked through the microscope eyepiece, comparing a slide of rat cells with human cells. Both tissue samples were skin cells and both had high levels of telomerase. But that was where the similarities ended. The human cells were otherwise completely normal and healthy; the rat cells were clearly cancerous—jammed together haphazardly, huge nuclei, irregular shapes.

Obviously, he was doing something wrong—probably multiple things—but what? There were any number of possibilities. Elijah had over a decade of trial and error to draw on. Dr. Stein had had only a few weeks.

And he was unlikely to get much more. Someday soon, whoever had hired those spies—and he had a good idea who that was—would burst in and raid the lab. Dr. Stein had a contingency plan for when that happened, but it would require destroying everything he had done so far and might mean a permanent end to his efforts to re-create Enoch.

Frustration boiled in him. Locked in those cells was the secret to curing not just cancer, but death itself. He could finish Elijah's work if he had more time. He knew it. If only he had Elijah's research notes, his years of results, the protocols he had used. And he had come so close to getting them. So very close. They had been right there in Elijah's laptop—before the Rubinellis snatched it away.

He needed Elijah's hard drive. Needed it badly and needed it now.

CHAPTER 61

Leigh had never been to the Waterbar before, and she was dreading it a little. The place had all the hallmarks of a San Francisco tourist trap: waterfront location, view of a bridge, laughably high prices, and a seafood-heavy menu. At least they didn't serve chowder in a sourdough bowl.

But her fears were misplaced. The ambience was great, the view of the Bay Bridge was spectacular, and the weather was warm and sunny enough for them to sit outside. Plus, the food was so good that it almost justified what they charged for it—though she still couldn't quite wrap her head around the fact that a side order of fries cost nine dollars.

"Good call on the restaurant," she said to Daniel after the first bite of their Dungeness crab appetizers. "There are some benefits to living on the coast. I do miss Chicago food, though."

He smiled and leaned back. The bright sun brought out little flecks of gold in his eyes that she hadn't noticed before. "What do you miss most? For me, it's real deep dish pizza."

She nodded. "So what's the best Chicago pizza place—Uno, Giordano's, or Malnati's?"

His smile faded somewhat and a nostalgic expression came over his face. "Mama's."

Leigh cocked her head. "I don't think I've been there. Is it on the West Side around Little Italy?"

He chuckled softly. "It used to be. My mama made the best deep dish pizza I ever had. She was from Italy, and she did it differently—less cheese, fresher ingredients, a different kind of sausage—I think. She didn't use a written recipe, so I'm not really sure."

"I'll bet it was delicious."

"Oh, yeah. She was quite a cook." He patted his flat stomach. "I used to put on ten pounds every time I'd go home for more than a day."

"Sounds like me and my secretary," Leigh said. "It must have been tough to move this far away from your mom's kitchen."

"It was, but Brown & Enersen made me an offer I couldn't refuse. And like you said, there are benefits to living out here," he said, gesturing expansively at the sparkling sapphire bay spread out in front of them. "What brought you out here?"

"Stanford."

"College or law school?" he asked.

"College—though law school was a foregone conclusion, so I was looking for a college with a good law school attached. My dad was a big firm litigator in Chicago, and everyone just assumed I'd be one too. But I rebelled," she said with a smile. "I'm a boutique firm litigator in San Francisco."

He laughed. "Your parents must be so disappointed."

"They managed to forgive me eventually, though my dad still tries to recruit me every now and then. He claims practice at a big firm is a cut above anything else. Speaking of which, why did you leave Brown & Enersen? I'd always heard it's a good place to work."

He nodded. "It is—or at least it was when I left. I did labor and employment litigation when I was there, and I enjoyed it. But after Mama died . . ." He shrugged and looked up in the direction of the Bay Bridge for a moment. "Well, my work seemed kind of inconsequential. I went looking for something a little more meaningful. Cancer killed her, so I decided to help kill it. I started looking for a company that was as dedicated to beating cancer as I was and that had an opening for a lawyer. I'm not in the lab designing new drugs, of course, but I'm doing what I can. How about you? How did you wind up at Diamond & Wang?"

"Nothing quite that noble," she said, picking at a nearly empty crab shell. "They're an excellent firm, and I got experience faster than I would have at a big firm." That sounded kind of weak after what he said, so she decided to shift the conversation to business. "Like this case, for example. I never would have gotten to handle it on my own at a big firm."

"Speaking of which, do you have a settlement offer for us?"

She nodded. "My client remains convinced that they have strong defenses, but they're willing to go up to twenty million to resolve this case."

He kept his expression neutral, but she thought he looked pleased. Which he should be—twenty million was a generous opening offer. Jack Diamond had suggested ten, but Leigh had decided to go higher to keep the negotiations friendly. That was in American Guaranty's best interests at this point because there was no way they would pay less than $50 million if the case went to trial, which Daniel probably saw as clearly as she did. Trying to chisel Biosolutions would simply poison the atmosphere during settlement negotiations. And friendly negotiations happened to advance Leigh's personal interests as well.

"All right. I'll take that back to Biosolutions," Daniel said. "Twenty million won't settle this case, but I think it's a good-faith offer and I'll recommend that we make a counteroffer."

"When do you think you'll have a response?"

"I'll need to talk to the board, so it will probably take a couple of weeks."

Good. Phyllis expected that her work with Bruno should wrap up in the next week, so there wasn't much risk that the case would settle before Leigh got the answers she wanted. And if she did need to slow negotiations down, she was confident that she'd be able to find an excuse.

Their main courses arrived then, and they ate in silence for a few minutes. Leigh silently congratulated herself on ordering the yellowtail tacos, which were awesome.

"So, how's Bruno?" she asked, watching his reaction carefully.

To her surprise, he wasn't at all reticent. "He's doing great. You know what he and Phyllis have been up to, right?"

"Yes," she said. "According to Phyllis, they're—"

Daniel's cell phone interrupted her.

"Sorry," he said as he fished it out of his pants pocket. He grinned. "Speak of the devil," he said, holding the phone up to show Bruno's name.

"Oh—go ahead and take it," Leigh said.

He smiled his thanks and held the phone to his ear. "Hey, B. We were just talking—"

His smile vanished and his eyes widened as he listened, staring into space.

"Okay," he said after half a minute. He swiveled his head from side to side, his eyes darting around the restaurant and along the bike path between their table and the water. "I don't see anyone."

He listened in silence again, then nodded and stood up. "Okay, we're moving," he said, glancing at Leigh and motioning for her to get up.

She pushed back her chair and got to her feet, giving him a questioning look—but he was already walking toward the tall brick wall at the edge of the restaurant patio. He dropped the phone in his pocket and gestured for her to join him.

She reached his side. "What's going on?"

"Stillwater just tried to kill Bruno. They may be after us too. Bruno's on his way."

CHAPTER 62

Daniel pressed against the brick wall, ignoring the curious looks of the staff and other diners. His attention was focused on the Embarcadero, which was around the corner from where he and Leigh hid. He was looking for two cars: Bruno's black BMW and the gray Toyota Camry Bruno warned him the Stillwater killers were now driving.

"Can I help you, sir?" a voice said behind him.

Daniel whirled and saw a man wearing a tie and a look of polite concern. A nameplate over his left shirt pocket read "Antonio Lopez, Assistant Manager."

"No," Daniel said, turning back to the street. "We're just, uh, waiting for someone."

"Would you like your meals boxed?"

"No," Daniel said. He pulled out his wallet and shoved bills at the man. "Here, this will cover our meals. Keep the change."

The assistant manager retreated reluctantly and Daniel turned his full attention back to the street. His brain buzzed with adrenaline and the whole scene felt unreal. Five minutes ago, he was having a pleasant lunch with opposing counsel in his biggest case. Now he was hiding from assassins just outside a five-star restaurant—and feeling more than a little foolish.

Bruno pulled up and waved them over. Daniel got in the passenger seat and Leigh jumped in the back.

"Phyllis isn't answering her phone," Leigh announced.

"I know," Bruno said, his eyes continually moving between the mirrors and the road. He drew a shaky breath. "I called her as soon as I got off the phone with Danny. I've got someone checking on her."

Daniel pulled out his phone. Bruno glanced over. "What are you doing?"

"Calling Sandy."

"No."

"Why not? She could be in danger."

"No—she's not investigating Stillwater; we are. And her phone could be bugged."

"We need help," Daniel said, starting to dial. "We need her professionals."

Bruno snatched the phone out of his hand. "No! Not until we know more. We've been compromised. I don't know how, but it happened. We're not making any calls or sending any e-mails or texts until I figure that out."

Daniel's muscles tensed and he almost made a grab for his phone. But he restrained himself. Bruno was rattled. Badly. Daniel had never seen his cousin like this. The best thing to do was to cut Bruno some slack and let him drive.

So Daniel left his phone in Bruno's skinny fist—which might not be the best place for it. "Hey, B. Shouldn't all our phones go in that box of yours?"

"Yeah—shoulda thought of that." Bruno frowned and shook his head. "It's in the back. Leigh, do you see it?"

"I do," she said. "Do you think they're tracking our cell phones?"

Bruno nodded sharply. "Oh, yeah. Probably not mine, but yours for sure."

"Okay—wouldn't it be better to let them keep tracking the phones, but send them in the wrong direction?" she asked.

"What did you have in mind?" Bruno asked.

"Put our phones in a car or truck that's headed somewhere we aren't." She leaned forward and pointed to a pickup truck in the lane to their right. "Like that one."

Bruno and Daniel both looked over. It was a well-used Ford F-150 with "Modesto Orchards" painted on the side and a load of boxes and farm implements in the bed.

"Excellent idea," Daniel said. "B, could I have my phone back?"

Bruno handed the phone over wordlessly. Leigh tapped Daniel's shoulder and handed him her phone.

Traffic on the Embarcadero is always stop-and-go, and it was more stop than go at the moment. Daniel rolled down his window and waited until they were beside the truck's bed and moving about five miles per hour—fast enough that the pickup driver would be focused on the road in front of him, but slow enough that it would be an easy throw.

With a twinge of regret, he tossed his month-old iPhone away. It arced over the side of the truck's bed and landed noiselessly between two boxes. A quick glance at the driver to make sure he hadn't noticed, then Leigh's phone followed.

"Nice," Bruno said as he pulled into the left turn lane. The Modesto Orchards truck kept going straight, and a few seconds later they and their phones were heading in different directions.

They drove through San Francisco's tech-heavy SoMa district as fast as they could—which was little more than walking speed. It was a harrowing trip. Daniel sat hunched forward, the back of his neck constantly tingling. Any second a bullet could smash through the window and into his skull. Every tenth car seemed to be a gray Camry, and they were always boxed in by traffic when they spotted one. But then every third car was a BMW or Mercedes and plenty of them were black, so at least they had some cover as they crawled through the city.

Finally they pulled onto I-80. Traffic thinned out some and their speed picked up to sixty. Daniel heaved a sigh of relief and sat back. "So, where are we headed?"

"Marin," Bruno said as he merged onto 101 North. "We need a new ride. This was fine in the city or the valley, but it'll stick out anywhere else. And Stillwater probably knows it's mine and knows the plate. So I'm going to park this in a garage someplace and borrow Dad's van."

"The Mystery Machine?" Daniel asked. "He still owns that thing?"

Bruno smiled for the first time since he had picked them up outside the Waterbar. "Well, technically. He was going to junk it about five years ago, but I kinda bought it from him. I put about twenty grand into a new engine and some other stuff, but it's still in his name and he mostly drives it, so they may not expect us to be in it. At least not until they find this thing," he said, patting the dashboard.

"It wasn't worth twenty grand, even when it was new," Daniel said.

"Yeah, well, I'm a nostalgic guy."

"Wouldn't have called that," Daniel said. "So, where do we go once we have the van?"

Bruno shrugged. "Don't know, man. I haven't really thought that through. I'm still pretty freaked out. Someplace safe. Someplace we can plan our next move."

CHAPTER 63

Leigh eyed the Mystery Machine dubiously. It was a dumpy 1970s vintage van painted pastel green with blue trim. She doubted that they'd be able to outrun a bicycle if someone chased them.

"I could rent a car for us," she volunteered. "Or have the firm do it if you're worried about having my name on the paperwork."

Bruno laughed and turned to Daniel. "Can't believe she's disrespecting the Mystery Machine like that."

Daniel shook his head. "No kidding. She hasn't even had to push it anywhere."

"New engine," Bruno reminded them. He put a duffel bag in the back and shut the door. "Come on, let's go."

Bruno got into the driver's seat and Daniel rode shotgun—literally. Bruno's father had donated a much-used double-barreled gun and a box of shells. Leigh climbed in back, where she was pleasantly surprised to find comfortable leather seats, a small fridge, and a built-in cabinet filled with snacks.

Bruno started the engine, which had a reassuringly powerful rumble. Leigh buckled herself in and hoped for the best.

They pulled out of the driveway and headed north. Bruno's father had a friend who owned a remote cabin on the Oregon coast. After a flurry of calls on his father's balky old landline phone, they had managed to rent it for the week under the name Andrew Jackson.

"You never told us what happened," Daniel said as they pulled onto the highway.

Bruno took a deep breath and blew it out. "I was alone at Whacktastic doing some government work. Someone disabled our main security system, which isn't easy. Taking the system offline triggered an alarm. I grabbed Rhodes's hard drive and ran—but I almost wasn't fast enough. Two guys were coming up the stairs and another was watching the back door. They all had guns, and one of them had a toolbox—not sure what that was for. Maybe they were gonna throw me off the roof and mess with the railing to make it look like an accident. Maybe they were gonna try to torture me into talking. Anyway, I set off the sprinklers and fire alarm and got out through an emergency exit."

"Wow," Leigh said. "That's pretty intense." She paused. "Any word on Phyllis?"

Bruno shook his head. "I didn't want to make too many calls from Dad's landline, particularly to numbers that might be under surveillance. I'll check from a pay phone when we stop."

"I thought you said your cell phone was probably safe," Leigh said.

Bruno's bald head bobbed. "But *probably* and *certainly* are very different. That's why my phone is off and I took the battery out as soon as I got off the phone with Danny. Not taking any risks I can avoid—especially when I don't know how big the risks are. Didn't think sitting behind my desk at Whacktastic in the middle of the day was a serious risk, but here we are."

They drove in silence for a few minutes. Then Daniel said, "You have Dr. Rhodes's hard drive?"

"Yep." Bruno pointed back with a thumb. "In the duffel."

"I thought it was in a safe at Biosolutions."

Bruno shrugged. "They have a hard drive that says 'Rhodes' on the label. They'll never know the difference."

Daniel shook his head. "Dude, why?"

"My security is better."

"You seriously think it's more secure in the back of the Mystery Machine than in a safe in Dr. Gupta's office?"

Bruno was quiet for a moment. "Maybe I was wrong."

Daniel scoffed. "Maybe. And maybe you don't like corporate suits telling you what to do. So you blew them off. But guess what? I work for those suits. I vouched for you when they hired you. If there's blowback from this, who's it going to hit?"

"There's not gonna be blowback because they'll never know. They'll never break the encryption on the dummy I gave them. I'll finish working on the real hard drive and switch them out when I'm ready."

"What if you're wrong about that too?" Daniel snapped. "What if they *do* manage to decrypt it somehow?"

"They won't," Bruno insisted. "They'd need a second-generation Meyers-Richard quantum computer to do that, and they don't have one."

"How can you be so sure?"

"Because I happen to know where all of them are. Can't say any more. Sorry."

"So, I'll just have to trust you on this," Daniel said.

"Yeah."

"And that's been working out so well."

Bruno said nothing.

Daniel rubbed his temples and sighed. "Humor me. If they miraculously break the encryption, what will happen?"

"They, ah, they'll watch a Rick Astley video."

Daniel groaned and slouched back in his seat, staring at the ceiling.

Leigh couldn't help laughing. "You Rickrolled Biosolutions?"

Bruno shrugged. "Technically, it's only Rickrolling if they watch it, which they won't." He turned and shot her a grin. "But yeah."

"I was afraid you'd pull a stunt like that." Daniel sighed again, then chuckled. "If I get fired, Whacktastic had better have an opening for general counsel that pays at least as much as what I'm getting now."

They pulled off at a rest stop and Bruno went in search of a pay phone while Leigh bought toiletries and Daniel filled up with gas.

Ten minutes later, Leigh came back to the van, carrying a plastic bag containing her purchases. "Bruno's not back yet?"

"No," Daniel said. "Maybe I should go looking for him."

Before she could reply, Bruno appeared around the side of the van. His face was slack and pale.

"What is it?" she asked.

"Phyllis. They ambushed her in her parking garage. Shot her three times. She's in surgery now."

CHAPTER 64

Another time, Daniel would have thought the cabin was scenic and rugged. Now it looked ominous and isolated. It was a small wooden building with an outhouse and an old-fashioned hand-operated water pump. It sat in a tiny clearing surrounded by a thick forest of young pine trees. There was only one road in—a winding, muddy dirt track that appeared to be an old logging road. At one point, Daniel feared that he'd have to get out and push despite the Mystery Machine's new engine.

As he got out of the van, Daniel could hear the dim susurration of ocean waves crashing a few hundred yards away. The only other sound was the whispering of a breeze in the tops of the trees.

Bruno surveyed the scene and frowned. "Easy to get real close to the cabin without us knowing."

"Well, sort of," Daniel said. "Either they drive up the same road we did or they'd have to park five miles away and hike in."

"Unless they come in from the beach," Leigh said.

"Good point," Bruno said and walked in the direction of the waves, followed by Daniel and Leigh.

They found a narrow path leading to the water's edge. There was no beach to speak of—just a steep tumble of rocks that vanished into gray waves and foam. A chill, wet wind hit them as they stepped out of the forest.

Daniel looked up and down the coast. "No place to land a boat, but I guess they could use one of those inflatable things."

"Zodiacs," Bruno said. "Yeah, that might be possible." He shivered as the breeze whipped his thin black T-shirt, then shoved his hands in his jeans pockets and held his arms against his sides. "If they come from the sea, we can drive out, but if they come from the land, we'll have to hope we can lose them in the forest."

Daniel nodded. "How long do you think you'll need?"

"Not sure," Bruno said. "Need to hack into Stillwater first and see what's there." He took a deep breath and rubbed his arms. "Getting into their system is harder than I thought it would be. Probably need another day or two at least. Once I'm in, we figure out what step two is."

"Okay," Daniel said. "One of us can watch the water, one can watch the road, and one can sleep. You'll be able to work while you watch?"

Bruno nodded.

"But first, we need to find someplace to buy food," Leigh said. She glanced at Bruno. "And we could use some warmer clothing. I'm cold now, and it'll be freezing out here at night."

They headed back to the cabin and opened the door. Brief scurrying noises came from the dimly lit interior and Daniel caught a glimpse of something small vanishing into a gap between a wall and the floor. Leigh shivered. "Add rat poison and traps to the shopping list."

The cabin was a single large room with two folding cots, a stone fireplace, and a battered propane stove. A rusty ax and camp saw leaned in one corner. The only light came from the open door and a small window in one wall.

"Home sweet home for the next week or two," Daniel said.

"If we're lucky," Leigh added. She turned to Bruno. "I'm guessing they'll find your car in Marin eventually. After that, it's probably just a matter of time before they figure out that you visited your dad and called his friend who owns this cabin."

"Should we move to a motel?" Daniel asked.

Bruno shook his head. "Too many people and cameras—and I'm not the only one who knows how to hack those. It's hard to disappear, Danny. Lots of people try; very few succeed."

"And as you start trying to hack them," Leigh said, "the risk that they'll find us starts going up."

Bruno nodded. "Yep. I'll be as careful as I can, of course, but there's always a risk." He frowned and stared into the shadows for a moment. "It's personal for these guys. Maybe it was just business before, even after Phyllis slashed their tires. But it's personal now. That's why they're not just surveilling us anymore. They know we're trying to break into their most secret files. By the time this is over, we'll be on a first-name basis with every skeleton in their closet. Unless they kill me first."

Leigh nodded grimly. "Phyllis said these are bad guys who have probably been doing bad stuff for a long time. Stuff that could land them all in prison for a very long time. They're going to come after us with everything they've got."

They were all silent for a moment as that realization sank in. Then Daniel cleared his throat. "Well, if they're coming after us, we need to get to work as soon as possible. Like now. I'll take the first watch down by the water."

"I'll find someplace with cell reception where I can watch the road," Bruno said.

Leigh gave the cabin floor a suspicious look. "And I'll go into town and do some shopping."

CHAPTER 65

Three hours later, Leigh was done shopping in a little town that they had driven through on the way in. It wasn't much more than a large truck stop, a smallish Walmart, a McDonald's, a Starbucks, and about ten houses. She burned through all their cash, but between the truck stop and the Walmart, she had managed to find a decent assortment of granola bars, fruit, ramen noodles, instant coffee, tea, and serviceable clothing. And rat poison and traps, of course.

When she arrived back at the cabin, she found Bruno waiting for her.

"Want to talk to Phyllis?" he asked as soon as she opened the van door.

She gaped at him for a second. "Of course! Where is she?"

He turned and started walking into the woods. "She's still in the hospital, but she's stable and awake."

"How . . . how is she?"

He hesitated briefly. "Better than she was. They shot her in the back and severed her spine. She'll live, but she's not going to walk again." He glanced back. "I'm really sorry."

They walked in silence while Leigh absorbed the news. Pine needles crackled faintly under their feet. They reached a small, sun-dappled hillock overlooking the entrance road. Bruno led them to the top, where his laptop sat in the shade, connected to a row of miniature solar panels laid out in the sun.

"Okay, one second while I get us connected," he said. "Doing this securely takes a few steps."

A moment later, the sound of a phone dialing came through his speakers and he motioned for Leigh to sit down next to him. The phone rang once, then clicked. "Hello?" Phyllis said. Her voice sounded tired.

"Phyllis!" Leigh said. "It's Leigh and Bruno. How . . . how are you doing?"

"I've been better, but I'm on the mend. Did Bruno tell you about my back?"

"He did. I'm so sorry. I feel terrible that this happened to you."

"It's not your fault," Phyllis said. "And it could have been worse. I could be dead or paralyzed from the neck down. This just means I'll never have to stand up again. I'll bet I can get used to that."

Phyllis's tone was light and upbeat, but Leigh knew she was trying to make her feel better. "Does it hurt much?"

"It doesn't hurt at all," Phyllis said. "They've got me on some outstanding painkillers. I feel great."

"I wish I could be there," Leigh said.

"And I wish I could be *there*," Phyllis said. "Bruno told me what happened. Stay safe."

"We're doing our best," Leigh said. "And we're going to try to take down Stillwater in the process."

"That would be the best get-well present you can give me," Phyllis said. "Don't bother sending flowers. Just send me Bill Stillwater's head on a platter. And if there's anything I can do to help you get it—anything at all—just let me know. You'll know where to find me."

Chapter 66

It was Daniel's off shift, but it was the middle of the day and he didn't feel the least bit sleepy. He decided to visit Bruno and see how he was doing.

Daniel found his cousin on top of the small hillock, his head slowly bobbing up and down as his gaze alternated between his computer screen and the road stretched out below him, which twisted haphazardly to a two-lane county road a mile and a half away. Although Bruno had a good view of it, the narrow trunks of the trees would make him virtually impossible to see from the road.

"Good spot," Daniel said as he walked up.

Bruno glanced over. "Only place I could get a decent connection." He turned back to his computer and started typing rapidly. "Not that it's doing much good."

"How come? I thought you could hack into any system."

"I got in. That's not the problem." Bruno pointed to the screen of his laptop, which was crowded with lines of code that were meaningless to Daniel. "They left an admin backdoor, which I found yesterday. But this is all that's on the other side."

"And what exactly is that, B?"

"A customer-facing website—and basically nothing else. There's a contact form, but it just connects to a standalone Gmail account. There's no company e-mail system, no client files, no billing records, no nothing. They pay their phone and utility bills online, but that's it. Everything else must be on paper or a computer that's not connected to the 'net."

"Very 1980," Daniel said.

"It worked then," Bruno replied. "And it's more or less unhackable. I've heard that some companies do this, particularly in the security business. Never run into one before, but I'm guessing this won't be the last time."

"More or less unhackable," Daniel repeated. "Does *more or less* mean that there *is* something you can do?"

"I can't hack them, but I can hack their phone company," Bruno replied, still bent over the screen. "I've slapped pen registers on all of the phones that the company pays for."

"Pen registers?"

Bruno nodded. "Programs that record the numbers for every call that a phone makes or receives. It's not much, but it's something. Big news so far is that these guys still have lots of buddies in the FBI and SFPD—or at least they're on the phone with them a lot."

"Not surprising, but not reassuring," Daniel said. "I'd been thinking about just calling the cops at some point, but that might not turn out well."

"I always tell people you're the smart one and I'm the pretty one, but they never believe me."

Daniel chuckled. "Can't imagine why not. You working on anything else?"

"Gonna try to get their texts, but that's harder."

"And it assumes they send texts to each other," Daniel observed. "If they keep everything offline, they probably don't text."

"True." Bruno twisted to the left and right, eliciting a series of cracks and pops from his spine. "That's why I'm also trying to find some personal e-mail addresses and phone numbers. That'll set me up to do some spear phishing. If I can get a couple of 'em to download a keystroke logger, we may be in business."

"But we may not, right?"

Bruno took a deep breath and blew it out. "Sorry, but this sort of thing can take time, Danny. A lot of time. You just keep trying one thing after another until boom, you're in. Sometimes the first tactic works, sometimes the hundred and first, and sometimes the thousand and first. I've always been able to get what I want, but it can take months."

Months? "B, we don't have—"

"Yeah, I know," Bruno said, cutting him off. He stopped typing and shot a tense glare at Daniel. "I'm working as fast as I possibly can, okay?"

"Okay," Daniel said. "Anything I can do to help—other than leave you alone?"

"Wish there was, man," Bruno said as he hunched over the laptop once again.

Daniel walked down the hill and back to the cabin. He lay down on a cot and closed his eyes. Peaceful forest sounds drifted in through door and window, but he could not sleep.

CHAPTER 67

The three of them developed a rough routine. Bruno would trudge up to his little hill as soon as it was light and work until his battery ran out, which was always well after dark. Then he would stagger back to the cabin and one of the others would relieve him while he slept the few hours remaining before dawn. Leigh and Daniel took turns watching the ocean from just inside the tree line, where they would be practically invisible from the water.

Daniel and Bruno each took one of the cots in the cabin. They both offered their beds to Leigh, but she chose to sleep in the Mystery Machine during her off shift. It was stuffy and uncomfortable in the van, but they caught two large mice during the first day, so she knew she wouldn't be able to sleep in the cabin.

She woke up one night with a crick in the right side of her neck. She tried turning over, but immediately felt another crick start to develop in the left side of her neck. She yawned and sat up. The Mystery Machine's seats were built to make long drives comfortable, and Leigh could testify that they were great for that. But they were terrible beds.

She slid open the van door, stepped out into the cold night air, and pulled on the oversize Oregon State Beavers sweatshirt she had bought at the truck stop.

She glanced at the dimly glowing face of her watch. Eleven thirty. She wasn't due to relieve Daniel for another hour and a half and Bruno wouldn't be back until at least then, but the fresh breeze was waking her up and she didn't think she'd be able to go back to sleep.

She walked around the little clearing to the path that led to the ocean, choosing her steps carefully to avoid twisting her still-tender ankle. The moon was almost full and the sky was cloudless, so she had little trouble seeing where she was going.

Daniel was silhouetted against the moon-silvered water. He sat facing the ocean, leaning against a tree with his arms folded. His head drooped toward his chest, jerked up, and then drooped again. A notebook with a half-finished pencil drawing of the rocky coastline and moonlit ocean lay on his knees.

Leigh walked up softly behind him, taking care not to step on any twigs. "Boo!"

He jumped up and whirled around, nearly losing his balance in the process. When he saw her, he smiled and spread his hands. "Busted," he said sheepishly.

"No worries." The moonlight now fell directly on his drawing. It was an impressionistic sketch that evoked the scene rather than precisely recording it. "That's beautiful. I didn't know you were an artist."

He yawned and stretched until his joints cracked. "Thanks. Drawing and painting relax me—which may not be the best thing when I'm supposed to be on guard duty."

"I'll bet sleeping in the cabin is a lot more comfortable," she said, pointing back up the path with her chin. "Go ahead. I don't mind taking over a little early."

"No way I'll be able to sleep after you scared me like that."

"Liar. You'll be out thirty seconds after you lie down. I remember the trip up here." Daniel had fallen asleep in the van around the time they crossed the Oregon border, to Leigh and Bruno's surprise and amusement.

"Well, I'll try," he said, "but no promises. And I'll be back for you an hour and a half early."

He walked back up the path and Leigh sat down and settled against the tree he had just left. It was still warm from him and surprisingly comfortable. She had a good view of the ocean. The moon was about three-quarters of the way through its journey across the sky, and its light turned the wind-roughened water into ten million shards of ethereal glass. The waves thrummed rhythmically on the rocks thirty yards below her. It was a beautiful and peaceful place. Soothing, really. But for the chilly breeze—stronger here than at the cabin—she'd be afraid that she might fall asleep too.

She pulled her knees up and stretched her sweatshirt over them. Better. She folded her arms on her knees and rested her chin on them. This was actually more comfortable than the Mystery Machine. Dangerously comfortable.

She scanned the sea to keep herself alert, looking for lights or telltale black shapes speeding across the empty water.

Was that how all this would end? A speedboat spotted too late, followed by a desperate and futile flight through the dark forest? A bullet in her back if she was lucky, torture and interrogation if she wasn't?

Leigh shivered and hugged her knees, feeling small and alone. She had never really considered the possibility that she might die, but now there wasn't much else to think about. There were no plans to make, nothing to do. Just long hours of watching, waiting, and wondering whether Bruno would get to Stillwater before Stillwater got to them.

She never would have guessed that the secret to eternal life would bring her so close to death.

"Boo!"

Her head whipped around. Daniel stood behind her, holding a steel travel mug in each hand. A broad grin stretched his stubbled cheeks. The notebook was tucked under his left arm.

"I wasn't sleeping," she announced.

"Maybe not, but I'm pretty sure you were cold," he said, handing one of the mugs to her. "I couldn't sleep, and I thought you might want some peppermint tea."

"Thanks," she said, taking the mug with both hands. It felt good in her chilled fingers. "I wouldn't mind some company too—if you're really not going back to bed."

"I'm not," he said. "And I never finished my drawing. So I fired up the stove and made something hot to drink."

He sat down cross-legged at a right angle to her. He put his notebook in his lap and eyed the scene critically. Leigh couldn't be sure if he was looking at her or the coastline beyond her.

"I've sketched this same exact scene half a dozen times," he commented. "Mind if I draw you?"

She jerked upright. "What? I look terrible."

He gave a crooked smile. "I beg to differ."

"Seriously. I haven't washed my hair or put on makeup in days."

"I promise to draw you with clean hair and makeup," he said. "And I'll give you the drawing when I'm done, so you can burn it if you want."

The thought of him drawing her was still uncomfortable. But it was also intriguing. "Well, okay. But only if I really can burn it when you're done."

"Deal." He picked up the pencil and braced the notebook against one knee.

She sat perfectly still, feeling intensely self-conscious. "Do you want me sit like this, or should I do something different?"

"Just be yourself," he said. "Talk. Move around. Act natural. I'm not drawing exactly what you look like. It's more like I'm drawing your personality—or trying to anyway."

Oh, great. She forced a chuckle. "So I should just make conversation or something?"

"Sure."

"Okay, um, how are things with you?"

"I'm fine," he said nonchalantly, looking down at the paper. His pencil scratched faintly on the page.

"Seriously?" she said, trying to ignore what he was doing. "Here we are on the run from murdering thugs, hiding in a vermin-infested cabin, and praying that your hacker cousin can somehow beat them before they find us. And if he fails, all we've got is a Scooby van and an old shotgun. And you're *fine*?"

He shrugged. "Could be worse."

"How?" she demanded.

He looked up and winked. "I could be stuck here with just Bruno."

"He's not so bad," Leigh said. "I like him."

"Oh, so do I," Daniel replied. "But he's being a gentleman—relatively speaking—because you're here."

Leigh took a sip of her tea. "Well, I'm glad I bring out the best in him."

They were silent together for several minutes, Daniel sketching and Leigh alternately watching the quicksilver water and trying to sneak looks at his artwork.

"I never would have guessed things would turn out like this when I filed that complaint against American Guaranty," he said. "Especially not after our first couple of court hearings. If someone told me I'd end up running for my life because of something related to the case, I would've figured you'd be chasing me."

She gave an embarrassed little laugh. "I have a confession to make. A friend of mine set up this zombie-hunting game so that I could put different people's faces on the zombies I fight. I killed a lot of undead Rubinellis for a while."

He looked up from his drawing. "That is awesome! I need that game. What's it called?"

"Zombie Hunter 3."

"Really? I've already got it. Good game. Send me that face hack when we get back, okay?"

"Okay." She paused for a heartbeat. "If we get back."

"We will," he said. He reached over and put his hand on her arm. It felt warm and strong, even through her sleeve. "And even if we don't, I'm glad I met you."

She put her hand on his and squeezed, then released it. "Me too."

He withdrew his hand and held the notepad up, examining it critically in the moonlight. He added a few lines, then carefully detached the top sheet and handed it to her. "There you go," he said. "A starter for the next time you light the camp stove." His words were nonchalant, but she heard the nervousness in his voice.

The drawing showed a three-quarters profile of her. She was looking sidelong out of the picture, and a smile that was both mischievous and warm played at the corners of her lips. A few tendrils of hair had escaped from her ponytail and framed her face. The moon cast soft shadows, highlighting her cheekbones and turning her eyes into soulful pools. She was beautiful.

Her heart raced and alarm bells went off in the part of her brain where her career control center was located. How could she possibly let herself feel this way about her opponent in a $100 million case? What would Jack say if he saw her now? Would her partnership prospects survive?

But then again, would she survive?

She looked up at him. "Thank you for seeing me this way."

"How else could I see you?"

He smiled at her and his eyes shone in the moonlight, but she saw in them the same conflict that she felt.

The moment hung between them, undecided.

Then Leigh noticed a movement out of the corner of her eye. A tiny shadow creased the silver sea. A speedboat about a mile down the coast, coming toward them.

CHAPTER 68

Daniel saw the sudden fear in Leigh's face and turned to follow her gaze.

The next instant, he was on his feet and helping Leigh to hers. They needed to get out of here this instant. Then they'd have to ditch the Mystery Machine in the next town, someplace out of the way where no one would find it for at least a day or two. And then they'd need to find another—and better—place to hide. Somehow.

Leigh stuffed the drawing in her pocket and they both turned to run back to the cabin. But before they could move, Daniel heard footsteps pelting down the path.

Bruno appeared out of a thicket of pine saplings, racing toward them. He skidded to a stop, gasping for breath. He clutched the shotgun in one hand and the hard drive in the other. "We gotta go," he said. "They're coming down the road. They'll be here in two minutes."

"And from the ocean," Leigh said, pointing to the approaching boat.

The stared at each other, frozen in fear and indecision. Panic began shouting in Daniel's brain, drowning out thought. They were trapped! They'd be caught in minutes, dead minutes after that!

He tried to force himself to think. Lessons his father repeated every Saturday at the firing range popped into his head. *In an emergency, a bad plan is better than no plan. Speed wins. In a gunfight, good cover wins more often than good aim.*

And then he knew what to do.

"Get off the path and lie down in the brush over there," Daniel said, pointing to the left, where the growth was thickest. "They'll go right past us." He reached out his hand. "And give me the gun."

Bruno handed it over wordlessly. Then he and Leigh forced their way about ten yards into the bushy growth that lined the border between the rocky coast and the forest. They lay down, and even Daniel couldn't see them.

He scanned the ground for the right spot. There—a thick, half-rotten log lying parallel to the water and a few feet inside the tree line. He lay down behind it, the shotgun by his side. He wasn't quite as well hidden as Leigh and Bruno. If someone happened to look directly at him from the path, they'd probably see him. He'd just have to hope that they didn't look his way.

The boat slowed as it approached the coast. It was a rubber inflatable craft with a vaguely military look. One man sat in the rear by the motor and two more were in front, ready to jump out. All were dressed in black, wore night vision goggles, and appeared to be carrying long guns and pistols.

The only noise the invaders made was the faint slap of the water against the sides of their boat. They didn't speak and their motor was entirely silent—and therefore presumably electric.

The two men in front jumped out as soon as the bow touched the rocks, then pulled the boat up with practiced efficiency. The third man got out and stood in front of the boat, head swiveling back and forth with his gun—it looked like an AR-15—at the ready. The first two men picked their way through the rocks and started up the path. Daniel tensed as they passed him, but they didn't look his way.

Daniel knew he only had a few minutes. The commandos would quickly realize that the cabin and the van were empty, but that their prey couldn't have gone far. Then they would start searching the area and it would just be a matter of time.

As soon as the two men were out of earshot, Daniel picked up the shotgun and laid the barrel across the log. His heart thundered in his ears as he aimed at the head of the man by the boat.

"Drop the gun into the boat," he said, just loud enough for the man to hear him.

The man raised his gun and looked around wildly, then spotted the gun barrel sticking out of the woods. He froze, staring at Daniel's hiding place, his gun raised but not aimed. Daniel could almost read the man's mind—he was standing up, completely exposed, and silhouetted against the sinking moon. In other words, he was an excellent target and Daniel was less than twenty yards away—can't-miss range for even a mediocre marksman. And Daniel was behind cover and had already drawn a bead on the man's head, while his opponent hadn't taken aim at Daniel.

After a few tense seconds, the man did the smart thing and reluctantly tossed his rifle into the boat.

"Pistol too," Daniel said.

The pistol went into the boat.

"Good," Daniel said. "Now step away and lie down."

The man obeyed.

"B, check the motor to make sure you can operate it," Daniel said more quietly, keeping his gun aimed at the prone figure. "And stay out of my line of fire."

There was a rustling sound to his right. A few seconds later, Bruno appeared in his peripheral vision, walking down to the boat in a wide arc that avoided the man lying on the rocks. Bruno got in, examined the motor for a few seconds, and then gave a thumbs-up. Without needing to be asked, he picked up the pistol and pointed it at the Stillwater thug.

"Okay, Leigh, get in the boat," Daniel said.

More rustling, then she appeared and followed Bruno's path down to the water and got in. She picked up the AR-15 and pointed it at the man on the beach.

Daniel got to his feet and stepped over the log, keeping the shotgun trained the entire time. He walked across the rocks, moving as quickly as he could without risking his balance or his aim. He paused as he passed the man. "Stay there until I say you can move."

He reached the boat and handed the shotgun to Leigh, who put the AR-15 down. "Just point it at his head and pull the trigger if he even twitches," he said, loud enough for the man to hear. "Both barrels are loaded with deer slugs, and he knows what those will do to him."

He bent down and braced his hands against the bow of the boat to push it back into the water. Then several things happened at once. He shoved the boat, Leigh shouted something, and he heard the firecracker sound of gunshots behind him.

The boat slipped into the water just as someone slammed into Daniel from behind and pulled at him. Daniel grabbed the side of the boat with his right hand and swung his left elbow back as hard as he could. He felt an electric crack as it connected with something hard. His arm went numb, but the grip on him slackened.

The familiar blast of a shotgun roared over his head as Leigh returned fire. Bullets thunked into the rubber sides of the boat. Several people shouted at the same time.

He pulled himself over the side of the boat as the shotgun fired a second time. He landed on the AR-15. He grabbed it and pulled it to his shoulder. He flipped the safety selector to "fire" and laid the rifle's barrel over the side of the boat. His left arm was still numb, but he was able to brace the gun against an oarlock.

He now had his first view of what was happening. They were about twenty yards from shore now. About half a dozen figures in black lay or crouched at the edge of the woods and among the rocks, taking advantage of whatever cover they could find. Gunfire flashed and bullets slapped the water and thudded into the sides of the boat, which had some sort of armor attached to the sides and bow.

Daniel started firing as rapidly as he could pull the trigger. Shooting that fast meant that he couldn't really aim, just point in the general direction of his targets. That was fine—he mostly wanted to make them keep their heads down.

The fire from the shore lessened. They had put over a hundred yards of water between them and their attackers, and the bullets were mostly hitting the water now.

The boat jerked and veered sharply to the left. Daniel turned and saw Bruno slumped in the stern. The right side of his hoodie gleamed wetly in the fading moonlight.

Daniel scrambled back and pulled the tiller straight. They were now headed north along the coastline, toward a small promontory that would hide them from their attackers.

They rounded the promontory a few seconds later and the gunfire ceased. Daniel relaxed slightly. "Bruno's been shot," he said to Leigh, who lay curled in the bottom of the boat. "Could you check him?"

"Okay," she said faintly. She crawled over to Bruno, and Daniel saw that her right shoulder was covered with blood.

"You too?" he said. "How bad?"

"I can use my arm," she said, demonstrating. "So I think it must have just grazed me." She bent down to examine Bruno, who groaned. "Looks like a bullet went straight through his arm. No other wounds, but he's bleeding a lot."

"Hold his injured arm up and put pressure on the wound," Daniel said.

Bruno groaned as she followed Daniel's instructions. He batted weakly at her hand. "Ow! Hey, what're you doin'?"

"Keeping you from bleeding to death," Daniel said. He unbuckled his belt with one hand, pulled it out of his pants, and tossed it to Leigh. "Use this as a tourniquet up by his shoulder."

She did, and Bruno didn't resist this time. The flow of blood reduced to a slow trickle.

"Bruno, you still with us?" Daniel asked.

His cousin nodded. He tried to push himself up with his good arm, but collapsed back into the bottom of the boat.

"Relax," Daniel said. "You've lost a lot of blood. You'll probably pass out again if you try to sit up."

"Okay." Bruno moved his injured arm tentatively. "At least the bone doesn't seem broken."

"Good," Daniel said. "We've got to get you two to a hospital."

"No hospital," Bruno said. "Not yet. We go to the hospital, the hospital calls the cops. And I'll bet Stillwater has friends in the local PD."

They rode in silence for several minutes. The moon set and the mile after mile of sea cliffs and sandy or stony beaches slid by, lit only by faint starlight. They were far enough from shore that the waves were only gentle swells rolling them rhythmically from side to side. They moved fairly fast, but the motor was so quiet that Daniel could barely hear it above the muted slap of the bow against the water. He noticed a faint hiss and poked at the inflated rubber beside him. It was softer than before. One or more of the bullets must have hit a vulnerable spot in the boat's armor. If they didn't land soon, they would sink.

"We're losing air," Daniel announced as he steered them into a small inlet. It held a rickety dock and a fishing cabin that appeared to be deserted. The lights of a town glowed on the horizon, but the shore was completely dark and silent. Daniel guided the boat up to the end of the dock and helped Bruno out. Leigh got out on her own and joined them on the dock.

"So what do we do?" Daniel asked. "Plan A is now officially a dumpster fire. What's Plan B?"

No one answered.

CHAPTER 69

Bruno flinched and grunted when Leigh swabbed his wound with disinfectant from the first-aid kit Daniel found in the bottom of their boat. "Sorry," she said, trying to be as gentle as she could.

Daniel had also found a leak sealing kit, but they didn't have an air compressor to reinflate the boat. Besides, Stillwater would be looking for it. So they decided to load it with rocks and sink it, which Daniel was doing now.

Bruno stiffened again.

"So, how far had you gotten when the Stillwater guys showed up?" Leigh asked, partly out of curiosity and partly to take his mind off the pain.

He told her about Stillwater's deliberately obsolete record system while she finished cleaning his arm, then covered it with sterile pads and wrapped it with gauze. It continued to ooze blood slowly, but the flow had reduced considerably.

Bruno had just finished explaining how pen registers worked when Daniel returned, carrying the guns. "So, any progress on Plan B?" he asked.

Bruno held his good hand palm up in a gesture of helplessness. "Dude, my laptop is probably in the back of a Stillwater SUV right now. Even if I had it with me, it would take too long to get anywhere. I'd need to hack into the personal phones and e-mail accounts of everyone at Stillwater, or at least the top guys. I can probably do it, but it'll take time—like weeks. Maybe months."

"Which we don't have," Daniel said. "They found us in three days. I'll bet it won't take them that long to find us again." He looked at Bruno's arm, eyeing Leigh's handiwork. "And we do need to get you to a doctor sooner rather than later."

Leigh worked on her shoulder while they talked, biting her lip against the pain. The disinfectant really did hurt. The bullet had torn an inch-wide furrow across her shoulder, which she now had to douse with what felt like acid.

She decided that it was clean enough and bandaged it. It still stung, now with a sort of throbbing ache underneath. She wished she had some of Phyllis's painkillers.

Phyllis. Pen registers. "Guys, I think I know what Plan B is."

They both turned to her. "Great," Daniel said. "What do you have in mind?"

"We need to get Stillwater to make some incriminating calls and then do something that will get them busted."

"But Stillwater is wired into every law enforcement agency around," Bruno objected. "Who's gonna bust them?"

"We've got Phyllis," Leigh said. "She's wired in too."

"Yeah, in Oakland," Bruno responded.

Leigh nodded. "Which is where we have to go."

"How exactly are we gonna get there?" Bruno asked.

"I'm not sure," she conceded. "But I'll bet the first thing we have to do is get to that town." She pointed toward the lights in the distance.

"Oh, joy," Bruno said, wincing and nearly losing his balance as he stood up.

Daniel scrambled to his feet. "Hey, B, let me give you a hand," he said, holding out his arm for Bruno to lean on.

Bruno shot his cousin a withering glare and walked down the dock with an unsteady but determined stride.

CHAPTER 70

Thirty hours later, the three of them were in the main public library in Oakland. Bruno and Leigh were both at computer terminals. Daniel watched the door with increasing nervousness. He was exhausted, but in no danger of falling asleep.

The town whose lights they had seen from the dock turned out to be only about three miles away—but it had taken almost three hours to walk there due to the terrain and Bruno's frequent need to rest. They picked up new clothes, food, and fresh medical supplies. Then they took a long—and expensive—cab ride to Brookings, which had a Greyhound station. After that came almost a day on buses and in stations waiting for connections as they made their way to Oakland.

They had no cash left, so all of their expenses had gone on Daniel's credit card. That increased the risk that they could be tracked, of course, but speed mattered more than secrecy at this point. And soon secrecy wouldn't matter at all.

"Found him," Bruno announced, scribbling awkwardly on a scrap of paper with his left hand. He held it out to Daniel. "He's in a Safeway. Here's the number. Good luck."

Heart pounding, Daniel took the paper and jogged out to the pay phone. They had checked it before they went in, so he knew it would work.

He took a deep breath, dropped in quarters, and dialed.

"Safeway," a man's voice said a moment later. "How may I direct your call?"

"I'm calling for a customer who is in your store right now. His name is Rich Johnson. There's been a medical emergency, and I need to talk to him immediately. Could you page him, please? Tell him Daniel Rubinelli is on the line."

"Certainly, sir. One moment."

The line went silent for what seemed like an eternity. Daniel looked up and down the street, feeling eyes on his back no matter which way he turned. Bruno didn't think Stillwater would be able to trace a call from one untapped phone to another, at least not quickly. But then Bruno had been wrong before and now sported a bullet hole as a result.

Would Rich—or whatever his real name was—even take the bait? He would know it was a trap, of course. But he would also know that if he could get to Daniel, he would be a lot closer to the hard drive—so he would probably take the bait and gamble that he could beat the trap. Or at least that's what Daniel, Bruno, and Leigh had decided was most likely to happen.

And if Rich decided not to take Daniel's call . . . well, they'd have to figure out what Plan C was.

The phone clattered. "So, what's the emergency, Daniel?" Rich asked.

"Take your pick. How about Phyllis Higgins lying in a hospital with three bullet wounds in her back? Or Anya Rhodes being kidnapped? Or a guns-blazing commando raid on a cabin where I was staying?" He paused, but Rich said nothing. "Maybe those weren't emergencies to you or Professor Stein, but here's something that I'll bet is: I have Dr. Rhodes's hard drive, and I'm going to destroy it unless you do exactly what I say."

Silence for a long moment, then, "What do you want?"

"I'm about to give you detailed instructions and you'll need to follow them precisely. Do you have something to write with?"

"One second." The line was briefly silent, then Rich said, "Okay, go ahead."

"At eight o'clock tonight, you will go to the McDonald's at 14th and Jackson in Oakland," Daniel said, speaking rapidly. "You will have Anya Rhodes with you. You will be ready to wire transfer five million dollars. Other than Anya, you will be alone—and unarmed. You will be met by one of my representatives, who will hand you wire instructions. My representative will then leave McDonald's with Anya. This representative will not have the hard drive and will not know where it is, so don't bother asking. You will then have one hour in which to complete the wire transfer. You will then return to the McDonald's, at which time someone will call the restaurant and ask for you. That person will then tell you where the hard drive is."

"Daniel, let's talk about this," Rich said urgently. "I—"

Daniel wasn't going to stand there a second longer than was necessary to deliver his message. "We are talking, Rich—and we're almost done. If you don't follow those instructions exactly, the hard drive will be destroyed. If you, Stein, or your Stillwater thugs do anything the least bit suspicious, the hard drive will be destroyed. Don't be late."

He hung up, feeling vulnerable and exposed. This had better work.

CHAPTER 71

Dr. Stein shoved his human and rat tissue samples into a cooler and took it out to the SUV waiting at the building's loading dock—which was invisible from the street. The smaller pieces of equipment were already there, packed together with the cages holding the more valuable test subjects. He could fit everything that he truly needed to set up a new lab elsewhere, but he still wished a rental truck would have been possible so that he could take more. But a truck might have drawn attention, whereas the street was dotted with SUVs similar to the one he was now packing.

He went back into the building, picked up the last of his equipment, and took one last look around to make sure he hadn't forgotten anything. Then he left for the last time. He got into the SUV and started the engine.

The Safeway call to "Rich" had been a surprise, but Dr. Stein had been expecting something like that ever since he discovered that his lab was being watched. He had an exit plan ready and he intended to follow it, regardless of Daniel Rubinelli's instructions.

It was a pity that Rubinelli had decided to force the issue. Dr. Stein obviously wasn't going to hand over Anya or five million dollars, but that didn't mean they had nothing to talk about. Quite the contrary—Daniel Rubinelli seemed like he genuinely believed in Elijah's work. Rubinelli could have been a useful ally but instead he chose to be a problem that needed to be dealt with. Too bad.

Dr. Stein sighed. No use putting off the inevitable.

CHAPTER 72

There was one more call Daniel needed to make—a call he wished he'd made as soon as he got off the phone with Bruno at the Waterbar. He braced himself, dropped in his quarters, and dialed.

She picked up on the second ring. "Hello, Sandra Hampton speaking."

"Sandy, it's Daniel."

"Daniel! Where are you? We've been really worried about you."

"I'm sorry, but I can't tell you. There are people after me, and they've already tried to kill me once."

"Tried to kill you?" she echoed, disbelief in her voice. "Have you called the police?"

"We can't. Stillwater Security is chasing us, and they've got too many connections with the police and FBI."

"Let me help," she pleaded. "I can have someone pick you up in ten minutes, maybe less. Just tell me where you are."

"I can't. I . . . Sandy, I called to say good-bye. I've got Dr. Rhodes's hard drive, and I need to deal with it."

"Wait—the drive is in Dr. Gupta's safe, isn't it?"

"No. That's a fake. Bruno didn't trust Biosolutions' security, and I'm afraid I agree with him."

"Daniel, you need to give me that hard drive," Sandy said, her voice urgent. "You know how important it is. If you won't let me protect you, at least let me protect that."

"I wish I could, but I don't think it will be any safer with you—and you'll be a lot less safe if you have it. Trust me."

"What if they don't know I have it?" she asked. "What if you leave it someplace hidden and I have someone pick it up?"

"That won't work, but . . . Actually, there is something you can do."

"Of course—just tell me."

"Well, I'm going to be meeting with Rich Johnson at eight o'clock tonight at the McDonald's at 14th and Jackson in Oakland. We think Rich is working for Professor Frederick Stein, who probably hired Stillwater. We're going to try to make a deal. If you could have some people there to make sure they don't try anything, that would be great."

"Done. They'll be there and they'll blend in. Rich will never notice them."

"Thanks, I really appreciate it." He glanced around. The conversation had gone on too long already, and Bruno and Leigh would start to wonder where he was. "I've got to go. Bye."

"Stay safe," she said. "And keep that hard drive safe."

"I'll do what I can."

CHAPTER 73

Leigh had never been particularly patient. She paced and fidgeted whenever one of her juries was deliberating. She hit refresh every five minutes when she was waiting for a court to post a ruling on its website. It drove her nuts to have some big uncertainty hanging over her.

And now the mother of all uncertainties loomed toward her—but it wasn't here yet. Daniel's call had set things in motion, but they still had over two hours to kill, and all they could do was wait. It drove her nuts.

Daniel sat in a chair with a good view of the library entrance, his eyes constantly moving. Bruno was at one of the public computer terminals, staring intently at the screen and moving the mouse rapidly. Leigh walked up and looked over his shoulder. He was playing Minesweeper.

"Seriously?" she said.

He jumped and hit a mine, ending the game. "I know," he said, shaking his head in disgust. "Used to be a lot faster back in college. Held the record for a while, but I got rusty."

"You know what I mean."

He shrugged and turned away from the screen to face her. "I got nothing better to do. No more planning or hacking. Nothing. This plan works or it doesn't. I'm too freaked out to read or watch a movie, so I do this." He gestured at the computer. "Keeps me from bouncing off the walls. You might want to try it."

He turned back to the terminal and started a new game.

Leigh walked off and began to pace up and down the rows of bookshelves. Bruno was right, of course. They had all memorized the area around the McDonald's and the internal layout of the restaurant. They had talked through every tactical and strategic detail with Phyllis, gamed out every scenario they could think of. Now they had made their first move and they had little choice but to follow through with their plan. As Bruno said, it would either work or it wouldn't.

Her ankle gave a warning twinge, and Leigh grudgingly admitted to herself that she should sit down. She went back to the computer terminals, found a free one, and started searching for a decent online zombie-fighting game.

◆ ◆ ◆

Several hundred mangled zombies later, it was finally time. At seven thirty, she got up and walked over to Bruno, who nodded and rose. Daniel arrived a few seconds later. He took a deep breath and blew it out. "It really should be me," he said to Leigh. "I'm pretty sure I'm the only one of us who likes McDonald's."

Bruno shook his head vigorously. "Best fries on the planet—and I'm hungry."

"Thanks, but we've been over this," Leigh said. "It's my plan and I insist."

She turned and walked toward the door, relieved to finally be doing something. It would all be over soon, one way or the other. Her role was very straightforward: all she needed to do was walk two blocks to the McDonald's, go in, and sit down. Then she would walk out twenty or thirty minutes later. Simple. Not necessarily safe, but simple.

The three of them walked out of the library and down the front steps. The real danger wouldn't start until Leigh got close to the restaurant, but she could already feel the adrenaline humming in her blood. She felt a little lightheaded and giddy—almost reckless.

Should she buy Bruno an order of fries while she was there? A smile twitched her lips at the thought. She would have at least twenty minutes before Rich was supposed to arrive. It was probably a bad idea, but the thought of the look on Bruno's and Daniel's faces when she came out carrying fries was—

A sudden movement flashed in her peripheral vision as she passed a tall cement planter. Before she could react, a hand grabbed her and yanked her behind the planter. A cloth clamped over her mouth. Muffled sounds of fighting came from behind her. She struggled and tried to draw a breath to scream—but choked on chemical fumes from the cloth. Black spots clouded her vision and roaring filled her ears.

She felt herself falling.

CHAPTER 74

Daniel's head hurt. That was the first thing he noticed. The second was that he was moving. The surface under him rattled and shook, and for a second he thought it was an earthquake.

He opened his eyes and realized that he was in the back of a van. He lay on his left side, facing forward. Bruno and Leigh lay in front of him. Buildings rolled past outside the sliver of windshield he could see over the driver's shoulder.

Daniel tried to sit up, but his legs seemed to be tangled in something and his arms were stuck behind his back.

A sharp blow struck him between the shoulder blades. "Don't move," a man's voice commanded from somewhere behind him.

Daniel lay still. His head cleared and his memory returned. A man had grabbed Leigh two feet in front of him. Then, while Daniel's attention was focused on Leigh, someone hit him from behind. Something similar must have happened to Bruno, though Daniel hadn't seen it. The whole thing had been over in a few seconds.

It was a good move, he had to admit. The McDonald's meeting was an obvious setup, even if Stillwater and company didn't know exactly what Daniel and his allies had planned. So somehow their attackers had figured out that they were at the library and got them before they could get anywhere near the restaurant.

Daniel knew he was probably responsible. He took a chance by calling Sandy's phone, even though it might be bugged. He had been careful not to say where he was, but the call might have been traced. In retrospect, he was almost certain that it had been. He wondered whether he would live long enough to be able to apologize to Leigh and Bruno.

He was a little surprised that he was alive at all. Stillwater had tried to kill him once, so why hadn't they finished the job?

Because they didn't have the hard drive, he realized. Bruno had hidden it behind a row of particularly dusty books at the library, and it must still be there. So they still needed Daniel, Bruno, and Leigh—or at least one of them.

Daniel had to operate on the assumption that Plan B had failed, but it might be possible to come up with a Plan C. He stared out the window, struggling to think. They were on a city street that he didn't immediately recognize. If they were headed for Dr. Stein's building in Berkeley, they only had a few minutes. He paid more attention to the narrow view he had, trying to figure out where they were.

A sign flashed past: Adeline Street. They weren't in Berkeley after all, but Oakland. And they were headed toward the docks and warehouses of the Port of Oakland. The port had been slowly dying for years, so there were plenty of empty buildings and semi-deserted areas even during the day. At night, it would be even emptier. The perfect place to have a private and brutal conversation without interruption—and to dispose of bodies afterward.

He needed a plan before they arrived. Assuming that Stillwater didn't have the hard drive, they would need to get one of their three prisoners to tell them where it was. He doubted Stillwater would have any compunction about using torture, but they might be willing to negotiate. Would they be willing to let Leigh and Bruno go in return for the location of the hard drive? That would obviously pose risks for Stillwater, Dr. Stein, and Rich—but if it were their only option, maybe they'd agree. He realized with a chill that it wouldn't be their only option until they had tried a lot of torture.

The SUV turned into a dimly lit side street. Then it pulled into the loading bay of a cavernous, rust-streaked warehouse. The van stopped and the driver shut off the engine. Metal squealed and rattled outside—presumably the sound of the warehouse doors closing behind them.

They were out of time.

CHAPTER 75

Leigh's heart sank as the warehouse door clanged shut. Phyllis had promised that there would be an OPD detective watching and ready to intervene, but they had only talked about the McDonald's meeting. Phyllis knew they would be walking from the library to the restaurant, so it was possible that the detective had been outside the library, ready to start tailing them there. And it was also possible that they had a car—probably unmarked to avoid giving them away—ready in case some of the Stillwater thugs escaped.

Leigh had hoped that was the case, hoped it desperately. But her hope faded with every mile they traveled without being pulled over. And it died entirely when they pulled into this place and the door closed.

The van door slid open and two men wearing ski masks and black gloves grabbed Leigh and pulled her out. Her feet and hands were both bound with zip ties, so she couldn't brace herself when she landed on the cement floor. It knocked the wind out of her and she gasped, inhaling exhaust fumes and chemical smells. It was cold and dark, lit only by the interior light of the van and flashlights carried by their captors.

Bruno followed a few seconds later. He grunted in pain as they dropped him on his injured arm.

They were hauling Daniel out when she heard running steps and a man shouted, "Put 'em back in! Open the door!"

The two men froze for an instant, then grabbed Leigh and tossed her back in like a sack of potatoes. She landed on Daniel, and Bruno landed on her an instant later. More men got in and she heard the warehouse door opening. The van door slammed shut and the engine roared to life.

The driver threw the vehicle into reverse, then slammed on the brakes, turned, and sped off. They were hurled around the back like human pinballs for what felt like an eternity. Sirens, shouts, and a cacophony of vehicle noises assaulted her ears and brain.

A crunching impact threw her into the back of the seat so hard that she saw stars. The van came to a sudden stop. For a moment, everything was still. Then the door flew open, revealing several men wearing helmets and body armor. They all had guns, which were pointed at the Stillwater men.

"Out!" one of their rescuers shouted at their captors. "Hands on your heads!"

Someone cut the ties on Leigh's wrists and ankles and helped her out of the van. She blinked in the glare of a circle of headlights and a dozen flashing red, blue, and amber lights. A few minutes later, she found herself sitting in the back of an ambulance, trying to answer questions from an EMT.

Then it hit her: it was over. It was really over. She sobbed with relief.

CHAPTER 76

Daniel sat on the bumper of an ambulance while a paramedic finished examining him. There was a throbbing lump on the back of his skull and he had symptoms of a mild concussion, but other than that the paramedic thought he was okay. She nodded to a police detective, who had been waiting more or less patiently while the paramedic checked Daniel for any injuries requiring urgent care.

"Do you feel up to answering a few questions, Mr. Rubinelli?" the detective asked.

"Sure."

"Do you think you could recognize any of the individuals who attacked you in Oregon?"

Daniel started to shake his head, but stopped when a little flare of pain erupted in his skull. "No, they were all wearing masks. Also, it was dark and I never got a close look at any of them."

"All right, how about the ones who attacked you tonight?"

"Also masked," Daniel replied. He thought for a moment. "I think one of them had blue eyes."

The detective jotted down a note. "Do you recall how many attackers there were in Oregon?"

Before Daniel could answer, another EMT walked up. "Daniel Rubinelli?"

"Yes?"

"We're about to take your cousin, Bruno, to the hospital, but he wanted to talk to you first."

"Sure." Daniel turned to the officer. "Excuse me for a minute."

The EMT guided Daniel over to another ambulance. Bruno lay inside, his shirt off and fresh bandages on his arm. As always when he saw his cousin's bony torso, Daniel felt a strong urge to feed Bruno PowerBars and take him to the gym.

Daniel climbed into the ambulance and crouched next to Bruno. "How are you doing, B?"

"It worked," Bruno said without preamble.

"What worked?"

"Plan B. The pen registers."

"Really? How do you know already?"

"I borrowed a cop's cell phone and checked." He looked down. "I know who called Stillwater. The cops are on their way to pick them up now."

"That's great!"

"Yeah," Bruno said without enthusiasm.

"Who was it?"

"I really thought it was going to be Rich, calling from that burner phone he bought," Bruno said. "Or maybe calling from a pay phone in Berkeley."

"But it wasn't?"

Bruno shook his head. "Nope."

A hard knot of fear began to grow in Daniel's stomach. "Who was it?" he repeated.

Bruno glanced up at Daniel, then dropped his gaze again. "It was Sandy."

"Sandy?" Daniel heard himself say.

Bruno nodded. "As soon as she hung up with you today, she called Bill Stillwater's cell phone."

The bottom fell out of Daniel's stomach. He didn't doubt Bruno, but he couldn't make himself believe what he had just heard. The magnitude of Sandy's betrayal numbed and overwhelmed him.

After the three of them first started developing Plan B up in Oregon, Leigh had diplomatically mentioned that it was conceivable that someone at Biosolutions was involved. The company was interested in Dr. Rhodes's research, of course, and Rhodes had been trying to hide Enoch from somebody in the company. Maybe that somebody grabbed Anya and shipped her to Dr. Stein's lab for experimentation, Leigh had speculated. And maybe that same somebody sent Stillwater after them when they got too close to finding Anya. Daniel had agreed that all of that was indeed hypothetically conceivable—but the thought that Sandy might be involved never entered his darkest nightmares.

Bruno reached out and put his hand on Daniel's arm. "I'm sorry, man. I'm really sorry."

CHAPTER 77

"What's your name?" a disembodied male voice asked.

Anya opened her eyes. She was lying on something. A man she had never seen before was leaning over her. He wore a short-sleeved blue shirt and he had a nameplate over the right pocket, though Anya couldn't focus her eyes enough to read it.

"What is your name?" the man repeated more slowly.

"Where am I?" she asked.

"You're in an ambulance," the man said. "We're taking you to ValleyCare hospital."

Her mind was fuzzy and she couldn't quite piece together what his words meant. ValleyCare? What was that? Why was she here?

Her nose itched. She tried to reach up and scratch it, but she couldn't move her hands. She lifted her head and looked down. She was on a gurney—and her wrists were in restraints. An IV bag hung by the gurney, swaying slightly.

Horror flooded her as her last memory resurfaced in her mind. Restraints. Needles in her arm. They had caught her again.

She had to get away! She tried to sit up, to pull herself free.

The man pushed her back down. "Hey, relax. You're okay now. Just relax."

She tried to tug her hands out of the restraints. "Please let me go," she begged.

"It's okay," he repeated, taking hold of her wrist with one hand and continuing to push her down with the other. He nodded and another blue-shirted man appeared. He injected something into the tube connecting the IV bag to her arm.

Then the world went dark again as she slipped back into unconsciousness.

CHAPTER 78

Leigh hated hospitals, and she had dreaded visiting Aunt Phyllis. She visualized the motherly detective lying in a bed, connected to tubes and heavily drugged, her skin pasty and her eyes glazed. Plus, Leigh knew that she'd get a gut punch of guilt the instant she walked in the room—not because of anything Phyllis would say, but because seeing her would make what happened real.

But she had to visit, of course, so she enlisted Andrea for moral support and bit the bullet. Andrea baked a batch of her aunt's favorite scones and they stopped by Starbucks to pick up several varieties of hot liquid caffeine. Then they went in.

To Leigh's relief, Phyllis was alert and seemed to be in good spirits. Her makeup was done and her hair had been washed and braided. She was happy to see them, particularly once she spotted the scones and coffee. "Mmm, you girls are the best," she said after the first bite. "I was wasting away to a size ten on the food they serve here."

"You poor thing!" Andrea said, patting her aunt's arm. "I'll make sure to bring cookies next time."

"How are you feeling?" Leigh asked.

"Better," Phyllis said. "Especially now that Bill Stillwater and his boys are in jail. That's been a long time coming. What's the word from the DA's office?"

"They can't say too much, of course, but it sounds like there's a big indictment coming," Leigh replied. "Multiple counts of attempted murder and assault with a deadly weapon, plus kidnapping and conspiracy."

"They'll probably try to plea bargain," Phyllis mused. "Did you get any hint of whether the DA will need their testimony against Biosolutions?"

Leigh shook her head. "No, but it's only been a couple of days. I don't think they know yet. I'll keep you posted."

Phyllis nodded. "Thanks. And thanks for coming over."

"Of course," Leigh said. "It's wonderful to see you." She paused. "I . . . I'm really sorry about this, Phyllis. Once I knew about Stillwater, I should have hired some ex–Special Forces guys of my own. If I had, you never would have gotten hurt."

Phyllis gave her a gentle smile. "It's not your fault. At all. I knew Stillwater a lot better than you, and I never recommended bringing in reinforcements. To be honest, I wanted to take them on myself. That's my fault, not yours."

"That's nice of you to say, but—"

"No *buts*," Phyllis said. "Don't blame yourself. And I really do appreciate your coming in here and chatting about something other than my back. I was getting very, very tired of talking about nothing but physical therapy and what they keep calling 'mobility options' and stuff like that. They've already given me four catalogs of electric chairs," she said with a glance at a pile of glossy brochures on her bedside table. "This is a nice change of pace."

"Well, if you'd like, I'd be happy to help you pick out a chair when you're ready," Andrea said. "Maybe a fun red one with a basket for Nutmeg," referring to Phyllis's dog.

Phyllis smiled. "That would be great—especially if you bring some of those quadruple chocolate cookies you made for my book club last year."

"Of course," Andrea said. "I've been looking for an excuse to bake those again. But I didn't mean to make you talk about 'mobility options.'" She turned to Leigh. "You were saying something about Biosolutions—how is that nice Mr. Rubinelli doing?"

"I'm not sure," Leigh replied. "I've talked to him for maybe five minutes total since the police raided Biosolutions. I think he's been in crisis mode pretty much nonstop. His boss is in jail. So is their chief science officer and about half a dozen other people. The company might even get indicted. They've hired outside counsel to handle the investigation, but Daniel is still their lawyer—and also a key prosecution witness against them. He's in an absolutely surreal position. I feel sorry for him. You might want to make him some cookies."

"I'd be happy to," Andrea said. "I'll bet he likes oatmeal-chocolate-chip-walnut. He looks like the type. By the way, speaking of people in absolutely surreal positions, is there any news about Anya Rhodes?"

CHAPTER 79

Anya woke. The sun shone on her face, warm and bright. She opened her eyes, blinked, and looked around.

She was in what appeared to be a hospital room. A nice hospital room. An overstuffed red leather armchair and matching ottoman sat next to the bedside table. Fresh flowers on the table filled the room with a faint perfume. Crisp, fresh sheets covered the bed, brilliant white in the light pouring in through the window. Outside, she could see the top of a rosebush. Best of all, there were no restraints on her arms, legs, or waist.

She sat up, grunting with surprise and pain when she did. Her insides felt like they were full of razors.

A thirtyish woman with her hair back hurried in. "Oh, you're awake already! I'll let the doctors know. Please lie down—you've been through a lot. My name is Janet and I'm one of the nurses. I'll go get the doctor."

Anya lay back, wondering just how much they knew about what she had been through. Her eyes fell on the flowers. A lovely arrangement of mixed roses. And there was a card. She picked it up and read: "Dear Anya, I hope you have a speedy and full recovery. Please call me when you feel ready to talk. We have much to discuss. Very truly yours, Fred Stein." There was a number under his name.

Fred Stein. How did he know she was here? And where was he now?

Her train of thought was interrupted when Janet came in, accompanied by an older woman in a white coat, who gave Anya a friendly smile. "Hello, Ms. Rhodes, my name is Liz Sykes, and I'm one of the doctors who have been taking care of you since the police brought you in. I'm sure you have lots of questions, but there's one very important thing I want to tell you first: you're safe. The people who kidnapped you and hurt you are all in prison."

"That's a relief," Anya said. "What did they do to me?"

Dr. Sykes's face grew serious. "We're not entirely sure. It looks like you were subjected to numerous illegal surgeries—mostly laparoscopies and endoscopies designed to take biopsies from various organs. But confirming that would require more surgeries to examine the sites where biopsies may have been taken. We haven't done that, of course." She paused and her smile returned. "How are you feeling?"

"Not too bad, as long as I don't move."

Dr. Sykes nodded. "The less you move, the better. You should make a full recovery, but you need rest. You've got some healing to do, and we wouldn't want to risk any internal bleeding." She touched Janet lightly on the arm. "If you need help going to the bathroom or anything else, just push the call button at the head of your bed and a nurse will come right in."

Janet nodded and pointed out the door. "The nursing station is right outside."

"Thank you," Anya said. "You mentioned that the police arrested the people who held me prisoner. I never knew who they were or where they were holding me."

"They worked for a company called Biosolutions," Dr. Sykes replied. "I believe they kept you in the basement of one of their buildings."

"I see." So it was Elijah's company. She remembered going to events at Biosolutions before her health deteriorated. They had an annual picnic where smiling executives in aprons served bratwursts and hamburgers to their employees. Once they held a dinner honoring Elijah for inventing a drug that saved thousands of lives and earned the company billions of dollars. Anya had met at least a dozen top corporate leaders from Biosolutions over the years. They had struck her as good and respectable people. She wondered which of them had ordered that she be used as a human lab experiment.

"The police would like to talk to you when you feel up for it," Dr. Sykes said. "I've told them that you need rest, and they've been understanding."

"Thank you." Anya paused and gave a slightly embarrassed smile. "Before I talk to them, would it be possible to get some clothes? I feel a little awkward wearing nothing but a hospital gown."

"Of course," Janet said. "Is there someone who could bring you what you need?"

"I'm afraid there isn't," Anya said, tinging her voice with sadness that she didn't have to feign. "I don't live nearby. Would it be possible for someone to buy something very cheap and simple? I promise to pay for it when I can get to an ATM, of course."

"We'd be happy to," Janet said.

Anya gave her sizes and found herself stifling a yawn before she was through.

"We'll let you relax," Dr. Sykes said. "By the way, are you hungry? I don't think you've had anything to eat for quite some time."

"Now that you mention it, I am," Anya replied.

"I'll have a tray sent up. Eat slowly—your stomach is out of practice."

Janet and Dr. Sykes left and Anya closed her eyes.

When she opened them again, her room was dark. A tray sat on her bedside table with a covered plate and a plastic cup of water with cellophane stretched across the top. A Target bag was on the chair.

She opened the bag and found leggings, two T-shirts, a sweatshirt, undergarments, socks, and slip-on sneakers. Perfect. She dressed quickly without turning on the light. She looked wistfully at the tray, but decided she didn't have time.

She took the card from the flowers, walked around to the window, and looked out. As she hoped, the room was on the ground floor. She opened the window as quietly as she could and slipped out, taking care not to step in the rosebush.

Then she stepped into the shadows and limped off into the night.

Chapter 80

March

Leigh shivered and took a sip from a cup of hot spiced cider, taking care not to burn her tongue. Andrea sat across a small wooden table, nursing a steaming cup of whipped-cream-topped cocoa and complaining about the weather. Outside the window of the coffee shop, a cold wind blew down Market Street, carrying a chill mist that was halfway between fog and rain. Even ten minutes after coming inside, Leigh still hadn't completely warmed up.

She let out a happy sigh as the hot cider slid down her throat. When she first moved to California, Leigh used to scoff at the natives for complaining about fifty-degree weather in December. *If it can't kill you, it's not bad weather,* she would say. *There's no such thing as bad weather, just bad clothes* had been another favorite of hers. But since then her blood had thinned and she had bought a lot of bad clothes. So now she sat huddled next to a heating vent, gripping a paper cup with both hands, and wishing she had worn something more substantial than a dress and a too-thin denim jacket.

"Five years ago, I'd be mocking you right now," she said.

"But you've grown as a person," Andrea replied. "Now you understand that if we're going to have to be this cold, we should at least be skiing."

"Not that I've ever gone skiing," Leigh said.

"How come?" Andrea asked. "It's lots of fun."

Leigh watched the water bead on the outside of the window and run down in little rivulets. "I had other things on my mind."

Andrea nodded. "Like making partner by thirty-one, the billion-dollar club by thirty-five, and having your name on the door by forty, right?"

"Exactly, and winning every case I got, no matter how bad it was."

"And you've done it," Andrea said. "Congratulations! To your success." She lifted her cup in a toast.

"Thanks," Leigh said as she tapped her cup against Andrea's. "But I wonder whether maybe . . ." Her voice trailed off as the thought failed to take concrete shape in her mind. "I don't know. Maybe I should have learned to ski or something."

Andrea chuckled. "If you had, you'd be spending eighty hours a week training and you'd have a wall full of medals. And you'd probably be wondering whether maybe you should have gone to law school or something."

Leigh laughed. "Yeah, I guess you're right. I'm not too good at the whole hobby thing. Everything in my life has to have a point. If it's not worth putting on my résumé, it's not worth doing." She paused. "Maybe that's not quite the right approach."

Andrea looked surprised. "That's not what you thought last year."

Leigh shrugged and touched her right shoulder, which now bore a jagged pink scar that was still tender. "Getting shot changed my perspective, I guess."

"I can imagine."

"Or maybe my perspective started to change before that," Leigh said, thinking back. "Right before we started running from those Stillwater guys, I was having lunch with Daniel. We were talking about how we wound up in our jobs, and he said he went to Biosolutions because his mom died from cancer. So he quit his big firm job and went to work for a company that fights cancer."

"Impressive," Andrea commented.

Leigh nodded. "Next to that, being a Rising Star with a lot of wins on my résumé didn't seem like such a big deal. And it seemed like an even smaller deal when we were hiding in a cabin in Oregon."

"I'll bet," Andrea said. "What was it like up there? You've never told me what happened."

Leigh shrugged. "Most of the time, nothing happened. Bruno went up on a hill and worked on his computer. Daniel and I took turns watching from the coast and sleeping."

An inquisitive light came into Andrea's eyes. "So it was really you and Daniel alone in the woods? I didn't know about that."

Leigh felt herself blush and took a long sip of her cider so she could hide behind the cup. "That's not how it was," she said, looking down into her cup and fiddling with a cinnamon stick. "One of us was watching for bad guys and the other one was back in the cabin. We were almost never together."

"It wasn't the least bit romantic?" Andrea persisted.

Leigh remembered that last night, sitting with Daniel in the moonlight. Him drawing her. That seemed so far away now. And it *was* far away—they had been on the run, unsure whether they would survive. Now they were back in the real world. Daniel was coping with a corporate crisis that he couldn't talk about, so they had barely spoken in the last two weeks, even though they had a case management conference coming up. And she didn't know what would happen when their paths crossed again in the real world. But she still had his drawing. It sat in a dresser drawer in her apartment. It was stained, creased, and crumpled from their flight, but she had no intention of throwing it away. Or telling Andrea about it.

"Trust me," she said. "Nothing is romantic when you haven't showered for three days."

CHAPTER 81

Bruno looked around Daniel's new fifteenth-floor office and whistled through his teeth. "Not bad, Danny Boy. How exactly did you score this?"

"After Sandy and our CSO got arrested, the board was afraid the company would get indicted too. They needed to do something to show the government that they were taking steps to make sure nothing like this ever happened again. So they created a new C-level position for ethics and compliance."

"And they picked *you*?" Bruno asked, his voice incredulous. "They must not know you cheat at poker."

"Hey, you having a terrible poker face is not the same thing as me cheating."

"Yeah. Sure." Bruno stared into space for a moment. "Maybe it's not that crazy, now that I think about it. They need someone they can prove wasn't part of the problem. Not an outsider who'll come in and try to change how the company does everything. Probably should be a lawyer. So you."

Daniel nodded. "Yeah, that's basically what they said. And to show the government they were serious about this new position, they figured they had to give me a serious-looking office."

"Uh-huh," Bruno said as he strolled around the office. He stopped in front of Daniel's framed Notre Dame poster. "If they were going for a serious look, why'd they let you hang this thing?"

"They make me take it down when I have serious guests."

Bruno grinned at the implied dig. "Nicely played, cuz." He walked over to one of Daniel's guest chairs and flopped down. "I'm guessing that you didn't ask me to come out here just so you could show off your new office. What's up?"

"A couple of things. First, Rich Johnson and Dr. Stein. We need to decide what we're going to do about them."

Bruno shrugged. "Not sure there's much to do. Your IT guys patched the hole that let them into your e-mail system, and they haven't tried to hack back in. Nothing ties Stein or Johnson to Anya's kidnapping, so the police and FBI aren't interested in finding them. And whatever they were doing in that old Berkeley building is over. An SUV left the building on the same day the police raided Biosolutions, and it's empty now. There's been no sign of either Rich or Stein in California since then. The SUV's plate popped up in Fort Collins, Colorado, two weeks later when someone sold it—probably one of them, though neither of their names was on the vehicle title, of course. I've still got facial recognition software looking for them around the Bay Area, but no hits. I think they're gone."

Daniel brooded on that for moment. It bothered him that they were still out there and that he didn't know where they were or what they were doing. But there wasn't much he could do about it. Plus, he had bigger issues to worry about.

"What about Anya Rhodes?" Daniel asked.

"Disappeared from the hospital where the police took her. Then she took out as much money as she could before she hit the ATM withdrawal limits. She must have gone back to her apartment to get the ATM card, but she's not living there. And wherever she *is* living, she's not showing her face." Bruno held his hands palm up. "We may have seen the last of her too."

Daniel shook his head. "Not while we have Rhodes's hard drive. And that's the main thing I wanted to talk to you about. The CEO and a few of the board members are asking about it. They know something about what's on there, but not the details. Since I'm the new ethics and compliance officer, they want a recommendation from me on what the company should do."

Bruno cocked his head. "And you're coming to me for advice? Aren't there, like, medical or legal ethics rules or something?"

"Oh, sure," Daniel said. "There are all sorts of ethical rules and compliance best practices. I'm just starting to discover how many there are. But none of them covers a situation like this. Not by a long shot."

Bruno nodded thoughtfully. "Yeah, I can see why maybe this kind of thing doesn't come up too often."

"So what do you think?"

Bruno was silent for a moment, then shook his head. "I don't know, man. The whole world would change. Not sure whether that's good or bad."

"Shouldn't we let people make up their own minds?" Daniel asked. "If they want to never get old, they can take the Enoch treatment. If they want to live normal lives and die at eighty or ninety, they can do that."

"Normal lives? Nothing would be normal anymore. The world would be run by the people who live forever, right? How many CEOs or presidents or prime ministers resign if they don't have to? And what will they do afterwards? If you're twenty-five forever, you can't really retire permanently, and you won't want to."

"Is that a bad thing?" Daniel countered. "I'd like to live in a world where Mother Teresa and Nelson Mandela never got old and died."

"How about Josef Stalin and Attila the Hun?"

"Just imagine the advances in science and technology," Daniel persisted. "Think of Einstein, Newton, and Hawking all working together."

Bruno shook his head. "They wouldn't work together. They'd all be arguing and trying to prove the pet theory they had when they were twenty-five. Trust me, I know a lot more geeks than you do. Old guys never come up with anything really new. At best, they come up with new twists on ideas they had when they were young." He paused. "Then there's the whole overpopulation angle. Almost no one could have kids. Can you imagine what it would be like to enforce that law, how ugly it would get?"

Daniel regarded his cousin in silence for a second. "So you think I should recommend that we lock that hard drive in a basement closet somewhere and throw away the key? We sentence everyone on Earth to die of old age just because the alternative has some issues?"

Bruno shook his head. "Not what I said, dude. I said I wasn't sure whether Enoch would be good or bad. And that's all I'm saying." He paused. "So what do *you* think?"

Daniel thought for a long moment, then slowly shook his head. "I'm not sure."

CHAPTER 82

Leigh's desk phone rang and Daniel's office number appeared. She pushed the speakerphone button. "Hi, Daniel. What's up?"

"I just got chewed out by Judge Bovarnick's clerk for not filing a case management statement for our conference with the judge on Thursday."

"That was due last week."

"I know," he said. "I've been distracted. Anyway, the clerk wants a joint statement from us by tomorrow morning. And he specifically mentioned that we should include a section on settlement negotiations."

"Did you mention that our last negotiating session ended with a slow-motion car chase?"

He laughed. "It slipped my mind. I'll make sure to include that."

"Is there anything else you want to include?" she asked.

"Like what?"

"Like your response to our offer."

The line was silent for a heartbeat. "Oh, that's right. I'd forgotten the ball was in my court. What was it you offered—thirty million?"

"Nice try. Twenty."

"Really? Huh. Well, if you say so. The case would be easier to settle if you were at thirty, though."

Leigh smiled. She had authority from American Guaranty to pay as much as sixty million if she had to—but she didn't intend to have to.

Not even for him. These were friendly negotiations, but they were still negotiations. And this was her client's money, not hers.

"I'm not going to negotiate against myself, Daniel," she said.

"But you'll negotiate against eighty million," he said. "I mean, you're a great lawyer, but there's no way you're winning on the building insurance policy. No way at all. And the life insurance policy isn't a slam dunk for you."

Leigh leaned back in her chair and swiveled to look out the window at the twilit San Francisco skyline. This was going to be fun.

CHAPTER 83

"*Biosolutions versus American Guaranty*," Judge Bovarnick's clerk called.

Daniel walked up and took his seat at the table to the left of the lectern while Leigh sat down at the table to the right.

Judge Bovarnick beamed at both of them. "I see that this case has settled for fifty million dollars."

Daniel stood. "Yes, Your Honor." He had felt a little guilty about negotiating so hard with Leigh, but it was Biosolutions' money, not his. So he couldn't just settle for his bottom line, which had been forty million. It had been important for him to get every penny American Guaranty had authorized Leigh to put on the table—and he was pretty sure that he had done so.

"Congratulations to both of you," the judge said, smiling broadly. "I suspected that this case might sort itself out if the lawyers on each side could cooperate and stop sniping at each other."

Daniel nodded. "Thank you, Your Honor. We were able to make a lot of progress once Ms. Collins and I were both aiming our fire at the real problem."

Leigh made a noise between a choke and a cough. Judge Bovarnick looked in her direction.

Leigh got to her feet. "For once I agree with Mr. Rubinelli, Your Honor. After we started working together and stopped running from our problems, a couple of key phone calls made all the difference."

Now it was Daniel's turn to stifle a laugh.

The judge looked a little confused, but she smiled benevolently. "Well, good. I'm glad things went smoothly after my 'play nice' order." She held up the stipulated dismissal they had submitted with the case management statement. "In light of the parties' settlement and in accordance with their agreement, this case is hereby dismissed." She signed the dismissal with a flourish and handed it to the court clerk. "We're done here."

◆ ◆ ◆

"That's the first time opposing counsel made me laugh in court," Leigh said as they walked down the courthouse hall.

"I'm not opposing counsel anymore, remember?" Daniel said as they arrived at the elevator lobby.

"That's true," she said as she pushed the down button. "What do you say we go out to dinner tonight to celebrate not being enemies anymore?"

"Good idea," he replied. The elevator to their left pinged and the doors slid open. "How about the Waterbar?" he said as they stepped in. "It might be fun to actually eat a full meal there."

She gave him a warm smile as the doors closed. "I'd like that."

CHAPTER 84

They sat inside this time, next to an enormous aquarium that rose from the floor of the Waterbar to the ceiling. Angelfish, blue darters, and a living bouquet of other tropical species drifted lazily past, ignoring the humans just outside the glass that enclosed their little world.

Daniel sat opposite Leigh. He wore a white oxford that set off the deep tan he had developed from hours of watching the Oregon coast. He held a glass of pinot noir that he swirled idly as they talked while dining on excellent swordfish steaks. They were chatting about the now-safe topic of the case they had just settled—and the loose ends it had left.

"So how did Dr. Rhodes die?" Leigh asked. "Do you think he committed suicide?"

He shrugged. "It's possible that Rhodes killed himself, but we never found anything indicating that he was depressed or going through a crisis. He was definitely odd, and you might have been able to convince a jury that he was unstable—but that's not the same thing as suicidal. So, no, I don't think he committed suicide. I think he was murdered and the murderer tried to make it look like a suicide."

"Who do you think killed him? Not Anya?" Leigh asked as she speared a bite with her fork.

Daniel shook his head. "She wouldn't kill her own son. If I had to guess—and it is only a guess—I'd say someone else killed him and she found him dead. She didn't like Enoch—and maybe his death was somehow related to it—so she burned down the lab."

"Do you think she knows who killed him?"

He took a sip of his wine and nodded slowly.

She thought she knew who he suspected. "Rich?"

He smiled and gave her a sidelong look. "Now why would you say that?"

"Because he worked in Rhodes's lab, but he was actually spying for Stein. Rhodes and Stein worked together on some papers, so Stein may have known about Enoch—or guessed about it anyway. He sent Rich to steal it. Once Stein got what he wanted, he killed Rhodes to remove a competitor. Or maybe Rhodes caught Rich and threatened to turn him in, so Rich killed Rhodes to protect himself. Either way, Rich is the most likely suspect—if Rhodes was murdered."

He nodded. "That was going to be my theory at trial. The evidence was thin, but it did point that way."

"True." She paused as a new thought occurred to her. "So let's assume Rich killed Dr. Rhodes. Why do you think Anya knew about it?"

"Because I think she's the one who burned down our lab. If that's right, she must have gotten there shortly after Dr. Rhodes died. And the most likely reason for her to be there is that she got a call from him as he was dying. So somebody just injected him with a lethal dose of barbiturates. He knows he's going to die, and he somehow manages to get a message to her. I'm guessing that message included the name of his killer."

She thought about that for a moment. There was a lot of speculation in what he said, but it did make some sense. Some. "Why didn't he dial 911?"

"Maybe he knew they wouldn't be able to save him. He only had time to make one call before he lost consciousness, so he called her." He shrugged and stabbed the last bite on his plate. "Just a guess."

This was an entertaining mental exercise—but it was also a little unnerving. "Hmm. So what's your guess as to what she decided to do—after she burned down the lab, of course?"

"Well, she probably felt she couldn't go to the police, and she may not have wanted to."

Leigh took a sip of her wine. "It wouldn't be the first time she killed an enemy," she observed. "Or the second. Or the third."

Daniel nodded. "Right. I'll bet she planned to deal with Rich and Stein after she got the hard drive and burned Dr. Rhodes's second lab, but she never got the chance."

A little chill went up Leigh's spine. "Until now."

"Yep. Maybe that's the reason all three of them dropped off the grid. The two guys are hiding from her and she's hunting them."

"Or they're dead and she's hiding," Leigh said.

"Also possible," he said. "How likely it is, I don't really know. Bruno or Phyllis may be able to tell us eventually. Speaking of Phyllis, how is she doing?" His face and voice held real concern. "If there's anything I can do to help, please let me know."

"She's doing as well as can be expected—better actually. She's out of the hospital and back at work, zipping around on her little electric cart. There's some stuff she can't do anymore, of course, but she's dead set on keeping her agency going."

"Good. I'll see if I can send her some work."

"That would be great. I'm sure she'd appreciate it. By the way, how's Bruno?"

"Fully recovered—and always looking for an excuse to show off his scar and explain how he got it. Apparently, he was saving his helpless cousin and another lawyer from assassins."

She laughed. "Seriously?"

He grinned and shrugged one shoulder. "Sort of. He said the scar and story made him something of a rock star at Comic-Con this year. I'm extrapolating from there."

"By the way, what's Biosolutions going to do with Dr. Rhodes's hard drive?"

Daniel slowly drained his glass and set it down. "How about them Cubbies? They're looking pretty good in spring training," he said with a smile and a wink.

She chuckled. "Okay, fine. Tell me when you can."

"I will," he said more seriously. "After all we've been through, you deserve to know."

The server arrived with the bill, momentarily interrupting their conversation. After a brief negotiation, Leigh agreed to let Daniel pay.

Five minutes later, they were strolling along the Embarcadero. The sun had set and a crescent moon rode high, but the sky still held a hint of deep blue between shreds of dark gray cloud. The slightly odd public art dotting the Embarcadero loomed out of the twilight like the playthings of a giant with surrealist tastes—an enormous bow and arrow half buried in the grass, lights that turned the Bay Bridge's support cables into enormous glow sticks, and so on. Leigh and Daniel weren't the only ones out for an evening stroll or jog, but the path was mostly empty.

She decided this was as good a time as any to pop the surprise she'd been sitting on for the past few days. "By the way, I lined up opening-day seats for you and your dad. Have you ever seen a game from a Wrigley Rooftop?" she asked, referring to the elaborate seating built on the roofs of some of the taller buildings surrounding Wrigley Field.

He stopped and turned to her. "You really did that? I thought we were just joking around."

She shook her head firmly. "Opening day is never a joke in Wrigleyville. Do you still need tickets?"

"Uh, yeah. Thanks. I was afraid I was going to have to pay a scalper two hundred bucks each for obstructed view seating or something. I've never seen a game from a rooftop, but I've heard some of them can be great."

"This one is," she said. "Excellent view from Sheffield Avenue, leather armchair seating with umbrellas, complimentary—and first-rate—food and drink menu, servers bring your orders to your seat. It's a real VIP experience."

He nodded appreciatively. "That's awesome. Dad will love it." He hesitated. "How much is it going to set me back?"

"Nothing. My parents are part owners of the building. Our treat."

She wished she could pull out her phone and snap a picture of the expression on his face. The mixture of surprise, joy, and gratitude was just what she'd hoped for. "That's . . . wow, that's very generous. But I can't accept. Those seats must be worth a thousand dollars on opening day."

"We insist," she said, putting a hand on his arm. "Seriously. They insist. I insist. The seats are reserved in your name. It's happening."

"I . . ." For a second, she thought he was going to keep arguing, but instead he simply smiled and looked into her eyes. "That's really, really nice. Thank you. I owe you one."

"No, I've owed you one ever since our visit to Ratopia. Now we're even."

Her heartbeat quickened when she saw the look in his eyes—the same look he had given her in Oregon, just before Stillwater interrupted them. But this time there was no uncertainty in his gaze. He took her in his arms and kissed her.

CHAPTER 85

April

The seats were everything Leigh had promised. Most Wrigley Rooftops featured hard folding seats similar to those in the ballpark, but the one part-owned by Leigh's parents had a luxury section that was like a cross between an upscale sports bar and a living room. Except that it had a view that was way better than any big-screen TV.

The in-seat service was also great. Daniel and Dad had both finished off excellent brats, and a mostly empty plate of stuffed potato skins sat on a little table between them. Daniel was drinking Sierra Nevada Summerfest lager and had tried to get his father to try one. But Dad gave him a slightly scandalized look and said, "We're at a Cubs game. You drink Old Style at a Cubs game." And that's what he did.

Leigh's parents had stopped by before the game to meet them and chat briefly, but they had other guests and soon retreated to their seats a few yards away. Plus, Daniel suspected Leigh had told them that this was a father-son bonding time rather than simply a day at the ballgame.

By the sixth inning, the Cubs were ahead by four runs and the crowd, including the Rubinellis, was in high spirits. And then it happened. The Cubs hit a two-run homer and everyone got to their feet to cheer.

Dad's deep roar was cut short by a coughing spasm. He covered his mouth with a big fist, but he couldn't stop. He pulled an inhaler out of his coat pocket, but he couldn't stop coughing long enough to use it.

He bent over and Daniel patted him on the back. Every time he tried to get a breath, the coughing started again.

Dad collapsed into his seat, gasping and almost choking. The useless inhaler clattered onto the table. Their server rushed up and asked if she should call an ambulance. Daniel started to say yes, but Dad shook his head and waved her away.

Finally, mercifully, it stopped. The hacking convulsion eased enough for Dad to use the inhaler. Then he sat back, exhausted and breathing in wheezy gulps. He wiped his mouth with his napkin, ignoring the concerned looks of the fans sitting around them. He cleared his throat, took a sip of his beer, and went back to watching the game.

Daniel slowly slipped back into his seat and turned his eyes to the game, but he wasn't really watching anymore. That was the worst fit he had seen Dad have. The COPD was killing him. Despite the shots, the pills, the doctor visits, and the inhaler, it was still inexorably getting worse. And even without the COPD, the men in his family generally died in their seventies from something—cancer, heart attack, stroke.

Would Enoch help? COPD hit older people hardest and it made age-related conditions like high blood pressure worse. So maybe having younger, healthier cells would reverse it. Could Biosolutions put together the pieces of Dr. Rhodes's research fast enough to save Dad?

Daniel remembered his father when he was younger and healthier. Even ten years ago, he had been a bull of a man, full of life and health and energy. What Daniel wouldn't give to have those days back.

"This is terrific," Dad said. His voice was a little rough, but strong.

"What's terrific?" Daniel asked.

"This," Dad said, waving an arm at the rooftop around them. "That," he said, now pointing to the game. "All of it. What a great day."

"It's great to be here with you."

"It is," Dad said, clapping a hand on Daniel's shoulder. "I'm glad you could come out. And this place is fantastic. This is the way to see a ball game."

"It is," Daniel agreed. "I'm going to reserve these same seats for next year, except this time I'm going to insist on paying."

"You're a good boy, Danny, taking care of your old man like this." He sighed with contentment. "Ah, I could do this forever."

"Could you?" Daniel asked.

"Sure. There's nothing like having a good time with my son and watching the Cubs win on opening day. This is special."

"But would you want to do it forever?"

Dad gave him a confused look. "What do you mean?"

Daniel hadn't told his father about Enoch, so he chose his words carefully. "I was just thinking about how we've been coming here since I was a kid, and how much fun it could be if we could keep doing it forever—especially if you were, you know, healthy again. We could be watching the Cubs together a century from now. Who knows how many times they'll win the World Series now that they broke the Curse of the Billy Goat."

Dad chuckled, low and gravelly. "The optimism of youth." Then he grew more serious. "You're worried about me, aren't you?"

"No," Daniel lied. "You look great. You're still as strong as a horse. The COPD thing just acts up every now and then, but you're fine five minutes later."

"Nice of you to say that, but we both know it's not true."

Daniel said nothing.

Dad swiped the air with a hand. "Ah, don't let it ruin the game. Days like this are special *because* they don't go on forever. And the fewer of them there are left, the more special they become. You'll learn that as you get older."

Daniel forced a smile. "Well, I hope there are still a lot of them left."

"Me too," Dad said. "But if there aren't . . ." He shrugged. "That's all right too. It means I'm going to see your mom again sooner. And until then, I get to do things like this with you. And I'll treasure every minute." He patted Daniel's knee and smiled. "It's okay."

Daniel smiled back. But it wasn't okay.

CHAPTER 86

Anya slipped into one of the computer carrels at the Mariposa County Library. The library was a lovely little building in a lovely little town nestled into the Sierra Nevada mountains near Yosemite National Park. Many of the buildings dated from the 1800s, and the entire area had an intentionally rustic feel. But not so rustic that the library lacked public computers and Internet.

She liked the town, but she knew that coming here wasn't safe. There were more security cameras and people here, and therefore more risk that she would be spotted. She would have preferred to remain at the Yosemite campground where she had been staying, but that wasn't really an option anymore.

Yosemite had been an excellent base of operation while she recuperated. She could live cheaply and inconspicuously, and she had always enjoyed the outdoors. Her young body healed quickly, and the hundreds of miles of trails gave her plenty of opportunities to regain her stamina and exercise muscles that had gone unused for weeks while she lay unconscious. She wished she could stay.

But she had unfinished business. Elijah's hard drive was probably still in the hands of Daniel or Bruno Rubinelli, and she had no idea what they planned to do with it. Maybe they could be reasoned with; maybe not. She had come up with contingency plans for both options during her weeks of solitude, and now was the time to act. After that, she would deal with Frederick Stein—and she would need to do it quickly. The longer she took, the greater the chance that she would be recaptured—particularly now that she had left the relative safety of the campground.

First, she needed to update her research. A quick Google search told her that a lot had happened since she vanished into the wilderness. Over a dozen people had been arrested, and several of them had already entered guilty pleas. In fact, Biosolutions' former general counsel, whom Anya guessed had been Daniel Rubinelli's superior, just pled guilty to conspiracy and kidnapping charges. Another article reported that Daniel Rubinelli had been promoted to chief ethics and compliance officer, a position that the press release described as "the conscience of the company." How very interesting.

Time to make her first call.

She cleared the computer's search history, got up, and briskly walked to the nearest pay phone. She pulled out the card Daniel had given her when they first met and dialed. Hopefully his number had not changed with his promotion.

It hadn't. He picked up after the third ring. "Daniel Rubinelli."

"Hello, Daniel. It's Anne Smith. Congratulations on your promotion."

The line was silent for a few seconds. "Hello, Anya Rhodes. What can I do for you?"

So he knew. Well, that was hardly a surprise. "It's a matter of conscience, and as you are now the conscience of the company, I thought you might be able to help me. Elijah Rhodes's hard drive and all of his Enoch research must be destroyed. I will be happy to explain why."

More silence. Then, "I'll listen. But only in person."

Her stomach muscles clenched. "Why?"

"Partly because I'm on my way out the door and don't have time to talk now. But mostly because I never make big decisions without a face-to-face meeting. It tells me a lot about whether I can trust what I'm being told."

She thought for a moment. "All right. We can meet tomorrow between one and three p.m. in San Francisco. I'll call you thirty minutes in advance with the exact time and location."

"Okay. Call my cell number. Do you have it?"

She looked down at the card, which listed his cell. "Yes. One more thing: you must bring the hard drive."

He didn't answer immediately. "I'll see you tomorrow."

Then he hung up.

She hung up the phone and walked back to the library, slightly nonplussed. He had agreed to hear her out, which was good. She would rather not meet him in person, of course, but his rationale hadn't sounded contrived and he hadn't objected to her ambush-prevention conditions. And more generally, she hadn't gotten the impression that he was trying to set her up somehow. He hadn't tried to keep the phone call going so it could be traced, for example. Quite the opposite—he had rushed to get off the phone and had seemed distracted. And that's what bothered her, she realized. What was on his mind that was more important than Enoch? Had she missed something in her research?

She was back at the computer carrel now, and she was tempted to do a little more digging into what might be going on at Biosolutions or in Daniel's life. But she had a more pressing matter to deal with. Frederick Stein, to be specific.

She had been racking her memory and had reread the card a hundred times, but couldn't place the name. Now she could finally Google him.

The search results came up and she started through them. So he had been a longtime professor at UC Berkeley and had authored papers with Elijah. That explained it. She thought she remembered him now. He had been one of the younger faculty members when Elijah was a graduate student—a slender and handsome man of about forty with bright blue eyes. She liked him, possibly because he had been cordially flirtatious with her. She had been a fifty-year-old widow at the time and had enjoyed the attention.

She smiled at the memory and went hunting for photos of him. She couldn't quite see him in her mind's eye, but she thought she would recognize him—if he were indeed the man she remembered. Most of the search results were impenetrable research papers or patent filings, neither of which had pictures. Finally, she came across an old copy of his faculty biography. The smiling gray-haired professor in the picture was several decades older than the one she remembered. But it was the same man.

Something clicked in her memory and she looked closer at the picture. Then she stared. Her smile vanished and her heart pounded.

CHAPTER 87

Daniel texted Leigh with the news as he rode the elevator down. As soon as the doors opened, he jogged to his car. He had been on his way out the door when Anya called, and he couldn't afford to be late.

He was going to Santa Rita Jail to talk to Sandy. When he made the appointment, the jail staff had been very clear it could be canceled if he was at all late. Sandy was being transferred tomorrow, so this was effectively his last chance to visit her.

Daniel hadn't seen her since the day he told her that Bruno had discovered that Anya had been kidnapped by Stillwater and that he was hacking into Stillwater's files. According to the police, Sandy had called Stillwater as soon as Daniel left her office. Hours later, they shot Phyllis and tried to kill Bruno.

The DA had asked Daniel to testify at Sandy's trial. Daniel had agreed. He had been both dreading and looking forward to taking the stand. It would be difficult and painful, but he had wanted to confront her in court. To look her in the face and tell what happened. And after he had testified, he would sit in the gallery and listen to as much of the rest of the case as he could. He doubted that Sandy would testify, but he wanted to hear the whole truth—not just the little snippets that the DA had been willing to share.

But then she pled guilty. The evidence against her had been strong, and it got stronger when several of the Stillwater defendants agreed to testify against her and Dr. Gupta in return for lighter sentences. Once her trial was canceled, there was no longer any reason to keep her at Santa Rita, so the California Department of Corrections promptly scheduled her for transfer.

When Daniel heard the news, part of him had been tempted to simply let her go and say good riddance. But he knew that he needed to talk to her first. To find out why she did what she did.

He pulled into the visitor lot and hurried inside. He went through a previsit security check and surrendered his cell phone. Then he was ushered into the visiting room and directed to a seat facing a large window. A dingy phone handset hung from the wall beside the window.

The seat on the other side of the window was empty when Daniel sat down, but a minute later, Sandy walked in. She looked tired, small, and old. In place of her perfectly tailored professional suits and heels, she wore a baggy blue prison uniform and floppy flat shoes. Her hair was pulled back in a ponytail, and he could see the gray roots as she sat down. She wore no makeup, and her face was pale and lined.

Daniel picked up the phone and Sandy did the same. For a moment, neither of them spoke. Then Sandy said, "I'm sorry."

"So am I," Daniel said. "What happened? Why did you do it?"

"I . . . First, I want you to know that I never meant to hurt you."

"Did you mean to hurt Phyllis? And Bruno? And Leigh?" he asked, hearing the cold anger in his voice.

Her eyes hardened and the lines around her mouth tightened. "I never meant to hurt anyone. None of us did, except maybe those gunslingers from Stillwater. No, all we wanted to do was get control of what was left of Dr. Rhodes's research. His death was a tremendous setback. The fire was another. And then his laptop was stolen. We were just trying to gather the pieces that were left before someone else could destroy them too."

"Is that why you hired Stillwater?"

She nodded heavily. "We thought that Rhodes's death and the fire might be industrial espionage, and we were sure the theft of his laptop was. So we brought in Stillwater to do some digging and provide security. I didn't tell you because . . ." She sighed and shook her head slightly. "It was a mistake. Dr. Rhodes's geriatrics research was Biosolutions' most valuable secret. We kept it on a need-to-know basis, and you didn't need to know. Your insurance case was separate from what they were doing, so I didn't say anything. Stillwater handles a lot of sensitive and high-profile matters, so I didn't monitor them as closely as I should have. And we wanted to make sure they were motivated to work hard for us, so we promised them a large bonus if they could retrieve all of Dr. Rhodes's research quickly and quietly. But if I had known what they would do, I never would have hired them." She paused. "I'm sorry."

"And what about Anya Rhodes?"

She rubbed her eyes. "Another mistake. The Stillwater guys were still at Rhodes's second lab changing the tires on their car when she came back. They didn't see her until after she set that fire. That was another big blow, of course. But they caught her as she was leaving, and we knew she had been responsible for the other fire and the laptop. It seemed only fitting that she might be able to help us rebuild what she had destroyed."

"Fitting?" He stared at her. "You kept her unconscious in a basement and cut pieces out of her. You think that's fitting?"

She pressed her lips together and looked away for a moment. Then her gaze locked on his. "You have to put this in perspective, Daniel. You're young, so I know that's hard. It was hard for me when I was your age. You don't understand what it's like to have nothing to look forward to except growing old and dying."

She smiled grimly. "I've fought the calendar as hard as I can, but the calendar always wins in the end. Or it did until Elijah Rhodes discovered how to beat it. Now the calendar doesn't have to win. Now we can all be like Anya Rhodes. Imagine a world where everyone is young and healthy forever. Or we could be if she didn't keep the secret to herself. That was incredibly selfish of her. So since she wasn't willing to help us—help all of humanity—voluntarily, we . . . made her. As I said, what we did was a mistake, but it was a mistake she forced us to make."

She leaned forward and an eager, almost hungry, look came into her face. "And because we made that mistake—that unfortunately necessary mistake—you don't have to. You can finish the work. The tissue samples we took should still be in the freezer. And you still have the hard drive, right?"

He sat in shocked silence, unable to quite believe what she was saying. The fevered hope in her eyes vanished and her face went as neutral and blank as a closed door.

"I don't know you anymore," he said. "Maybe I never knew you."

CHAPTER 88

Leigh's cell phone buzzed on her desk and Daniel's smiling face appeared on the screen. It was the same picture she had Photoshopped onto undead hordes just eight months ago. She needed to get a different one, preferably of her and Daniel doing something fun together. But that would have to wait until they actually *did* something fun together. They hadn't had time since The Kiss. Both of them had been working twelve-hour days since then—except for Daniel's trip to Chicago, of course. And it didn't help that they worked thirty miles away from each other, so having lunch together or grabbing a cup of coffee wasn't really an option.

But at least they could text and call a few times a day, which they did. Actually, Leigh had done both more than a few times over the past hour and a half since she got his message about Anya.

She answered his call. "About time. You can't just send a text like that and then go silent."

She expected a chuckle and a snappy comeback, but instead he said, "I'm sorry. I've been at the Santa Rita Jail and they took my phone. I'm sitting in my car in the parking lot right now."

Oh, yeah. He'd mentioned that he was going to be saying good-bye to his former boss today. Maybe that was a bigger deal than she had assumed. "Don't worry about it," she said in a gentler and more serious tone. "How did it go?"

He sighed. "Not well. I wanted to hear her side of the story. And when I did, it was a shock."

"What did she say?"

"Basically, that she was sorry and she didn't mean to hurt anyone. They hired Stillwater because they needed security after Anya burned down the lab and stole the laptop. She didn't realize what they would do."

That didn't sound particularly shocking to Leigh. Lame and self-exculpatory certainly, but basically what she would have expected. But then she hadn't worked with this woman. She would have been horrified if Jack Diamond did something similar, and she got the impression that Daniel and his boss had been pretty tight.

"Were you two close?" she asked.

"Yeah," he said, sounding tired. "I looked up to her, respected her. She was a role model for me." He was silent for a heartbeat. "I trusted her."

Ouch. "I'm sorry. That must really hurt."

"Thanks. I just . . . maybe I should have seen it coming, but I didn't. It's still hard to believe that at the same time she was joking around with me in her office, she had Anya Rhodes locked in a basement."

"Did she say anything about Anya?" Leigh asked.

"She said that Enoch was so important that it justified everything." He paused. "And it wasn't just what she said, but how she said it. When she talked about Enoch, there was this look in her face like Gollum when he saw the One Ring."

He took a short breath and blew it out. He went on in a brisk, businesslike tone. "Speaking of Anya, let's talk about tomorrow. Would you like to come?"

"Of course!"

"I thought you might." She could hear the smile in his voice. "Since we're going to be meeting her in San Francisco, I should be downtown.

Do you have an empty office or conference room I could work in while we're waiting for her to call?"

"Sure. What do you think she's going to do?"

"She *says* she just wants to talk," he replied with a dry chuckle. "But the last time we talked with her about the hard drive, the conversation began with her pulling a gun on Bruno."

"So where will the hard drive be this time?"

"With Bruno in a safe location. She wanted me to bring it, but there's no way I'm going to do that."

"Of course not," she said. "Any other guesses about what will happen tomorrow?"

"Nope, but I bet it will be interesting."

CHAPTER 89

Anya's call came at one thirty. "Meet me at Schroeder's at two o'clock," she said. "Do you know it?"

"I do." It was private enough that they wouldn't be overheard, but public enough that she presumably wouldn't try to mug them.

"Remember to bring the hard drive."

"We'll see you at two."

"We? Who else is coming?"

"Leigh Collins."

She was silent for a moment. "That is acceptable."

The line went dead.

Daniel put away the new lab proposal he had been trying to read for the past hour. He walked down the hall to Leigh's office, dialing Bruno's cell as he went. Bruno answered just as Daniel knocked on Leigh's door. "Showtime," he said to both of them. "We're meeting her at two at Schroeder's. It's about five blocks from here."

"So let's get there early," Leigh said.

Daniel nodded. "Does that work for you, B?" he said into the phone.

"No problem. I'll be ready."

Ten minutes later, Leigh and Daniel walked into Schroeder's. It was a cavernous old place with rathskeller-style seating, German-themed murals, and a complicated layout that made it hard to see all the seats from the door. Daniel scanned the interior for a moment, then saw Anya watching them from a table in a corner of the restaurant by the front window, a small smile on her face. A coffee cup and a half-finished piece of heavy-looking chocolate cake sat in front of her. Her left hand was on the table, her right somewhere beneath it.

Daniel and Leigh walked over. "Sorry to interrupt your meal," Daniel said.

"Not at all," she said. "I thought you might be early." She gestured to the chairs around the table. "Please sit down."

They did. Once they were seated, Daniel put his phone on the table and said, "I'm very sorry about what Biosolutions did to you. I had no idea what was happening. If I knew, I would have found a way to stop it."

"I believe you," Anya said. "If I didn't, we wouldn't be meeting."

"How are you doing?" Leigh asked. "Have you recovered?"

Anya nodded. "Thank you for asking. Yes, I am quite well. If I wasn't, we also wouldn't be having this meeting."

"You said you wanted to discuss Enoch," Daniel said. "I'm listening."

"Did you bring the hard drive?"

He shook his head. "It tends to attract guns, so no."

She frowned and appeared to do a swift mental calculation. "That's unfortunate. However, it's still important that we speak."

Daniel nodded. "I agree. So tell us what you have to say."

"All right." She thought for a moment. "I suppose the best place to start is when Elijah discovered that his new gene therapy had some unexpected side effects. I don't know the details, but he had developed a new technique that was supposed to cure cancers by fixing the problems that made the cells multiply out of control. His new technique did that, but it did something else too. The organism's cells stopped aging, so the organism did too."

She smiled. "He was so excited. He had been looking for a drug that cured cancer. Instead, he discovered something that cured old age and even death—or at least it did in rats. Then he got permission to try it on cats. When he did, the drug stopped some tumors, but it caused others. He asked for permission to experiment with dogs, and again the company gave it to him. But the drug caused the same problem in dogs that it did in cats. In fact, it was worse. It caused far more tumors than it cured."

Daniel had seen a hint of this in Dr. Rhodes's personnel file. "So they cut him off, right?"

She sighed and nodded. "The company stopped his experiments until he could fix the problem. He went back to his lab to find out what was going on. He worked very hard, so hard it worried me. I would call at eleven at night and he would be there. Then I would call at six the next morning, and he would still be there. He wouldn't even realize that he had worked through the night. Finally, he found the problem—or he thought he had. Cats and dogs share a lot of genes with each other that humans and monkeys do not have. One of those genes was interacting with the drug to cause cancer."

Her smile returned, though it was touched with regret. "He was so happy. When he was working on a problem, he could be very intense. Even I didn't want to be with him sometimes. But when he was happy, he was like a big puppy. He had to share his happiness. He needed to tell everybody right away about the thing that had made him happy. So that's what he did—he went straight to the Biosolutions executives. They were having a meeting, and he just walked in and started talking to them. I don't think he even bothered to shave or change out of the old sweatpants and T-shirt he wore in his lab."

"Did they let him work with monkeys after that?" Leigh asked.

Anya shook her head. "They wanted to see all his research, have it verified by other scientists who worked for the company. Elijah said no.

He thought they were trying to steal his discovery, take it away from him and give it to someone they liked better."

Daniel leaned forward. "So, what did he do then? Is that when he created his second lab?"

Anya shrugged. "Perhaps. I didn't know about that until you told me. All I know is that he became very frustrated—and secretive."

"Did he ask you to help him?" Leigh said.

The regret in Anya's face and voice deepened. "Actually, I volunteered. I hated to see him like that, unhappy and boxed in. He was a brilliant scientist, and I so much wanted him to be successful and happy. Besides, I had little to lose. I had cancer, slow growing but inoperable. I also had osteoporosis, cataracts, and arthritis that was so bad I could barely walk. In a word, I was dying slowly. If Elijah's drug killed me quickly, so be it." She gave a dry chuckle. "My only real fear was that stopping my cells from aging would also slow down my death. Little did I know."

She looked down into her coffee. "He came to my apartment one night after my nurse had gone home. He had a bag full of needles, some of them quite long so they could reach internal organs. He gave me at least twenty injections all over my body." She gave a vague shrug without looking up. "Then he did other things that I don't remember clearly. It hurt, but I was used to pain—older people with health problems usually are."

She grimaced. "The pain got worse. Soon everything hurt, even the places he hadn't given me shots. He gave me a painkiller and a sedative, and I must have fallen asleep or passed out. The next thing I knew, it was morning. Elijah was still there, sitting by my bed. I don't know if he slept at all. 'Mom, how do you feel?' he asked me. I told him I felt fine, better than I had for days, in fact. I was still sore from all of the shots, but other than that I felt wonderful. He gave me a quick checkup and then left before my nurse arrived."

"Was the nurse surprised to see you like this?" Leigh made a sweeping gesture that captured everything from Anya's lustrous jet-black hair to her lithe legs. "What did she say?"

"Oh, I didn't look like this," Anya said with a little laugh. "Not at first. I just felt better. I had more energy during the day and slept better at night. Then I noticed that my eyes were getting better and I could go down the hall without a walker. My appetite came back and I didn't have as much trouble hearing conversations around me. When I noticed that the roots of my hair were black, I began to realize the full extent of what was happening to me."

She sighed and smiled. "At first, it was wonderful. I could take walks in Golden Gate Park again. I went to the symphony and ate at all my favorite restaurants. I could read a book without my hands hurting. I didn't even need large-print editions anymore. I could live on my own without a nurse."

"It sounds idyllic," Daniel said. "What was the problem?"

"After a couple of weeks, Elijah said, 'You know, we'll have to hide you.' Once he said it, I realized it was true, of course. I couldn't possibly keep living like I was, under my old name and in my old apartment. People would start asking questions. Already I was getting strange looks."

She looked into her coffee. "So Elijah rented a new apartment for me in a different part of town. After about six months, I looked like I do now. He set up a trust to pay all the bills. That worked for ten years. Until you found me."

"But that was only a problem because you were the only one like this," Daniel countered. "If everyone in the world could get Enoch treatments, then you wouldn't have to live in hiding."

"True," Anya said.

"That would be a pretty amazing world, don't you think?" Daniel said, watching her reaction closely. Her body language made him suspect that she had been less than completely honest in describing the Enoch treatments, but the rest of her story rang true. So far.

"That's what Elijah thought," Anya said, a frown twisting the corners of her mouth. "After his success with me, he renamed his research Project Enoch after the Enoch in the Bible who never died, but went straight to heaven."

"But you disagreed," he observed.

She nodded. "Elijah and I argued often over the years. To live forever is . . . well, it's not heaven. I got close enough to the real thing to know the difference. I was months, maybe weeks, from leaving this world behind. I was ready. I still am ready. By the time Elijah gave me those injections, most of the people I cared about had already left. I had done everything I wanted to do, seen everything I wanted to see." She paused and a yearning look came into her face. "No, that's not true. There was still one thing I desperately wanted to do. I wanted to see the face of God. I had caught glimpses of eternity—hints, really—from time to time. An Easter sunrise when I was a child. A Christmas night years later when I was in the Italian Alps with the man I would marry. The sky was so deep I felt I could look straight into the heart of the universe. A few years after that, holding Elijah in my arms for the first time."

Anya's eyes lost their focus as she wandered in memories. "As I got closer to death, I began to see these moments for what they were: postcards from heaven. All I wanted to do was go there, to be with God and to begin the next chapter of my life with Him."

She came back from wherever she had been and looked at them. "Have you ever been just about to leave on a trip you have looked forward to for a long time? You're all packed, the reservations have been confirmed, maybe you're even already at the airport or the dock, waiting to board. Then the trip is canceled at the last minute. That's how I felt, how I still feel. Now I may be here for a thousand years. Do you understand?" Her eyes darted back and forth, pleading with Leigh and Daniel. "Tell me you understand."

Leigh nodded. "You'll spend the rest of your life on the run from people who want to make you a lab rat again."

"If I'm lucky. If we're all lucky." Anya looked at them with an intensity that drilled into Daniel. "If we aren't, someone will manage to finish Elijah's work. They'll take that hard drive and pick up where he left off. Except they won't be just one brilliant scientist working in secret. Thousands of scientists will work night and day on figuring out how to make Enoch work on everyone, not just one sick old lady. Eventually, they'll succeed."

Her look grew grim. "Then the endless end will begin. We'll be like those rats in Elijah's hidden lab. The population will explode and there will be an eternal struggle of all against all as everyone fights for food, water, even air."

She paused and shook her head. "Worse, immortality will destroy their souls. They will lose the chance for unending joy. And for what? Endless days of youth? But what is youth when the world is no longer new and you have already done what you were placed on Earth to do? We are not meant to live forever, not as we are. We must be remade. We're seeds that need to sprout and grow into something new—not stay like this for all time."

Anya looked at them with piercing, insistent eyes. "Look at me!" she demanded. "Look at how I really am! I'm world-weary and crackling with energy, mortally sick at heart and in perfect health, full of life and yearning for death. Is that how you want to spend the next hundred years? The next thousand? The next ten thousand? And maybe still more? Is that how you want everyone on the planet to spend all those years? Elijah was wrong, don't you see that? He plucked the story of Enoch out of Genesis, but he should have read the whole book. God cast Adam and Eve out of Eden before they could eat from the tree of life—*and it was a mercy that he did.* Elijah's invention won't create a deathless heaven. It will create an unending hell on Earth."

Her words shook Daniel, but he kept his face and voice carefully neutral. "How did Elijah die?"

Her face softened with remembered pain. "Two years ago, he was diagnosed with colon cancer. He decided to treat himself with Enoch. But for some reason it didn't work. In fact, it left him in permanent pain and made the cancer much more aggressive."

She sniffed and blinked tears from her eyes. "He called me one night to say good-bye. He said he had just given himself a massive overdose of barbiturates, so massive that he'd be dead in minutes. I rushed to the lab to be with him. It was a short trip, but I was too late. He—" Her voice broke and she stopped.

She took a deep breath and went on. "He was dead when I got there. I set fire to the lab, hoping to destroy Enoch forever. I think you know the rest of the story."

The table was silent. Light rain made a faint patter on the window. A car passed. Then a bus full of tourists.

At last, Leigh cleared her throat. "Do you know how long this will last? Will you look twenty-five forever?"

Anya shrugged. "I don't know. Neither did Elijah. His rats never aged, and he thought I might not either. I haven't changed for nearly a decade."

She turned to Daniel. "Do you have any other questions?"

He opened his mouth, then closed it and slowly shook his head. "I was going to ask what will happen to you, but I realized we're probably all safer if you don't tell us."

She nodded. "So what are you going to do?"

He was silent for a long moment, pondering. "I don't know," he said at last.

She nodded, looking slightly disappointed but unsurprised. "When you decide, please send a message to this e-mail address." She slid a scrap of paper across the table to him.

CHAPTER 90

Leigh walked into Whacktastic with Daniel and found Bruno playing Space Invaders on the giant TV. A Polycom phone sat on the coffee table in front of him. Bruno had been their insurance policy in case anything went wrong in the restaurant. He had been listening in on Daniel's iPhone, ostensibly ready to leap into action if a problem came up.

"So, what did you think, B?" Daniel asked.

The invaders landed on him. He tossed the game controller on the sofa and looked up at Daniel. "I think I'm glad I'm not you. You've got a tough decision to make."

Daniel collapsed into one of the overstuffed leather armchairs, sprawling his muscular frame haphazardly over it. "No kidding. I haven't slept more than a few hours any night in the past week." He closed his eyes. "I wonder if I should just punt to the board—give them the hard drive with a nonrecommendation that just lays out the pros and cons. It's their hard drive. Let them figure out what to do with it."

Bruno snorted derisively. "You know what they'll do, Danny."

Daniel lifted his head. "What?"

Bruno rolled his eyes. "What boards always do when they have a hard choice. They'll say all sorts of pompous crap about how they have a fiduciary duty to their shareholders. Then they'll do whatever makes the most money."

"Yeah, you're probably right." Daniel sighed and dropped his head back down. "What do you think, Leigh?"

She sat down on the arm of a sofa next to Daniel's chair. "Anya made a good point about what would happen if no one ever got old. We really would be like those rats." She tensed at the memory. "That would be hell on Earth."

Daniel nodded. "I know," he said softly. "But I watched my mom die, and I buried her. That was less than three years ago. I'm not ready to do the same thing with my dad."

Silence fell in the room and a lump formed in Leigh's throat. She had heard about what happened on opening day. She reached over and squeezed Daniel's shoulder.

Daniel took a deep breath. "But he's okay with it, so maybe I should be too. He almost seemed to look forward to death, at least a little. Or not death, but what comes after."

"Maybe he's been getting postcards from heaven too," Leigh said. "I never really thought about it before, but listening to Anya talk, it was like . . ." She paused, not really sure how to express it. "I don't know—like I'm homesick for a place I've never been."

"I felt it too," Daniel said. "But then I think of Dad coughing his lungs out at the ball game and billions like him slowly dying. It's wrong. Death is wrong." He shook his head. "But Enoch is worse."

"So what are you going to do?" Leigh asked.

"I think I have to destroy the hard drive," he said. "Maybe it will be possible to restart Rhodes's cancer research without the Enoch data. Maybe not. But his Enoch research has to go. Do either of you disagree?"

Leigh shook her head. "I know it's a hard decision, but it's the right one."

"You know they're gonna fire you, right?" Bruno said.

"Maybe," Daniel said. "It won't look good for them to fire 'the conscience of the company' for making an ethical decision that they don't like—particularly not if that decision involves the very same research that almost got them indicted." He shrugged. "But if they do, they're not a company I want to work for."

Bruno nodded and got up. "I'll go get the hard drive and a hammer." He returned a moment later with both. "You make me proud to be a Rubinelli, man."

Chapter 91

The cemetery took good care of Theodore's and Elijah's graves, which comforted Anya. The grass was green and well trimmed. The old flowers she left when she visited last time were gone. She had brought new lilies to take their place.

She laid the flowers against the headstone, a broad slab of black granite. It was over forty years old, but it had weathered the decades well. She bought it and the double grave plot when Theodore died. He had suffered a massive heart attack over dinner two weeks after their thirtieth wedding anniversary. She had grieved him deeply and intended to be buried next to him. She had often imagined the two of them rising together at the resurrection and embracing. But Elijah had taken her place in the ground.

Bitter tears stung her eyes. Visiting her husband's grave had always been hard. Visiting her son's was unbearable.

She wiped her eyes. This was probably the last trip she would be able to make to this place, at least for a very long time. The Bay Area was not safe for her. Too many people here knew her story or pieces of it. She needed to leave soon, and she would. She was hopeful that Daniel Rubinelli would make the right decision, and if he didn't, she had a backup plan. Either way, she would be gone soon.

After that, she needed to go someplace where no one had ever seen her face or heard her name. And of course she wouldn't be able to stay anywhere for long. She was cursed to wander the Earth, forever and alone.

"Good-bye," she said. Then she turned and left.

CHAPTER 92

Daniel and Leigh waited outside of the Ferry Building at eight thirty the next morning. They stood together in a little corner where they were outside the flood of rush-hour foot traffic as commuters headed from their ferries to their Financial District jobs. Daniel carried a black nylon messenger bag.

Daniel had sent a message to the e-mail address Anya gave him at Schroeder's that said, "Meet us in front of the Ferry Building @ 8:45 am tomorrow. We have a present for you."

They had decided to get there fifteen minutes early to look around. Not that they had any particular reason to suspect that anything bad would happen—but then they didn't need a particular reason when Anya Rhodes was involved. Bruno was back at Whacktastic monitoring nearby security cameras.

Leigh looked up at him, a slight frown creasing her forehead. "What will you do if Biosolutions fires you?"

"Probably go out on my own. Bruno called me last night to say that Whacktastic doesn't need a conscience, but it could always use a good lawyer." He paused. "Come to think of it, since this is Bruno we're talking about, there may be more work than one lawyer can handle. I could use a partner. What do you think of Rubinelli & Collins?"

She gave him a startled look. Then her face broke into a mischievous smile. "I think you mean Collins & Rubinelli."

Before he could respond, Anya slipped up beside Leigh, seeming to materialize out of the crowd. "Good morning, Mr. Rubinelli, Ms. Collins."

"Good morning," Daniel said, reaching into his bag as he spoke. "We thought you should have this."

He pulled out a plastic freezer bag containing the remains of the hard drive. "Here you go," he said. "This is the copy of Elijah's hard drive, or what's left of it anyway. This was the last of the Enoch research."

She took it with trembling hands, her green eyes luminous. "Thank you," she said softly.

They stood like that for a moment, a tableau in an eddy of the stream of humanity. Then Anya came to herself and looked around quickly. "I should go. Thank you again."

She turned and disappeared into the crowd.

CHAPTER 93

Anya stood with her back to the wall in the middle of Midway Airport's passenger terminal. People streamed past on their way to and from hundreds of destinations. A restored World War II torpedo bomber hung from the ceiling overhead.

She had picked the location for her meeting with Dr. Stein. She insisted on meeting in an airport because it meant that before he could get to her, he would have to go through a full-body scan. And if he wanted to kidnap her, he would need to do it in front of dozens of strangers and then somehow get her past a gauntlet of armed TSA agents.

Dr. Stein, however, had picked the particular spot in the airport. She had to admit that it was a natural meeting location, and it seemed safe enough. Still, the fact that he had chosen it made her nervous.

The meeting itself made her even more nervous. She suspected that she knew at least one reason why he wanted this meeting, but was she right? Moreover, was she right about *him*?

She had her doubts, and they had only grown stronger as the minutes ticked past. They were supposed to meet at half past two, and it was now nearly three. She considered leaving, but decided against it—at least for the moment. A string of storms had passed through the Rockies, snarling air traffic and delaying hundreds of flights. Perhaps his was one of them. Still, she wasn't going to wait too much longer. If someone had gotten to him, they might be on their way to her. They—

There he was.

She saw him before he spotted her. He hurried in from Concourse A, scanning the crowd with glacial blue eyes. She congratulated herself as she watched him, savoring the fact that she had been right.

He noticed her and a wide, relieved grin split his face. He walked over and studied the antique plane, craning his neck. "A very well-preserved old relic," he commented. Then he looked at Anya and winked. "An appropriate place for us to meet, don't you think?"

She smiled. "Very witty, Dr. Stein. Or do you prefer to go by Rich Johnson these days?"

He inclined his head. "Fred is fine for now, though you probably shouldn't call me that in public. Don't call me Rich Johnson either. Rich got himself in trouble at Biosolutions, so I needed to create a new identity. I'm Michael Smith now."

"I *thought* I recognized you at that Starbucks," she said. "I just couldn't place your face."

"I'm glad you didn't," he said with a chuckle. "You had me scared for a second."

"But you recognized me," she observed. "So you know my story, no?"

He shrugged. "To a certain extent. Elijah used to tell tales of his mother the lethal resistance fighter. He was quite proud of you, and understandably so."

She inclined her head. "The feeling was mutual."

"And he eventually told me about your treatment, at least in broad strokes," he said. "He kept the details to himself."

That surprised her. "Even from you? I thought you two worked together."

"We did, but he was always protective of his research. And of you. He never fully trusted anyone, at least not after Biosolutions tried to force him to turn over all his data. He never told me about his second lab, for example."

"But he must have told you enough for you to trust the treatment," she said. "Otherwise, you wouldn't look like this." He had smooth, tanned skin, a full head of sandy-brown hair, and a willowy, athletic build. He looked like he could be a grad student—and he dressed like one too: baggy jeans, slightly faded UC Berkeley T-shirt with a light jacket over it, and Vans sneakers.

His face grew serious and she could see his age in his eyes. "I was desperate. I had been diagnosed with Alzheimer's. It's a horrible disease. I could feel pages being erased from my memory. They'd be there one day and gone the next. To gradually lose your mind and know it's happening . . ." He shook his head. "I told Elijah, and he actually seemed relieved. He said that he thought I was just getting stupid and unreliable."

She chuckled. "How very like him."

"Indeed. Elijah said he thought he could help. I said yes, of course. I don't remember much about the treatment itself except that it hurt a lot."

"Yes, it did," she said, remembering her own agony. "How did you come to work in the legal department of Biosolutions?"

"Shortly after I went through the Enoch protocol, I created a new identity for myself—Richard C. Johnson, recent Berkeley graduate. Elijah hired me as a lab assistant." He gave a short laugh. "I think he enjoyed giving orders to his old professor. I worked directly with him, mostly doing cancer research. I also did some Enoch work and I helped him with what he called countersurveillance—monitoring Biosolutions e-mail traffic that mentioned him, me, or Enoch."

"He spied on his own company?"

He grinned, flashing even white teeth. "Of course he did. He had built a program that would make the NSA proud. Everything went fine for about five years." He paused. "And then one day he told me he had cancer and was treating himself with Enoch. It did not go well."

She nodded gravely. "Yes, he told me. Do you know what went wrong?"

He shook his head and sighed. "So much of science is trial and error, particularly in the field of human genetics. Maybe he wasn't old enough, so his telomeres were too long for the process to work properly. Maybe he had a version of some key gene that was different from the version you and I have. We'll probably never know."

"So how did you wind up working with Daniel Rubinelli?" she prompted.

"Sorry, old professors sometimes have trouble coming to the point. One night, Elijah sent me an e-mail saying that he wanted me to take over his research. He had just taken an overdose of barbiturates and left a package in my desk that contained encryption keys and all of his Enoch research—including much that he had never shared with me. The package also held the keys to his car, where he had left his laptop and work papers. I went straight to the lab, but it was already on fire. I barely got out alive. He didn't tell me where he parked, so the police found his car before I did. After that, all of Elijah's research—or what was left of it anyway—was in Legal's hands. And more importantly, they were the ones investigating the death of a man who was my student and my friend—and who had saved me from a fate I felt was worse than death."

That last comment worried her. "And what do you think of the fate he has saved you *to*?"

He looked at her silently for a long moment. "It's interesting that you should ask that," he said at last. "At first, I loved it. My mind was back." He smiled and patted the top of his head. "So was my hair, my hearing, and so many other things. But now I'm starting to feel almost . . . almost tired of it all."

"Like there's nothing new under the sun," she said.

"Yes, exactly." He gave a weary half smile. "Like the feeling you get when you've eaten at the same restaurant too many times. Except the whole world feels that way." He sighed. "Maybe another city or another country will feel different, at least for a while."

"Maybe," she said doubtfully. "Are we the only two?"

He nodded. "As far as I know. Elijah had his secrets, but I think I would have known if he tried Enoch on anyone else."

She decided to ask the question that troubled her most. "So what's next? Do you still want to continue Elijah's research on Enoch?"

He opened his mouth to answer, but then closed it. Then he stared into the middle distance for several heartbeats. "You know, if you'd asked me that question two months ago, I would have said yes. I was hiding in an abandoned lab building, trying to re-create his results, using my own cells. But even then I had misgivings, and they've grown since. Now I'm not sure I'll try again. I wasn't making progress, and it will be hard to accomplish much if I'm always in hiding or on the move. But that's only part of the reason. I've seen what the desire for eternal youth can do to people. I've also felt the price of getting it—and I feel it more every day." He paused and pressed his lips together. "I'm no longer sure that Enoch is something the world needs or should have."

Relief flooded through her. "I absolutely agree. So do the Rubinellis and Ms. Collins. They destroyed Elijah's hard drive."

"I'm glad to hear it." A wistful look came over his face. "Or mostly glad at least. Every scientist dreams of working on something big, a new breakthrough that could change the world. I'll miss that."

"Maybe you can find a way to continue some of Elijah's other work. His cancer research, for example. You could work at a lab, make some progress, and then move on after a few years. Then you could do the same thing at another lab, and then another. And each time, you would leave behind ideas and experiments that they could develop—just so long as none of it could lead to re-creating Enoch."

He stroked his chin. "That might work," he said slowly. "What about you? What are your plans?"

"I'll disappear," she said. "Live an anonymous life, always moving on before anyone gets too curious about me."

The corners of his mouth twitched and he winked. "Not to be forward, but I'll bet that you can't even go out to dinner alone without men getting curious about you."

She blushed, and was amused at herself for doing so. "I don't eat out much."

"Well, then let me take you to dinner tonight."

She smiled. "Thank you. I'd enjoy that."

Author's Afterword

This is the part of the book where I separate fact from fiction to the best of my ability.

Enoch. Elijah Rhodes's invention is very likely science fiction, of course—but with the emphasis on *science* rather than *fiction*. All of the gene therapy successes described in Chapter 4 are nonfiction. So is the discussion of the relationship between telomeres, aging, and cancer in Chapter 46. Likewise the description of telomere-related anti-aging experiments mentioned later in Chapter 46. It's not at all impossible that research in these interconnected fields could lead to the discovery of something very similar to Enoch. In fact, a company called BioViva claims to have already developed an Enoch-like gene therapy—*and is testing it on their own CEO, Elizabeth Parrish*. Watch for her name in the news. And if you're interested in learning more about this rapidly developing area of medicine, check out the University of Utah's website. They've got some excellent plain English materials on genetics, gene therapy, and the importance of telomeres.

Comic-Con. San Diego Comic-Con International, generally known simply as Comic-Con, is an enormous convention of comic book enthusiasts, superhero buffs, science fiction and fantasy fans, and other people who are likely to travel in the same social circles as Bruno Rubinelli. While Comic-Con has been held as early as March, it generally occurs in late July. However, I decided that it wasn't reasonable to make Bruno wait that long to show off his new scar.

Meyers-Richard quantum computers. To learn more about these nifty (but fictional) devices, you'll need to read *Double Vision*, a highly entertaining novel by Randy Ingermanson.

San Francisco. As always, I have stuck to describing real locations in my adopted home city and its environs. Except that there is no Señor Fishface truck selling fish tacos in the Financial District. But there really should be.

Acknowledgments

Many, many thanks to everyone who contributed to this book. Dozens of people helped me throughout the plotting, writing, and editing process, but the following individuals played particularly significant roles:

Lee Hough (former agent)—for helping brainstorm the plot and providing crucial early feedback.

Anette (wife)—for being my partner in creating this book at every step along the way.

Amy Hosford, Sheryl Zajechowski, and the rest of the Waterfall team—for giving this book the perfect home.

Peggy Hageman and Rachel Fudge (editors)—for numerous suggestions and revisions that corrected errors and significantly improved the flow of the story.

John Olson, PhD (author and biochemistry expert)—for giving me an early reality check on the scientific aspects of the book.

Charlotte Spink, Suneeta Fernandes, Gail and Bubba Pettit, Chris Ames, Rob Schultz, Kathy Engel, Jody Wallem, Per Kjeldaas, Randy

Ingermanson, and Cindy and Fred Acker (test readers)—for reading a beta version of the manuscript and helping me polish it into something publishable.

ABOUT THE AUTHOR

Photo © Anette Acker

Bestselling author Rick Acker is supervising deputy attorney general in the California Department of Justice. Most recently, he and his team won a string of unprecedented recoveries against the Wall Street players who triggered the Great Recession. Acker has authored several legal thrillers, including *Death in the Mind's Eye*, an RT Book Reviews Top Pick. He spends most of his free time with his wife and children. You can learn more about Acker and his books at www.rickacker.com.